AF575244

STRINGS

First edition published March 2021

Editor Charlie Knight
Cover design by Jonas Steger, cover designer at Fantasy and Coffee Design
Book design by Eliott Griffen

ISBN: 978-0-578-75721-6

RYAN HICKEY

Book One of the Winter Saga

For all those who needed a hero growing up

Table of Contents

Content Warning

Mild gore
Childhood abuse
Abuse scars
Suicidal ideation
Fantasy violence
Death

Part One

Chapter One

Snow flurried over the barren farm fields of Orion, Illinois. The sound of sprinting paws and turning gears tore through the otherwise silent night. Caleb Fleischer pedaled down an icy, gravel road on a rusted bicycle that was far too small for him. His knees rammed against his chest, but he didn't slow his pace. The residents of his small town were in danger, and he couldn't afford any delay.

He squinted past the snow assaulting his face, keeping his gaze glued on the German Shepherd that ran in front of him. Oppenheimer, like most dogs, had a keen sense of smell. But while most dogs were trained to locate explosives or other contraband, Opp's skills were far more unique.

Opp barked twice and sprinted down a paved road to the left. Caleb skidded as he turned, barely keeping his balance. The dim light of infrequent streetlamps was all that battled the darkness, but he could navigate Orion blindfolded.

The rural landscape faded as they approached town. Empty pastures yielded to rundown homes with unlocked doors and darkened windows. Oppenheimer barked twice again and jolted down a new path. Caleb followed him towards the familiar brick buildings of Main Street.

They approached an intersection bathed red in the glow of a stoplight when Opp came to an abrupt halt. Caleb pulled the brakes and slid to a stop. His heart pounded in his chest, but he kept his breathing steady and controlled. Bringing his hands up to his mouth, he blew warm air into his palms and rubbed them together, wishing he hadn't foolishly left his gloves at home.

Opp trotted in a circle with his nose tilted up. After a few paces, he let out a soft whimper and looked to his owner. Caleb frowned, and his grandfather's voice crept into the back of his mind. It berated him, accused him of failure, and claimed he was worthless. He had to try harder. Move faster. Be better.

"Come on, Opp," Caleb said. "We don't know how long it's been feasting." They had to make it in time.

With a whine, Opp paced once more and continued to smell the freezing air. A cold wind swept over Orion and past them both. Opp's ears perked up, and his sniffing intensified. Turning right, the dog stiffened and barked twice before sprinting down the next street.

Caleb took a deep breath and patted the leather satchel that hung at his side, ensuring its contents were secure. Satisfied, he remounted his bicycle and pedaled after his companion.

It took five minutes for Opp to lead them to the town's only park. An aging baseball field sat in front of them, flanked by vast, snow-covered terrain. A row of houses stood at the far end, barely visible through the downfall. Opp barked twice and stopped. The target was nearby.

Hopping off his bike, Caleb knelt in front of Oppenheimer. He rested his head against the dog's fur, petting him gently. "You've done your part, buddy. Now stay here and let me do mine."

Standing, he unbuckled the main flap of his satchel. He crept across the field, his feet crunching the white powder with every step. More snow fell around him like a tempest, obstructing his vision and biting his skin.

Three-quarters of the way across the vacant field, he found what he was looking for. Two strands of purple light emerged from one of the homes and floated to a nearby row of pine trees.

Soul strings. The tools of monsters, appearing as nothing more than harmless decoration.

His heart racing, Caleb closed his eyes and directed his mind inward. Deep into his chest, past his skin, past his muscles, and beyond his bones to the depths of his consciousness where one hides memories best forgotten. There resided a blazing golden flame that all living things possessed. A soul.

With his mind, he stoked the fire, expanding and spreading it throughout his body and opening it to the outside world. Where the houses and been empty to his perceptions just moments ago, he could now see and feel the souls of the occupants. They were all significantly smaller than his own. The souls of normal humans.

He focused his attention on the home with the strings. Each string flowed through the house and into one of the two sleeping residents, wrapping around their flames. Like a straw, they pulled the life of their victims towards some source. Their fires had nearly vanished. Unbeknownst to them, these people had been chosen as prey and had about half an hour to live.

Unless Caleb saved them.

Bringing his mind from his soul, he shifted his eyes to the pine tree. Past the snow-covered branches dwelled the source of the strings.

A demonic beast, seven feet long, with orange, leathery skin rested with its claws torn into the trunk of the tree. Jagged, purple bones tore through the skin at its joints, and its spine protruded from its back. Its hind legs were double-jointed and reminded Caleb of a frog.

Caleb's hands relaxed, and his pulse slowed. "Only a filken," he whispered to himself. It could have been so much worse.

He stepped closer to it, taking no care to conceal his presence. Fifteen yards from the tree, he cleared his throat.

Its head snapped towards him. No mouth nor eyes rested upon its face. Two slits served as a nose, and a pair of holes on the side of its head acted as ears. In the center of the creature's forehead existed a smooth, black orb.

The filken jumped from the tree, the strings following it and passing through the branches. It landed in a puff of snow, the orb on its face vibrating. A venomous, telepathic voice filled Caleb's mind. "Some more food has sought me out."

Caleb snapped his fingers. A leather-clad tome shot out of his satchel and hovered in front of him. The familiar sight of the floating book slowed his heart back to normal, but he made no further move against the creature. Not yet.

"I see...a Scribe," the filken seethed. The beast tilted its head back and sniffed between its slits. It faced its orb back down at him. "No, not a Scribe. Not entirely. What are you?"

Caleb's eyes drifted to the snow, his breath clinging to the air. "Someone who doesn't want anyone to die, including you. So, please, release your victims, and return to the Speculon. If you do, I give you my word that no harm will come to you."

The filken cackled. "Your word? No, Mystery Scribe, I will never trust a human."

It sprang off its hind legs, launching straight at Caleb. It opened one of its three-toed hands and slashed at his jugular.

Eyes focused, Caleb ducked under the attack. Rolling to the side, he hopped back to his feet. Snow clung to his windbreaker, and his tome remained floating in front of him.

Twirling through the air, the filken landed. Caleb sighed and formed a phrase in his mind memorized long ago. He siphoned away a portion of his soul as the tome flipped through pages of red text. The fiend circled around him, snarling telepathically. No doubt, it was waiting for an opening. Caleb had no intention of giving it one.

The tome opened to the page containing the incantation he held in his mind. He funneled his soul into the words, giving them power. The text glowed crimson, and he brought out the words from his thoughts. *"From sky to page; Feel the storm's rage."*

His soul manifested above the tome as a golden flame. It morphed into a ball of electricity and shot out at the filken. The beast hissed and jumped back, narrowly avoiding the attack.

As it slid across the snow, Caleb focused his soul on the tome's cover. An intricate etching in the leather glowed gold and projected onto his hands. In a flash, a yellow crystalline scythe appeared in his grasp. The weapon was translucent, yet solid. He held its weight with a familiarity born from countless years of training.

The beast charged. Caleb readied his scythe and brought a new incantation into his mind, his tome flipping through its pages. The filken brandished both sets of claws and hacked at him. He blocked the attacks with the polearm of his weapon, his muscles straining against the beast's strength.

The force of the blows sent him skidding back. His tome finished opening, and he brought the words to his lips. *"With blood of iron and heart of coal; Make my body stronger than my soul."*

A surge of strength and stamina flooded him. His scythe felt weightless in his hands, and all fatigue left his body.

The filken sprang at him with a snarl. Caleb raised his scythe and caught the monster's claws with the staff. He planted his feet in the snow, his newfound power allowing him to stop the beast in its tracks. Its pungent, acidic smell assaulted Caleb's nostrils, and his eyes watered. His muscles strained against his too-tight jacket as he brought his scythe over his head and vaulted the filken into the air.

It soared forty yards through flurrying snow before landing against a pine tree. Scrunching its hind legs like a spring, the filken launched off the trunk with a powerful snap. It landed ten yards from Caleb and charged, the strings dangling behind it.

But Caleb's attention wasn't on his foe. The force of its jump had sheared the tree trunk, and it teetered back and forth. Right in front of a row of houses.

He sprinted forward and unsummoned his scythe. The filken slashed, and Caleb dove and slid across the snow under the attack, bringing a new phrase into his thoughts. His mind strained from the burden of holding two incantations at once. The tome only turned a few pages, and he poured his soul into the words: *"Lightning and wind carry me; I am too fast to see."*

His body suddenly felt light as a feather, and his lungs seemed to hold limitless reserves of air. The tree fell towards a house. He sprinted across the snow, pushing the speed incantation to its limit. His surroundings blurred, and air whirled past him.

He skidded to a halt. Caleb raised a single hand, and the tree crashed down upon it. The bark cracked against his palm and the tree stopped in an instant, not budging him an inch. With deliberate care, he grabbed the tree with both hands and set it on the ground.

The filken faced him from across the field, tilting its head to the side. Caleb stared it down and held his hands out, summoning his weapon once more. Pouring more of his soul into the speed enhancement, he charged.

It tried to slash him as he approached, but its claws only ever reached the air where he had been moments before. Caleb danced around the beast, letting his movements confound it.

The filken spun, trying to keep up with him. He jumped to the left to find the beast's ribs exposed and unguarded. His grandfather's voice yelled in his mind, urging him to kill the monster now.

Spinning his scythe, he sliced at its orange skin. Keeping the wound deliberately shallow, he jumped away from his foe. Purple blood seeped from the cut and dripped onto the snow. It faced him, black orb tremoring.

Caleb unsummoned his scythe and softened his expression. Cutting his soul off from his speed and strength enhancements, he released the phrases from his thoughts, and his body returned to normal. His mind relaxed from the strain of holding both at once, like taking a fresh breath of air after being underwater.

He lifted both hands, palms up, and stepped towards the beast. "Please, this is your last chance. Let them go and return home."

The filken dug its claws into the ground and growled. A crimson ball of energy formed in front of its orb. Static crackled from the sphere, and the air suddenly smelled of burnt plastic.

Caleb sagged his shoulders and sighed. He brought a new incantation into his mind, and his tome flipped back a few pages. The filken launched an attack as he opened his mouth to speak. *"No matter the power you may wield; Stand firm against my mighty shield."*

His tome glowed, and a dome of golden light formed around him. The filken's attack tore across the ground, vaporizing the snow in its path and leaving steam in its wake. The energy crashed into Caleb's shield in a blast of red, snow, and dirt.

Keeping his soul tied to the shield, he closed his eyes as debris fell to the ground and clenched his hands. Why didn't they take his offer? Not ever. Not once.

The filken cackled telepathically. "Your soul is mine, Mystery Scribe."

His eyes snapped open. The debris had cleared, but snow still fell. Through it dangled a new purple soul string. It jutted out of the filken's chest, snaked across the field, and led into his own.

The string was siphoning the golden flame of Caleb's soul.

A dangerous cold seeped into his chest, and his legs trembled. The ground swayed under his feet, and he shook his head, desperate to keep focus.

The filken's laughter continued. "I will avenge my kin tonight."

Caleb bit his lip and flared his soul. Its warmth spread through his body before the string siphoned it out of him. His grandfather's voice urged him to resist, to fight against its influence.

He ignored it.

Taking in a deep breath, he embraced the string's parasitic presence. Accepting it as a part of him, he allowed the connection to deepen. The string drained his soul even faster, and he lost sensation in much of his body.

He fell to a knee and struggled to take a breath. But he kept his gaze steady on the purple strand, waiting. Snow pummeled down on the field, and the filken's laughter finally quieted.

The string hummed and faded from a deep purple to a radiant gold. Warmth flooded his chest, and he rose to his feet as both his and the filken's soul grew exponentially. He flared his flame once more and forced it into the golden string. Molding his soul into a sharp edge, he severed the strand of light, removing his connection with the beast.

Both their souls returned to normal.

The filken took a hesitant step back. Its body shook, and it gasped. "It's not possible...how did you...what are you?"

Caleb frowned and looked down, his grandfather's voice providing the answer in his mind. "A mistake."

A new phrase entered his thoughts, and his tome opened to a new page. *"I am king of this stage; Chains will be your cage."*

A golden, circular glyph manifested beneath the filken. Chains of yellow light flew out, coiling and wrapping around the bewildered beast. They pulled it to the ground, trapping it completely.

Maintaining the incantation in his thoughts, he held out his hands and summoned his scythe. He hesitated a moment before inching over to the constrained beast. It thrashed against the chains, its desperate whimpers filling his mind. It clawed at the dirt and tried to crawl away. The chains didn't budge.

Caleb stood over the filken, glancing down on it with misty eyes. The snow barraged them both and quickly piled upon the restrained creature.

It looked up at him, its black orb pulsating softly. "Please, don't kill me. Please. I was just so hungry."

His grip on his scythe tightened. In the back of his mind, his grandfather's voice screamed at him to kill the monster. The voice then asked a question that Caleb had heard a thousand times: What does Fleischer mean?

"Please," it pleaded again.

His focus shifted to the two remaining purple soul strings. He followed them to the house where two innocent residents of Orion slept, none the wiser to the current threat on their life. Returning his gaze to the filken, he raised his scythe above his head.

"I gave you two chances," he whispered. "You'll never stop killing."

It screamed. Forcing his eyes to stay open, Caleb heaved his weapon down and buried the blade into its skull. The filken twitched violently before going limp, purple blood spreading through the white snow.

The two soul strings vanished. Caleb released the incantation, and the chains disappeared as well. But the job wasn't finished.

Closing his eyes, he opened his soul to the world around him. Searching out the former victims, he found both souls were now steady. They were smaller than normal, but in a few days, they'd make a full recovery.

Satisfied, he closed off his soul and opened his eyes. He knelt and placed a hand on the filken's orange hide. It was still warm to the touch. Bringing a new phrase to his mind, Caleb looked around to ensure no one was watching.

"Shadows hide me from my enemy's eyes; Make me impossible to recognize."

A purple veil spread from his tome and engulfed him, making him invisible to the outside world. He funneled a little more of his soul into the incantation, increasing the radius of the veil until it also covered the filken. It was only a precaution. Normal humans couldn't see a creature of the Speculon.

Caleb ran his hand along the creature's coarse skin, traveling around the jagged bones, and up to its head. He cupped its face, looking into the deep abyss of its black orb. His grandfather's voice congratulated him. Tears filled his eyes.

"I'm so sorry," he whispered. "I tried. I tried to tell you."

Time passed imperceptibly. Snow covered him, and his soul strained under the weight of the cloaking spell. Finally, he whispered new words and cast the incantation to dispose of the body. Yellow glyphs appeared over the corpse and dissolved it.

Certain that the job was finished, he released both incantations and stood. Blood rushed to his head, and he staggered a moment. His soul flickered in his chest, waning from excessive use. The ride home was going to be rough.

He stowed his tome in his satchel and walked back to the edge of the park to find Oppenheimer sitting obediently. Opp drummed his feet into the snow, panting eagerly. A small smile crept across Caleb's face, and he clicked his tongue twice. Opp barked and sprinted at him.

Caleb knelt and embraced his dog, rubbing his face into the warm fur. "You did good tonight, buddy. Let's go home."

The bike ride back was slow, his too-small bike doing him no favors. While he used his soul to power his incantations, it was his body that paid the toll of the fight. His legs felt like stone and resisted his commands. His eyelids were heavy and demanded rest.

Nevertheless, he pedaled onward, Opp trotting beside him. After half an hour, he reached the outskirts of the small town. All around him were empty fields, save a solitary, rundown home.

The once blue siding had long since faded and peeled. Boards covered both front windows. Single-storied, the house's roof was missing most of its shingles and looked as if a slight breeze might blow it down.

"Home," he said.

Walking to the front door, he unlocked the deadbolt and let Opp inside. Closing the door behind him, Caleb was thankful to have finally escaped the snow. Winter was just the worst. He brushed himself off and threw his thin jacket to the floor.

Opp strutted into the conjoining living room and climbed upon a worn-down couch. Caleb smiled and crept past the kitchen, down a short hallway. Opening a door on the right, he tiptoed into his father's bedroom.

A familiar stale odor confronted him. Soft green light emanated from a medical monitor next to a twin bed. Not wanting to risk waking his father, he stayed where he was and read the vitals displayed on the screen. Everything was stable. He visually verified the IV bag hanging from the stand still held medication.

Satisfied, Caleb left and shuffled to his room. Dirty clothes littered the floor, and the only notable piece of furniture was his bed. He took off his satchel and threw it to the ground.

He didn't bother undressing and climbed onto his mattress. Laying on his stomach, he glanced at the alarm clock that rested next to his pillow. Thirteen minutes after midnight. Only then did he realize what day it was.

"Twenty-four years old," he sighed.

Sleep didn't come easy. His mind replayed the fight over and over. His attempts to convince the filken to leave, it begging for mercy, his grandfather's voice.

Caleb grabbed his pillow and stuffed it over his head, trying to smother the thoughts. There was no use in thinking about any of it. This was the life that had been forced upon him. There was nothing he could do to change that.

Chapter Two

The alarm blared a few hours later. Without opening his eyes, Caleb shut off the incessant ringing. Every fiber of his being wanted to pull up the covers and hide from the world, but his father needed him, and his growling stomach demanded food.

He rolled out of bed and glanced at the clock. Four in the morning. His head pounded, and his muscles ached. The previous night had taken its toll, and he craved more sleep. But he'd have to tough it out.

Turning towards the door, Caleb found himself face-to-face with a figure in a black cloak. His heart nearly tore out of his chest. Stumbling back, he slammed into the wall and readied his fingers to snap.

But he didn't.

"Can you not just appear like that?" he told her.

A hood rested over the figure's head. The shadow cast by its cowl obscured her face completely. Coldness seeped from the figure, and Caleb's breath clung to the air. The figure stepped towards him and reached out a pale hand. A soft light emanated from her skin, illuminating the room.

Caleb shook his head. "No, I'm not doing this today. I had to kill a filken last night, I got three hours of sleep, and I have to get ready for my shift. Please, just go." He didn't have the patience for one of her cryptic messages. Not now.

The figure's shoulders slumped. She remained for a moment before vanishing into thin air. He let out a long, belabored sigh. It was too early for drama.

Once his pulse returned to normal, he stepped out into the hallway. Pattering paws preceded eighty pounds of fur jumping straight at him. Oppenheimer licked at his face. Hugging Opp, Caleb rested his forehead against the brown and black of his dog's coat.

Opp followed him into the living room and let out a soft whimper. In the middle of the floor sat a tattered, leather collar. Sighing, Caleb picked it up and caught a glimpse of red on the inner strap.

He put the collar back on Opp, looking the dog in the eyes. "Come on, bud. You know how important it is you wear this at all times."

Opp whimpered again and looked down.

Caleb smiled softly and embraced his companion. "I can't stay mad at you. Come on, let's get you outside."

Turning on the exterior lights, he let Opp into the front yard. The snow had finally stopped falling, but a thick blanket covered the ground.

Exiting the hallway, the soft green light of the medical monitor greeted Caleb as he entered his father's room. He scanned his father's vitals and checked the IV bag. Perched in a basket attached to the stand sat a small journal with "Scott Fleischer" engraved upon it.

Placing a hand on the man's bony shoulder, Caleb gently shook him awake. "Time to get up."

Scott opened his glassy, gray eyes. With a wheeze, he rolled onto his back and stared at the ceiling. Bags hung heavy under his eyes with only a few wisps of sickly hair remaining on his head. Bones poked against deathly pale skin, yellow splotches the only hint of color. It looked as if a papercut might do the man in.

His hands shook as he tried to sit. Caleb assisted, helping his father through a coughing spasm.

Scott wiped his mouth and looked up. "Good morning. How are. You doing?" He took painful, wheezing breaths every few syllables.

"I'm okay. Tired. How are you feeling?"

"Invincible," Scott said with a smirk and a wink.

Caleb smiled softly and helped his father up. He kept a firm hand on the man's back and shuffled him across the floor, rolling the medical stand behind them. "Let's get you cleaned."

It took them a few minutes to reach the cramped bathroom. He undressed his father and disconnected him from the monitor. A cheap plastic chair rested against the shower wall. Sitting his father down, Caleb turned on the water and let it warm. With gentle hands, he rubbed a bar of soap over his father's skin.

Scott met his eye line. "I heard you. Leave last. Night. Was it a. Filken?"

"Yeah."

"It refused your. Offer?"

The filken's pleas for mercy filled Caleb's mind. "Twice."

"I didn't hear. Sirens. Everyone was okay?"

Caleb nodded. "Opp got me there fast enough."

Scott smiled from ear to ear. "The Guild. Couldn't have done. Better. I'm proud of you."

His grandfather's voice fought against his father's, accusing Caleb of failure. He shook his head and tried to push the thought away. "Thanks, Dad."

He finished cleaning his father, dressed him in fresh clothes, and reconnected him to the monitor and IV. He then brought him into the kitchen. He filled Opp's bowl and let the dog back into the house. Scott sat at a shabby two-person table and pulled out the journal from the medical stand.

"How's the incantation coming?" Caleb asked as his father began to scribble on one of the pages.

Scott took a long, labored breath. "It's coming. I'll need at. Least six or. Seven more months. To finish this one."

A mountain of dirty dishes occupied most of the kitchen sink. Caleb opened the fridge, finding it barren save an empty carton of orange juice. Unsurprised, he checked the cabinets and found a single packet of instant oatmeal.

Wiping off a dirty pot, he boiled some water and prepared

the solitary meal. With a spoon in hand, he set the oatmeal in front of his dad.

"You need help eating?" he asked.

Scott shook his head. "You're not having. Any?"

Caleb kept a straight face. "I'm not hungry."

His father shot him a skeptical look, but Caleb retreated to the bathroom before another question could surface. He took off his dirty clothes and caught sight of himself in the mirror.

At six foot one, he was an inch shorter than his father and three inches shorter than his grandfather. His curly, platinum blond hair hung just past his ears. But his torso drew his gaze. Dozens of scars ran across the pale skin on his stomach, chest, and back. His body was a tapestry of lessons he'd sooner forget.

Pulling himself from his reflection, he stepped into the shower and removed the chair. The water came at barely more than a trickle and stabbed at his skin like freezing daggers. Teeth chattering, he cleaned himself as fast as he could manage. When he finished, he dried himself off and changed into his only other pair of jeans and a clean shirt.

After grabbing his satchel off the floor and verifying his tome was inside, he hustled into the living room. He picked up his jacket and threw it on. Opp was lying at his father's feet, and Caleb was about to say his farewells, but Scott beat him to the punch.

"I think I. Heard something. Outback."

Caleb arched an eyebrow and glanced at Opp. No barking. Still, if his father heard something, he'd check it out. Underestimating the Guild was the same as asking for tragedy.

He unbuckled the main flap of his satchel and darted out the front door. Using the dim light of the exterior bulbs, he worked his way around the house, cold air nipping at his face. Coming to the corner, he peered into the backyard. There wasn't a living thing in sight, Scribe or beast. But leaning against the back of the house was a brand new, yellow bicycle with a red bow taped to its seat.

His eyes grew wide, and he stared at the bike in confusion. Running his hand down the cold, polished metal, he admired the gift. He brushed the snow off it and wheeled it to the front yard. Stepping back inside, he shot his father a curious glance.

A sheepish grin spread across the man's face. "Happy birthday. Caleb."

"Thanks, Dad." Caleb reached across his body and grabbed his own arm. "Where did you get the money for this?"

"I called JJ. Got you a raise. And took out. An advance."

Caleb looked down. "I appreciate this, I do. But...we could have used that money for food. Or to get you an extra dose of medicine."

His father's smile softened. "Don't get so. Caught up in our. Hardships. That you forget. That you are still alive. Enjoy it. It won't last. Forever."

Caleb tried to smile but failed. His grandfather's voice reminded him that he didn't deserve gifts. Not after he tried to negotiate with a filken. For a brief moment, Caleb's blood began to boil, and he clenched his jaw. He wanted to yell back at the imagined voice. To tell it that it was wrong.

"Son?" his father asked.

Snapping back into the moment, Caleb tried to bring his thoughts under control. "Thanks again, Dad. I should head to work. I'll bring home some dinner." The mention of food brought a rumble to his stomach. He ignored the sensation and knelt next to Opp. He gave his companion a reassuring pat. "Take care of Dad while I'm gone, buddy."

Opp licked at his face, and Caleb managed a sincere smile. He said a farewell to his father and exited the house. Mounting his new bike, he pedaled down the driveway. Even through snow, having a bicycle that fit him made pedaling so much easier.

It only took him twenty minutes to reach downtown Orion, half the time it would have taken on his old bike. Once the brick buildings of Main Street greeted him, it didn't take long to reach a mundane, square structure that served as the town's only grocer.

He pulled up to the rear of the establishment and secured his bike with a lock that had rested there for the last nine years. Unlocking the back door, he stepped into the employee office. He threw his satchel underneath the metal desk to his left. Part of him enjoyed it when its weight wasn't around his shoulder, but another felt unsafe without it.

With the flip of a switch, he turned on all the lights in the store. He then dialed the radio to his favorite station and let the music consume him. Whistling along with the tunes, he mopped the floors and stocked the shelves. His stomach growled as he handled the food, and he imagined the dinner he was going to cook that night.

The back door opened and brought him out of his trance. Poking his head into the backroom, a familiar face greeted him.

A young woman his age took off a blue knitted beanie to reveal black, frizzy hair. Snow clung to her dark skin before she brushed it off. She looked at him and gave him a warm smile. “Good morning, Caleb. Happy birthday!”

He grinned back. “Hey, Sally. Thanks.”

Sally pulled a bagel with cream cheese from her purse and handed it to him. “Cause you forget to eat breakfast most of the time.”

He snatched it from her and took a large bite. He muttered a gracious thank you with a full mouth.

Taking off her coat, she stepped into the store and looked around. “You almost got everything done already.”

Still clutching his breakfast, he placed his hands on his hips and took a practiced, heroic pose. “I am nothing if not a miracle worker.”

She chuckled as he scarfed down the rest of the food. Together, they prepared the store for the day. As opening time approached, they arranged a newspaper stand by the main entrance.

Sally held up one of the papers. “It’s too bad we’re gonna miss President Davis’ Inauguration. Everyone says he’s going to be amazing.”

He shrugged. “He’ll probably be the same as all the others.”

“I hear ya. But he won by thirty-five percent. That’s gotta count for something. Maybe he’ll actually be good.”

The front doors slid open, its chimes cutting their conversation short. A stocky, bald man wearing a green flannel shirt entered. The midnight of his beard matched his complexion, though a bit of gray was starting to nip at the ends.

“Morning, you two,” the man said.

“Hey, Dad,” Sally chimed.

Caleb faced the man and grabbed his own arm. “Good morning, Mister Jackson. Thank you for the raise.”

Mister Jackson placed a steady, reassuring hand on Caleb’s shoulder and looked him square in the eye. “Caleb, first, you and

Sally have been friends since second grade; please call me Jordan. Second, you're a solid worker. You deserve it. Happy birthday, son."

"Thank you, sir."

Mister Jackson chuckled. "No more formality. No sirs or misters. Understood?"

"Yes...JJ."

"There you go. Speaking of which..." Mister Jackson reached into his back pocket and produced an envelope stuffed with cash. "This is everything minus the advance your father took out."

Caleb stuffed the envelope into his pocket. "Thank you."

"That's the third time you've thanked me in the last minute. No more for the rest of the week." Mister Jackson laughed and patted him on the shoulder before vanishing into the back room.

Within fifteen minutes, they opened the store. A modest influx of customers visited them throughout the day. They managed them with little issue, even helping some of the elderly townsfolk through the aisles.

The warm atmosphere of the store made the work easy. Smiles and pleasantries were routinely exchanged. Late in the afternoon, each customer was in a buzz over the president's speech. If they were to be believed, it was nothing short of inspirational.

Caleb's shift came to an end at a quarter past two. After he clocked out, he used his paycheck to gather a modest amount of groceries, though he made sure to splurge on supplies for spaghetti and meatballs. He brought his basket of food to the register Sally worked.

"Your usual birthday dinner tonight?" she asked him.

"That's right. Been looking forward to it for three hundred and sixty-four days."

"Last year was a leap year."

He gave her a deadpan look, and she laughed.

She finished bagging his items before clearing her throat. "A bunch of us are gonna head to Patch's tomorrow night. I'm gonna finally ask Rachel out. I feel good about my chances. You wanna come?"

Caleb blinked several times, words escaping him. His first instinct was to say yes, but his grandfather's voice crept into his thoughts. It reminded him that he was a Scribe. He had no business being with normal humans. His powers, the beasts of the Speculon, all of it was beyond them. He had to keep his life a secret. He was alone.

"I'm sorry, Sally," he muttered. "I need to take care of my dad."

Grabbing the two bags of groceries, he retreated from the register before she could respond. His eyes grew hot and began to sting.

He almost made it to the backroom, but a customer's voice stopped him. "Caleb, dear?"

Missus Gentry stood crouched over a rusty cart, waving at him to come closer. He approached, and she said, "I ran into your cousin. They're on their way to your house now."

His eyes widened, and he nearly dropped the groceries. "My cousin?"

"Yes, dear. I ran into her at the library. She said her GPS wasn't working, so I gave her directions."

Murmuring thanks, he grabbed his satchel and raced out to his bike. He didn't have a cousin.

His shaking hands slowed his attempts to tie the grocery bags to the handlebars, but soon he was pedaling down Main Street. He took every conceivable shortcut he could think of. Anything that could give him a small edge against a vehicle. Every so often, he'd come across a car driving into town, preventing him from casting an incantation to aid him.

His mind raced as he pedaled. Who would pose as his cousin? Why were they here? How did they find him and his father? He wasn't entirely sure, but he knew the Guild had to be involved somehow. Who else could it be?

Turning onto the gravel road that ran in front of his home, he found a black SUV parked in his driveway. Tinted windows obscured him from seeing if anyone was inside the vehicle. He abandoned his bike fifty yards from his house, taking care with the food. Crouching low to the ground, he darted through the snow. Trees provided him with cover, allowing him to remain hidden during his approach.

He came up to the rear of the SUV, leaning against it. The exhaust was still warm, and it had government plates. That suggested the Guild. Peeking his head up to the rear window, he glanced through the tint. Empty.

Disappearing inside of himself, he opened his soul to the outside world. He confirmed that no one resided in the SUV before focusing on his home. Three souls revealed themselves to him. The first was the small, golden flame belonging to Oppenheimer. The second was the smoldering timber of his father's brittle spirit. The third, however, was a massive wildfire. Not the soul of a normal human. The soul of a Scribe. And they were standing at his front door.

A knock sounded.

His heart raced against his chest. Holding his breath, he peered around the corner of the SUV. A young woman stood at his door. Her wavy, golden hair blew in the wind, and her peach skin was blushed slightly from the cold. If he had to guess, she was his age, maybe a year older. Did that powerful soul truly belong to someone so young?

She knocked again.

No tome floated in front of her, nor was she holding anything that could have one. Something was off. Yet his grandfather's voice screamed at him to act.

He unbuckled the flap of his satchel but didn't take his tome out. He had to investigate.

He snuck up to his house as quietly as he could. When he was ten yards away from the woman, her shoulders perked up, and she spun around to face him. He met the gaze of her green eyes and froze.

"Who are you?" she asked in a fearful tone.

Why was she the one who was afraid? Caleb took a second to gather his breath. None of this made sense. He brought his thumb and middle finger together, ready to snap at a moment's notice. "This is my home. Who are you?"

The young woman stood up straight and raised her chin. Fierce determination burned in her eyes. "My name is Heather O'Brien. I'm looking for Scott Fleischer. I desperately need his help."

Chapter Three

Caleb suspected the Guild had come to kill him and his father. He hadn't expected to find someone asking for help. That didn't sound like the tactic of a Guild Scribe.

Studying Heather, he didn't find any deception in her demeanor. "Are you with the Guild?" he asked her.

A confused expression painted her face. "The what now?"

"The Guild of Life. Are you a member of the Guild of Life?"

She shook her head. "I have no idea what that is."

Her eyes were sincere. A cold breeze swept over the yard, and he tried to calm himself. It didn't appear that she was here to attack, yet she didn't have the soul of a normal human. And it was still troubling she knew about his father and where to find him. No matter her intentions, that was a problem. Caleb had to figure out what she knew and how.

Looking back at his bike down the street, he motioned for Heather to wait a moment. He kept an eye on her as he retrieved it along with the groceries. Untying both bags, he brought them to the front door.

"Come on in," he said after unlocking it.

He scanned outside one last time before locking the door. He led Heather into the kitchen and motioned to the cheap table. She took a seat and waited as he unpacked the food.

"I see supplies for spaghetti and meatballs," she said.

"I'm making it for dinner tonight. It's... a special occasion."

Oppenheimer trotted into the room, approached Heather, and began to sniff. Caleb watched the dog with a careful eye, waiting, ready to snap his fingers. There were no barks. She truly didn't have anything on her that could cast an incantation. He relaxed slightly as she began to pet Opp.

"Hey there, cutie," she said, looking at his collar. "Your name's Oppenheimer, huh? My name is Heather." She took one of Opp's paws into her hand and gave it a playful shake. She read Opp's collar. "I guess that makes you Caleb, then?"

He nodded. "It's nice to meet you. Would you like some tea?"

"Yes, please."

Grabbing a kettle from the sink, he began to boil some water, then returned to the table and set his satchel on his lap. He took a moment to look over his guest. A red sweater fell loosely over her plump figure and didn't strike him as an outfit worn by someone who would be driving a government vehicle. Then again, what did he know? Her golden hair was held back in a hairband that matched her clothing in color.

Swallowing past the lump in his throat, he dove straight in. "Why are you here?"

Her warm expression dulled slightly. "My mom... she's sick. Dying slowly."

"I'm sorry. But my dad isn't a doctor."

"My mom is. She's in the best hospital in Chicago, surrounded by the most skilled specialists money can buy."

He raised an eyebrow. "And then you decided to come to a nothing town in the middle of Illinois looking for help?"

Heather shifted in her seat and folded her hands on the table. Taking in a deep breath, she said, "One of the senior doctors treating my mom pulled me aside a couple months ago. He told me that when he worked in a Manhattan hospital a few decades back and came across a similar situation.

"A patient was dying, yet the staff had no idea why. Then,

one day, a young man named Scott Fleischer showed up. He spent a few minutes with the patient and then vanished for an hour. When he returned, the patient was completely healthy. He accepted no payment and offered no explanation, only winking at them before running off."

The kettle whistled behind them.

Caleb stood and prepared two cups of the tea he had bought. Her story sounded exactly like his father, the young man who went around saving everyone he could find. Scott Fleischer. But his grandfather's voice told Caleb he had to keep this under wraps. He had to keep their identities a secret. He was going to have to play this with care.

Both mugs in hand, he returned to the table and handed Heather her drink.

"Thank you."

He nodded, and they both took a sip. Letting the mug warm him, he thought of what to say. "My dad happened to show up in a hospital, and a patient happened to get better. Sounds like a coincidence to me."

Heather traced her finger along the rim of her mug. "I thought the same at first. But then I did some digging. It wasn't easy or cheap, but I found what I was looking for. Seven other times, Scott Fleischer appeared in a hospital somewhere across the country. Each time was the same as the first."

Caleb bit his lip and looked down. "You have the wrong Scott Fleischer."

She took a sip of her drink, her green eyes studying him. "I don't think so. If you thought I had the wrong place, you wouldn't have let me in. But you knew why someone would ask your father for help and let me in to convince me I had the wrong place."

His grip on his mug tightened, and he cursed under his breath.

Thinking about her mother's state, the most likely culprit was a soul string. All he'd have to do was follow it to the filken that created it and kill it. At least he hoped it was only a filken.

But it wasn't that simple. A massive city like Chicago would be packed with Guild Scribes. Every second he spent there would be a risk. If they ever caught him, his life would be forfeit. His father's life would be forfeit. Besides, this job was exactly what the Guild was created to do: keep humanity safe from the Speculon. It wasn't on him to solve a problem that they could solve in minutes, especially when it put his and his father's life at risk.

His heart began to beat faster in his chest. Sweat dripped down his temple, and his breath grew short. He couldn't go to Chicago.

Heather touched his wrist, her gaze overwhelming him. "Please. I'm desperate. I can pay you. A lot."

He pulled his arm away, his heart blasting in his ears. This was too much. He had to get away from this situation. Caleb stood, but his father's voice stopped him from moving.

"It seems. We have a guest." Scott leaned against his medical stand in the kitchen entrance. A sly grin painted his face. "I overheard. A bit of your story. I'm afraid. I would be. Unable to. Help you, my lady."

Heather looked over to his father, her eyes growing wide. She opened her mouth to say something, but no words came out. Her shoulders sank, and she looked down at the table. "I see."

"Thankfully. Caleb here is more than. Capable."

Caleb clenched his jeans with tight fists. His face remained stone, and he stared off at nothing. In his periphery, Heather smiled until she saw his expression.

"Please," she said, "she's my mom. I don't know what else to do."

Scott smiled and held up a shaking hand. "You don't need. To go. But please. Give us a moment."

Heather stood and looked around. Realizing there was nowhere to go, she exited the house. Scott shuffled over to the table and took a seat. His gray eyes pierced Caleb as he rubbed his chin. "You don't. Want to. Go."

Caleb shrugged. He did not. Staying in Orion and fighting the occasional filken was hard enough on him. But traveling to an unfamiliar, enormous city with someone he didn't know and running the risk of confronting the Guild? That was too much.

He didn't want to travel the world and be some famous Scribe. Was it so wrong to just want a normal life?

But he didn't know how to say any of this to his father. He was supposed to love being a Scribe. His last name was Fleischer, after all. He'd have to try a different approach. "I can't leave. I need to stay and take care of you. Plus, there's the store."

"I'll call JJ. And say. You need to travel for. Family reasons. And we can get your. Grandfather. To take care of me."

The very mention of his grandfather sent shivers down his spine. "We haven't talked to him in three years."

"He is. Stubborn. And resents me. But he'll come. If we ask."

Caleb clenched his jaw. His knuckles had gone white from gripping his pants for so long. Oppenheimer trotted over to him and rubbed his snout against Caleb's leg.

Scott tilted his head and arched an eyebrow. "Is there. Something else. On your mind?"

Caleb loosened his grip and placed his hands on the table. His thumbs circled each other. Was it worth protesting? Maybe his father would listen. Maybe he'd understand. But then his grandfather's voice echoed in the back of his mind.

His hands fell to his side, and any semblance of resistance faded from him. "No. I'll go pack."

He ran from the kitchen without another word. Closing his bedroom door behind him, Caleb slid down to the floor. He wrapped his arms around his shins and pulled his legs to his chest. A terrible weight pushed down on his shoulders, and he buried his face into his knees.

This was too much.

For ten minutes, he sat there, a statue overlooking nothing. Knowing he couldn't sit there forever, he rolled to his side and crawled to his bed. He pulled a wrinkled duffle bag from underneath his dirty mattress.

Packing the few clothes he owned, Caleb realized how empty his room was without them on the floor. He checked under his bed and shoveled out a pile of books. A dozen in total, he paged through them to decide which he should bring. If Heather's mother wasn't plagued by a soul string, then these would prove invaluable at helping cure her. Zipping up the bag, he slung it over his shoulder and verified he still had his satchel with him.

Oppenheimer was waiting for him in the kitchen, sitting patiently at his father's feet. Caleb knelt in front of him and put his forehead against the dog's temple. "We're going on a trip, buddy." Opp licked at his face and looked at him with bright eyes. Caleb smiled solemnly. "I don't know what I'd do without you."

Caleb stood and met his father's gaze. What was there to

say? Perhaps one last plea to stay? To escape this task that had been thrust upon him.

Scott cleared his throat. "Your grandfather. May be more agreeable. If you were to. Ask him to come."

Caleb dropped his duffle bag. Speaking to his grandfather? Was this day predestined to be his worst? Had he done something wrong?

There was no use in putting up a fight. Hands shaking, he tried to swallow past a dry throat as he walked over to the phone. Pulling it off its receiver, he untangled the cord before dialing the number labeled Karl Fleischer.

The phone rang. It rang. And rang. And rang.

"Scott. You've come crawling back," a gruff, unsympathetic voice said.

Caleb nearly crushed the phone. He squeezed his eyes shut and cleared his throat. "No, Grandpa. It's me."

A brief pause hung over the line. "Caleb? Did something happen to your father?"

"No. But we need your help."

Another pause. "Of course you do. What else could it be?" His voice dripped with venom.

Caleb shrunk into himself. "Please," he croaked.

His grandfather grumbled. "What is it?"

"We were approached by a stranger. I'm going to Chicago to help her. Can you come watch Dad until I return?"

Silence. More silence. "Have I taught you nothing? What does Fleischer mean?"

Caleb almost hung up. His knuckles burned white as his grip tightened around the phone. "You know I know what it means. It'll be a day or two at most. Please...sir."

Thirty seconds passed. He struggled to take a breath. Was his grandfather even still on the line?

His grandfather cleared his throat. "I'll be there at ten tomorrow morning." Before Caleb could respond, his grandfather hung up.

Caleb dropped the phone, his breathing frenzied and out of control. Looking down, he saw a spear made of golden light piercing his stomach. Blood gushed from his gut, and he nearly passed out. And then it was gone. There was no wound.

His grandfather's voice yelled at him in his mind, the words unclear. The room spun under his feet, and he fell against the wall. His chest tightened, and sweat poured down his face. He wrapped his arms around his torso and desperately tried to control his breathing.

A pair of bony hands grabbed his shoulders. They gently rocked him, and a soft voice spoke to him. What was it saying? Where was he? Why was there a spear sticking out of his stomach again?

But there wasn't. He was safe. That's what the voice said.

Caleb blinked repeatedly. He regained control of his breathing, and his pulse returned to normal. He was in Orion, Illinois. He was in his kitchen. His father's hands were holding him. His father's voice was telling him it was okay. He was safe.

"It's been a while. Since you've had. A panic attack," Scott said.

He looked up at his father and took a desperate breath. "You shouldn't have made me talk to him."

"I had hoped. It would produce. A favorable outcome."

Caleb's eyes drifted to the floor. A favorable outcome?

An uncomfortable silence hung in the kitchen. Opp licked at his hand, and Caleb pulled his dog close.

His father continued, "Is he. Coming?"

Using Opp for stability, Caleb came to his feet and hung up the phone. "He said he'll be here at ten tomorrow morning."

Scott shuffled back to his medical stand, using it for support. His gray eyes studied Caleb, a look of mild worry twinkling in his gaze. "Are you. Okay?"

Caleb grabbed his own arm. "If he's not gonna be here until the morning, is it fine if Heather sleeps on the couch?" It was hard to describe how much he didn't want to see his grandfather tomorrow, but it was unavoidable.

Scott closed his eyes and rubbed his temple. He fiddled with his monitor before giving Caleb a sheepish grin. "You know what? Leave with her. Now."

Caleb's eyes widened. "And leave you alone? I can't do that."

His father chuckled. "I can. Take care of. Myself for the night. I won't ask. You to endure. Seeing him if. It can be. Helped."

A massive weight fell from Caleb's chest. He wiped the sweat from his brow and shook his head, trying to remain in the present. Taking a few minutes, he ensured his anxiety wasn't going to flare again.

Satisfied, he picked the duffle bag off the ground and verified the presence of his tome within his satchel. "I guess I'm off."

"I'm glad you're. Going. You are meant. For great things. Son."

He shrugged. "Mom always said that when I was young."

Scott hobbled over to Caleb, placing a thin hand on his shoulder. "You'll do. Great."

Caleb moved to hug his father but stopped. Instead, he walked towards the front door. As he opened it, he looked back at the man. "Heather said you helped someone out in Manhattan a few decades back. Was it a soul string?"

Scott looked up and thought a moment. He then nodded. "Yes. It was. Do you think. That's what is. Wrong with her. Mother?"

"It's the most likely explanation." He shrugged again and turned to the door. "Bye, Dad."

"Give them. Hell, Caleb," Scott called out.

He looked back at his father and arched an eyebrow. "Who?"

"The world." His father gave him a wink and chuckled.

A smile forced its way across Caleb's face. Not wanting to put off the inevitable any longer, he signaled for Opp to follow and stepped outside. He looked back at his father briefly and then closed the door.

It wasn't snowing, but the January air was frigid as ever. It bit at him, and he zipped up his windbreaker. The setting sun did nothing to aid the falling temperature, but he admired the purple, red, and orange of the sky nonetheless.

Heather stood leaning against the SUV, her smartphone in hand.

"Hey," he said.

She looked up at him and eyed his bag. Her face brightened, and she came up to the tips of her toes. "Caleb! Thank you so much! I can't begin to express how much this means to me."

He held up a hand to quiet her and chose his next words with care. "My help comes with three conditions. First, Oppenheimer goes where I go, no exceptions. Second, as soon as I'm finished, I'm coming home. Third, once I'm home, you will never try to contact us again, and you will tell nobody about us."

Heather's head rocketed up and down. "I agree. I agree.

Thank you!"

She rushed forward and threw her arms around him, nearly knocking him over. Her level of energy overwhelmed him, and he began to wonder if he'd survive the drive to Chicago.

He pulled away from her embrace without returning it. He helped Opp into the SUV and took his spot in the passenger's seat. Heather pulled them out of the driveway and drove them down the street.

It was only then that Caleb realized how tired he was. His eyelids hung heavy, but he resisted their pleas for rest. He gave Heather a sideways glance. Opp still hadn't barked, so she didn't have a tome in the vehicle, but there still was no explanation for her soul. He was going to have to be cautious.

Despite his best efforts, though, not helped at all by the heaters warming the SUV, Caleb closed his eyes. It wasn't long before sleep descended upon him and took hold.

Chapter Four

"We're here," Heather called out.

Caleb jolted from his sleep. His hand shot to his satchel, and he looked around. It took him a moment to remember where he was. Glancing out the SUV window, he saw they were driving through a crowded city street. Concrete towers rose up around them, consuming the skyline. Even in the vehicle, he could hear the wind outside blaring down upon them. Lights, people, and noises engulfed them from every direction. This was a city.

Heather chuckled. "First time in Chicago?"

"It's my first time out of Orion."

Vehicles swarmed every inch of the roads. It seemed thirty seconds couldn't pass without at least one of them honking. Streams of people walked on both sidewalks, their combined conversations filling the air. Despite how dark it was, the city seemed that it was not even close to slowing down. It was only then that he realized how quiet Orion had been. This was maddening.

His eyes darted to the face of each pedestrian, studying them. His heart quickened its pace. Any one of these people could be an undercover Guild Scribe. They'd have no reason to find him suspicious, even if they were out there, but his stomach turned nonetheless. The potential for danger was everywhere.

To take his mind off it, he turned around to see Opp in the back seat. His dog's face was pressed against the window, completely transfixed by this new environment. Caleb reached back and scratched Opp's head before facing the front again.

Despite the dense traffic, they arrived at a large glass building shortly. The hospital treating Heather's mom. Thankfully, the parking lot wasn't as busy as the street. Heather pulled them into a reserved spot and parked.

"Okay, I need to grab something from the gift shop," Heather said as they exited. "You can either come with or wait for me at the front desk."

He pursed his lips, throwing his satchel and duffle bag over his shoulder. "Or I could just head straight to your mom's room and get started."

She grimaced. "Not a good idea. You'll need my help getting in at this hour."

"I'll figure it out. I really want to get started, so I can get home."

Heather gave him a sympathetic look and thought a moment. "Okay, okay. She's in ICU room three hundred and three." She gave him quick directions on how to find the room.

Making sure Opp was following him, he took off towards the main entrance. Heather left his side after they entered and beelined it to the shop.

An unfamiliar, sterile smell hung in the air of the hospital. Caleb wrinkled his nose as he walked past the information desk, his eyes set on the elevators down the hall.

A voice stopped him. "Can I help you, sir?" A middle-aged woman sat behind the desk, her steady gaze fixed on him.

He tried to fake a sincere smile. "No, I'm good. Thank you." He stepped forward.

"Excuse me, sir, can I ask where you're going?"

"The...the ICU."

She gave him a dry look. "I'm sorry, but it's past visiting hours. Further, only service animals are allowed in the hospital."

"Oh," was all he managed to mutter. He looked at Opp, his mind scrambling to try and think of a strategy. "Well, I only need to go up there for a quick minute."

"That's well and all, but you can do that tomorrow. Come back during visiting hours, and without a dog."

The woman's expression was stern and gave him the impression she wasn't going to change her mind. Heather approached the desk with a vase of tulips in hand. She gave him a concerned look and faced the woman behind the desk.

"Sorry, Molly, he's with me."

The woman looked at Heather, and her face softened a smidge. Her scowl returned once she looked back at Caleb. "Okay. Just make sure he stays out of trouble."

"I pinky promise," Heather responded with a warm smile.

Heather darted away from the desk and straight towards the elevators. Caleb clicked his tongue twice for Opp to follow and stayed on her heels. He kept his head on a swivel, ensuring no wandering eyes were watching them too closely.

Once they were inside, he looked to her. "Do you own the hospital?"

She giggled. "No. My mom is Head of Surgery, and my dad sits on the board. We donate a lot of money."

Caleb arched an eyebrow. What was it like to have money to spare?

After they exited, it was only a short walk to the ICU. Heather's shoulders drooped more and more the closer they came to room three hundred and three.

When they came to the door, she led him inside the cold room, and his eyes darted to the hospital bed. A middle-aged woman lay there, unconscious. A sickly gray hue had seeped into her otherwise peach-colored skin. Her body looked frail, and a myriad of sensors dotted her. He glanced at the familiar monitor. Her vitals were troubling but seemed to be stable at the moment.

What he did not see was a purple soul string protruding from her chest. He closed his eyes and pinched the bridge of his nose. His stomach sank. There was no chance he'd be able to return home tonight.

He opened his eyes and stood in silence. Heather walked over to her mother's bed. She replaced a vase of wilted tulips with the fresh ones she had just bought.

She gave her mom's hand a gentle squeeze. "Hey, Mom, this is Caleb. He's going to help you get better." She looked up at him and smiled weakly. "Her name is Cassandra. Don't call her Cassie, she hates it."

He nodded and grabbed his arm. "Listen...what's affecting her is not what I thought it was. This might take me a while."

Heather frowned. "You can already tell?"

"I would have been able to see what was wrong the moment I walked in. So now I have to try other methods. Would you mind stepping outside?"

She gave him an uneasy look. "I could stay and help."

"I work better alone."

She rocked back and forth on her toes, hesitating.

Caleb sighed. "Heather, you asked me to come here. Please."

Meeting his gaze, she opened her mouth but said nothing. With one last look at her mother, she left. Through the window on the door, he saw her take a seat outside, her back to the room.

He set his duffle bag and satchel on the cold tile floor. Sitting in one of the chairs in the room, he looked at Opp and sighed. "Take a seat, buddy. We could be here a while."

Opp plopped down and yawned. Caleb closed his eyes and delved into his mind. He found the golden flame of his soul and opened it to the outside world. Hundreds of souls throughout the hospital became visible to him.

Some were moving, others were lying in hospital beds. The overwhelming majority of them were the size of an average human soul. Two were as powerful as a Scribe's: his and Heather's. And one was weaker than it should have been. Cassandra's. It wasn't as small as his father's, but it was a pitiful flame nonetheless.

He observed the woman's soul for a moment. Like any flame, it flickered to and fro with life. But the way it did was...off. It wasn't consistent like a healthy soul would be. It danced like it was under strain like it was being attacked.

All of this pointed to a soul string. The way her soul moved, the fact that it was weaker than it should have been, it *had* to be a soul string. And yet, before his very eyes, there was no string. It didn't make any sense.

Standing, he walked past the bed and into the room's lavatory. He turned on the sink and splashed water across his face.

Bags hung heavy under his reflection's eyes. His stomach roared, demanding food, but he had a job to do.

He returned to his duffle bag and pulled out one of the books he had brought from Orion. The text detailed a list of known diseases from the Speculon. With a long sigh, he opened it up.

One by one, he read through the list. He compared Cassandra's symptoms with each disease. Most were easy to eliminate as potential causes, but each time he found one that may be the culprit, he delved into the red text of his tome. Nearly every incantation he had memorized was related to combat in some way. He'd have to look up the medical ones manually.

The first page of medical incantations bore no fruit. One steadied pulse but couldn't be used on patients with low blood pressure. Another helped a soul recover but ran the risk of damaging the liver so it could only be used in emergencies. Others didn't match Cassandra's symptoms at all.

On the second page, he found one that may be a correct match. It would lower the oxygen level in her blood, but her levels were high enough to compensate. It wouldn't matter, though, if it didn't eliminate whatever was causing the symptoms in the first place.

He held the phrase in his mind and spoke the words. The incantation glowed red, and circular yellow glyphs appeared over Cassandra's body.

Her oxygen level lowered as expected but stayed in a safe range. Wishing to be thorough, he kept the incantation active for five minutes, though thirty seconds would have sufficed. When he removed it, Cassandra's oxygen levels rose to their previous level, but nothing else had changed. The incantation had failed.

An hour passed, and he tried seven incantations. Each one failed to alleviate Cassandra's symptoms. Setting the book down, he rubbed his temples. His eyelids were heavy, and he considered taking a nap before continuing, but a knock came at the door. He quickly closed his tome.

"Sorry," Heather called in before entering. "I hope you don't mind, but your stomach growled the whole ride here, so I went and got us some sandwiches and chips." She held out a plain-looking sub and an individual bag of potato chips.

"Thank you." He accepted them both and took a bite of the sandwich. The bread was dry, but it was food, and he wasn't going to complain.

Heather sat down next to him. 'Is it okay if I join you for a moment?"

He shrugged. He pushed the books under his chair, hoping to obscure them.

"Haven't made any progress, huh?" She gave him a sideways glance.

"No. I've got a few things I can try. I may not heal her tonight, though."

"What exactly are you doing?"

He finished the first half of his sandwich and looked down at the duffle bag. His grandfather's voice scolded him, telling him to keep his mouth shut. And so, he would. He'd carry this weight alone. He glanced over to her and said, "I can't go into detail."

A concerned expression painted her face. She hadn't taken a bite of her food yet. "It's hard. I'm no fool, Caleb. I know this is irrational, asking a stranger to pull off some miraculous cure based on a rumor." Her eyes fixated on her mother, tears welling up in them. "My dad is never around much. My best friend, Aalia, works for him now, so she's gone too. All I had left were Wilson and my mom, and now she's sick. I'd do anything to save her, no matter how ridiculous it sounds."

Caleb's heart sank in his chest. If he didn't know anything about the world of Scribes, would he do the same for his father? Of course. Without a doubt. Maybe he should tell her the truth. Given the nature of her soul, she'd be able to see the full effect of his incantations. Perhaps it would give her some peace of mind.

Heather sighed. "Oh, well. I'll respect your boundaries if it means she'll get better." She exited the room, leaving her food behind, untouched.

Guilt bubbled in his stomach. He glanced at Cassandra. What if she had been his father? He couldn't fail to save her. Setting his food down, he returned to his book and continued to scan through the list of ailments.

Hours passed. Opp had fallen asleep long ago, and Caleb had reached the end of the book. In all, he had found nine incantations that may have been the cure, but none worked. Cassandra lay in her bed, unchanged and still dying. There were five more books he could try, but it was late, and the thought of more reading blurred his vision. He'd have to return tomorrow after resting.

He packed his stuff, double-checking his tome was back in his satchel. Exiting the room, he found Heather asleep in a chair. He gently shook her. It took a moment for her to return to reality, but she shot up and looked at him, a smile sweeping her face. It faded when she saw his expression.

"I'm sorry, Heather, I haven't figured out what is wrong with her. I'll have to come back tomorrow. Is there a hotel you could bring me to?" The words terrified him. How on earth was he going to afford a hotel in the middle of Chicago?

Heather remained motionless for a long moment, her eyes fixated on ICU room three hundred and three. Eventually, she shook her head, and a false smile crawled back on her face. "Don't be silly. You can stay at my place. We have more than enough room. And once you're rested, we can come back."

Despite the hopeful facade she tried to portray, the car ride was silent. The streets had emptied significantly, and it took them half an hour to reach the base of a black skyscraper. They unloaded the vehicle as a man in a suit approached and entered the driver's seat.

Caleb arched an eyebrow. "Is this normal?"

"Oh, he's just the valet. He works for the building."

Clicking his tongue for Opp to follow, Caleb stuck close to Heather as they scurried into the building. The main foyer had a black marble floor with a plush purple rug guiding them further inside. White square pillars rose high to the ceiling. Between each hung rich, artistic tapestries of varying, vibrant colors. In the center of the room stood a round, stone desk. A short man dressed in blue stood there, glancing at them with a polite smile.

"Good evening, Ms. O'Brien, how are we tonight?"

Heather raised her shoulders and beamed at the man. "Hey, Paul. Just coming home from the hospital."

The man tsked. "Oh, I am terribly sorry. No good news yet?"

"Not yet." She motioned to Caleb. "This is Caleb. He's a welcome guest. Can you have a keycard made up for him?"

"Yes, ma'am, right away."

"Also, please keep him off the official manifest."

"Of course, ma'am."

"Thank you."

Heather shuffled past the desk and moved to the gold-trimmed elevators at the other end of the foyer. Caleb kept pace with her, trying to process all the new information. She pulled out a white plastic card and held it up to a console next to the elevator. With a ding, one of the doors opened for them.

"So, you're rich, huh?" he asked as the elevator ascended.

She gave him a nervous smile. "My dad runs some company that contracts with the government. We've been wealthy for a few generations."

Wealthy for a few generations. The Fleischers had been the same until his grandfather disinherited his father. But Caleb didn't want that money. He'd bag groceries the rest of his life, and he'd do it with a smile on his face.

The elevator stopped and opened with a ding. They stepped out into a lavish penthouse. Polished hardwood covered the floor of the extensive entryway, and the entire right wall was a massive window that overlooked the Chicago skyline. Entrances to two other rooms dotted either end of the left wall.

Caleb looked down at Opp. Still no barking. Did Heather really not know about the nature of her own soul?

A stocky, elderly man dressed in a magenta sweater vest and slacks appeared from the nearest room. His tanned white skin was a mild contrast to his well-trimmed hair and beard. "Miss O'Brien," the man said anxiously, "you had me worried sick."

Heather looked down and dug her toes into the floor. "Sorry, Wilson. I had to do some stuff."

"Shall I go into a lengthy explanation of how upset I am?"

Heather sauntered over to the man and nudged him in the ribs with her elbow. "I already said sorry. Plus, you love me too much to stay mad at me. It's your weakness."

A faint smile curled at the corner of Wilson's mouth. He then glanced over to Caleb, as if he were noticing him for the first time. "And who are our guests?"

"This is Caleb Fleischer and Oppenheimer. They're here to help with Mom."

Wilson's eyes narrowed. Caleb grabbed his arm and kept his gaze downwards. He had nothing to add.

"I see. I'm not sure if it is a wise decision to bring them to the hospital, Miss O'Brien."

"Well...I already did."

Wilson huffed.

"Come on, Wilson, it's fine. Just don't tell my dad."

"You know I don't appreciate keeping secrets from my employer, even for you."

"I know, but you're gonna anyway, right?"

A sigh escaped the old man. "I'll give it some thought, Miss O'Brien."

She stood on the tips of her toes and kissed Wilson's cheek. "Thank you. Now, I have barely slept in a few days, so I'm gonna go crash. Could you show Caleb to his room?"

"Very well. But I think we should talk about this tomorrow."

Heather rolled her eyes. "I can't wait." She gave Caleb a warm smile before disappearing through the far entrance.

Wilson nodded courteously as she left, but his fierce gaze remained on Caleb. Once she was safely out of earshot, he cleared his throat. "Mister Fleischer, perhaps we can have a word in the kitchen."

Caleb closed his eyes. He knew when a request wasn't a request.

Without putting up a fight, he followed the old man into the nearer room. The kitchen that opened before him was near twice the size of his kitchen and living room back in Orion combined. Fancy cabinets and molding lined the walls, and an ornately carved table sat at the opposite end of the room.

Wilson took a seat at the end of the table. A disassembled pistol lay in front of him, along with a folded towel and cleaning supplies. The old man methodically wiped down the barrel with a thin cloth scrubber.

Caleb sat at the opposite end of the table, setting his duffle bag on the ground but keeping his satchel on his lap.

Without looking up at him, Wilson spoke. "I've known Miss O'Brien since the day she was born. Her father was always traveling, and her mother was always at the hospital, so I raised her. She's one of the most good-natured people I know. She's also young and desperate. Combined, this can make her easily swayed by the promises of a charlatan."

Wilson paused, his eyes still glued to his gun. Caleb assumed it was his turn to defend himself, but he kept his mouth shut.

The old man finally looked up and gave him a long, hard stare. "I don't know what you've promised her, but I can't make you leave. This is her home, and she makes the rules. So, go to the hospital and wave your magic wand. Spin whatever web of lies you must and accept your payment. Then leave, and never come back. The sooner she can accept Cassandra's eventual death, the sooner she can begin coping."

Caleb looked up and met the man's eyes at last. They were hard, cold, and brown. But, for a moment, he thought he saw the icy blue eyes of his grandfather. Shaking his head, he tried to keep his breathing under control.

"Thank you for welcoming me into your home," was all he could squeak out.

Wilson motioned to the door behind him. "The den is through there. Turn right, and you'll see a metal, spiral staircase. Take it to the lower level. The first door on your left will be your guest bedroom." Wilson studied him for a moment. "Get some rest, Mister Fleischer. You look exhausted."

Caleb grabbed his duffle bag and stood. Opp right on his heels, he made his way through the door into what looked like a fancy living room. Taking the spiral staircase down, he found himself in a long hallway. Following Wilson's instructions, he entered the first door on the left.

The guest room was somehow both elegant and simple at the same time. The right wall was one giant window, giving him a clear view of the city. An open door on his left led to a large bathroom. The only two significant objects were a king-sized mattress and a fancy wardrobe.

Too tired to explore further, Caleb dropped his satchel and duffle bag and shuffled over to the bed. Collapsing upon it, he closed his eyes and drifted off to sleep.

Chapter Five

Heated voices woke Caleb some hours later. Was his grandfather yelling at his father? His heart raced, and he shot up in the bed. Wait. But he wasn't in Orion. This was Heather's penthouse. Those were hers and Wilson's voices.

He shook his head, trying to snap back to reality. The raised voices continued, shouting back and forth, though he couldn't make out what they were saying. Wishing to drown out the argument, he shuffled to the bathroom. The white walls, tiles, and counters were blinding.

Turning on the shower, he couldn't believe the pressure. Undressing, he stepped under the powerful, warm stream. Steam surrounded him, and he remained under the water for some time. It relaxed his muscles, and his stress melted away. But, just as important, it drowned out the yelling.

How long had it been since a shower had felt relaxing?

He put on a new shirt but slipped into his old jeans once he finished. Heather and Wilson were still arguing. Should he just stay in the guest room until they stopped? No, he wanted to get to the hospital as soon as possible. Showing up in the middle of an argument never stopped his grandfather and father from fighting, but maybe things with Heather and Wilson would be different.

His stomach growled on his way up the spiral stairs, Opp right on his heels. The voices grew louder.

"Miss O'Brien, I am not comfortable with it," Wilson said sternly.

"It's not your decision," Heather responded.

Caleb stepped into the entryway to see them standing a few feet apart. They hadn't noticed him yet.

"No, but I could call your father."

"Wilson! You said you wouldn't."

"I said I'd give it some thought, Miss O'Brien. But I have to put your safety above—"

They both looked over at him.

He grabbed his arm. "I'm guessing this is about me."

Heather took a step towards him. "Caleb, I'm sorry if we woke you."

Wilson cleared his throat. "Mister Fleischer, I do not trust the safety of Missus O'Brien nor Miss O'Brien while you reside here or work in the hospital."

Heather spun and glared at the man. "Wilson, stop."

The old man's eyes bore into him. "Answer me one question, Mister Fleischer. How are you planning on healing Missus O'Brien?"

Caleb waited for Heather to say something. Instead, she glanced at him, curiosity evident in her gaze. His grandfather's voice screamed at him to keep his mouth shut. To never to speak of this. "I'm sorry. I can't say."

Wilson straightened his tie. Despite Caleb's response, the man didn't have a satisfied look upon his face. It was bittersweet. "Miss O'Brien, mysterious promises aren't going to save your mother's life. I am asking you, please, think with your head and not your heart."

Heather dug her toes into the floor. She looked at Caleb from the corner of her eyes. "I want to believe. More than you know. I need to. Can I?"

He met her gaze. Yesterday she had shown up to his house already trusting him. Or perhaps she had been lying to herself.

But now, she was asking. If he lied, here and now, he could go home. He'd never see Chicago again.

He'd be safe.

But Cassandra would die. Images of Heather sitting next to her deceased mother in the hospital flooded his mind. Yesterday, in Orion, those thoughts hadn't bothered him. He was willing to stay home instead of helping some nameless individual. But now he'd seen her face. He'd felt Cassandra's decaying soul. How could he leave?

But what did that make him if he'd only save someone after seeing them? Just the thought of someone in danger wasn't enough. Did he have to be personally invested to do the right thing? Those questions plagued him, but one last thought came to his mind.

Sally. Yesterday, she had asked him to hang out, and his grandfather's voice demanded he refuse. That he had to be separate from everyone else. Keep his life a secret. Never trust anyone.

He didn't want to be alone anymore.

Caleb snapped his fingers. His tome shot out of his satchel and floated in front of him. Heather fell to the floor, staring up at the book in horror. Wilson took a step back, his eyes growing wide.

"I'm what's called a Scribe," Caleb said. "This is my tome. I use it to cast incantations with my soul."

Heather's mouth hung open, her face having gone pale. Wilson rubbed his eyes and stepped forward. The old man waved his hands around the tome, apparently checking for wires.

"How are you doing this?" Wilson asked.

"Take a step back, and I'll show you something." Once Wilson complied, Caleb brought a phrase into his mind. His tome flipped through its pages, and he flared his soul. *"With birds, I'd like to share; Being lighter than air."*

The text glowed, and a golden glyph formed around his waist. His stomach lurched as he started to rise off the ground, the glyph remaining around his gut. He swayed back and forth and gritted his teeth. His full concentration went to trying to remain balanced, and he was failing. After nearly tumbling backward, he released the incantation and came back to the floor.

"That one isn't very practical," he admitted. "I hardly ever use it."

Heather and Wilson were silent.

"I'll show you one more." Bringing a new phrase to his thoughts, he spoke the words. *"Traveling through time and space; Fly me to another place."*

Static crackled. A hole tore in the air in front of him and formed a golden portal. Through it, he could see the other side of the entryway. He stepped through the hole and emerged through a second portal on the other side of the room.

Caleb released the incantation, and the portals vanished. Heather was already staring at him, but Wilson focused on where he had been.

"I'm over here," Caleb said.

Wilson spun, his eyes growing even wider. "You teleported."

Heather shook her head. "No, he stepped through a hole and came out another one."

"She's right," Caleb said.

"I didn't see any hole." The old man lowered his brow.

Caleb nodded. "That's because you're not a Scribe."

"And what does that mean, exactly?"

Caleb grabbed his tome from the air and returned it to his satchel. "Every living thing has a soul. A Scribe, however, is born with a far more powerful and advanced soul. And we can use them to create these tomes." He paused, giving them a moment to digest the information. The next bit might not be easy for them. "When Heather showed up at my home, I looked at her soul. She has the soul of a Scribe."

Wilson took in a long breath. "You're sure of this?"

Heather looked down to her hands, then glanced up at the old man. "I saw what you couldn't, didn't I?"

"I need a moment." Wilson retreated to the kitchen.

Sighing, Caleb walked to Heather and helped her to her feet. "You okay?"

She smiled nervously and rubbed the back of her neck. "You know, you'd think the fact that I spent large amounts of time and money chasing down a nonsensical lead would make this easy to believe. But..." She trailed off, looking out at the Chicago skyline. "Is anyone really ever ready for their entire world view to change?"

"I can imagine." He studied her out of his peripheries. She

did seem to be genuinely surprised, but she wasn't casting him out. There were no insults or attacks. He had told her the truth, and she had accepted him. His grandfather had been wrong.

"And..." She hesitated. "I can learn all of this?"

"Oh," he said, peering out at the city beneath them, "you could. But you shouldn't. Being a Scribe is...difficult." Unconsciously, his finger traced up a scar on his chest.

She tilted her head to the side. "You don't like it?"

"It's what I was born to be."

"What would you want to be instead?" she asked, her soft green eyes washing over him.

Grabbing his arm, he said nothing. It was a fruitless question. He was a Scribe. It's what his grandfather trained him to be, what he had been forced to be. There wasn't any other life available to him.

She was silent for a long moment before saying, "We should go check on Wilson."

In the kitchen, they saw the old man sitting with his head resting on the table. Heather walked over and embraced him.

"You okay, Mister Wilson, sir?" she said in a playful tone.

A chuckle escaped the man. "I shall always be swell when I have the world's greatest caretaker watching over me." Wilson stood and wrapped his burly arms around her. They held the embrace for a moment before parting. "I must distract myself."

Straightening his waistcoat, the old man stepped to the cupboard and pulled out a cutting board. "Perhaps you would care to assist me in preparing a meal, Mister Fleischer?"

The question took Caleb by surprise. Was this a peace offering? If so, he relished the opportunity. But there was a slight problem. "Actually," he said, looking down, "I really only know how to cook cheap stuff."

"I can show you the ropes well enough if you're willing," the old man responded.

Heather nudged Caleb's ribs. "Come on, it'll be fun."

His stomach tumbled at the thought of embarrassing himself, but he nodded, nonetheless.

Wilson held a red pot out towards him. "Could you bring six cups of water to boil, Mister Fleischer?"

Caleb's gut eased slightly. That he could do. After measuring out the water, he set the pot on the stove and turned on the heat.

As the glass surface warmed, his stomach let out a thunderous growl.

Wilson chuckled. "It appears we are starting at the appropriate time."

Caleb smiled weakly. "Sorry for shattering your grasp on reality," he said, trying to change the subject.

The old man grabbed a handful of some sort of leaf from the fridge before returning to the cutting board. He began to dice the leaves before finally saying, "Magic, is it? If I'm being honest, Mister Fleischer, I haven't the faintest idea what to make of any of this. But only a fool denies evidence before their very eyes."

"How opened minded of you," Heather teased as she made her way to the fridge. "Shall I beat some eggs?"

"That would be quite helpful, Miss O'Brien. And Mister Fleischer, perhaps you could tenderize the chicken in the refrigerator."

Heather cracked four eggs into a bowl and stirred with a whisk. "So," she said, "you're a Scribe. And I'm a Scribe...or wait. I have the soul of one?"

"Oh, well," Caleb said. "Mostly the same thing. Scribe's are born, not made. You've just never had someone train you." His grandfather's screams filled his mind the moment the words left his mouth.

Heather twisted her mouth. "Oh, okay. So how many of us are there?"

Caleb thought for a moment as he gathered the chicken. "My grandfather always said the Guild's forces were three million strong."

"You mentioned them yesterday. You called them The Guild of Life?" Heather said, tilting her head. "Who are they?"

"They're a massive organization that employs almost every Scribe. It's their job to keep us safe from the beasts of the Speculon."

Wilson looked over from the cutting board and offered him a metallic, flat hammer-like instrument. "Speculon?"

Caleb accepted the tool and narrowed his eyes at it.

Wilson chuckled. "Use the flat end to pound the chicken. Making it flatter and less firm allows for a more even cooking of the meat."

Nodding, Caleb followed the instructions as he recalled the

stories his mother had told him of the Speculon as a kid. "There are two planes of existence. Ours, and the Speculon. A barrier separates us, though some of the smaller beasts still sneak through." The filken's pleas from a few nights ago crept into his mind.

Heather set her whisk in the sink. "It sounds like this guild protects us. But you seem so afraid of them."

He sighed, recalling the stories his grandfather told him as a child, his hammering growing firmer. "They do protect us. But they're a powerful organization, and many covet leading it. My grandfather used to be in charge over twenty years ago, then someone staged a coup against him. My family has been on the run ever since, and I've lived my life looking over my shoulder."

She looked down. "And coming here has increased the chance they may find you, hasn't it?"

He nodded.

"I'm sorry."

"No," he said, stopping his hammering. "I'm sorry it was so hard to get me to say yes. It's a risk being here, and I miss Orion already, but I want to be the kind of person who does the right thing. I want to help."

Wilson dumped the now finely chopped leaves onto a plate before giving Caleb a long stare, studying him. "Well said, Mister Fleischer."

Caleb looked away, his face growing warm.

"The chicken appears properly tenderized," the man continued. "Now we need to apply the rub and breading. Come, Mister Fleischer."

Together with the old man, Caleb mixed the chopped leaves with flour and an assortment of other spices. After cutting the chicken into smaller pieces, they rubbed them in the flour and dipped them in the eggs Heather had prepared. After applying a hearty coat of breadcrumbs, they fried the chicken and set it in the oven.

A smile spread across Caleb's face. It was strange how much cooking took his mind off of everything else. The simple task of taking a group of random food and combining them into a meal allowed him to disappear. The thought caused Caleb's heart to dip, however. If only he and his father had owned the money to eat proper meals all these years.

"Very good," Wilson exclaimed. "I shall prepare the rice and asparagus while the chicken bakes. Feel free to take a seat, Mr. Fleischer."

As Wilson cooked, Heather asked Caleb to cast more incantations. Hoping it would help further convince them both and make them more comfortable with the idea, he complied. He summoned a small flame, produced water, created ice, and healed a small cut on his hand.

While Heather could see the entirety of each display, Wilson was unable to see the glowing text nor the resulting glyphs, only their effects.

Once Wilson finished cooking the meal, he set three plates at the table, and they dined together. Flavor burst in Caleb's mouth with every bite, easily outshining the microwave dinners, instant ramen, and peanut butter and jelly sandwiches that had served as most of his life's meals.

Wilson set his fork and knife upon his empty plate. "Today has me questioning my knowledge of...well, everything. But human history specifically. Have there always been Scribes, Mister Fleischer?"

Caleb placed his utensils down as well, pondering the question. What was the easiest way to explain the truth to them concisely?

"Well," he began, "we've been around for most of history. A long, long time ago, before the barrier separated us, the Speculon invaded Earth. But the Guardians of Life, Death, and Time saved us. They then passed a fraction of their power onto a handful of humans, creating the first Scribes."

Heather hung on his every word with wide eyes. "So, we're descended from those people?"

He nodded.

A moment passed, and Wilson cleared his throat. "You mentioned your normal cuisine, Mister Fleischer. I assume you struggle to make ends meet?"

Caleb glanced down at his empty plate. "I work most days at Orion's grocer. Even then, it's always tough."

The old man frowned. "Are your parents able to assist?"

"My mom was never really around much," he said. "And my dad has been sick since before I was born."

Heather reached out a comforting hand, but Caleb reflexively shied from her touch. He muttered a quick apology and did his best to avoid their gazes.

The three were silent as Wilson cleaned off the table and washed the dishes. No doubt they needed time to mull over everything he had told them in the last hour.

Once the old man had finished cleaning, he cleared his throat. "Miss O'Brien, perhaps it is time we made our way to the hospital."

She perked up with a bright smile. "Does this mean you aren't calling my dad?"

Wilson took a measured breath. "It seems to me that Mister Fleischer has good intentions and a kind character. If he truly can help your mother, I want to give him that chance."

Heather shot up from the table and darted to Wilson, wrapping her arms around him. "Thank you, Wilson."

"Of course, Miss O'Brien."

Caleb looked down, a small bit of relief washing over him. He wasn't sure how he had managed it, but he gained a bit of Wilson's trust. Now he had to prove worthy of it.

The three prepared to depart, and Caleb asked Heather if she had a backpack he could borrow. Lugging his duffle bag around the hospital each visit wasn't a task he relished. Better to only bring a single book or two at a time.

Heather disappeared upstairs and returned with a worn, red backpack. He accepted it and retrieved the book he thought would be more helpful for the day's task. As he did, he noticed a button reading "Johns Hopkins" pinned to one of the backpack's straps.

Once they were ready, they left for the hospital.

ICU room three hundred and three was still frigid. Wilson stood guard outside the room while Caleb, Heather, and Opp sat inside. Pulling out his tome and the academic book he had retrieved, he walked Heather through what he was doing in more detail. For a few hours, she watched him page through the text, trying one incantation after another. Frustratingly, the results were the same as they had been the day before.

"Yesterday, you said you thought you'd be able to see what was wrong with my mom right away. What would you have seen?" she asked him.

"I would have bet a lot of money I don't have that she had a soul string."

She arched an eyebrow at him.

"The beasts of the Speculon use the strings to feed off people's souls." He decided to leave off the Guardians from the explanation. He didn't want to overwhelm her.

"Gotcha," she said with a puzzled look plain upon her face. "These beasts sound scary."

Caleb nodded. "My grandfather always called them monsters."

"And you've fought them?"

He looked down. The pleading from the filken a few nights ago filled his mind yet again. "I've killed more filken than I care to think about. But I'm lucky. I've never had to face an elderon. Or worse, a hydran."

She put a hand on his shoulder, staring at him for a full minute. "Those ones are worse than filken?"

"They appear far less often. But it would normally take four or five Scribes to take one down."

She brought a finger to her chin but didn't open her mouth. When no additional question came, he refocused on her mother. All this talk of the beasts, of killing and fighting, wasn't where he wanted his thoughts to lie. Right now, he wanted to focus on healing. On saving.

Caleb finished scanning the book hours later. Still no cure for Cassandra. After he closed the book, he looked over to Heather and gave her a disappointed look. "Try again tomorrow?" he asked her.

"Try again tomorrow."

Chapter Six

Four days had passed since Caleb arrived in Chicago. A powerful wind barraged the window of the penthouse guest bedroom like a howling train. He sat on the hardwood with books open around him. Oppenheimer lay in the corner of the room, sound asleep.

He pinched the bridge of his nose. He could feel the bags that hung under his eyes, a testament to the hours upon hours of studying he had endured, but he was no closer to curing Cassandra than he had been his first night here. Only one book remained untested. If he didn't find a solution in it tonight, he didn't know what he was going to do.

A knock brought him from his thoughts. "Mister Fleischer, are you decent?"

Caleb set aside the book and nodded. Only after a moment did he realize Wilson couldn't see him through the closed door and said, "Yeah."

The door cracked open, and Wilson's head poked through.

The man's mouth was already open to speak, but he remained silent. His steady eyes studied the condition of the room, his expression transitioning from confused to concerned. "Would you like lunch, Mister Fleischer?"

Caleb's stomach balled tight. He doubted food would even fit. "No, thank you, Wilson."

The old man retreated a step. "Mister Fleischer...do you require any assistance?"

He shook his head. "Is Heather awake?"

"Miss O'Brien is studying in the living room. She wouldn't say it, but I know she's eager to make her way to the hospital."

"I'll be up soon."

"Very good, sir."

Caleb kept his eyes closed as Wilson drove them to the hospital. A banging pain drummed in his head, and he squeezed his eyes tighter. His lack of sleep was catching up with him. Heather's phone chimed, not helping at all.

"Is that Miss Laghari?" Wilson asked.

"Yeah," Heather said. "Aalia found out I dropped out this semester. She's not too happy about it. Reminded me my dad won't be either."

The name sounded familiar to Caleb. As he tried to recall where he had heard it, a question came to mind. "You're going to school still?"

"Yeah. Well, not this semester. I'm studying to be a surgeon at Hopkins. It's what my parents always wanted from me."

Wilson shifted in his seat but kept his eyes on the road.

A brief silence hung in the air until Heather cleared her throat. "So, what happened to the other two Guilds? You said there were three Guardians, but only one Guild..."

Opening his eyes, he gave her a sideways glance. "The three Guilds worked together for thousands of years. Then, a few centuries ago, the Guild of Life decided all Scribes should unite. They launched a surprise attack against the leaders of the other two and killed them. Then they offered the remaining Scribes a choice: join or die. Most joined."

"The Guardians of Time and Death didn't stop them?"

He shook his head. "They only interfere in the affairs of mortals if the world is at stake."

"Sorry for the questions," she said. "You look really tired."

"I *am* really tired," he said, closing his eyes again.

None of them spoke for the rest of the journey to ICU room three hundred and three. Heather joined him inside, and he pulled out the only book he hadn't tested yet. He tried to force himself to feel hopeful, but his grandfather's voice drowned out the attempt. Today was going to end in failure.

Feigning determination, he read over every ailment, parasite, condition, disease, and sickness. Shadows danced across the tiled floor as the hours passed. Each page brought him closer to defeat, and he could have sworn the room was shrinking.

Sweat dripped from his hands, and his breathing grew labored. He double-checked. Triple checked. He begged for a solution to reveal itself. But each incantation he cast left Cassandra unchanged.

An hour past sundown, he reached the final page. He didn't even read it. How could he? If he did, it would become real. He'll have failed. Heather would be shattered. Cassandra's fate would be sealed. And his grandfather would be right.

He tried to swallow past the lump lodged in his throat. With dry eyes, he read the page. No cure. No cure. No cure.

His stomach sank. Cassandra lay in her bed, still dying. He closed the book, letting it slide from his lap. It landed with a thump, and Heather jolted.

He opened his mouth to speak, but she beat him to the punch. "Caleb, what's your favorite color?"

Narrowing his eyes at the sudden question, he hesitated before saying, "Yellow, I suppose."

"Mine's red. I always liked how fierce it felt. Whenever I wear it, I feel so powerful." Tears welled up in her eyes, though she tried to blink them away. Her gaze remained fixated on her mother. "My parents always seemed so strong to me. My mom is so accomplished, kind, and smart. My dad is decisive and hardworking. I look up to them so much, and I want to be as strong as them. As strong as red."

"Heather..."

"But she's dying. You were my last hope. I don't know what else to do."

He didn't know what to say. What words could make this better? Instead, he stood and called Wilson into the room.

Caleb couldn't look at either of them. "I finished the last book. I'm so sorry, but I couldn't figure out what was wrong with her."

Gathering his nerves, he glanced up. Heather was trying to smile, but her mouth would twitch up only to droop. She stared at her mother with misty eyes. Wilson put a calloused hand on her shoulder, staying silent.

Caleb moved towards her and raised a hand, stopping it halfway to her shoulder. It wasn't his place to try and comfort her.

Oppenheimer trotted forward, nuzzling her leg. She looked to the dog and then to Caleb, tears welling up in her eyes. "Is there anything else you can do?"

He wracked his mind. If it wasn't a soul string, and it wasn't in these books, what else was there?

"I guess I could give my dad a call, but I don't know how much good it would do."

Heather blinked away tears and walked over to Cassandra's side. Holding the woman's hand, she said, "You've spent enough time in Chicago on my behalf. I'll bring you home tonight."

He grabbed his arm. "Heather—"

Oppenheimer barked three distinct times.

Caleb's head snapped to his dog, then to the door. His eyes grew wide, and his hands clenched into fists.

Three barks. Three.

He gathered his belongings and double-checked he wasn't leaving anything lying around. Satisfied, he darted to the corner of the room farthest from the door. Signaling for Opp to join him and stay quiet, he snapped his fingers. His tome shot out of his satchel and floated in front of him.

It flipped through its pages, and he shot Heather a desperate glance. "No matter who comes through that door, you can't say anything. Nothing about me, my dad, or what I've been doing here."

Heather exchanged a glance with Wilson before asking, "Caleb, what's going on?"

"Do you understand?"

She nodded, though her worried expression did not dissipate.

Caleb didn't waste a moment. His tome opened to the correct page, and he spoke the phrase he held in his mind. "*Shadows hide me from my enemy's eyes; Make me impossible to recognize.*"

A purple veil sprang from his tome and enveloped him. Pouring the golden flame of his soul into the words, he expanded it to cover Opp as well. His heart drummed in his ears. Sweat dripped down his face, and he kept his gaze glued to the door.

Two minutes passed. More than once, Heather and Wilson looked to the corner where he stood, despite him being invisible to them.

Finally, a knock rapped against the door. After a courteous pause, a man and woman dressed in black suits strolled in. Each carried large, official-looking briefcases and no firearms at their side.

The man stood over six and a half feet tall. His black, buzzed hair rested upon a large head with a chiseled jaw. The UV lighting radiated off his tan skin and accentuated the veins popping on his neck. Capped off with arms as thick as tree trunks, the man reminded Caleb of an 80's action star.

The woman was short and wiry, but clearly the one in charge. She held her light brown hair up in a bun, and her thin mouth seemed to be stuck in a permanent scowl. Her milky skin was a deep contrast to her dark suit.

The woman focused on Heather while her partner slowly scanned the room. Reaching into her breast pocket, the woman produced a badge and showed it to both Heather and Wilson. Caleb couldn't make out what the badge said from where he stood, but he guessed either FBI or DHS.

"Good evening, Ms. O'Brien," the woman said. "I'm Agent Megan Trenton. This is my partner, Dom Eckerson. We're with the Department of Homeland Security, and we'd like to ask you a few questions."

Heather wiped her eyes, but it was Wilson who spoke. "Excuse me, Agents, but we are here with Miss O'Brien's sick mother. This hardly seems appropriate."

"Actually, this is about her mother," Trenton responded.

Agent Eckerson advanced towards Cassandra's bedside and

scrutinized the comatose woman. Heather shot him an uneasy glance, but he didn't acknowledge her.

Caleb only took a breath when he absolutely needed to. His hands trembled, but he was otherwise as still as stone. The Guild had come.

Trenton sat at one of the chairs and produced a small notepad. "Now, Ms. O'Brien, do you know what is wrong with your mother?"

"If the doctors don't know, then I certainly don't."

"You're a pre-med student, are you not?"

Heather tilted her head. "Yeah, pre-med, not a doctor."

"Fair enough. How long has she been sick?"

"Five months."

"Has anyone tried to contact you about her condition?"

"What do you mean?" Heather asked.

"Has someone approached you and offered help? Promised to cure her?"

"As far as I know, the only people who have had contact with my mom are myself, Wilson here, and the hospital staff."

Eckerson opened the bathroom door and stepped inside.

Wilson marched over and kept an eye on him. He then looked at Trenton. "Are we nearly finished here?"

"Nearly," Trenton said. "I can't help but notice you didn't mention your father as people who have seen your mother."

"He's been away for work. He calls sometimes, though."

"How does that make you feel?"

Heather arched an eyebrow.

Eckerson emerged from the bathroom. Briefcase still in hand, the man walked around the bed and towards Caleb's corner.

Caleb's pulse quickened. The time between his breaths grew shorter, and perspiration soaked into his shirt. He held out his hands, ready to summon his scythe, but he desperately hoped it wouldn't come to blows. He had never taken a human life.

"I'm sorry," Heather said, "but what is this about?"

"Dangerous individuals may be contacting family members of certain hospital patients. They may be trying to take advantage of their desperation and exploit them. We're here for your safety, Ms. O'Brien."

Eckerson was steps from the purple veil. Caleb's heart exploded in his ears. A fight was coming. He didn't want to hurt anyone. He didn't want to be like his grandfather.

Wilson's hand appeared on Eckerson's shoulder, stopping the man. "Excuse me," Wilson said, "I'm afraid I must ask you both to leave. Now."

Trenton narrowed her eyes at the old man and flipped through her notepad a few pages. "Wilson Price, correct? Former Army Captain? Lived homeless a few years after returning from Vietnam, then bounced from one job to the next before meeting Michael O'Brien, whom you've been employed by for thirty years now."

Wilson furrowed his brow and crossed his arms. "Yes, that's correct, ma'am."

"Well, Mr. Price, I'm afraid we'll leave when we're good and—" A ringing phone sounded from the woman's suit. Taking it out, she answered, "This is Trenton. Yes, sir. Yes, sir. No, sir. Understood."

Trenton ended the call and stood. She motioned her head to the door. Eckerson nodded and made his way towards the exit, stepping away from Caleb's veil.

Opening the door, Trenton faced Heather. "Thank you for answering our questions, Ms. O'Brien. We'll be in touch."

Both agents departed.

Caleb kept the incantation intact, the phrase fresh in his thoughts. His soul continued to feed the words, keeping him and Opp invisible. Heather glanced in his direction, but she remained silent.

Ten minutes passed, and his soul and mind began to strain from the effort. Convinced the agents weren't going to return, he released the words. He became visible once more, relieved from the massive weight that had been removed from his head.

Heather jumped back the moment he reappeared. "I knew you were there, and I still freaked out. I don't know if I'll ever get used to this."

Caleb signaled to Opp that it was okay to move. Taking a seat in one of the chairs, he looked at both Wilson and Heather. "Thank you, both of you."

Wilson adjusted his tie and met Caleb's gaze. "Mister Fleischer, perhaps you can offer an explanation of what just transpired."

"Those two are Scribes, and they work for the Guild."

Heather walked away from her mom and towards him. "Are you sure? I really want to think I didn't just lie to the government."

Caleb nodded. "It was Opp. Incantations are written in a Scribe's blood. Among other things, he's trained to smell the scent of blood on paper. When he barked three times, he was telling me that a Scribe was nearby. Two barks mean a beast of the Speculon is close."

"Oh, okay. That's why you insist he always be near you."

He shrugged. "It's one of the reasons."

Wilson leaned against the wall and looked up at the ceiling. "And what you just did, that was some sort of cloaking spell?"

"An illusionary one. A Scribe can make themselves invisible, hide other objects, or even conceal incantations or creatures of the—"

Caleb shot out of his chair and stared at Cassandra. His stomach turned as he considered an improbable, terrible possibility. Snapping his fingers, he brought a new phrase to mind.

"Caleb?" Heather asked. "What's going on?"

He didn't answer.

"Wise, I shall not be deceived; I see past illusions weaved."

As the red text glowed, a small yellow orb formed over his tome. The sphere spun and hummed before growing. It expanded outward, past the walls of the hospital room, seemingly without end.

He shielded his eyes from the bright light. When he lowered his hand, he noticed Heather had closed her eyes, but Wilson had not reacted at all. But Caleb quickly shifted his focus to Cassandra.

His eyes widened.

A purple soul string emerged from her chest. One of the deadliest things in the world, it danced softly in the air. He couldn't believe it. His instincts had been right, after all.

But his spirits fell. Scribes couldn't create soul strings, and beasts of the Speculon couldn't cast incantations. Either one of the Guardians had cast both on Cassandra, or a Scribe was somehow in league with one of the beasts. The more he dwelled on it, the more one thought stood out from the rest: the Guild had to be involved. He nearly vomited from the implication.

Just as strange, Heather had mentioned her mother had been sick for five months. At worst, a filken could consume a soul in a few hours. What was going on?

Heather took a nervous step back. "So...that's a soul string?"

Wilson looked at both their faces. "What's happening?"

She waved her hand through the string, passing through it. "It's a strand of purple light coming out of her body."

"It's consuming her soul," Caleb added.

Wilson rubbed his chin. "And you two couldn't see it before?"

"A Scribe cloaked it, but my incantation canceled it out."

Caleb moved forward and stumbled. Heather grabbed him, helping him stay up. Lightheaded, he pinched the bridge of his nose. It had been a long couple of days.

Keeping a hand on his back, Heather asked, "So, does this mean you can save her?"

Blinking several times, he nodded. "Yeah. All I have to do is follow the string and kill the creature that is feeding off it. Then she should wake up and recover."

Heather's face lit up, and she jumped up and down. She wrapped her arms around him, squeezing him tight. Caleb stood as still as stone, not sure what to do.

After a moment, she pulled away. "I know you're tired, and you've already done so much. But...can we go look for it now?"

Caleb nodded. He was exhausted, and he knew fighting now wasn't the best idea, but he was ready for this to be over. He craved the safety of Orion, especially now that the Guild had shown itself. At worst, he could scout and retreat if he found something he couldn't handle.

"You ready?" he asked.

She nodded eagerly and looked at Wilson. "Can you keep an eye on Mom?"

"Of course, Miss O'Brien."

They left the hospital room and headed for the stairwell. At a sprint, they made their way up to the roof and flung the door open.

A cold wind assaulted their faces. Keeping his eyes glued to the roof, Caleb tried to find Cassandra's soul string. Instead, he found three coming from the building.

"Three?" Heather asked. "Other people are sick too?"

Caleb barely registered her words. He hobbled forward, dropping his satchel. His legs shook underneath him. With wide eyes, he turned in a slow circle, his jaw hanging open. It couldn't be. This...this was impossible.

All around them were tens of thousands of purple soul strings, engulfing the city like a spider's web.

"What does this mean?"

Caleb didn't answer. In his gut, however, he instantly knew three things. First, he was in over his head. Second, the whole city was in danger. And third, he wasn't going home anytime soon.

End of Part One

Part Two

Chapter Seven

Soul strings were the weapons of monsters. That's what Caleb's grandfather had always said. The tens of thousands of strings strangling the Chicago skyline only reaffirmed this. So many lives were in danger, and he had no idea how to save them.

Six months had passed since Heather whisked him off to Chicago. A blazing summer wind assaulted him, almost sending him tumbling off the skyscraper he stood upon. The morning sun washed over the countless pedestrians below, none of them fully aware of the silent threat surrounding them.

Opp sat at his feet, exhausted. Another ten hours of patrolling the city, and they had failed to find the source of the strings. For half a year, he had been searching every night trying to find what was creating them. The strings were knotted, bunched, and threaded expertly across Chicago. They wove in and out of buildings, disappeared beneath the ground, making it impossible to follow any single strand. It seemed fruitless, but he didn't know how else he could save Cassandra. Or this city.

Closing his eyes, he opened his soul to the world around him. All at once, the energy given off by the cacophony of strings overwhelmed his senses. He couldn't feel souls past his immediate vicinity. Another solution blocked.

He reached into his satchel and dug past his tome, producing a crumpled newspaper. The headline read "Sleeping Plague Panics Chicago." The web of strings hospitalized more and more people every day, and the city had recognized the pattern.

Every few days or so, they'd travel to the ICU to visit Heather's mother. While there, he'd cast a few incantations to stabilize Cassandra's soul and limit the effects of the soul string as much as possible. It was a small change, but it would prolong her life. But he couldn't do that for all the victims.

His pocket buzzed. He pulled out the cell phone Heather had insisted she buy for him. He had been reluctant at first but finally compromised on getting a flip phone. He found a text from Sally.

Hey Caleb. Just got to the store, it's still weird not seeing you here. I hope you and your aunt are ok

His grip on the device tightened. He missed Sally and JJ and the simple work of the store. Sighing, he recalled the cover story his dad had given them about a supposed sick aunt in Chicago.

Using both hands, he slowly typed his response back to her.

Thanks, Sal. Hopefully, she'll recover soon, and I can come home

Exiting from the text, he checked the time. Nine-thirty in the morning. If he remembered correctly, Heather had said her friend Aalia would be visiting at eleven. Plenty of time to return and hide in the guest bedroom before she arrived. Explaining his presence was not a conversation he cared to have.

Instead of closing his phone, he checked the call history. It had been over a week since he called home. His grandfather would be furious if he didn't check in today. Then again, when wasn't he?

Attempting to keep his pulse under control, he dialed the number.

"Report," his grandfather's voice came over the line.

"I still haven't found the source of the strings."

"Why aren't I surprised? How many months of failure is that now?"

He gritted his teeth and tried not to crush the phone. "Thank you for taking care of my dad."

"One of us has to do real work while you're off playing hero."

"I'm sorry." Without waiting for a response, Caleb hung up.

Squeezing his eyes shut, he tried to keep his breathing under control, fighting off the encroaching flashbacks. The sunflower field, being dropped from unfathomable heights, and constant, searing pain.

Opp barked twice.

The sound tore him from his thoughts. He spun on his heels just as a filken climbed over the top of the skyscraper. Yellow glyphs dotted the beast's orange skin. He narrowed his eyes at the sight. It was being controlled like the thirteen others he had fought in Chicago.

Snapping his fingers, he brought forth his tome and summoned his scythe. But the filken didn't move. Its black orb stared straight at him, not vibrating at all. Something was off. Caleb put a foot forward, preparing to charge.

Everything happened at once. The hairs on the back of his neck stood. Opp barked twice again. Caleb dove to the ground. A second filken passed over him, its claws missing the back of his head by an inch.

An ambush.

Caleb sprang back to his feet as the second filken landed next to the first. Yellow glyphs covered this one as well, but it didn't matter. Two filken weren't anything he couldn't handle.

Bringing both phrases to mind, he spoke the words for his strength and speed enhancements. *"Lightning and wind carry me; I am too fast to see. With blood of iron and heart of coal; Make my body stronger than my soul."* His muscles swelled with familiar power, and his body felt impossibly light.

They weren't going to have a chance to make the second move. In a flash, he came upon the first filken and rammed the butt of his scythe into its face. It howled in pain and jumped back.

Caleb danced on his toes and faced the second beast. Spinning his scythe, he lashed out three times. It narrowly avoided the first two blows, but the third left a shallow gash across its chest.

Leaping back, he let them both recover from the attacks. "I'll say this once. Help me, please. If you do, I won't harm you anymore." It was a pointless effort; the incantations controlling them were too powerful. But he couldn't kill them without trying.

The filken faced each other. The orbs in their heads quaked. A golden soul string emerged from the first beast's chest and shot into the other.

Caleb's eyes grew wide. A *golden* string.

His stomach turned, and he nearly dropped his scythe. It was a sight he never thought he'd see. Opening his soul, he felt each of their spirits. The golden connection grew both their souls exponentially until they easily outshone his.

The first filken charged. His eyes darted around as he tried to track its movements. The beast flashed in his peripheries, and he jumped back. Its claws raked across his chest. Red hot blood seeped from the wound and stained his shirt as pain surged through his mind.

He flooded his soul into the speed incantation as the second filken galloped from the left. Razor-sharp nails shot out in a swarm. They tore at his clothes, just missing his skin as he barely managed to weave around them.

He gritted his teeth and raised his scythe, but before he could swing, the first filken rammed its thick skull into his side. The blow knocked the wind out of Caleb, and he skidded across the roof.

Despite the enhancements, he felt at least two of his ribs bruise. He poured more of his soul into the strength incantation, trying to dull the pain spreading through his chest.

Taking ragged breaths, he assessed his foes. Beating them in open combat wasn't going to work. Instead, he thought of another phrase, his mind straining from the burden of three simultaneous incantations.

His tome flipped through its pages. A ball of crimson energy formed in front of the first filken's orb. He quickly spoke the words before the filken could attack. *"From sky to page; Feel the storm's rage."*

Electricity formed above his tome as the beast launched the sphere of energy. Lightning shot out to meet it. The two blasts collided and exploded. A shockwave tore across the concrete and threw Caleb off the roof.

Air rushed past him as he plummeted towards the street. His

stomach turned, and he tumbled over himself. With seconds to act, he thought of a desperate phrase, the strain threatening to fracture his mind.

"Traveling through time and space; Fly me to another place."

Screams erupted from below. He plunged towards the sidewalk, moments away from crashing.

A golden hole tore in the air beneath him. Falling through it, his downward trajectory shifted to upward momentum as he launched out of a second portal high in the sky.

His stomach lurched, and he nearly wretched. His path carried him over the building and back onto the roof. Landing with a thud, he scanned for Opp, finding his dog hiding behind a metal duct.

Relief flooding him, he held his scythe in a defensive stance as both filken circled him. His heart thundered in his chest. The golden string was overwhelming. What could he do?

Both filken charged, their black orbs quaking. Caleb spun his scythe and stumbled around the onslaught of claws, barely able to stay out of their reach. Each passing second brought their attacks closer to shredding him.

Clenching his jaw, he brought a new phrase into his mind. He ducked and leaped across the roof as his tome flipped through its pages. Rolling to his knees, he faced one of the filken and called out, *"From breeze to gale; Feel the sky's wail."*

A typhoon of wind blew out of his tome and consumed the filken. The torrent lifted the beast off its feet and threw it to the roof of the next building.

His thoughts racing, Caleb held a new phrase as the remaining filken charged him. The three incantations thrashed in his head, painfully splitting his consciousness. He barely deflected its attacks with his scythe, his vision blurring.

His tome reached a new page. *"No matter the power you may wield; Stand firm against my mighty shield."*

A dome of golden light formed around him. He bit his lip and flooded his soul into the shield, expanding it until it covered the entire roof.

The filken he had sent to the other building jumped at them, landing on the shield and snarling. The golden string still connected the two filken, but the barrier would allow him to fight them one at a time. A small victory.

The filken trapped with him darted across the roof. Its movements blurred, and Caleb's legs shook. His breaths grew ragged, and sweat dripped down his head. He was exhausting his soul too quickly.

But as the filken closed in on him, he took a risk and released his speed incantation. To replace it, he brought a new passage to mind.

The filken moved in for an attack as he muttered, *"Summoned from frozen Hell; The winter citadel."*

A frigid wind burst from his tome and covered the roof in a sheet of ice. The filken lost its footing and slid across the freezing plane.

Ignoring the blood running down his chest, Caleb jumped forward. His grandfather's voice screamed to kill it now. In a single, swift swing, he buried his scythe into the beast's skull. Purple blood painted the ice, and the filken went limp. The glyphs covering its orange skin vanished, and the golden soul string dissipated.

The living filken's soul returned to its normal size. Panicked, it jumped away from the golden barrier and fled across rooftops.

Caleb released both incantations, and his mind was finally allowed to relax. But now wasn't the time to dawdle. He brought one last phrase into his mind and kept his eyes on the escaping filken.

When the creature was in the middle of a jump, he spoke the words. *"Traveling through time and space; Fly me to another place."*

Two portals opened, one in front of the filken and one next to him. The filken flew through the first and shot out the second. Spinning his scythe, Caleb swung the blade into the beast's chest.

It fell to the roof, and the yellow glyphs dotting it disappeared. Purple blood pooled beneath it, and it gasped for air.

"Finally...free," it said telepathically.

Caleb unsummoned his scythe and knelt next to the creature. This was the first time the glyphs controlling one of them vanished before it died. He had to take advantage of the opportunity. He needed answers. "Where is the source of the strings?"

But the filken was paying no attention to him. It was fixated on the other filken's corpse. Its orb shook softly. "They...they were my best friend. We grew up together."

Best friend? But filken weren't capable of love. Or trust. Or anything human. That's what his grandfather had always told him.

It was difficult to describe the sounds that filled his mind next. Was the filken crying? What was going on? But its cries made his heart twist. He reached out and touched its shoulder. "I'm sorry."

It faced him, its orb studying him. Taking a long breath between its slits, it said, "You don't have the smell of a normal Scribe. Why are they forcing us to hunt you?" It began to convulse as its purple blood spread further across the roof.

Caleb's shoulders sank at its words. He knew what it was like being forced into an unwanted life. "Because I'm trying to save this city. So, please, do you know what the strings are for? If you help me, I can heal you."

It shook its head. "Don't heal me. Kill me. I beg you. If they find me again, they'll control me once more. I cannot bear that any longer."

"But—"

The filken retracted the claws of one of its bulbous paws and placed it on his chest. "I do...not know where the strings go. Nor do I know their purpose." It convulsed once more, and Caleb tried to steady it. "But I do know that the Guild is responsible."

His eyes widened. He had long suspected the Guild of Life were the culprits, but to have it confirmed was still shocking. Their job was to protect humanity, and yet they were harming tens of thousands of people.

Pulling him closer, the filken placed its orb against Caleb's chest. "Forgive the crimes you have seen my kin commit. It is easy to sin when you are starving to death."

Caleb looked down. He knew that pain all too well. But why were they starving? Was something wrong with the Speculon?

Stretching out its legs, the filken crawled through its blood to its dead companion, lying next to it. "Please, take my life now. I do not wish to suffer any longer."

Caleb hesitated. How many times had he hoped to have a real conversation with a filken? To learn about them. To reach an agreement so he didn't have to kill. And now that he had, he still had to take its life.

Standing, he summoned his scythe. His legs shook under him as he shuffled to the dying beast. He refused to close his eyes as he raised his weapon; the filken deserved the respect of him watching its final moments.

Then a question came to him. "Do you have a name?"

The filken looked up at him, studying him momentarily. "Iibere."

"I hope you find some peace, Iibere." He swung the blade down and decapitated it, killing it as painlessly as he knew how.

Unsummoning his scythe, Caleb fell to his rear and buried his head into his arms. Six months in Chicago, and he was no closer to getting rid of the strings. And now this? What did the world want from him?

Opp sat next to him, resting his head on his lap. Caleb wanted to enjoy the momentary rest, but sirens began to echo from the streets below. Not a moment later, several helicopters approached from different directions. He must have garnered more attention than he thought.

Gritting his teeth, he stood and brought two incantations into his mind. There wasn't enough time to decompose the filken bodies. He'd have to focus only on escape. He cast the incantations to make him and Opp invisible and created a portal to another rooftop.

His vision blurred as he brought them from one building to another, making their way back to the penthouse. He'd have to wait to heal until he was safely back inside and away from any potential pursuers.

But there had to be another way. A way to bring this struggle to an end. To bring the fight to the Guild. He'd have to sleep on it, but he was committed to finding it.

Chapter Eight

Chicago was her home, and it was under siege. Heather wasn't reading the book she held, too distracted by her own thoughts. She glanced out the living room window, peering at the canopy of strings that suffocated her city.

Wilson stood across the room, dusting a bookshelf. She had tried to convince him to relax with her, but he refused.

"I'll rest when I'm dead," she muttered, doing her best to imitate the old man.

"Did you say something, Miss O'Brien?"

She looked up at him and grinned. "Just making fun of you."

A sly smile curled up at the corners of his mouth. "Very good, ma'am."

With a sigh, she tried to refocus on her book, but her mind drifted to Caleb. He should have been back by now. Was something wrong? Should she go look for him? She didn't want to worry, but the longer she tried to remain calm, the more her thoughts began to race.

To distract herself, she removed the folded piece of paper

that was serving as a bookmark. Opening it revealed a registration form for psychology classes at a local school. She had partially filled it out and reached for a pen that rested on the coffee table.

She stopped her hand halfway there. Her mother's hospital room flashed through her mind. Her parents expected her to become a surgeon, and who was she to deny them? The weight of her medical textbooks seemed to stack up against her, threatening to crush her. With indignant resignation, she folded the registration form back up and stuffed it into the book.

No matter what problems plagued her, they were unimportant. Her mother was dying. Mystical forces were attacking the city. And every night Caleb went out, risking his life to try and stop it.

She wanted to help him, but he still refused to teach her anything. He never gave a concrete reason, but he always shriveled up whenever she brought up training to be a Scribe.

A crash erupted from the kitchen, startling her from her thoughts. Wilson knelt and drew the pistol strapped to his ankle. He darted to the kitchen entrance, placing his back against the wall.

Heather's eyes fixated on a crystal bowl upon the coffee table. She poured the smooth, colorful stones out of it and made her way to the kitchen entryway. Wilson shot her a questioning look before storming into the room, clearing the corners as he did.

Her heart pounded in her ears, but she refused to stand idly by. Taking a powerful breath, she rolled around the frame and jumped into the kitchen.

Inside, Wilson lowered his pistol. Caleb stood in the center of the room, tattered and injured. Opp sat next to him, sniffing at the blood pooling across the tile floor.

Heather's heart leaped into her throat and her eyes widened. Her gaze fixated on the claw marks gashed across his chest. Lips quivering, she wanted to rush to Caleb's side, but she could only manage small steps.

"I'll call an ambulance," Wilson said and pulled out his cellphone.

"Don't," Caleb said, sitting at the table.

Wilson shot him a skeptical look. "Are you certain, Mister

Fleischer?"

He nodded and pulled out his tome. "A hospital will only mean questions. I have to heal myself."

Heather's slow hobbling finally brought her to the table. She took a seat, her eyes still scanning Caleb. The wound across his chest was deep, and his shirt was stained crimson. And she was helpless. She could do nothing for him. "What happened?"

"I was attacked by two filken," he said, flipping through his tome.

Why was he turning the pages manually? His hands shook as he did, and he was struggling to keep his eyelids open.

"I didn't think two filken would give you this much trouble."

Caleb scanned the pages more thoroughly now. "Normally, they wouldn't. These two were connected with a golden soul string, though."

A golden soul string? The ones strangling the city were purple. Somewhere in her memory, she remembered Caleb mentioning a golden connection once, but she couldn't recall much. "Is a golden string different?"

Caleb nodded and winced. "A purple string is made through aggression. As an attack on someone's soul. It's one-sided. But a golden string is a mutual connection. Fostered between two souls, it greatly elevates both participant's power."

Heather frowned. The golden connection sounded far more dangerous than the purple, no matter how they were made.

"It made that much of a difference?" she asked.

"Yeah. It caught me off guard, too. It's the best advantage the beasts of the Speculon have over Scribes, but I was always told filken couldn't trust enough to make one. That we've only ever recorded the Guardians using them." He looked suddenly troubled.

She placed her hand on his wrist, trying to catch his eye line. "What is it?"

"Both of the filken were being controlled like all the others. But when I fatally wounded one of them, the glyphs controlling it vanished, and it returned to normal."

Heather sat up. Maybe he was able to learn something. "Did it say anything?"

He flipped another page, a cough escaping him. "It didn't know what the strings were for or where they're going. But it did confirm that the Guild is responsible."

That wasn't surprising. From what Caleb had told her, they seemed the only ones capable of doing something this massive.

"There was another thing," he continued. "It told me its name. Iibere."

Sitting back in her chair, she looked down at the polished wood of the table, seeing a messy reflection in it. She had never considered those creatures having names. They had only ever been the beasts who created strings.

Wilson cleared his throat. "What does this mean?"

"I'm not sure," Caleb said, then held up a finger to silence them. His gaze was fixated on an incantation. He closed his eyes and spoke the words, *"This life, you cannot steal; These wounds, they will be healed."*

The tome glowed red. Yellow, circular symbols appeared around his wounds. Heather glanced at Wilson, knowing that he couldn't see this portion of the display. Focusing back on Caleb, the symbols began to spin, and the wound began to heal very slowly.

"That is a handy talent, Mister Fleischer," Wilson said at the closing skin.

"It is, but dangerous," Caleb said. "It takes a while to heal serious wounds, and some Scribes make the mistake of trying to do it in the middle of a fight. I almost got myself killed healing a wound my soul couldn't handle."

True to his word, the claw marks across his chest healed at a crawling rate. Sweat dripped down his brow as the seconds passed. Heather remained silent, not wanting to disturb his concentration. Opp slept under the table by both their feet.

Ten minutes had gone by before he had finally healed the wounds, leaving no traces behind. His breathing was ragged, and sweat now drenched his shirt along with blood. "There, all finished," he said.

Despite his injuries having vanished, he still looked in poor condition. His skin was even paler than normal, and his entire body sagged as if it were under tremendous pressure. She rubbed his shoulder softly. "You okay?"

His eyes flickered to Wilson briefly. "I'm fine. I just need to rest." He packed his tome and stood but stumbled.

Heather shot out of her chair and caught him, supporting his weight. “I got you,” she whispered to him.

“Thanks.”

She helped him out of the kitchen and down the stairs. Caleb could barely move faster than a shuffle, and she made sure to keep pace with him.

Anticipation bubbled in her stomach when they reached the guest bedroom. She opened the door and led him inside. Her eyes darted to a neatly wrapped present upon the nightstand.

It took him a moment to notice it. “What’s that?”

“I’ll grab it for you.” Helping him to the bed, she grabbed the gift and handed it to him.

He gave her a questioning look. She shrugged and grinned, beckoning him to open it. Tearing off the red wrapping paper, Caleb revealed a new, yellow dog collar.

She beamed at him. “I noticed Opp’s was getting pretty old, so I thought I’d surprise you with this. You know, as a thank you for everything you’re doing.”

Her smile faded. He didn’t appear excited. Instead, he gingerly held the collar, giving it a skeptical look.

“Sorry, Heather,” he said, “but Opp’s collar is...special. I can’t replace it. I really appreciate the thought, though.”

She accepted it back. Her shoulders sagged, but she forced a smile back on her face. “It’s okay, I understand.”

“Besides,” he continued, “you already got me a phone, new clothes, and have fed both me and Opp for several months. You don’t owe me any more than that.”

She nodded and prepared to leave, but the state of his shirt caught her eyes. “You probably shouldn’t sleep in that.”

He glanced down and chuckled before breaking out into a coughing fit. “Yeah, you’re right,” he said when he had regained control of his body.

She strolled across the room to the wardrobe and picked out a new shirt. She turned to hand it to him and saw he had taken off his shirt. Dozens of scars tore across his torso. Some jagged, some smooth. Some long, some short. But they were everywhere.

She gasped and dropped the shirt. “Caleb...”

He grabbed his own arm. “Oh yeah, sorry. I should have warned you first.” Reaching down, he picked up the fresh shirt and put it on.

What had he been through? She was about to ask when a thought popped in her mind. "Why do you have so many scars? Couldn't you have healed them?"

Caleb sat back down on the bed. He clutched his stomach and avoided her gaze. "My grandpa had...high standards when it came to training. If I got injured, it meant I had failed. Refusing to let me heal myself was my punishment."

Heather sprang forward and wrapped her arms around Caleb. Who could do such a thing to their own family? To a child? Tears welled up in her eyes, but she quickly stepped away from him. Early on, she noticed that he seemed uncomfortable anytime she embraced him. She had stopped because of this, but it slipped her mind in the moment.

"I'm so sorry, Caleb," she muttered. "Is there anything I can do?"

He shook his head. "I just need to shut my eyes for a bit. That fight took a lot out of me. But, when I wake up, we may have to think of a new plan. I can't just wander the city following the strings anymore."

"Okay," she said as she reached the door. Digging her toes into the ground, she mulled over a question that burned hot in her stomach. "You know, if you taught me how to be a Scribe, I could help you."

"Heather—"

"Listen," she cut him off, "I'm beginning to understand why this is a difficult subject for you. But you can't keep trying to do everything yourself. It's okay to accept help."

He stared at her for a long moment. Sighing, he said, "How about this? After I sleep, we can have a real, open discussion about it?"

It wasn't a yes, but it wasn't a no either. She'd take it what she could get. "Okay, I hope you sleep well."

Shutting the door behind her, she made her way back to the kitchen. Wilson knelt next to a bucket of cleaning supplies, mopping up the crimson blood that covered the once spotless tile floor.

"Oh, sorry, Wilson," she said, digging her toes into the floor.

"It's quite alright, Miss O'Brien. I'm just thankful Mister Fleischer is well."

She mulled over his words, transfixed on the red pools. It

was Caleb's blood. Blood from wounds he suffered trying to cure her mom. And he was only in Chicago because she had dragged him here.

The more Wilson cleaned, the more her mind raced. She drummed her fingers against her thigh. This wasn't fair to Caleb. This wasn't his problem. She needed to do something. Anything. Everything. Waiting on the sidelines wasn't something she could bear any longer.

Springing forward, she grabbed a rag out of the bucket and scrubbed the floor.

Wilson's head snapped towards her. "Miss O'Brien, please. It is not your place to be cleaning the floor."

"I have to do something, Wilson! My mom is the one who is dying, and yet Caleb is the one getting attacked. And you're the one cleaning up his blood. Am I supposed to just watch while others do all the work?"

She scrubbed until her knuckles turned white. Wilson stared at her with an open mouth, but she didn't stop. Her arms moved faster and faster, the rag grating against the tile. Her eyes began to sting, and she squeezed them shut. She imagined her mother's hospital bed. Caleb's wounds. The unanswered texts to her father. What else could she do?

A firm hand touched her shoulder, finally getting her to stop. "Heather. There's no shame in living a happy, comfortable life. There are those who can't who wish they could."

She gave him a hard look. "That's a nice thing to put on a card, but it doesn't help. Back in the day, how would you have felt if Bobby's name had been called for the draft and yours hadn't? How would it have felt knowing he was fighting and getting hurt while you were doing nothing?"

"That was a war, not everyday life."

Her eyes flickered to the canopy of strings hanging outside the window. "This *is* a war, Wilson. I know you can't, but I see the strings every day. The news outlets always talking about the Sleeping Plague, and thousands of people are slowly dying. And Caleb is the only person fighting against it. I want to help him, but until I can, at least I can help you clean."

Wilson took his hand from her shoulder and nodded. He picked up his rag, and the two cleaned in silence.

A half an hour passed, and the two of them finished disinfecting the surfaces in the kitchen. Wilson began putting away the supplies, and she noticed that she hadn't filled Opp's bowl yet. Grabbing a bag of food, she poured a healthy amount in and was surprised that the sound of pattering paws didn't fill the penthouse. Glancing under the table, she found Opp sound asleep. The day's events must have really worn him out.

An electronic bell sounded at the penthouse intercom.

She and Wilson exchanged a confused glance. Then she remembered.

"Aalia is here!" she called out. How could she have forgotten?

"Go on, Miss O'Brien," Wilson said, "I'll finish up here."

She nodded and buzzed Aalia up. When the elevator opened, the sight of her oldest friend greeted her.

The young woman stood four inches taller than Heather and had black hair pulled back in a single, long braid. Her bronzed skin brought out the shades of her acorn colored eyes. Aalia wore a yellow summer dress and held her signature, giant violet purse.

Heather lunged forward and embraced her friend. "It's been so long!"

Aalia laughed and returned her hug. "Blame your dad. He keeps us busy."

They separated, and Heather led her upstairs. "Am I allowed to ask you where you've been working?"

"We've been all over. My mom and I were able to visit my great-granddad in New Delhi. We also spent a few months in London, a couple of weeks in Berlin, and most recently, we've been in D.C. That's all I can say, though."

They walked into Heather's colorful bedroom. Various book posters covered most of the white walls. Multiple bookshelves hugged the exterior of the room, save for her bed with crimson, velvet sheets.

Sitting on the bed, Heather asked, "Did your mom come home, too?"

Aalia plopped onto the windowsill, setting her humongous purse on the red carpet. Something outside caught her eyes for a moment before she answered, "No, she had to stay with your dad. Too much work to be done."

Heather pouted. "It's been so long since I've seen her. Do

you remember when my dad wanted her to run for mayor?"

Aalia chuckled. "Yeah. She wasn't pleased with that at all. Don't tell your dad, but she was happy she lost to Mayor Ivers."

Heather remembered her father's rant on that election night. Hugging her body pillow, she stared up at the ceiling. "So, how'd you manage to sneak back home?"

"I got assigned to take care of some small tasks here, but I wasn't not going to visit you too."

"It means a lot. Between my mom being sick and you and my dad traveling for the better part of a year, I feel like a big part of my life has been removed."

Aalia looked away and rubbed her hands together. A moment of silence passed before she asked, "Are you gonna sign up for classes next semester?"

Heather squeezed her pillow tighter. "No. I can't leave Chicago while my mom's sick. And..." She trailed off.

"What is it?"

"I'm considering not becoming a surgeon." She glanced over at Aalia's widened eyes.

"Your parents won't be happy with that one bit. What do you want to do instead?"

"I want to become a therapist. I really want to work with kids who come from troubled homes, try and help them, you know?"

Aalia rested her head against the window, looking up at the ceiling. "I'm guessing your dad knows nothing about this?"

Heather buried her head into the pillow.

Smacking her lips, Aalia said, "I thought as much. You never stood up to your parents directly."

Knowing her friend was right, Heather kept smothering her face. The mattress sagged as Aalia joined her, wrapping a strong arm around her.

"Hey," Aalia said, "I found this new song last week."

Pulling out her phone, Aalia passed her an earbud. A soft, melancholic tune caressed Heather. It had a harmonious duet with a male and female singer. It was beautiful, and she finally freed her face from the pillow.

For another hour, they listened to music in silence, enjoying each other's company. After a while, Aalia regaled her with stories of her recent travels. The usual sights in Europe. Members of government. All the women she had hooked up with.

Hours passed, a good portion of it spent in content silence. Eventually, Aalia sat up, a nervous look on her face. Heather raised an eyebrow, and Aalia avoided her gaze.

"Heather..." Aalia began, "There's something I need to talk to you about. I'm not really sure—"

Oppenheimer's barks sounded from the main level of the penthouse. For a moment, Heather thought nothing of it. She could hear Opp sprint up the stairs and paw at her bedroom door.

And then it clicked.

He was barking. Three times. Three barks over and over. She struggled to take a breath as she slowly looked over to Aalia. Her eyes drifted down to her best friend's massive purse.

No. Please no. It couldn't be true.

A knock sounded at her door. "Miss O'Brien, Miss Laghari, is everything well?"

After struggling to take a deep breath, Heather forced a smile and said, "One sec, okay?"

Aalia tilted her head. "You got a dog?"

"I'll be right back," Heather said, avoiding the question. She stepped out of her room to find Wilson holding Opp by his collar, having managed to calm the dog down.

In a hushed tone, he said, "Three barks, Miss O'Brien."

"I know. My heart is racing, Wilson. I don't want to believe it."

He rubbed his beard. "What do you want to do?"

She placed a hand on her chest, feeling the rapid thud of her pulse. "Wake up Caleb, tell him what's going on. I'll bring Aalia to the kitchen."

"Yes, ma'am."

Wilson vanished down the stairs with Opp. Taking a moment for herself, she shuffled back into her room. Aalia held up her hands in confusion. Heather barely registered the gesture, her eyes glued to the strings outside the window. Was her best friend in league with those responsible for the Sleeping Plague?

"Heather?" Aalia asked.

Snapping back into the moment, Heather said, "Sorry. Wilson is dog sitting for a friend. Anyway, I'm hungry, let's go to the kitchen."

"Is everything okay?"

"Yeah, of course. Come on."

Aalia grabbed her purse before they made their way downstairs. Heather snatched apples for them both but didn't take a bite of hers. The seconds passed slowly as she waited for Wilson and Caleb to come. Aalia stared at her, giving her a questioning look.

But Heather couldn't wait. She had to know. Stopping her forced smile, she returned her friend's gaze. "Are you in the Guild of Life?"

Aalia took a step back. "What?"

"Answer the question, Aalia."

A pause. Aalia looked down. "Yes."

Chapter Nine

Caleb snapped awake. He wasn't sure what woke him, but he was thankful to be free from the nightmare. Parts were of Iibere; others were of memories best left forgotten. Wiping the sweat from his face, he got out of bed only to realize he wasn't alone in the penthouse guest bedroom.

The familiar figure in the black cloak stood in the corner of the room. A soft light emanated from her pale hands, though the shadow of her cowl kept her face concealed. She strolled towards him.

He held up a hand. "What do you want?"

She stopped. Looking up at the ceiling, she remained silent for a long moment. "Do you hate me, Caleb?"

The question took him back. Surely she wasn't here just to ask that. Grabbing his arm, he said, "Of course I don't, not really. It's just...you're the reason he's sick, you know?" His father flashed through his mind.

The figure looked down. "I am sorry. But he made his own

choice. To him, it was a price worth paying. For you."

That didn't make him feel better.

"Something is troubling you," she said. "Tell me about it."

He thought of the fight that morning. Of Iibere. "I fought two filken this morning. They were being controlled, but one managed to get free after I injured it. It cried. It talked about its friend. It had a name."

The figure took a long breath. "And this surprises you?"

"Well...yeah? Everything I've been taught labeled them as monsters. Incapable of love."

She sighed. "You must remember, history is written by the victors. Those that lose are stigmatized and blamed."

He recalled all the books he had read throughout his life. Certainly, they all weren't full of lies...right?

"Listen," she said. "Events have been set in motion that I have known about for some time. I know it has already been hard on you, but you have only taken the first steps on a journey beyond your comprehension. It shall not be an easy one."

He ran his hands through his hair and dragged them down his face. She was always like this. "Can you not be so cryptic, just once?"

"Our time is short, Caleb." She walked to him and placed a hand on his shoulder. "You can trust her."

"Trust who?"

But then she was gone, just like that. He shook his head and waved his hand through the cold air she had just occupied.

Sighing, he pushed the encounter out of his mind. He peeked down his shirt, happy to find his wounds were still healed. All too often, as a kid, he did a poor job, and the wounds reopened as he slept. He'd wake up covered in blood with his grandfather yelling at him.

An urgent knock sounded at his door.

Instinctively, he grabbed his satchel from the floor and jogged to the door. Wilson and Opp were on the other side. A rare expression painted the old man's face. Worry.

"What is it?" Caleb asked.

Wilson filled him in. Aalia. Opp's barking. She was a Scribe.

Not wasting a moment, the three hurried upstairs. Caleb found Heather with a horrified expression on her face. She stood across the kitchen from a young woman he assumed was Aalia.

Snapping his fingers, he brought out his tome and summoned his scythe. He walked to Heather's side, holding his weapon out towards Aalia.

"Who the hell are you?" Aalia asked, bringing her fingers together.

"Don't," he warned.

She lowered her hand.

"She's in the Guild," Heather said, her eyes growing misty. "I asked her."

And she told the truth? That didn't seem right. He stared at the woman, a look of bewilderment and fear apparent on her.

"Where's your tome?" he asked her.

She nodded at a large violet purse on the table.

"Wilson, do you mind?" he asked.

The old man retrieved the bag and produced a book with a silver cover. Gold metal trimmed the edge, giving it a far more elegant look than Caleb's gnarled, brown leather.

Caleb looked over to Wilson. "Hold on to it tight, please."

Nodding, Wilson wrapped his arms around the book, clinging to it with all his might.

Aalia crossed her arms. "You're the one the Guild is looking for, aren't you? Who are you? Why are you in Chicago?"

He couldn't tell her his name, that much was obvious. But what was he to do? He certainly couldn't kill her, but neither could he let her go. Was he to take her prisoner? At the very least, he could try and get some answers.

"I ask, you answer," he said. "What are the strings for?"

"Are you the one that kept dissolving the cloaking incantation?" she countered.

"Aalia!" Heather said, slamming a foot down. "Answer him."

The Scribe pursed her lips. "I don't know what their purpose is. Only the top officers do."

He shook his head. Why had he expected to get answers now all of a sudden? "What *do* you know?"

Her gaze shifted amongst each of the room's occupants. She bit her lip and closed her eyes. Sighing, she opened them and said, "I know I want to stop this plan, no matter what it is."

His eyes widened. That, he hadn't expected. He narrowed his gaze at her, his grip on weapon tightening. "Why? The Guild is the one responsible for it."

She looked down. "The Guild isn't as monolithic as you might think. A good number of us in the lower ranks don't support what's happening here. But no one is brave enough to move against Michael and his captains."

"Michael?" Heather blurted.

Caleb glanced at her. She had gone deathly white and took a step towards her friend. Aalia covered her mouth.

Wilson cleared his throat. "Miss Laghari, do you mean to say..."

She nodded. "Heather...your dad is the head of the Guild."

Heather's eyes rolled back in her head as she fell. Wilson dropped Aalia's tome and sprang forward just in time to catch her.

There was a snap. The silver tome shot to its owner, floating in front of her. A yellow, crystalline staff appeared in her outstretched hands.

Caleb cursed under his breath. His grandfather's voice told him to strike first. But he didn't want to fight. "Stand down, Aalia."

"I'm not going down without a fight," she seethed.

She thought he was going to kill her. Would he have assumed any different? He couldn't lower his weapon, but he didn't want conflict either. What were his options?

And then a different voice rang in his mind. *You can trust her.*

He gritted his teeth. His every instinct fought against the notion. His grandfather's voice screamed at him to ignore it.

Taking a careful breath, he unsummoned his scythe and set his tome down. He locked eyes with Aalia and held out his hands in a gesture of peace. "You say you want to stop the strings? Prove it. Let's talk, not fight."

She hesitated, then nodded. Her staff vanished, and she too set her tome down. "Alright. Can you make sure she's okay?" She motioned to her friend.

Wilson helped Heather back to her feet, steadying her. Heather shook her head and thanked him. Taking a seat, she gave Aalia a long, hard stare. "You and I need to have a lengthy talk. But, right now, tell me if you're serious about my dad."

"I am. He's run the Guild for nearly twenty-five years."

Now that things had deescalated, Caleb thought on the new

information. Heather's father was the Guild leader. The man who betrayed his grandfather and took control from him. The man behind the strings. But wait.

"My dad always said the family that leads the Guild were the Lancasters."

Wilson cleared his throat. "Shortly after you were born, Miss O'Brien, your father legally changed your family's name from Lancaster to O'Brien. With this new information presented, it appears the two events may be connected."

Heather slammed her fists onto the table. Her face was fire-engine red, and her entire body tense. He had never seen her like this before. It was scary. She produced her cell phone and dialed a contact.

Aalia's mouth hung agape. "What are you doing?" Her question was quick and panicked.

"I'm calling him," she said as it rang.

"Please don't!" Aalia begged.

"You just told me he's the reason my mom and everyone is sick. You think I'm going to let him get away with this?"

"Heather!" Aalia yelled. "Hang up the phone."

She did so, glaring at Aalia.

"I'm sorry, but you don't understand the Guild. You don't know what I'm risking by even telling you this. If Michael finds out, I'll be killed. My family will be killed. The Guild doesn't tolerate disloyalty."

Heather looked down, her face returning to its normal color. "I'm sorry, I didn't think about that. It's just...I don't..." She trailed off.

Caleb sat down next to her and put a reassuring hand on her shoulder. "You okay?"

She shook her head. "No. No, I'm not."

What was there to say? He had grown up knowing his family was abnormal. She just had her world shattered. Again. And that was on top of everything else she was struggling with.

Heather rested her face in her hand. She sat there in silence for several minutes. Finally, she looked up at Aalia. "Can we go upstairs and talk?"

Wilson cleared his throat. "Are you sure that is wise, Miss O'Brien?"

"Trust me, Wilson."

"Very well. Miss Laghari, please leave your book down here."

The request didn't seem to sit well with her, but she obliged. She and Heather walked upstairs, leaving Caleb and Wilson alone with Opp.

Pinching the bridge of his nose, Caleb let out a sigh. Between the fight with Iibere that morning and everything that had happened since waking up...he was overwhelmed.

"Are you well, Mister Fleischer?"

"Yeah, thanks, Wilson. Just need a moment to adjust."

"I understand." The old man stood and grabbed a box from one of the living room cabinets. Sitting back at the table, he opened it to reveal cleaning supplies. He removed the pistol from his ankle and began to disassemble it. "When I am stressed, I find it helpful to keep busy. Makes me quite suitable for my job."

Caleb chuckled. "I usually just crumble when I'm too stressed."

Wilson flashed him a warm smile. His steady hands began to clean the barrel of the firearm. "You need to develop more beneficial coping mechanisms, Mister Fleischer. Back in the war, my...best friend Bobby and I tried everything to cope. He was much better at it than I was. He could make anyone laugh, even when we were in a blistering jungle surrounded by people trying to kill us."

The man seemed to slip into the past, his hands slowly stopping their work. After a moment, his eyes flickered with life again, and he continued.

"There's something I want to discuss with you, Mister Fleischer. It's about Miss O'Brien. This morning, she was expressing her concerns about being unable to assist you in this struggle. She wants to save her mother. She wants to save this city. And she wants to help you. As such, I know she's going to insist you teach her to be a Scribe."

Caleb held up a hand. "Don't worry, Wilson. I have no intention of dragging her any further into this conflict."

Wilson shook his head. "No, that's not what I mean to say. Both you and Miss O'Brien are intelligent, determined, and capable adults. It is not my place to enforce what either of you should or should not do. What I do ask is, if you teach Miss O'Brien, give her the tools she needs. Teach her to be safe, to be effective, and absolutely do not underestimate her."

Looking down, Caleb considered the man's words. He hadn't expected the conversation to go in that direction. "I will," he promised.

"One more thing." Wilson shifted uncomfortably in his seat, setting the gun barrel down. "I wish to apologize. When you first arrived in Chicago, I was abrasive towards you. While I believe my skepticism was justified, you have since proven yourself several times over. So, I am sorry, and I thank you for trying to save Mrs. O'Brien and this city."

Caleb grabbed his arm and avoided the man's gaze. "You don't have to thank me."

Wilson placed a gentle hand on his shoulder. "I do, Caleb. I know better than most the difference between someone who volunteered for war and someone who was drafted."

Meeting the old man's gaze, Caleb tried to swallow past a lump in his throat. His eyes stung, and a response escaped him. Why had those words hit him so hard?

Silence fell between them, and Wilson returned to his cleaning. Unsure of what else to do, Caleb pulled out his phone. He had a text from Sally asking how he was. Over the next hour, the two of them exchanged pleasantries. She tried to get some details about Chicago out of him, but he managed to dodge the questions.

A door opened upstairs. Heather and Aalia rejoined them in the kitchen, both looking far more at ease.

Sitting next to Caleb, Heather said, "We talked about everything, except for your identity."

"Thank you," he said.

"But," she continued, "Aalia didn't know I was a Scribe, not for sure, at least. I asked her why she didn't look at my soul, and she said Scribes can't do that."

He looked away. This problem was going to creep up eventually. It was the other reason he had put off teaching her.

"Well...it's something only I can do."

Aalia's brown eyes pierced him. He could practically see the gears turning in her head. Would it be better to get ahead of this? The familiar voice sounded in his mind once more. *You can trust her.*

He met Aalia's gaze. "My name is Caleb Fleischer."

She jumped back. "No. No." She shook her head. "Caleb Fleischer is dead."

"My grandfather lied to the Guild. To keep me and my father safe."

"So then...that means...you're really the—"

"Yes, I am," he said, cutting her off. His gaze flickered to Heather and Wilson. He wasn't ready for them to know the truth. Not this truth. His grandfather's cold, judgmental eyes flashed through his memory. He wouldn't survive if they looked at him like that. It wasn't his fault. He didn't ask for it.

A sympathetic look crossed Aalia's face. "Caleb, could we speak in the other room?"

The request caught him off guard. Still, he didn't think she was going to try anything, so he followed her into the entryway where she stood staring out the large window.

"They don't know, then?" she asked him.

"No."

"Is what they say about you true?"

He looked down. "What kind of words do they use?"

"Monster. Abomination. That sorta thing."

The words stung, though it was not the first time he had heard them. "I'm not a monster. I'm just someone attempting to do the right thing for once."

She looked over to him. "Heather seems to deeply trust you. I won't tell them about this, 'cause I'm choosing to believe in you. In exchange, I'd like to ask for your help with stopping the strings." She held out her hand to him.

His gaze shifted between her face and hand. He could trust her. Reaching out, he shook it. "Deal." He looked back out at the canopy of strings. "So, you're a member of the Guild...but you're going to work against it?"

"Do you know the difference between patriotism and nationalism?"

He shook his head.

"Patriotism is loving your country and wanting it to be the best it can be. And that involves acknowledging its shortcomings and striving to improve them. Nationalism is blindly thinking your country is the best no matter what and is already perfect. It's a foolish mindset, and it's how I feel about the Guild. I want it to be a force for good. I want it to truly serve and protect all of humanity. But right now, it's failing at that. So, I'll fight to change it."

He had never thought of it that way. His whole life, he was raised to fear and hate the Guild. He had always thought of each Guild Scribe as the same. He had much to learn.

"Now that we have that squared away," she said, "let's get back in there."

They returned to the kitchen table. Heather raised an eyebrow at him, and a shrug was his only response.

"Okay," Aalia said. "Our first goal should be figuring out exactly what the strings are for."

"Does this mean you have a plan, Miss Laghari?"

"Maybe. The three ranking agents on this operation are Megan Trenton, Dom Eckerson, and Miranda Cross. I think you've met the first two?"

All three of them nodded. Wilson cleared his throat. "Are they the three highest-ranking officers beneath Mister O'Brien?"

"No. Most of the really senior staff are working on something called Operation Chimera. But Trenton and Eckerson were the ones who assigned me to this task. I was supposed to come and check to see if Heather was having any contact with a rogue Scribe. Since you are, I'm guessing at the very least they suspected it was true."

Caleb ran a hand through his hair. The Guild was closing in. How much longer would he be safe? His heart began to convulse.

"So," Aalia continued, "by taking advantage of my connection to them, I think we can lay a trap and question them."

Wilson folded his hands on the table. "If we believe it to be necessary, the army gave me a very...focused training back in the war. I could give them a more intimate form of interrogation."

Heather shifted in her seat. "I'm not sure I'm comfortable with that euphemism."

"I understand, Miss O'Brien, but if we weigh the safety of your mother and the rest of the city, it may be worth it."

"No," Caleb said, "I agree with Heather. If we do this, no torture and no killing."

"It'll make it more difficult," Aalia said, "but I accept. I'll reach out to them and ask for a meeting. I think they're both out of the city, so it may take a week or two. In the meantime, we can prepare."

They all chimed in with their agreements.

"I'll make some inquiries to old friends," Wilson said, "and acquire some more serious hardware, just in case."

Aalia stood and grabbed her tome. "On that note, I need to get going. I have other meetings to attend, but I'll stop back by tonight to continue planning."

They said their farewells before she disappeared into the elevator.

"I shall go make those calls," Wilson said before heading to the lower level of the penthouse.

Oppenheimer trotted forward and rested his snout on Caleb's lap. Caleb scratched his head and looked over to Heather. Her head was buried into her arms, resting on the table.

"It's been a tough day, huh?" he said.

She nodded without looking up.

"So, I've been thinking," he said, "and I've talked with Wilson about it. And, well...if we're going to start taking more active steps against the Guild, I think it is about time I taught you to be a Scribe."

Her head rocketed up. "Really?"

"Really. Though I want to be clear: this is going to be a long and slow process. You won't be casting incantations anytime soon."

"That's okay!" she exclaimed eagerly. "Progress is progress. I'm ready."

He smiled softly, recalling how uneager he had been when it was his turn to learn. "You want to start now?"

"Yes. Yes. Yes, please."

"Alright," he said, and he slid his tome in front of her.

Chapter Ten

"I've given you a rough history of the Speculon and Scribes," Caleb said to Heather. "What you need to know is that if a Scribe doesn't have their tome or some equivalent, they are no more capable than a normal human."

She paged through the pages of red text as he spoke. "So, if I tore up your tome right now, you'd lose all your power?"

"Yes. Well, at least until I made a new one. But go ahead, try and tear it up."

Grabbing a page between her hands, she gave him a questioning look to see if it was really okay. He nodded. She gave it a gentle tug. It didn't wrinkle.

Tilting her head, she pulled on it more forcefully. It held firm once again. She bit her lips and tried to tear the page down the middle. Her face turned red as she pulled with all her might. It didn't give an inch.

He chuckled. "The first things any competent Scribe puts in their tome are passive incantations to keep it safe. It would take an advanced Scribe days to destroy mine."

She let go of the page and examined the book. "What exactly is a tome? How do you make one?"

"First, an incantation can be written on any non-living material. So, it doesn't necessarily have to be a tome, it just happens to be a very effective way. But mine started off as a normal, old book, and over the years, I filled it with incantations."

"And an incantation is..."

"I told you incantations are written in blood," he said. "We seep our soul into our blood while forming the incantation, then write the words with it. When we attune our soul to that same incantation in the future, the tome turns to that page, and our soul activates its effects. Let's do a quick exercise."

She nodded.

"Close your eyes," he instructed. "We're going to do a meditation exercise my dad taught me. A common mistake with meditation is trying to not think at all. That's not practical, though. Instead, imagine yourself standing in a gently flowing river.

"The river is your mind. You can do your best to empty it, but thoughts will still come. When they do, don't fight them. Imagine them like a leaf floating on the water. Let them flow around you and down the stream."

He fell silent and let her perform the task. She breathed slowly in and out.

After several minutes, he continued, "Now, I want you to dive into the river. Direct your mind inward, towards the center of your chest. Travel deeper and deeper until you feel a warm presence. When you find it, embrace it."

Her face contorted. It couldn't be easy, especially for an adult raised away from this world. To suspend one's disbelief on their perceived reality was easy for a child but became much more difficult the older one became.

"I can't," she said after ten minutes.

"Don't worry, I'm not surprised. It'll take you multiple attempts. Take a quick break, then try again."

Over the next hour, she tried and failed several times. They took a longer break that involved ice cream and laughs. He did his best to keep her distracted. No doubt, a mountain of crap was on her mind at the moment.

Finally, she tried the exercise again. A few minutes passed, and she jolted in her chair, her eyes flying open.

He chuckled. "I had the same reaction my first time, too. What you just felt is your soul."

"I can't believe it," she said, looking down at her chest. "That's been inside me this whole time?"

"Yeah. It's a lot to come to terms with. We can stop here if you want."

She shook her head. "Heck no. I want to keep going. So you use that warmth to create incantations?"

"Yeah. You use your soul to craft them and to give them power the moment you use them. When casting an incantation, a Scribe must hold the words in their mind during the duration of its use. By doing this, when they speak the words, their soul serves as a connection between the tome and the incantation."

"If you have to hold the words in your head the whole time, does that mean you can only cast one at a time?"

"It depends on the Scribe. If you want to perform two at a time, you'd have to hold them in your mind simultaneously. An experienced Scribe can do this. A rare one can do three. My grandfather can do four."

"I can't imagine doing that and fighting at the same time."

The countless thousands of hours his grandfather forced him to practice flashed through his mind. "There's a trick to it, but it's certainly not easy. Most Scribes spend most of their time training their body. And of course, it's important to be in peak shape. But the real skill that separates a good Scribe from a great one is their mind. You're incredibly intelligent and educated. Adding your naturally large soul, you have a lot of potential."

She smiled at his words. He then offered to take her through more exercises. Once she was comfortable with finding her soul, he walked her through manipulating it. He helped her change its shape, intensity, and to move it to different parts of her body. After an hour of this, he let her rest.

"For now," he said, "only do that with me around. That way, I can watch your soul to make sure you don't use up too much of it. Exhausting your soul will kill you."

She wiped sweat from her brow and grinned. "Gotcha. We can do some more tomorrow."

Aalia returned later that night. She told them that Trenton and Eckerson would be returning to Chicago in a week and a half. When they did, she'd ask for a meeting at a Guild safehouse. There, Caleb, Heather, and Wilson would ambush and capture them. Wilson had successfully contacted his old war buddies and acquired equipment for the mission.

As they waited for the appointed day, Caleb and Heather spent hours on soul training. He let her page through his tome, explaining various incantations to her. She picked up things far faster than he had back in the day, and he ventured to guess she could start making incantations in a month or two. Gifted didn't even begin to describe her.

Each night, Aalia would stop by the penthouse. They'd all spend roughly half an hour going over the plan before the evening would devolve into merriment. Heather and Aalia did the majority of talking, while Wilson and Caleb usually listened.

The two women would regale them with stories of their youth. About how Aalia would get them into trouble, and Heather would talk them out of it. Wilson poured wine for them all. After a glass, the old man told a few stories about the misadventures he and his friend Bobby got into at West Point.

"Hey, Fleischer," Aalia called out. "Is it true your dad and gramps took down an elderon, just the two of them?"

Caleb nodded. How many times had his grandfather told him that story?

"That's so badass! And your gramps trained you?"

"Aalia," Heather said, changing the subject. "Try and guess what Caleb's favorite color is."

Aalia gave him a long stare before declaring, "Blue."

He arched an eyebrow. "Why blue?"

"I dunno," she shrugged. "Every guys' favorite color is blue."

Heather shot him a sheepish grin and said, "It's actually yellow."

"Really, why?"

Looking down, he felt his cheeks grow warm. "Every summer, this field of sunflowers grows behind my house. When I was a kid, I hid in it all the time. I always thought they were so beautiful."

The room had gone quiet. All three of them stared at him.

"What?" he questioned.

"That was strangely..." Aalia paused. "Touching."

His cheeks burned red hot. "Oh."

Wilson chuckled and pulled out a green camouflage bag. Unzipping it, he produced three military-grade radios. "Let's change the subject before Mister Fleischer bursts into flames." He handed a radio to him and Heather. "We'll use these to communicate tomorrow should the plan fall through, and we separate. Each of us should pick a codename."

Heather placed a finger on her chin. "Let's see...I want to be called Athena. And Caleb will be Sunflower!"

"Oh, boy," he said.

"I'll use my old Army nickname, Bloodhound," Wilson said.

"I know I won't be using a radio tomorrow," Aalia said, "but I still want a cool codename. I'll be...Firecracker!"

They all laughed. But with the wine bottle empty, a silence soon fell. Tomorrow was the day. Caleb would be taking the fight to the Guild, something he thought he'd never do. It could go so wrong.

Aalia smacked her lips. "Listen, there's something else we should discuss. Tomorrow, they're expecting me to report on several things, including my investigation of Heather. If I say no one is with her, and then she shows up with someone, it could end poorly for me and my family."

"What do you propose?" Wilson asked.

"I think I can get away with keeping your name secret. But I think I'll have to mention finding a young male and a dog. That should be enough to keep my cover intact." She looked to Caleb for agreement.

The thought made him uncomfortable. But he supposed it was a risk they'd have to take. And if they were careful, Trenton and Eckerson wouldn't be able to report to the Guild. "Do what you have to."

They finalized and reviewed the plan. Once they were all satisfied, Aalia returned home, and Wilson retired for the evening.

Heather scooched closer to Caleb on the couch. "You ready for tomorrow?"

A simple question that had a difficult answer. "Not really. But if we're ever going to save your mom, we have to take risks."

"Caleb...it means so much to me that you're doing all of this. For my mom. For me. For the city. It's really admirable."

Her green eyes studied him, and he looked away. Where was this coming from all of a sudden? His stomach fluttered, and his cheeks grew warm once more. "Thanks, Heather. I think it's really great that you're becoming a Scribe to help."

She smiled and leaned back, setting down her empty wine glass. "Hey. How come you hid in the sunflower field when you were a kid?"

Retching replaced the flutters in his stomach. He could nearly hear his grandfather yelling out his name. "I hid from my grandpa there."

"Oh," she said, looking at him with concerned eyes. "Your grandfather...he's not a good man, is he?"

Another difficult question. Or at least it felt difficult, though the answer seemed so obvious. "He's a man of high standards." He stood and walked towards the stairs, Opp following him.

"You know that doesn't answer the question," she called out.

He stopped and looked back at her. "I know."

"Caleb," she called out, "I won't pressure you to open up. I can't imagine how difficult this might be. But if you let this bottle up inside, it's gonna come out anyway, just in a negative way."

He locked eyes with her briefly before retreating to the guest room. He changed into his pajamas and climbed into bed. Sleep did not come easy, and even when he slept, it wasn't restful. Tomorrow certainly was going to be a challenging day.

No one spoke as they ate breakfast the next morning. Wilson checked over his weaponry and equipment, and Caleb paged through his tome. Heather checked her phone every few seconds. They were waiting on Aalia's signal that the meeting was happening.

Caleb hated it. The fearful anticipation. Not knowing when, or even if, she'd text them. But there was nothing he could do, so he continued to read through the pages of red text. He studied incantations he hadn't checked in a while, recommitting them to memory. Who knew what he may need today?

It wasn't until half-past three in the afternoon that they finally got their message. Aalia told them the meeting was taking place in an hour and gave them the address. They wasted no time. Wilson gathered his gear, and Caleb triple checked his tome was in his satchel.

The drive across the city was silent. Caleb sat in the back with Opp, his gaze glued to the concrete jungle around him. Hundreds of pedestrians strolled around them without a care in the world, none the wiser to the canopy of soul strings hanging above their heads. No idea how much danger they were all in.

They arrived twenty minutes early and parked several blocks back. While it had been a hindrance in Orion, Caleb was now thankful for the SUV's tinted windows.

"To review," Wilson said, "Mister Fleischer will unlock the door, and I'll throw in a flashbang. While the agents are stunned, we'll storm in and each grab a tome and secure them. After that, the questioning will be up to you, Mister Fleischer. Should events go awry, and we separate, our rendezvous point will be that alley there."

Wind barraged them as they exited the vehicle. Caleb verified the presence of his tome and helped Opp out. Wilson slung his camouflage bag over his shoulder and led the way.

Pedestrians flowed around them. Every few blocks, a purple soul string jutted from one of the citizen's chests. How long until they were in a hospital bed, surrounded by doctors who couldn't save them? Caleb didn't want to think about it.

He clenched his hands to stop them from shaking. The Guild wasn't meant to be fought, only fled from. That's what he had always been taught. And yet, here he was, confronting them head-on. This plot, whatever it was, had to be stopped. What other choice did he have?

A rundown, brick apartment building rose up before them. Caleb signaled to Opp to remain quiet. A moldy smell greeted them as they stepped inside and walked up to the third floor. The building was silent. How many people actually lived here?

Boards covered most of the doors, but not the one labeled A303. They tiptoed up to it, ensuring each step they took made no sound. Muffled voices came from inside the apartment, but Caleb couldn't hear what the occupants were saying.

Manually taking out his tome, he brought a phrase to his mind. As his tome flipped through its pages, Wilson handed them all earplugs and removed a rifle from his bag. He then grabbed a small canister that Caleb assumed was the flashbang. Both of them approached the door. Heather stood behind them, keeping a hand on Opp's collar.

Once everyone nodded, Caleb focused his soul onto the incantation. His heart raced, and he struggled to keep his breathing regular. After this, there would be no going back.

He spoke the words barely above a whisper. *"Bound tight by lock and key; I set this passage free."*

The door unlocked with a soft click. Wilson swung it open and threw in the flashbang. The grenade landed with a thud, and he slammed the door shut.

Even with plugs, the piercing explosion rattled Caleb. His ears rang, and his vision blurred for a moment.

But when Wilson opened the door again, they poured inside. Trenton, Eckerson, and Aalia stood around a table, each looking completely disorientated.

Caleb immediately grabbed Eckerson's briefcase while Wilson snatched Trenton's. They threw both on the ground at the far side of the living room they found themselves in, with Heather tossing Aalia's in to join them.

Snapping his fingers, he brought a new phrase to his mind. *"Run, hide, and cower; Weak, without power."*

A glyph appeared beneath the Guild tomes. A purple dome of light sprang up and surrounded all three.

Caleb's breathing relaxed. With this incantation in place, their tomes might as well have been a thousand miles away, their connection to them temporarily severed. He had to be careful, however. They could physically recover their tomes at any time. He'd have to keep on guard.

Wilson closed and locked the front door. The old man forced the agents and Aalia down into their chairs and raised his rifle against the back of Eckerson's head. "Don't move," he ordered.

The Guild members gained their bearing and glanced around. Heather stood near Aalia, giving her friend a manufactured glare. All part of the act.

Caleb walked to the opposite side of the ratty table, his tome still floating in front of him. Opp stood at his side, the dog's brown eyes locked on the two agents.

"So," Trenton said, locking her eyes with his, "you're him. We've been looking for you. Agent Laghari here was just telling us there was a young man staying at the O'Brien residence."

A pile of manila folders rested on the table in front of Trenton. Squinting, he saw the top one was labeled "Operation Chimera." Hadn't Aalia mentioned something about that?

"This is how this is going to work," he said. "Please just answer our questions, and we won't kill you." A desperate bluff.

"Please." Eckerson snorted. "Have you ever threatened anyone before? I doubt a wet noodle like you could even take a human life."

The corners of Trenton's mouth turned into a venomous smile. "We saw how much killing the filken on the roof made you weep. I expected a Fleischer to have a harder heart."

Caleb stepped back. His stomach ran cold, and he struggled to take a breath. They knew? How? His gaze darted to Aalia. She looked just as surprised as him. She hadn't told them.

Trenton chuckled. "You really are new at this." She pulled out one of the folders from the bottom of the pile and tossed it at him.

Keeping an eye on the agents, he opened it. Inside were several pictures of him and Opp over the last couple months. One photo, from his fight the other day, was zoomed in on Opp's collar. It showed his name.

Shit.

"It was quite a shock," Trenton continued, "to learn that Caleb Fleischer had come back from the dead. We should have known better than to think your grandfather would actually hold up his end of the bargain."

How much did they know? Had they figured out the location of his Orion home? Was his father in danger? Underestimating the Guild was the same as asking for tragedy.

His grandfather's voice screamed at him, accusing him of failure. And it was right.

Chapter Eleven

The coldness spread from Caleb's stomach to his chest. Not only had he failed to establish psychological control over the two agents, but they had immediately regained it. How had it gone wrong so fast?

Above all else, he needed to make sure his father was safe. He stepped towards a door to the right of the table, finding a sparsely decorated bedroom inside. Leaving the door open a crack, he kept an eye on the agents as he pulled out his phone and called home.

It rang. "Report," his grandfather's voice said.

Immediate relief flooded him. They were safe. Not wanting the agents to overhear them, his response came in fluent German. "We have a problem."

His grandfather hesitated before responding in kind. "Don't be coy, what is it?"

"I cornered two Guild Scribes with the hopes of extracting information. They know who I am. By name."

"You damn fool," the man spat. "Did you not think to consult me before pulling a stunt like this?"

"I had to try something! The strings—"

"This is what happens when you try and play hero. I shouldn't have expected better from you."

The words cut through him like daggers. "I'm sorry, sir."

"Your home won't be safe long now that they know to look for you and your father. I'll sneak him into Chicago, but then he's going to be your problem again. I wash my hands of this rash endeavor."

"Fine."

"We'll be there in two hours. Meet at Millennium Park."

Karl hung up before he could respond. Caleb's heart rate skyrocketed as he put away his phone. He was going to be around his grandfather again, and the Guild knew who he was. How could this get any worse?

He stepped back into the main room, sweat dripping down his temple. His vision blurred, and his grandfather's voice screamed incoherently at him.

"Mister Fleischer?"

All eyes were on him. He couldn't lose control. Not now. He had to ground himself. He was in Chicago. He was with Wilson and Heather. He was not safe. But he had a job to do.

Placing a hand on Opp, he gritted his teeth and brought his breathing under control.

Eckerson shot a glance to his partner. "This is the kid that's been a thorn in our side for half a year?"

She tsked, her hand moving from the fancy watch on her wrist. "It seems the Fleischers are no longer a family to be feared. I can't believe Karl would let his grandson turn out like this, even if he were an abomination."

There it was. Abomination. Monster. Mistake. It didn't matter what word they used, it always tore him apart.

It wasn't his fault. He hadn't asked for any of this.

"Enough," he said. "Tell us what the strings are for. Now." He had never heard his own voice sound less threatening.

"Or what? You won't kill us," Eckerson said, the man's hard eyes accusing him.

They were right. Lying had never been his strong suit. He had never managed to fool his grandfather.

Holding out his hands, he summoned his scythe and swung it down into the table. Neither agent flinched.

A police siren sounded in the distance. He tried not to focus on it, and instead tried to think of a plan. How was he going to extract information from them? This was their only solid idea, and it was slipping right through his hands.

More sirens sounded from a different part of the city.

"So, mutt," Trenton said, "how do you see this ending?"

The sirens grew louder, and his eyes darted to the windows. The sounds were coming towards them from multiple directions.

"You're in way over your head, kid," Eckerson said, crossing his muscular arms.

Police cars flooded the street below. Officers poured out, guns at the ready. Why were they here? How did the agents contact them? This plan couldn't have gone worse. What should he do?

Wilson retreated from the front door and came to their side of the table, standing in front of Heather.

She leaned across the table, eyeing the agents. "You work for my dad, don't you?"

Surprise flickered across both their faces.

"When we figured out Aalia was a Scribe, it wasn't a hard leap to make," Heather said, keeping her friend's cover intact.

"Ms. O'Brien," Trenton said, motioning at Caleb, "this monster is the enemy. You should stop working with him."

Heather's face flashed red. "You all are the reason my mom is sick! He's trying to save her. Am I missing something here?"

Trenton's eyes narrowed. "He hasn't told you, has he?"

The front door splintered open. Police officers filed in, guns immediately trained on the three of them. Oppenheimer barked at the new intruders, a rare break in his training.

"Don't shoot the girl!" Trenton ordered.

Heather grabbed Caleb and Wilson by the collar, forcing them behind her, using her body as a shield.

Wilson placed a hand on her shoulder, guiding her towards the bedroom. Caleb grabbed Opp by the collar and followed along, doing his best to stay behind Heather.

He unsummoned his scythe and slammed the bedroom door shut the second they passed through. His mind raced, trying to catch up on everything that had just happened. Their plan had entirely fallen apart, and the only new information they had gleaned was that the Guild had influence over the police.

"Focus, Mister Fleischer," Wilson called out.

Caleb snapped back to reality. He had to get them away from this situation. He muttered the strength incantation and felt his whole body swell with power. Holding the bedroom door shut, his eyes darted out the window to a distant alley.

Several bodies slammed against the door, trying to open it. Pouring his soul into his enhancement, Caleb held it closed. His mind raced. He had to be quick. The sealing incantation only stopped the agents from summoning their tome with their soul. They could physically remove them with ease.

A splitting headache tore through him as he brought a third incantation into his mind. Speaking the words, he created a portal from the room to an alley in the distance.

"Heather," he said. "Help Wilson and Opp through it. I'll follow."

She nodded and guided them into the portal. Once all three were in the alley, she turned back to him. "Come on!"

His shoulders slumped. "I'm sorry," he said before releasing the incantation. The portal vanished, separating them. They were after him. This was the best way to keep the others safe. Now he had to keep the Guild's attention solely on him.

The door slammed against him harder. If the agents hadn't recovered their tomes from his seal yet, they would soon. An enclosed space overrun with this many enemies was beyond dangerous. He needed to escape.

Eckerson's muffled voice sounded from the other room, ordering people to move. Caleb jumped back from the door. A yellow, double-headed ax split the wood clean in two. Eckerson stepped through the now open entryway, holding the crystalline weapon in two hands. The man's violet tome floated in front of him, pages flipping.

Releasing his sealing incantation, Caleb flooded his soul into his strength enhancement. Before Eckerson could cast anything, he sprinted towards the window. Gritting his teeth, Caleb smashed through the window. His stomach lurched, and air rushed past him as he fell to the street below.

Aiming his shoulder down, he crashed straight into a police car. Even with his enhancement, pain tore through his body, and the wind was knocked from his lungs. His brain rattled in his head, and he could barely make out the surprised shouting that surrounded him.

He rolled off the dented metal and onto the pavement. Officers surrounded him, guns at the ready. Blinking, he regained his bearings as an order came over their radios.

Shoot to kill.

Bullets tore through the air as he leaped from the ground. His enhanced body would deflect any lower caliber shots, but it wasn't worth the risk nor draining his soul. He landed and rolled to the side, casting the speed incantation. A slug bounced off his chest. Stumbling to his feet, he sprinted down the street in the opposite direction he had sent Heather and Wilson.

He ducked into an alley to avoid the hail of gunfire. His mind strained as he cast the portal incantation, traveling down several blocks. Moving as fast as his speed incantation would allow, he darted across the city.

Having temporarily lost the police, Caleb took a moment to catch his breath. Sirens echoed from every direction as the officers patrolled the city. His heart raced. Crouching behind a dumpster, he glanced down at the radio Wilson had given him. There was no way to know if they were hiding. It was better to maintain silence until the danger passed.

Pulling out his phone, he closed a text from Sally to check the time. His grandfather would be here in an hour and a half. He needed to continue evading the Guild and police, and reconnect with Heather by then. He could do this. He could.

He released his strength and speed enhancements, giving his soul rest. The cloaking incantation would make hiding a breeze, but there was no way he could maintain it for ninety minutes. Instead, with sirens surrounding him, he bounced from alley to alley. He remained in one spot for roughly ten minutes before moving on.

Then the sirens went silent. All of them. All at once.

Peeking around the corner to the street, he saw all the law enforcement vehicles leaving the area. Had the Guild given up? Something wasn't right.

Trusting his gut, he opened his soul to the world around him. Thousands upon thousands of small souls appeared around him. The people of Chicago. But there was something else.

A singular, powerful soul descended upon him from behind.

He leaped to the side. A double-headed ax crashed into the pavement, cracking it. Rolling through his jump, he cast his strength and speed incantations. He jumped to his feet to find himself facing Agent Eckerson.

"Found you, abomination," the man spat. "Looks like we won't need to bring out the big gun after all." He pulled his large, yellow ax from the concrete, bits of rubble falling from it.

Caleb summoned his scythe. His heart calmed down, and his breathing returned to normal. Running, evading, scheming, and interrogating...those were unfamiliar to him. But fighting? He knew how to fight, even if he hated it.

"Please," he begged the agent. "We don't have to do this."

Eckerson glared at him. "You will get no mercy, monster. I will be famous for putting down the Fleischer mutt." He charged.

Caleb spun his scythe, his eyes narrowing. His opponent swung that behemoth of a weapon again and again. Ducking in and around the slashes, Caleb didn't make a move to counterattack.

He could hear his grandfather's voice. The greatest weakness of a Guild Scribe is that they hold all the power. They train to fight the beasts of the Speculon, not other Scribes. For what Scribes were there to fight?

But how many thousands of hours had he trained? From sunrise to sunset, day after day for nearly two decades. Eckerson was slower than his grandfather. He was weaker than his grandfather. And his soul was smaller than his grandfather's.

The agent huffed in frustration. The man's tome flipped through its pages and glowed red. *"Water, life, and soot; My soul takes root,"* Eckerson growled.

Caleb jumped back. Vines constructed of golden light sprouted from the pavement where he had stood. His tome flipped through its pages as he landed on the ground. But more vines shot out and wrapped around his ankles, trapping him in place.

Eckerson sprinted towards him.

Staying calm, Caleb ignored his splitting mind and spoke the new incantation. *"With birds, I'd like to share; Being lighter than air."*

But he hadn't cast it on himself. A yellow glyph formed

around Eckerson's waist, lifting him helplessly into the air.

The man's focus on his incantation must have wavered for the vines around Caleb's ankles to vanish. Not wasting a moment, Caleb released his speed enhancement and brought a new phrase to mind. *"The land where you stand; Is only mud and sand."*

A black glyph formed on the pavement beneath the floating Guild Scribe. It spun in rapid circles, turning the concrete into a muddy pool.

Caleb released the flying incantation, letting Eckerson fall. He brought a final incantation into his mind as the agent landed in the artificial swamp, sinking in waist-deep. *"Summoned from frozen Hell; The winter citadel."*

Ice surged across the ground, freezing the slush around Eckerson. The agent growled in pain and struggled against the enclosure.

"Fucking abomination," the man seethed.

Caleb walked forward, scythe in hand. He watched as the large Scribe thrashed about. "I really wish you wouldn't call me that," he whispered.

Eckerson glared at him with brown eyes. "We call a spade a spade."

As Caleb reached his opponent, the man swung his ax haphazardly. Easily sidestepping the attack, he slashed out with his scythe and cut off the agent's right hand.

Crimson blood painted the ice as the man howled in pain. The large weapon vanished, and the man clutched his wounded stub.

"Quiet down," Caleb said. "I'm sure the Guild has medical Scribes to spare. You'll get a new hand in a few days."

He wanted to ask the man more questions, but the fight and scream would have caught someone's attention. It was time to flee. He began to walk away.

Eckerson laughed. "I knew you didn't have it in you to kill. Pathetic."

He kept walking.

"I can't wait for the day to come when you regret leaving me alive."

Caleb clenched his jaw. Part of him feared the man was right. And his grandfather's voice compelled him to finish off his opponent. *What does Fleischer mean?*

But he refused. Taking a human life was too much. A line that shouldn't be crossed lightly. Instead, he ran towards the setting sun.

For a quarter of an hour, he jumped from one alley to another, putting distance between himself and Eckerson, slowly making his way back towards Heather's SUV. Once he was satisfied he hadn't been followed, he took out his radio.

"Bloodhound, Athena, this is Sunflower."

Static came in on the other line. "Oh, thank goodness you're okay," Heather's voice came over. "I am so mad at you. Never do something like that again."

"I'm sorry."

"Sunflower," Wilson's voice said, "can you retreat to the rendezvous point?"

"Yes. I can get there in a few minutes."

"Understood. Athena and I are already close by. We'll meet with you."

Caleb stowed the radio and darted across the road. Still no sirens. Still no sign of any more Scribes. Had they truly gotten away?

Stepping into the predetermined alley, he let out a sigh of relief. Heather, Wilson, and Opp sat scrunched behind the corner of a building.

Heather ran at him, her face a strange mixture of sad, happy, and angry. "I swear," she said to him, "if I wasn't so happy to see you, I'd give you the talking to of your life."

He smiled and placed a hand on her shoulder. "I'm glad you three are okay."

Opp sprinted forward and jumped at him, licking at his face.

Caleb embraced his furry companion. "Hey, buddy. Did you keep Heather and Wilson safe?"

Wilson stepped forward. "I'm thankful we're all reunited, but we must not waste time. What's our next move, Mister Fleischer?"

"For whatever reason, the police have stopped pursuing us. It's suspicious, but we can't stand around scratching our heads. Our top priority has to be meeting up with my grandpa. How far away is Millennium Park?"

"About thirty minutes," Heather said, "depending on traffic."

"Then let's get going," he said. "We'll figure out the rest as we go."

Ensuring the coast was clear, they inconspicuously made their way to the SUV. Even as the sky darkened, pedestrians still overran the streets. As much as he hated crowds, the people made blending in easier.

They packed into the SUV. Caleb sat in the back with Opp, keeping his tome close.

"We didn't learn anything," Heather said dismally. "We failed today."

"We went up against the Guild and escaped with our lives. We should be thankful," he said.

She nodded. "I hope Aalia is okay."

Wilson drove them down the street. "We cannot return to the penthouse now that they know Miss O'Brien is involved. It'll be swarmed with agents. We'll have to lay low somewhere else."

Caleb lowered the car window, letting in fresh air. Perhaps his grandfather would know a place they could hide. Taking out his phone, he found two text messages waiting for him. One was Sally asking him how he was. The other was his grandfather saying he was twenty minutes away.

Sighing, he put the phone in the cupholder. He was ready for this day to be over. But there was still one obstacle. His grandfather. He wasn't ready to be around that man again. Not yet. Not ever.

Opp barked twice.

Caleb snapped out of his thoughts and looked to his dog. Opp barked twice again, then whimpered. Climbing into the space between the seats, he covered his snout with his paws and moaned.

What was going on? Opp never acted like this. His eyes grew wide. "Wilson!" he yelled. "Swerve left now!"

Without hesitation, the old man obliged. Caleb jerked against his seatbelt as they pulled into the opposing lane. Car horns blared, but his eyes were glued behind them.

A massive figure crashed into the street where they had been just moments before. The street cracked, and debris flew into the air. It rained down upon them as Wilson swerved in and out of oncoming vehicles.

"What's going on?" Heather screamed.

"Pull over," Caleb ordered.

Wilson brought them back into the right lane and swerved to a screeching stop. Caleb threw open the door and jumped out. Panicked pedestrians scrambled in every direction, fleeing from the mysterious explosion. Others crept towards the crater in the street, their phones out to record it.

Rising from the smoke and debris was a creature the size of a city bus. Coarse, green skin wrapped around its massive body and six legs. Dozens of squirming tendrils hung like a beard off a canine-like head, though it had no mouth.

Caleb's heart raced, threatening to tear out of his chest. Sweat dripped down his body, and he felt the color leave his face. His hands trembled, and he stumbled back, almost falling over. He managed to mutter only a single word: "Elderon."

Several yellow glyphs dotted the beast, covering it like the filken he had fought in the past. The Guild had managed to control such a creature. And they had sent it after him.

Heather joined him, her facing having gone ghostly pale. "So...that's an elderon. It's scarier than I imagined."

Wilson sprang from the vehicle, rifle in hand. "Miss O'Brien, Mister Fleischer," he said, looking at the crater in the road, "what is it?"

Caleb couldn't speak. His grandfather's voice ordered him to run. To flee to safety. An elderon couldn't be fought alone.

But then his eyes flickered to the hundreds of people either fleeing or approaching danger. If he ran, how many would die as the elderon rampaged behind him? He was its target. And he had to keep its attention on him and no one else.

Heather wrapped her hand around his, giving it a gentle squeeze. She was shaking as much as he was. "What are we going to do?"

Swallowing past the lump in his throat, he pulled away from her. "Get in the SUV. Get Opp and Wilson out of here, and find my grandpa."

"He's still so far away! I'm not leaving you—"

"Heather!" Caleb screamed. "Leave! This is not a debate."

She hesitated.

He snapped his fingers and walked towards the encroaching beast, his tome floating in front of him. "Go!" he yelled without looking back.

A moment passed before the SUV doors slammed shut. It skidded to life and drove down the street with screeching tires.

The elderon stalked forward, its razor-sharp claws carving up the pavement with every step. It growled in his mind, and the tendrils on its face squirmed in every direction.

Caleb had never felt more alone in his life. A coldness swept through him, threatening to freeze his body completely. His instincts implored him to run, but he couldn't abandon these people. Even if staying meant almost certain death.

Chapter Twelve

Caleb crouched in the sunflower field behind his home. Pulling his knees deep into his chest, he kept his eyes glued to the black dirt. The flowers rose like towers around him, protecting his small body from anything beyond their borders.

Everything ached. Splotches of blue and purple covered him from head to toe. Tears streamed down his cheeks, and snot dribbled out of his nose. What had he done wrong?

It had been his first day of combat training with his grandpa. So much yelling. So much pain. He had done everything he was told, and yet the hits kept coming. What should he have done differently? He sobbed, no answer coming to him.

He hid among the flowers for hours, unmoving. His cheeks had dried, but the bruises had only grown darker. As the sun set, parts of the sky soon matched the yellow and orange of the petals.

A trembling growl escaped his stomach. Hiding forever wasn't an option. He limped out of the field and back to his small, rundown home. Standing on the toes of his good foot, he peered inside to see if his grandpa was out and about.

With no sign of the man, he hobbled around to the front of the house. Creeping into the kitchen, he opened the fridge. He gingerly carried a milk carton over to the counter, barely able to place it on top of it. Using the drawers to form makeshift stairs, he climbed up.

He poured himself a glass. As he gulped it down, a familiar rolling sounded from the hallway. His dad shuffled into the room, using his medical stand as support.

Sad eyes painted the man's face. After a moment, his dad scuffled over and put a bony hand on his shoulder. "You hungry. Champ?"

He nodded. "Can I have a grilled cheese?"

His dad smiled weakly. "Of course. You can."

Gathering the necessary supplies, his dad cooked up a grilled cheese and handed it to him. Not waiting for it to cool, Caleb took a massive bite. Gooey cheese filled his mouth, and he puffed his cheeks out like a squirrel, then winced with pain.

"How are you. Feeling?"

He shrugged. "Okay. Grandpa hit me a lot today."

His dad pursed his lips together. "I know."

"What did I do wrong?" he asked, looking down at his sandwich.

An uncomfortable silence filled the room. Scott stared into his eyes, then looked away. Was his dad mad at him too?

"Do you. Remember. The story I told. About me and gramps. Fighting. The elderon?"

"You guys beat the scary monster no one else could. You were heroes."

"Yes. And because of. Who you are. And what you can do. One day you'll. Have to face. Scary monsters." A coughing spasm overcame his dad. Scott pulled out a handkerchief, spitting blood into it. "Your grandpa. Is doing what he. Thinks is best. To get you. Ready for it."

Caleb tried to smile but failed. He grabbed his own arm, avoiding his dad's gaze. "I don't like it," he whispered. Glancing up, he saw tears streaming down his dad's face.

His dad leaned down and wrapped his thin arms around him. Caleb hesitated a moment, then wrapped his arms as far around his dad's body as they would go.

"I know," Scott said. "But I need you. To be strong. For daddy."

Burying his face into his dad's chest, Caleb remained silent. He clutched his dad's shirt and accepted the safety of the man's arms. Tears fell down his cheeks, and he began to sob. He didn't want to get hurt again. He didn't want to fight. Ever. "Am I really going to have fight monsters?"

"You might," his dad told him. "Maybe even one. Of the scary. Monsters. Don't ever fight. Them alone. If you are. Alone. Run away. As fast as. You can."

Caleb nodded. Why wouldn't he run from a monster?

His father's words echoed in Caleb's mind. He faced the elderon, sweat dripping off his shaking hands. His grandfather was twenty minutes away and heading to a different part of the city. Delaying the elderon for that long was a fool's errand.

But more and more people flooded the street, trying to sneak a peek at the seemingly random display of destruction. He wanted to scream at them as they recorded with their phones, but his voice was trapped in his throat. He was utterly paralyzed.

The elderon took a step forward, its tendrils squirming like worms. Then, all at once, they grew rigid and pointed straight at him. A ball of red energy a yard in diameter grew in front of its snout.

The crimson sphere shot out from the beast and barreled down the street. It left a glowing trench in its wake, tearing up the pavement with ease.

Gritting his teeth and clenching his hand, Caleb drove a fist straight into his thigh. Pain shocked his system awake, and he regained control of his body. He jumped desperately to the side, narrowly avoiding the attack.

The blast sank into the street two blocks down and exploded. The shockwave shattered dozens of windows and threw him off his feet. People screamed as glass and debris rained from the sky.

"Run!" he screamed at the crowd around him. "Run!"

Fear finally spread across all their faces. Panicked yells filled the air as they fled in every direction, unable to see the creature that was the source of danger.

Vehicles screeched to life and horns blasted. An orange sedan sped straight towards the beast. Razor sharps claws cut the vehicle clean in two, each half falling apart. A perplexed, middle-aged man climbed out of the wreckage, overtaken with shock.

Caleb brought two phrases into his mind and sprinted forward. His tome opened to both pages simultaneously and cast the incantations for his speed and strength enhancements.

The elderon's tendrils pointed at the bystander. It raised a paw, the artificial lighting of the city gleaning off its nails.

Caleb sprang headfirst as the elderon brought its foot down. He wrapped his arms around the befuddled man and tackled him out of the way. A crash sounded behind him as the narrowly-avoided attack tore into the street. He landed on the pavement and pushed the man away, screaming at him to flee.

The elderon faced him, another ball of energy forming before its face. Jumping back to put distance between them, he summoned his scythe.

The attack hurtled towards him, the smell of burnt plastic and asphalt assaulting his nose. Ignoring the odor, he dumped his soul into his strength incantation. An onslaught of dust and debris swarmed him as the crimson sphere neared. Flexing, he planted his legs and swung his weapon.

The blade of his scythe caught the dense orb right in its elbow. It pushed him back, his feet tearing up the pavement. He gritted his teeth, his enhanced skin still singeing at the energy's heat.

A fierce roar bellowed from his gut as he swung his scythe up, flinging the attack up into the sky. The blast exploded high in the air, away from the city and its people.

The elderon's tendrils wriggled fanatically as it screeched telepathically. It galloped forward, its movements a blur. If he blinked, he'd lose it.

He diverted some of his soul into his speed enhancement

just as it slashed from his left. Fast as a whip, he still only barely raised his scythe in time. His staff caught the beast's claws, shielding his body. The force of the blow lifted him off his feet and sent him soaring back.

His stomach lurched, and he crashed through a brick wall. He slammed into a wooden floor and bounced straight off it. People screamed as he smashed through several tables before stopping.

He coughed up blood. Trying to stand, his vision blurred. Pain ruptured across his enhanced body, and he came to his knees. A confusing mess of sounds swirled around him as he stood, finding himself in a pub.

A dozen patrons stood against the establishment's walls, their horrified eyes fixated on him.

"R—" he coughed. "Run out the back!"

The elderon burst through the front of the building. Bricks flew, and terrified screams echoed.

Caleb hobbled forward, trying to keep the beast's attention on him. He slashed at its neck, but it dodged and whipped the back of its paw at him. The green, leathery skin crashed into him. It ripped him off his feet and sent him crashing through the side wall.

The blow knocked the wind from his lungs. He soared into the adjacent alley and collided with a dumpster, blowing through the metal and into the trash. Warm blood dripped down his temple. Taking a breath sent stabbing pain through his chest.

How many ribs were broken? The elderon was tearing apart his enhanced body as if it were putty. Three minutes into the fight, and he was already struggling to stand.

He flared his soul, stoking the flame that sat in his chest. He poured it into his strength incantation, allowing him to temporarily shrug off the pain.

Shooting to his feet, he jumped back into the pub. Blood painted the floor and walls. Six dismembered bodies littered the area, the elderon standing over them. Caleb had failed these people.

His grip on his scythe tightened, and he screamed to draw the creature's focus. As it spun to face him, he swung at its ribs. His blade only dug a quarter of an inch through the beast's thick hide. It didn't even draw blood.

It snarled. Taking advantage of its attention, he jumped back out onto the street and away from the remaining patrons. He had to keep them alive. He had to keep everyone alive.

The elderon screeched and followed. Crashing onto the street, it lunged at him, its front two claws flurried in a razor-sharp barrage.

He desperately retreated, continuously spinning his weapon around his body. The attacks missed by inches, tearing up his clothes with each swipe. No matter how fast he withdrew, the elderon was upon him a second later. Its front paws attacked without end.

This was unsustainable. One misstep and he was dead. His eyes drooped as he brought a third incantation into his thoughts, his mind screaming in agony.

The beast's middle feet slipped on rubble, creating a brief opening. This was his chance. *"By mark of brimstone; Be scorched to the bone!"* he yelled.

A plume of fire burst from his tome and consumed the elderon. It wouldn't do much damage, but as it shrieked, he knew it would buy him a few seconds.

Crouching low, he winced through the pain in his legs and jumped high into the air. He released his flame incantation and brought a new phrase into mind.

He landed on a building's ledge several stories up as images of his first day of combat training flashed through his memory. Opened to a new page, his tome glowed red. *"Plant of sunlight; Petals take flight."*

A glyph appeared in front of him. Golden light shot from it and formed a translucent sunflower. Dozens of petals flew off the plant and swarmed like daggers.

The elderon screeched and fled from the attack's path. Caleb gritted his teeth, struggling to maintain all three incantations. It was as if a knife was digging through his head. Sweat drenched his body, and his breathing grew labored.

He dumped his soul into the flower for over a minute, trying to ensnare his opponent. The petals divided into smaller and smaller pieces, trying to give the elderon no escape route. Three petals hit its back-right leg. Like his scythe, they barely pierced its skin.

His grip on the incantation faded, and the flower vanished.

How much of his soul had he just wasted for nothing? Legs wobbling, he leaned back against the building, afraid he'd fall off.

The elderon produced another sphere of red energy and shot it at him. Eyes growing wide, he cast the portal incantation. The attack passed through the first hole and shot out the second high into the sky before exploding.

Drawing ragged breaths, he glanced through the window behind him. Several families huddled in a hallway, shocked to see him. If he stayed near buildings, he was putting people at risk. Wiping the blood from his face, he jumped back down to the street, his enhanced legs absorbing the landing.

A volley of claws descended upon him. It took all his focus to just barely avoid them. But the blows were endless. From the left. Up. Down. Right. Right. Left. He couldn't keep this up.

The next set of slashes came, and instead of retreating, he sprang forward. The tips of its claws sliced his right thigh. Pouring his soul into his arms, Caleb swung his blade at the soft spot at the base of its skull. Its only weak point.

The elderon raised its head, and the scythe cut across its cheek instead. A few drops of purple blood leaked from the shallow injury, and the beast howled.

He jumped back. Warm blood spewed down his leg and stained his jeans. Warning bells sounded in his mind, and he tried not to panic, but his breathing grew frantic. His grandfather's voice crawled into his thoughts, asking him what he expected to happen after challenging an elderon alone.

"Shut up!" he yelled at the imagined question.

Anger burned in his chest. Screw his grandfather. Screw rationality. He wanted to do the right thing. He wanted to save people.

A perilous idea took shape in his mind. Gathering himself, he prepared for the final assault. It was going to be an all-or-nothing gamble.

The elderon charged, and his tome opened to a new page. He retreated as fast as his legs would carry him. *"Forty days all the way through; No ark can ever save you."*

A blue glyph appeared under the beast. A massive geyser of water ruptured out of it, lifting the elderon into the air. Water rained down and flooded the street. The creature landed in a splash, losing its footing.

Lungs burning, he released the flooding incantation and jumped up to a windowsill. It was time for the last incantation. *"From sky to page; Feel the storm's rage."*

A bolt of lightning sprang from his tome and shot at the beast. It jumped to the side and avoided the attack. The electricity crashed into the water and dispersed with violent arcs.

The elderon howled like nothing he had ever heard before. Its body convulsed, and it appeared unable to move as the lightning consumed it. It was paralyzed.

Hope bloomed inside him. Screaming, he launched himself at the immobile creature. Victory was within reach.

Feet away from the beast, a red ball formed in front of its snout, pointed at the ground. Caleb's eyes grew wide, and he desperately swung at the elderon's soft spot. The tip of his blade was inches from contact when the crimson sphere shot out.

It exploded into the ground.

The shockwave sent him flying. His arms burned, and he cried out. Pain scrambled his mind, and he barely maintained concentration on just his strength enhancement.

In an act of pure instinct, he raised his scythe in front of him. His weapon deflected the elderon's claws that he barely registered flying at him. They had aimed at his chest. Instead, they dug deep into his gut.

He screamed. White hot pain seared across his stomach.

Slamming into the ground, his head crashed into the pavement. His mind rang, and scarlet blood gushed from his gut. Reaching a hand down to the wound, his fingers slipped into his abdomen. His body grew cold and felt impossibly heavy. Was this death's grip?

But the elderon wasn't attacking. Using his polearm for support, Caleb struggled up to his knees. Through blurred vision, he saw the beast. Its front legs had snapped in two, no doubt from its own blast. It still howled in his head.

His tome fell to the ground, and his scythe vanished, his soul too exhausted to maintain the passive incantations. The strength enhancement faded from his mind. All the pain he had been able to ignore up to this point overwhelmed his body, and his vision blackened around the edges. Only a small flicker of a smoldering ember resided in his chest. Just like his father. His soul was all but spent.

The elderon refocused its attention on him. Another ball of red energy formed in front of its snout, though it grew noticeably slower.

Caleb knew the fight was over. His body barely responded to his commands. But his survival instincts had taken over. With a shaking hand, he manually flipped the pages of his tome, subconsciously holding a familiar phrase in his mind.

As the crimson sphere shot out at him, he whispered, *"No matter the power you may wield; Stand firm against my mighty shield."*

The cold timbers of his soul managed to form a golden dome around him just in time to absorb the attack. The force of the collision shook the ground and cracked his shield.

His eyelids drooped. Where was he? What was happening?

A second ball of energy formed, and his gaze drifted upwards. The canopy of purple strings dangled above him, taunting him. That's right, he was in Chicago. And he had failed to save the city.

The second sphere crashed into his barrier, cracking it further. He closed his eyes as tears streamed down his face. He fell forward, to his stomach, his body feeling weightless. He convulsed and sobbed. He didn't want to die.

A third blast all but shattered his shield.

Time slowed. His father crossed his mind. How the man had embraced him on the first day of combat training. All his dad's jokes and stories flashed from his memory.

He thought of Oppenheimer. His dearest pet. His most loyal comrade. His ever-faithful companion.

And then Sally and JJ came into view. All the years they worked together in the store. The warm laughs they had all shared. The time he had spent with her in school. His only childhood friend.

Lastly, he thought of Heather. Her smile. Her endless well of support and determination. And he had let her down. He hadn't taught her to be a Scribe. He hadn't gotten rid of the strings. And he hadn't saved her mother.

He was going to die a failure.

The sound of screeching tires jolted his eyes open. Several grenades rained down on the elderon, exploding into clouds of orange gas. The beast moaned and coughed as a hail of bullets descended upon it, bouncing off its hide.

A black SUV with tinted windows raced full speed at the elderon. Just before it reached the gaseous fog, someone jumped out of it.

Still coughing, the elderon didn't seem to notice the vehicle. It crashed into the beast and drove it into a nearby building. Bullets continued to fire, and more grenades landed where the SUV had pinned the elderon.

Soft hands clasped his shoulders and pulled him up. Someone yelled his name over and over. He focused his attention enough to see Heather's scraped up face. She cupped his cheek and covered the wound on his gut.

"H-Heather?" he asked weakly.

"I couldn't abandon you," she said, tears falling from her eyes.

He barely registered her words. The beast's screams still howled in his mind. "It's not. Dead."

"What do we do? Tell me what to do."

He looked into her green eyes. There was only one thing he could do. Disappearing into his mind, he accessed memories he had promised never to visit again. A part of him he loathed. The very thing that made him an abomination.

He opened his fledgling soul to the world around him. The souls of the city revealed themselves. Heather's raged and burned with ferocity. Only the elderon's was larger than hers.

Through sheer force of will, he kept himself conscious. "Heather...do you trust me?"

Her voice was weak. "Yes."

"Go to your soul. Open it to me."

She nodded, and her soul began to dance. As it did, the SUV was thrown out of the building. The elderon stepped out, battered and bruised. It wailed and limped down the street towards someone he couldn't make out.

Gritting his teeth, he extended his soul out towards Heather's, embracing it. Their souls flickered in unison. A golden soul string grew out of his chest and soared into hers. Her eyes grew wide.

Heather's energy flooded him, and his soul grew exponentially larger than it had ever been in his life. Power raged through him like a flooding stream, spreading to every inch of his body.

His tome floated once more, and fresh air filled his lungs. He shot to his feet, looking around with renewed clarity.

Wilson was firing his rifle at the beast, retreating with Opp as it hobbled towards them.

Heather let out a yelp and fell to the ground. His head snapped towards her. In his current state, he was drawing too much of her soul far too quickly. Her body couldn't handle it. He had to finish this before she lost consciousness.

His wounds hadn't healed, but her soul let him move despite them. He rushed down the street as the beast came upon Wilson and Opp. His surroundings blurred past him like he'd never experienced before.

This was the power of a golden connection?

In a flash, he scooped up Wilson and Opp before the elderon could reach them. In another blur of movement, he brought them a block away to safety.

"Mister...Fleischer?" Wilson asked, befuddled.

He said nothing. Facing the elderon, he summoned his scythe and charged forward. The beast struggled to keep balance but slashed out at him regardless. He weaved around the attacks with little effort.

Not sure about the limits of his strength, he focused on the beast's weak spot, the soft patch of skin towards the back of its skull. His grip tight, Caleb swung his scythe. The blade dug deep into its head, purple blood spewing out.

With a singular cry, the elderon convulsed and fell to the ground. The yellow glyphs covering its body vanished. It was dead.

Relief and despair flooded him. Another innocent life taken. But what choice had the Guild given him? For the briefest of moments, he thought of Iibere.

He pushed the memories away. There was no time to waste. He brought a healing incantation into his mind, and his tome flipped through its pages.

Then it fell to the ground. Pain ruptured through him, and he collapsed. The golden soul string had vanished. Down the block, Heather lay unconscious.

His vision blurred, and he rolled to his back. The canopy of purple strings hung above him, taunting him. They were ever-present. Ever haunting. A reminder of his failure.

But he didn't want that to be his final thought. Turning his head, he looked at Heather. He'd never see her smile again. He tried to imagine it as his vision faded black.

End of Part Two

Part Three

Chapter Thirteen

It was quiet. The kind of silence that persists for so long that time becomes imperceptible to the mind. When Caleb finally opened his eyes, he couldn't make out how long it had been since he had lost consciousness.

He shot up, taking in his surroundings. Expecting the Chicago streets, he instead found himself in an unfamiliar bedroom. It wasn't Heather's penthouse. Where was he? Had the Guild captured him? The accommodations seemed too lavish for that to be the case.

Now that he was grounded in the present, a thought occurred to him. He felt no pain. Throwing off his covers, he looked down. No wound covered his stomach, nor anywhere else on his body. His body was heavy and sluggish but otherwise was in excellent condition.

Clutching his head, he tried to remember what had happened. Flashes of the elderon fight tore through his mind. The beast's screams. Its claws ripping into him. What he had thought were his final moments.

He shuddered.

An IV stuck into his left hand, leading to a medical stand that wasn't too different from his father's. He reached out to remove the needle only to find he was not alone. In the dark corner opposite him was the ever-familiar figure in the black cloak.

Confused, he looked around again. "Did I not make it?"

She walked to the bed, sitting on the end of it. "You are alive," she assured him.

"Why are you here?"

"I wanted to thank you for trusting Aalia, and therefore me. I know your feelings towards me are...mixed. But I only want what is best for you and this world."

He tightened his mouth. "I know you didn't come here just for that. What do you really want?"

"I wished to make sure you were well, and to give you a message."

Frowning, he shook his head. "No. No, no, no. I'm fine, and I don't want one of your silly riddles. I just want to stop the strings and go home. If you aren't going to help with that, leave."

"You won't be returning to Orion anytime soon," she said. "Chicago is only the beginning. The first step. There is a larger game at play here, one that you will play a significant role in."

"Stop, I don't want to hear it. How many times have you tried to convince me of your tales of seasons and fate? I don't want any part of it." He jumped out of bed only to wince in pain. The IV needle tugged at his skin, and the medical stand toppled over. Cursing under his breath, he removed the needle.

The figure rose and stood in front of him. She put a cold hand on his shoulder. "Remember, Caleb. Autumn rises when Winter falls. Stand—"

He rolled his eyes. "That doesn't make any sense!"

A knock sounded behind him. His head snapped to the door. When he looked back, the figure was gone. Throwing on a shirt, he grabbed his satchel off the floor and pried open the door.

Heather's face greeted him. "You're awake. Thank goodness. Can I come in?"

He nodded and stepped out of the way.

She shuffled in, her eyes glued to the medical stand on the floor. "Everything okay? I thought I heard talking."

"Yeah, everything is fine."

Stepping closer to him, she looked him over. His face grew warm as she poked the places where his wounds had been. He was about to say something when she threw her arms around him, holding him tight.

"I'm so glad you're okay," she whispered. "Sorry, I know you don't like hugs. I've just been so worried."

She moved to pull away, but he stopped her. Wrapping his arms around her, Caleb pulled her close. Her warmth radiated over him, and he recalled the feeling of their souls connecting.

He wasn't sure how long they both stood there, but he finally pulled away. Grabbing his own arm, he looked down. "What happened? Where are we?"

She sat down on the bed. "You've been asleep for four days. We're in Aalia's apartment. After Wilson and I drove off, I noticed you left your phone in the car. So, I called your grandpa and told him what was happening. And then I convinced Wilson that we had to help you, so we came back."

"That was foolish, Heather."

She smiled weakly. "I wasn't going to stay and hide while you fought alone."

"I know," he said, sitting next to her. "Thank you. You saved my life."

"You and I, we're in this together, kiddo. Get used to it."

He smiled. "And Aalia's okay? Are we safe here?"

"Yeah, she managed to keep her cover intact. So hopefully, the Guild won't think to look for us here. My penthouse is under constant supervision, apparently."

"Okay," he said. "And my dad and grandpa are here?"

"Yupperooni. Your dad has been a delight to have around."

"And my grandpa?"

"Well...whenever he is around, he mostly sticks to himself. Or gives us mean looks."

"That sounds like him. Does he know about your dad?"

She shook her head. "Aalia told me it wasn't a good idea to tell him or your dad."

"She's right. My grandpa isn't a...forgiving man."

"Still," she said. "You should have seen him, Caleb. He brought out his tome, and, all at once, he concealed us, destroyed the elderon's body, shielded us, and healed you. I couldn't even make out the incantations he was using, he was casting them so quickly."

That also sounded just like his grandfather. "He's a very powerful Scribe. My dad always said he was the best." Moving to his feet, he walked over to the window and looked at the orange and red sky. The canopy of purple strings greeted him as the ever-present landmark of the Chicago skyline.

The Guild used the elderon to create strings, but it wasn't the one receiving all the soul-energy. Just like all the filken he had met thus far. All the souls being siphoned were going somewhere else.

"Caleb?"

The room suddenly felt confining, and he moved to the door. "I suppose we should go meet up with everyone else."

"Actually," she interjected, "I wanted to ask you something.

He stopped and met her green eyes.

"Well, before, you said something. And I confirmed it with Aalia. You said that only Guardians and beasts of the Speculon could create soul strings."

"That's true."

"Then...which are you?" she asked, seemingly afraid of the answer.

He didn't answer at first, his gaze steadfast. Both her question and the possible answers he could give ran through his mind. But he decided on the simplest truth. "Neither."

He knew it wasn't the response she was looking for. But he wasn't ready to open up about it. He glanced to where the cloaked figure had sat. No, not yet.

Instead, he left the room and found himself in a long hallway. Hearing voices to the left, he turned and walked out into a lavish living room. Apparently, Aalia's family was nearly as well off as Heather's.

Before he could take another step, eighty pounds of fur barraged him. Oppenheimer repeatedly licked his face.

Letting out a soft chuckle, he embraced his dog. "Hey, buddy, you miss me?"

Opp returned to all four legs but didn't calm down, rubbing his snout all over his jeans. Petting his dog's head, he heard laughter erupt from the next room.

He made his way into an ornately decorated study where

Wilson and his father sat at a large, mahogany table. Both men were red in the face, and Wilson was presently wiping joyous tears from his eyes.

"I. Swear. The whole town. Found me. Naked in the. Pasture." His dad grinned and took a long breath. "It didn't help that I. Spoke very. Broken French."

"Why would you wear such baggy clothing to a fight?" Wilson asked.

"The Guild. Only sent me. To meet with the. Constable. I didn't. Know two filken. Would show up."

"Did the citizens run you out of town?"

"No. Sir." Scott winked. "Talked my way. Outta it. Had drinks with. The whole town. That night."

"You talked your way out of that situation with broken French?"

"I am nothing. If not a. Miracle worker."

The corner of Caleb's mouth turned up as he recalled the story he had heard dozens of times. Every tale of his father was similar. A young, adventurous man who traveled the world to fight monsters, save people, and become a legend. It was exactly the kind of life Caleb didn't want to live.

"Ah, Mister Fleischer, you're awake," Wilson said, standing. "How are you feeling?"

Realizing they had noticed him, Caleb took an instinctive step back. Shaking his head, he headed to the table. "Fine, thanks, Wilson."

His father grabbed his medical stand and rose. Shuffling over, the sick man wrapped a pair of bony arms around Caleb. "Thank the. Guardians. That you're. Okay."

Hesitating a moment, he returned his father's embrace. "I'm okay, Dad."

"You had us worried, Mister Fleischer."

His father pulled away and placed a thin hand on his cheek. The man's glassy gray eyes pierced him. "You sure. You're. Well?"

He took a step away from his father's touch. "Yeah, I'm fine. Promise."

Hobbling back to the table, his father took a seat. "Come and. Sit."

Sighing, he complied and sat across from the man. Both his father's and Wilson's gaze bore into him. He shrunk into himself, unsure of what to do with the attention. Just as the silence was about to reach an uncomfortable level, his stomach let out a thunderous growl.

"Ah, perhaps you would like something to eat, Mister Fleischer?"

"Yes, please. I'm starving."

"Very good. I think it's time we all had some supper," Wilson said before disappearing into another room.

His father continued to stare, and Caleb finally arched an eyebrow at the man.

"Taking down. An elderon. I am so. Proud of. You," his dad said before coughing. "No other Scribe. Could have. Done that."

"That's only because I can do things no other Scribe can. And I still couldn't stop it before people died."

"You stopped it. From killing. Far more," his dad pointed out.

He shrugged. "It feels like I should have done more."

"That's because. You have a. Kind heart. But we must. Accept there is. Only so much. We can do in life. We are only. Human."

Only human. He could hear his grandfather using the same words in a derogatory manner. The man's voice criticized him for how he had handled the elderon. Telling him he should have abandoned the people in the streets. That survival was all that mattered.

He clenched his hands into fists, and then a question popped into his mind. "Where's Grandpa?"

"Probably out. Sulking. Somewhere," his father answered with a wink.

Laughter erupted from upstairs, shortly followed by Aalia and Heather entering the room.

"Oh man," Aalia said, her eyes locked on him. "You're up! How ya feeling?"

"Good, all things considered."

"I bet, you absolute beast," she said, sitting down across from him. "I got one of the Guild rooks to swipe all the nearby security footage to piece together the fight. You were amazing! Exactly what I'd expect from a Fleischer."

He looked down at her words, grabbing his arm. *What does Fleischer mean?* The legacy of his family's name.

His dad let out a hearty chuckle. "He's had. The best training. Around."

Slumping in his chair, he shied away from his father's playful pat.

"Aalia," Heather said, changing the subject, "tell Caleb what you told me."

Aalia played with a loose strand of hair, thinking. "Oh, right. The Guild is all in a fuss over you and the elderon. Rumors are spreading that the young Fleischer has come to stop the strings. The high-ranking officers are pissed."

That wouldn't make keeping a low profile any easier. "Also," he said, "the Guild has control of the police?"

"Wouldn't surprise. Me," Scott said. "The Guild. Always worked. To expand its. Influence."

"It's not just the police," Aalia said. "Ever since Michael took over, the Guild has really accelerated its infiltration. Heads of Government, high ranking military personnel, CEOs, any institution that has power, we've got people on the inside. All in preparation for some big plan."

His father shifted uncomfortably in his seat.

"Anyway," she continued, "that brings us to the other update that occurred while you were asleep. Chicago is under martial law."

Martial law? His mouth hung open. "That doesn't make any sense," he said. "Even if they thought the elderon incident was a terrorist attack or something, would that really justify this?"

Heather nodded. "A lot of people were shocked when it was announced. But the governor and president came out in favor of it, and that calmed down most of the vocal opponents of the decision."

Had this been part of the Guild's plan all along? Or were they turning a small defeat into a victory? His racing thoughts were interrupted by Wilson stepping back into the room, plates in hand.

"Supper is served."

The five of them chowed down on the meal, letting their woes temporarily fall away. Caleb was thankful to have warm food in his stomach again. It had been so long since he had been truly hungry, he was starting to get spoiled.

After a bottle of wine came into play, and his father began to regale the group with more stories of his youth. One tale involved him protecting a duchess for three months in England. Wilson followed suit and talked about Bobby and their time in the army. After much begging from Heather, Caleb even talked about his time at the store. Everyone seemed rather interested in the stories he considered mundane.

Reminded by a story, he pulled out his phone and shot a text to Sally, just to check in. Closing the phone, he looked to Heather. "How long has it been since we cast the incantations on your mom?"

"A week," she said, looking down. "But I don't know if we can go to the hospital anymore."

Aalia nodded. "The Guild has Scribes monitoring your mom's room now. You'd get caught."

Then the only way to save Cassandra was to get rid of the strings. Somehow.

Setting her silverware on her empty plate, Heather took a long glance around the table. "So, this is it, huh?" she said. "The five people who are going to save Chicago."

His father let out a mix of chuckles and coughs. "I don't know. How much use. I'll be."

Wilson shot him a skeptical look. "Are you not a Scribe as well, Mister Fleischer?"

"He is," Caleb interjected. "But his soul is too weak. It's unlikely he'd be able to endure casting an incantation."

"But I can. Provide. Moral support," the man said with a bow.

Heather chuckled, and Aalia snickered at the display.

His father pulled a small journal from the medical stand. Opening it, the man began to scribble inside.

"Still working on the new incantation?" he asked his father.

"I've almost. Wrapped my head. Around the. Theory."

The man's writing was barely legible, but he had grown up reading it. Since his father could no longer cast incantations without risk, creating the theories behind them was the man's only connection to being a Scribe. A good number of the incantations in Caleb's tome were a product of his father's mind.

After an hour of work, Scott set down the pen and let out a labored sigh.

"Finish it?" Caleb asked.

"Not. Quite. Soon though."

"The great masterpiece of Scott Fleischer," he said jokingly.

His father playfully ruffled Caleb's hair. "Nope. That would be. You."

A golden hole ripped through the middle of the room. Everyone but Wilson shot up, their eyes glued to the portal. Caleb and Aalia snapped their fingers and summoned their tomes.

A six-and-a-half-foot tall man lumbered into the room. His broad shoulders and muscular physique appeared like sharpened steel. The man's silver hair was pulled back into a neat mane. A jangling cage of black chains hung from his hip, housing a purple tome.

A permanent scowl was carved onto his face, and his icy blue eyes pierced everyone in the room. It was a look only Karl Fleischer could give. Utter disdain for everything and everyone in front of him.

"You're awake," the old man said to Caleb, venom dripping from the words. "It's about time."

Caleb avoided his grandfather's gaze. Running a finger along one of his scars, he tried to keep control of his breathing. "Thank you for saving me, sir."

His grandfather scoffed. "Someone had to clean up your mess."

His hands balled into fists. "My mess? I took down an elderon."

"You fought when you should have run," Karl snarled. "Have I taught you nothing?"

"You taught me plenty," he snapped, his blood beginning to boil.

His grandfather squared up to him and marched forward. "I taught you to be a survivor. But instead, you choose to be a child playing hero."

Images of the pub flashed through his mind. The blood-stained walls. The people he couldn't save. He wanted to yell at his grandfather. So many words swarmed at the tip of his tongue. His face burned hot, and his eyes stung. Hands shaking, he prepared to say everything in his heart.

Then, all at once, his body drooped. What would be the point? What good would saying anything do? His grandfather was right. He was just a boy playing hero. A failure. Instead, he shoved all the words, feelings, and actions, all of it, down deep into his soul. Down where it wouldn't bother anyone. Down where he wouldn't have to think about it.

"I'm sorry that I'm a disappointment," he said, barely above a whisper.

"I've gotten used to it."

"Come now. Dad," Scott said, trying to break up the situation. "Come and. Join us. There's still some. Wine left."

Karl scowled. "I don't have time to be playing house." The imposing man marched down the hall and into a guest room, leaving an uncomfortable silence in his wake.

Heather placed a hand on Caleb's shoulder. "You okay?"

He nodded slowly. What was there to say?

His dad cleared his throat. "Since the good. Times have already. Been stopped. I feel it's time. For me to tell. You all something."

Everyone glanced at the sickly man.

"I know. What the strings. Are for."

Chapter Fourteen

Caleb stared in disbelief. Had he misheard? After months of searching in vain, after their failed attempt to extract information from Trenton and Eckerson, his father had known the answer the whole time?

"You already know?" Heather asked, giving the man a confused look.

His father nodded. "The moment. I came here. And saw the strings."

Arching an eyebrow, he asked, "Grandpa never told you?"

"No. I'm guessing. That's why he. Refused to let me. Speak to you. He knew I'd. Tell you."

Aalia leaned forward. "Well, out with it! What are they for?"

"Operation. Moonlight. Sonata." Scott coughed violently. "Using strings to. Incubate. A hydran egg. In a major. City."

His heart skipped a beat. A hydran? It couldn't be. A creature of pure destruction. *No. Please no.* The Guild couldn't be that cruel.

"No," Aalia whispered. She stood, her face contorting in disbelief. "I don't believe you. The Guild has crossed some lines, but not this. You're wrong."

Wilson crossed his arms, his face giving no sign of reaction. "How do you know this?"

"I was there. When my dad made. The plans. Thirty. Years ago."

And then it made sense. Of course, it was his grandfather's plan. It was exactly the kind of undertaking that man would concoct.

Heather's face had faded to a ghostly white. Her green eyes stared straight ahead, looking a thousand yards into the distance. "How...how bad is a hydran?"

Aalia rested her head on the back of her chair. "If one were released in Chicago, it could level the city. Millions would die."

She was right. Every book Caleb had ever read, every story he had been told all passed on the same warning. Hydrans meant death.

"Wait," Wilson interjected, "normal people like me can't see these creatures. So, most of the world wouldn't even understand what was happening. They'd just see random destruction."

Scott shook his head. "We discovered. That birthing a. Creature of the. Speculon. On earth. Allowed non-Scribes to see them."

Aalia nodded in confirmation. "I've seen the Guild control filken and elderon. I guess they must have figured out how to control a hydran, too."

That didn't seem possible. Who could control such a force of nature?

"I don't understand," Heather said. "Why? What purpose could it possibly serve?"

"Just like. Aalia said. The Guild has been. Infiltrating. Now they just. Need a crisis. To justify. Taking over."

"I've heard rumors," Aalia said. "Jokes, really. Nothing I took seriously. About taking the war to the Speculon. Ending it once and for all."

Caleb shot out of his chair, knocking it over. It prattled across the wood floor as he charged to the sliding glass door. Stepping out to the patio, he took in some fresh air.

A hydran. The Guild takeover. War with the Speculon. Never had he wished he was bagging groceries more than at that moment. He wasn't meant to live this sort of life. What did the world want from him?

Then his thoughts drifted to Iibere and the filken's final words. It had wanted to stop the strings. It had loved its friend. It had been kind. And the Guild wanted to kill them all. It wasn't right.

The sliding door opened and closed again. Wheels rolled across the patio as his father joined his side.

"Caleb—"

"You helped make this plan?" he asked, cutting his father off. He stared out at the web of strings that strangled the city. Their sight had always been depressing, but now that he knew what they did, what they were bringing... They truly were a web, and Chicago was trapped.

His dad let out a long, cough-filled sigh. "I was there. When it was made. I voted against it. Convinced enough. Officers. To join me. It was tabled."

"But now it's happening," he said. He gripped the patio railing, wanting to rip it out of the concrete. Glancing down, he saw how high up they were. For a moment, he wondered how long the fall to the street would take. Closing his eyes, he brought his breathing back under control. Anger was dangerous. It threatened to consume him, and he refused to be like his grandfather. Looking to his father, he calmly asked, "How could you stand being a Guild Scribe?"

"It's hard. When you grow up. Immersed in. Something. It can all seem. Normal." His father ran a bony hand through the sparse hair atop his head. "I thought. I could do good. As a Guild Scribe. I hunted down. The monsters. And saved people. I figured. That was. Enough."

What if Caleb had grown up a part of the Guild instead of hiding from it? Would he be a part of this operation now? The thought sent shivers down his spine.

"After you were. Born. I finally saw. The Guild's true. Colors." The man's soft, gray eyes washed over him. "I devoted my life. To ensuring. You became a. Better man than me."

A brief pause hung between them. "Do you want war with the Speculon?"

His father shook his head. "It would be too. Costly. So many people would. Die."

"And them? The creatures?"

"What do. You. Mean?"

"Last week, I talked with a filken. It talked about having friends. It showed remorse. It acted...human."

"You actually held. A conversation. With one?" his father asked in disbelief.

"You never did?"

"No. I always just. Killed them."

That's what every Scribe did. No one had bothered learning about their supposed enemy. Instead, they all had listened to propaganda and succumbed to fear and hate. Even he had believed the creatures weren't capable of creating a golden soul a string, something deeply associated with trust and compassion. Not until Iibere had opened his eyes.

"You truly are. A better man. Than me."

Caleb avoided his father's gaze. Illustrations he'd seen of hydrans rushed through his mind. Then his first day of combat training. His grandfather's spear impaling him. His dad's laughter. Meeting Heather.

There were too many thoughts. How was he supposed to make sense of any of this?

"Come on," his father said. "Let's get back. Inside. There's more to. Discuss."

He followed the man back inside. Aalia, Heather, and Wilson appeared to be in the midst of a heated discussion.

"No," Aalia said, "we have to leave the city now. I have contacts in the Philippines. We can hide there."

Heather threw her hands into the air. "And what, just leave my mom here to die?"

"Heather, I'm sorry, but she's going to die no matter what. You don't understand, we can't stop a hydran. Our options are to join the Guild, flee them, or die."

"I don't accept that. I'm not abandoning my mom."

"Perhaps Miss Laghari has a point. As unfortunate as it may be, we may have to consider this pragmatically."

"I can't believe you two," Heather said. "We're just gonna let everyone here die?"

"We can't save them. It sucks, but it's true," Aalia said.

Caleb joined them at the table, sitting back down. He had

nothing to add to this discussion. Abandoning Chicago felt wrong, but Aalia was right. There was nothing they could do now.

His father cleared his throat. "By our. Calculations. It would take. Eighteen to. Twenty-four months. To gestate. The egg. We don't need. To be. Rash."

Caleb shot his father a disappointed glance. "People are dying, Dad."

His father frowned. "That's not. What I mean—"

Aalia shook her head and cut in. "What are we gonna figure out with more time, though? There's nothing we can do."

"If anyone will. Know what to do. It'll be. My dad."

A moment passed, and every pair of eyes in the room shifted to Caleb. They expected him to convince his grandfather to help. Of course they did.

"He's probably. Retired for the. Night. We'll approach him. Tomorrow."

Aalia sighed. "Whatever. I have a meeting to go to. But, for the record, I really think we should be on the first flight out of here in the morning." She stood and left the apartment.

"I'm going to. Head to bed. Myself."

He looked up at his father. "I'll give you a hand."

"No. No. I'm fine. You can stay." The sickly man rolled his medical stand out of the room, disappearing down the next hall.

Heather rested her head on the table. "We can't seem to catch a break."

"Do you think your grandfather will assist us, Mister Fleischer?"

"I don't know," he said. "If he'll listen to anyone, it'll be me. But he doesn't really care about other people."

That was only half of it. Was he even going to be able to ask that man? The last time he had asked his grandfather for help, it had sent him spiraling. Part of him would rather fight another elderon.

His eyelids hung heavy. His thoughts drifted to Orion, and his heart ached. Before coming to Chicago, he'd never had the opportunity to be homesick.

Then he recalled what Wilson had told him about keeping one's mind distracted. Looking to Heather, he asked, "You ready for some lessons?"

Her head shot up. "Oh goodness, yes. Anything but just sitting around and moping."

Over the next few hours, he helped her through some soul exercises. He had her move her golden flame throughout her body, forming and molding it into various shapes. They then spent some time paging through his tomes, going over a variety of incantations.

Once they finished, he brought Opp back to his room. He tossed and turned in his bed, sleep proving difficult to find. Even after he managed to drift off, he woke an hour later, covered in sweat. Images of the elderon, a golden spear, and the never-ending web of strings were fresh in his psyche.

Caleb still hadn't emerged from his room late in the afternoon the next day. Sequestering himself away, he tried to avoid what he knew was waiting for him. His grandfather. The strings. The Guild. A hydran.

His phone buzzed in his pocket. It was a text from Sally.

Hey Caleb hope all is well :p

Things have been tough lately. Hope Orion is okay, he typed back.

She responded in less than a minute. *You need to talk?*

He put the phone away, not knowing how to respond. His growling stomach reminded him that he couldn't hide forever. Sliding Opp off his lap, he stood and left the room.

Wilson, Heather, and his father awaited him in the study. A variety of snacks lay scattered across the table. Grabbing some jerky, he sat down next to Heather.

She nudged him in the ribs. "You don't think we should leave, do you?"

He took a bite of the jerky, thinking as he chewed. "I don't know what we should do. I wish I could go home, but I don't want to abandon everyone."

"Eventually," Wilson said, "we'll have to make a decision."

"A decision about what?" his grandfather's voice called from behind them.

Caleb nearly leaped from his chair, his pulse beating out of control.

Wilson locked eyes with the imposing man. "We were discussing how we're going to approach the current situation."

Karl scoffed. "Have you cast votes yet? Any heartfelt pleas of righteousness?"

"Come now. Dad," Scott said.

"Shall we all hold hands," Karl said, "and sing songs together? Count me out."

Heather stood from her chair, glaring at the old man. "Would it kill you to not be terrible for five minutes?"

"What did you say to me, girl?" He stormed across the room, towering over her.

Wilson shot up, getting up in Karl's face. "You will back away from Miss O'Brien, now."

"Dad," Scott coughed.

Karl's icy blue eyes darted from person to person before resting on Caleb. "Let's go. We're going on a patrol."

Caleb's satchel suddenly felt like it doubled in weight, and his shoulders sagged. Between the elderon fight and his lack of sleep the night before, he certainly didn't feel ready for a patrol.

"He's not going anywhere," Heather said with a stern face. "He still needs time to recover."

"She's right, Dad. He needs. To rest."

Karl crossed his arms. "I don't recall asking either of your opinions."

Several voices erupted at once, and Caleb couldn't make sense of them. Heather, Karl, and Wilson each shot volleys of words. The shouting melded into a singular, turbulent sound. One second, he was in Aalia's study; the next he was in his home in Orion. He sat in a pool of his own blood, his grandfather yelling incoherently at him.

He snapped back to the study. The yelling had to stop.

"Enough," he said. No one heard him. "Enough!" This time he shouted, and everyone quieted. "I'll go." He stood, verifying his satchel was secure around his shoulder.

Heather caught his wrist. "You don't have to."

He shrugged. "It's okay. I feel fine." A lie, but he knew better than to argue with his grandfather. Or worse, drag everyone into a confrontation. Appeasement was the preferable alternative.

Kneeling, he wrapped his arms around Opp. "Stay here and keep everyone safe, okay, buddy?" He kissed the dog's forehead and walked over to his grandfather.

Karl cast portal incantations for them, bringing them from rooftop to rooftop. A powerful wind assaulted them as the sun began to set.

They traveled far across the city to a section he had spent little time in. The strings coated the buildings as thickly here as in every other part of Chicago. For three hours, they moved across buildings in uncomfortable silence.

In the end, they wound up atop the tallest building in the heart of downtown. The setting sun had passed beyond the horizon, the sky fading from purple to black.

His grandfather paced around the roof, glancing at him every few minutes. The man's tome bounced against its cage, the chains clanking incessantly.

Caleb sat down on the edge of the skyscraper, looking down at a military convoy below. If he was going to ask his grandfather for help, now would be the time. How quickly would the man say no? Laugh at him. Yell at him. Hurt him. It was far from the first time.

His grandfather approached him and cleared his throat. "I watched the tape of your fight with the elderon. You're too reckless with your choice of incantations."

"Okay."

"Every decision you make, every incantation you cast, has to be for a specific purpose. And the benefits gained have to be worth the soul you expend."

"Okay."

"What does Fleischer mean?"

He sighed. The eternal question. "You know that I know."

Karl pounded a fist into his other hand. "It's been the philosophy of our family for generations. It's how we made it this far and rose to such prominence. We are survivors, not heroes."

Caleb dangled his feet over the side of the building. His grandfather stood next to him, and Caleb's eyes focused on the man's dangling tome. All he had to do was grab it and push the man off, and then he'd be free of him.

Clenching his jaw, he cursed in his head. He hated that he had even considered it.

Sighing, he responded, "We can be people who do the right thing and survive."

"You are young and idealistic," the man responded in a tone that was, at least for him, soft. "I'd be lying if I said I wasn't the same when I was young. My grandmother and father had this very talk with me."

He arched an eyebrow. "What talk is that?"

"About seeing the bigger picture. Look at the strings consuming this city. There's no saving it. No amount of effort by me, you, or anyone else, can prevent what is going to happen. It's a hard truth, but a truth nonetheless. It may make you sick and angry, but you will survive. Stay, and you'll die."

"Surviving isn't the only thing I care about."

"That's the problem right there," Karl countered, sitting next to him. "It's not about you. It's not about me. It's not about Scott. It's not about any individual. It's for our family. The Fleischers who came before us did whatever they had to to survive. I've done the same. Your father failed in this regard. He made choices for himself, not the family. But I've done my damnedest to ensure you don't fail. That you can carry this family to greater heights."

He remained silent as his grandfather spoke. His pocket buzzed, no doubt another text from Sally. He ignored it.

"You may disagree with my methods," the man continued. "The way I chose to train and raise you may seem harsh. But it was how I was raised, and it was necessary. So that you could become the man you needed to be for the family. You may not appreciate it now, and maybe you'll never appreciate it while I'm still alive. But one day you'll understand."

The words echoed in his mind. How could his grandfather even possibly try to justify his childhood? Caleb wanted to point to the scars that covered his body. To yell about the frequent nightmares he had, his anxiety attacks.

Instead, he felt nothing. His chest was empty. Hollow. There was no rage. No despair. No crying, wailing, or movement of any kind. There was only an emotionless void that sat like a broken house in his chest.

"Do you have anything to say?" the man asked him.

His throat was unbearably dry. He didn't want to respond. All he wanted was to flee this situation. To run away and never look back.

But he couldn't. Heather, Wilson, Aalia, all of Chicago, were relying on him to ask this man for help. To swallow the pain and do what had to be done. To carry more weight upon his shoulders.

"Grandpa...you're right. I understand what you're saying."

A look of genuine shock crossed the man's face.

"I'm ready. I'm ready to be a Fleischer, to do what I have to for the family." The words burned his throat. Vomit crept up from his stomach, but he swallowed it back down. He had to do this. For them. "But...only if you do something for me."

His grandfather narrowed his eyes. "And that would be?"

Caleb's hands shook. A frigid coldness swept through his chest, and his breathing nearly spiraled out of control. But he kept it under wraps. "Just this once, help me. Help stop the strings, and after we're done, I'll do anything you like. I'll be a true Fleischer."

His grandfather ran a hand over his cleanly shaven face. "You give me your word?"

Squeezing his eyes shut, he fought the tears that tried to escape. "I do."

The man stood and paced once more across the roof. "It wouldn't be easy. And it would require us to spill a lot of blood. But it's possible."

"We'd save so many people. All three million citizens, not to mention Heather, Wilson, Cassandra—"

His grandfather's head snapped to him. "Cassandra, who?"

"O'Brien? Heather's mom. The one I was brought here to save."

A slew of German profanity escaped the man. "Idiot boy. Did you not think to mention her name before?"

He stood up. "Does it matter?"

His grandfather ignored him and snapped his fingers. Speaking the incantation, he disappeared into a portal without another word.

Then there was silence. Once more, Caleb had failed. Despite his grandfather's absence, the hollow feeling inside him didn't subside. He wrapped his arm around his chest as his breathing quickened.

His childhood flashed through his mind. Screaming. Fighting. Pain. His father hiding inside the house. No one helping. Why hadn't anyone saved him?

The thought started small. A glance downwards, truly realizing how high above the street he was. How long would it take him to fall to the pavement? Then all the fighting, the emptiness, the struggling, the unwanted memories...they'd all go away. It would be over. It would be silence. There would be peace.

He put one foot forward.

His pocket buzzed.

Caleb froze. His phone continued to vibrate. Pulling it out, he saw it was Sally. "Hello?" he answered.

"Hey, sorry for the late call. I just got worried, and you weren't answering my texts."

He took a step away from the ledge. "Oh. Sorry."

"It's okay, ya goon. I just wanted to check in."

"Oh," he whispered. "Is everything okay?"

"Here? Well, yeah, it's Orion. I went on a few dates with Rachel before things fizzled. Other than that, this place never changes."

"Yeah."

She paused. "You okay? You don't sound too good."

He was about to respond, about to offer some comment to brush off her concern, but she was right. His eyes grew wet, and his throat cracked. "Sally, I don't know what to do. I don't want to be in Chicago anymore."

Her voice grew worried. "I'm sorry, Caleb. Is your aunt not getting any better?"

He paused, remembering the cover story. "No, she's not. She's getting worse, and there's nothing I can do to stop it. It feels like there's so much pressure on me."

"I can't imagine what that's like. But you'll get through this. Your strength is always what I've admired about you."

"It is?"

"Yeah! Do you remember the tornado warning during third grade?"

He furrowed his brow. "No, I don't."

"It was only a few days into the school year. We had been in the same class since first grade, but I had never really noticed you. I don't think you ever spoke more than a dozen words to anyone. But when the sirens went off, the teachers brought us all to the gym. And, you know, me being me, I bawled my eyes out. I was so scared. The wind sounded like a train, and the school was shaking.

"The teachers tried to calm me, but they couldn't. But then, out of nowhere, you appeared in your dorky little sweater and sat next to me. You started telling me some of your dad's jokes, and I laughed. You kept that up for the better part of an hour until the sirens finally stopped."

The memory returned to him as she spoke. "I can't believe you remember that."

"I'll never forget it."

He was about to respond when the canopy of strings caught his eye. "I'm sorry, Sally, but I should get going. But thank you for calling. Really."

"Yeah, anytime. Do you think you'll be coming home soon?"

"Maybe. I'm not sure how long I'll be here."

"You are coming home, though, right?"

"Yes. I promise."

They said their farewells, and she hung up. He let the phone slide from his hand and crash to the roof. Falling to his rear, he realized the hollow feeling had vanished. In its place was a knotted, cold, tempest. It tore at him from inside, and he fell to his side. His cheek rested against the chilled concrete, and his eyes stared at the purple soul strings dangling around him.

Would he ever see the Chicago skyline without them again?

Chapter Fifteen

Two days had passed since Caleb asked his grandfather for help. Both that and his call with Sally were fresh in his mind. As he struggled with the thoughts, he barely left the confines of his room. Twice he had emerged at night to scrounge for food and water, but that was it.

He sat with his back against the bed, his gaze glued out the window. His grandfather hadn't returned yet. What was that man up to? Whatever it was, it certainly wasn't good.

Oppenheimer had provided Caleb's only solace in the last few days. His dog was resting across his lap in a deep slumber. As he softly patted his companion, he thought of his last day in Orion. His shift with Sally. Heather appearing at his door. His father convincing him to come to Chicago and his call with his grandfather.

What if he'd never come? If he had stood against his father and said no to Heather. How long until he had heard news of the Sleeping Plague? It wouldn't have taken him long to figure out it was soul strings causing it.

Would he have remained in Orion once he figured out the truth? He certainly wouldn't have rushed off to Chicago of his own initiative. And that scared him. How many thousands of deaths would he have heard about? Would he had even felt a little bit guilty?

The only time these thoughts stopped was when he had flashbacks of childhood memories better left forgotten. That, and the small amount of sleep he managed to get. He could feel the bags that hung under his eyes, and it was as if molasses was clogging his mind.

But he knew he couldn't hide forever. Doing so had cost the city two days of progress. Brought it two days closer to disaster.

It was that thought that finally got him moving again. He took a shower that felt more obligatory than refreshing. Even changing into new clothes was less invigorating than he had hoped it would be.

He tried not to dwell on the dissatisfaction as he left the room. Both Aalia and Heather sat in the main living room, the former on the floor studying her tome. Heather sat on the couch, reading a book.

Shuffling across the room, he took a seat next to Heather.

She looked up at him, her green eyes soft and warm. "Hey, you. You feeling okay?"

"I'm fine."

A disapproving look crossed her face. "You want to talk about it?"

He shook his head.

"Okay. We wanted to give you your space, but we're always here."

"Thanks," he said, then trying to change the subject, he added. "What are you reading?"

She looked down at the book in her hands. "It's a book about trauma. There's so much to learn. When my mom wakes up and finds out I'm not going to be a surgeon, at least I'll be able to tell her I've put my effort fully into something else."

"You gonna tell your dad?"

She took a breath in through her teeth. "There's a lot he and I will have to talk about before we ever get to that."

He studied her. Unlike him, she was pursuing her dreams.

Striving to live the life she wanted to live. But he was trapped being a Scribe. And whenever his grandfather returned, he'd have to ask for his help again. The thought sent shivers down his spine.

The sound of a ringing phone filled the room. Aalia dug into her purse and pulled her smartphone out. She shot the device a confused look. "It's your dad," she said to Heather.

Heather let out a frustrating huff. "He still hasn't acknowledged me in the last few months."

Aalia answered. She remained silent for a long moment before her eyes went wide. Her grip on the phone tightened, and he thought she might break it. "Yes, sir." She listened. "Yes, sir." She listened. "I'm on my way."

She hung up and stuffed her phone into her purse. She didn't move until Heather called out her name.

Aalia snapped back to attention and stood. "Sorry, something came up. I have to go to an emergency meeting. I'll be back soon, hopefully." Without another word, she grabbed her purse and ran out the door.

Caleb barely registered the encounter, his eyes fixated on the floor.

"Mister Fleischer, you are with us once more." Wilson stood at the far end of the room, his hands folded behind his back.

"I am," he responded.

The old man marched across the room and took a seat in an armchair. "Is there anything I can do for you?"

"Not right now, thanks."

"Very good. Has your grandfather left the city?"

He shrugged. "I'm not sure. It's hard to tell with him."

Heather cleared her throat. "Did you get a chance to ask him for help?"

"Umm..." He looked down. "Yeah. I almost convinced him, then he stormed off. I don't think he's going to help." Images of his grandfather pressed against his mind. Screaming. A golden spear. Glowing red text.

Heather watched him from the corner of her eyes. "Let's talk about something else."

The sound of the rolling medical stand filled the hallway. His father emerged from it, a sheepish grin on his face. "Looks like I. Need to. Brighten some. Moods in here."

Caleb hardened his face at his father's words. The memories from his first day of combat training forced their way into his mind. Hiding in the sunflower field. The grilled cheese. Crying.

Standing, he headed into the study, closing the door behind him. He shut the blinds, refusing to look out at the strings.

The door to the room opened and shut again. Heather appeared at his side, her gaze fixated on a large bookcase. "Didn't want to be cheered up by your dad?"

He shook his head. Jokes were not what he needed right now.

"I know you don't want to talk about it. And I won't pressure you. But I'm here, Caleb. Should you ever need me."

He glanced over to her. She was always so supportive. If only her constant friendship made it easier to open up. He wanted to tell her. To try and get this vile storm out of his head. But what could he say? What words could he form to express these feelings? It was an impossible task. Especially for him.

They stood in silence for what felt like an eternity. Every so often, she'd pick a book off the shelf and page through it before returning it. It was strangely comforting, having her there even if neither of them was talking. It was like this room existed outside of the chaos that awaited him.

But the illusion couldn't last forever.

"Mister Fleischer!" Wilson called out from the living room.

He exchanged a worried glance with Heather, and they rushed back into the other room. The sight of his grandfather came into view. The man's tome floated before him, and he held a yellow, crystalline spear.

"Having fun, are we?" the man asked with narrowed eyes focused on Heather.

"Welcome back," Wilson said hesitantly, inching across the room to stand in front of her.

Karl ignored everyone else. "Did you know from the beginning? Did you purposefully lure my grandson here? Or are you just another pawn?"

Confusion spread across her face. "What are you talking about?"

Caleb's eyes sunk. His grandfather had figured out about her family. That's why he had been interested in her mother's name. This was his fault.

Karl stepped forward, but his gaze flickered to him. "Caleb... you already knew, didn't you?"

Scott rolled his medical stand forward. "Dad. What is this. About?"

"Heather O'Brien," the man seethed, his grip on the spear tightening, "daughter of Michael and Cassandra O'Brien. Formerly known as Michael and Cassandra Lancaster."

His father's head snapped to Heather, and understanding washed over him.

Wilson stepped forward. "Whatever grudge you may carry against Mister O'Brien, Miss O'Brien is innocent. She had nothing to do with her father's choices."

Caleb wanted to shrink back into the study. The sight of his grandfather's angry expression overwhelmed him. The golden spear and his stomach felt like it was ripping open.

His grandfather stared at him. "You wanted me to help, right? To stop the strings and the hydran? Well, this is how we do it. We use this young woman to leverage our way back into power. I still have friends in the Guild."

Wilson shot to the ground and removed the pistol strapped to his ankle, training it on his grandfather. "You will not lay a finger on Miss O'Brien."

It was no use, though. His grandfather would have had strength and speed enhancements active already. Everyone in this room could be killed at any minute. There was no standing against the man.

His father held up a hand. "Come on. Dad. Be reasonable. We're not. Going to take. A young girl. Hostage."

"Don't be a fool," Karl bellowed. "This is our opportunity to get back into power."

Caleb grabbed his arm and squeezed his eyes shut. There was too much yelling. Too much anger. It all needed to stop. Someone had to make it stop.

Heather took a confident step forward, her unblinking eyes staring at his grandfather. "All I want is for my mom to recover and to help Caleb save this city."

Karl let out a genuine laugh. "You're sincere, aren't you? You don't have the stomach to follow in your father's footsteps, that's for certain. Caleb, pack your things. We're leaving now, and she's coming with us."

He had received his orders. His affirmation sat on the tip of his tongue, a practiced response enforced by decades of pain.

But then he looked at Heather. They had connected their souls. They had embraced. She always stood by his side and supported him. She fought against an elderon for him.

Fixating his eyes on the ground, he whispered, "No."

"I'm not asking, boy. I'm ordering!" his grandfather shouted.

His hands balled into fists. He scowled at the man, his face flush and brow hard. "I said no."

"I will not repeat myself again."

Caleb slammed a foot into the ground. "I am done listening to you! I am not leaving, and you are not taking Heather!"

"You insolent brat," Karl spat. "After everything I've done for you. After you begged me to help you. After all I've sacrificed because of your father's mistake—"

"I am not a mistake!" he yelled, his eyes welling up with tears at the word. "And I didn't ask to be born."

"Then blame—"

"I am not finished yet!" he continued, cutting off his grandfather, tears streaming down his face. "You always go on about what you did for me. How you've given up so much for me. But you abused me. You tortured, beat, and broke a child so that you could craft him into a weapon!"

His father shuffled forward, placing a bony hand on his shoulder.

Caleb swatted it away. "Don't get me started on you. You sat around all those years and let him do it. You hid while I cried out for help. You're my dad, it was your job to keep me safe! And you failed."

Scott recoiled at the words, taking a few steps back.

He dug his nails into his palms. His whole body shook. "Neither of you ever, not once, asked me what I wanted out of my life. All you cared about is what you wanted from me. Nobody in this entire world ever asked me what I wanted. Not until Heather."

Looking over to her, he saw tears crawling down her cheeks. She walked toward him, taking one of his fists into her hand. His hand unfolded, interlocking with her fingers as she gave it a gentle squeeze.

Karl took a defiant step forward. "If you hate being a Scribe so much, then why stay in this hell hole?"

Gesturing to the strings out the window, he said, "Because someone has to stand up and do the right thing. So, I've decided. We don't need your help. Leave! We'll stop the Guild and strings without you."

His grandfather shook his head in disgust. "You've inherited your father's inclination for sentiment. If you want to stay and die, that's your prerogative. But your father and I are leaving, and I'm taking the girl."

Caleb snapped his fingers. He stepped in front of Heather and summoned his scythe. Holding it out towards his grandfather, he said, "The only way you're getting to her is if you kill me."

And then an emotion crossed his grandfather's face that he had never seen before. Sadness.

His grandfather returned his tome to its chain cage. "Scott, let's go."

Scott closed his eyes and took long, painful breaths. Leaning onto his monitor, he wheeled over to Caleb. "If he is. Going to stay. Then so will. I."

Karl shook his head in disbelief. Walking to the front door, he turned and faced them. "You both have forgotten what Fleischer means. When everything goes to shit, don't expect me to come save you."

And just like that, the man was gone. An eerie silence fell over the room. Heather ran her thumb over Caleb's palm, her soft eyes washing over him.

"Son," his father said, taking a step towards him.

He glared at the man. "Not a word!"

Taking his hand from Heather's, he walked away from the group and back to his guest room. He slammed the door behind him. Thoughts raged in his mind, and he paced in a large circle.

Unwanted memories barraged his psyche, driving him mad. Of being held underwater. Of lying in a pool of his own blood. Of endless screaming.

He had to make the thoughts stop.

Walking over to the wardrobe, he reeled back and drove his fist straight into it. The wood splintered, and pain shot through his fist and up his arm. Cursing under his breath, he grabbed his hand as the door to the room opened and closed again quickly.

Soft hands clasped his injured wrist, opening it up. Heather stood in front of him, her fingers caressing his hand. "It's sprained. Maybe broken," she said softly.

She let go of his injured hand and grabbed onto his good one. With a gentle tug, she led him over to the bed. They both sat, and she lowered her head to lock eyes with him. "Are you okay?"

He couldn't meet her gaze, looking at her chin instead. "I'm fine."

"Caleb," she whispered, placing a hand on his cheek. "Are you okay?"

Words escaped him, but tears returned to his eyes, and he buried his head into her shoulder. She wrapped her arms around his back and held him close, one of her hands making small circles on his spine.

All the emotions, pain, and memories he had kept caged for the last two decades boiled to the surface. He sobbed uncontrollably into her shoulder, gripping her shirt tightly with his good hand.

He wasn't sure how long he cried. Time became imperceptible. Somehow, they started talking. He told her everything. About his grandfather. His training. The abuse. All of it.

She held him tighter. "And we call those creatures out there monsters."

They laid down on the bed, embracing each other. He cried longer than he thought possible, and she didn't say another word, letting him get it all out. His tears eventually became silent, and they both rested there, though he wasn't sure for how long.

And finally, mercifully, he fell asleep.

Chapter Sixteen

Caleb opened his eyes to the sight of Heather's sleeping face. How long had they slept? The sun was already up, but his mind was in such a haze, it took him a moment to recall the previous night's events. It came back to him in one giant flood. His grandfather. The yelling. The crying. Reaching up, he found his face was as dry as his throat.

Despite everything, though, he didn't feel horrible. It was hard to describe, but he felt lighter. Like he had finally released some of the burdens he'd been dragging behind him his whole life.

But not all his problems had vanished. His mind drifted to his father and what he had yelled at the man. His words had been justified, yet guilt bubbled inside him nonetheless. Was his father going to be angry with him? Maybe he had decided to leave after all. He should go find out, sooner rather than later.

Caleb inched out of bed, trying not to wake Heather. Pain shot through his hand, and he recalled his injury. As quietly as he could manage, he brought out his tome and spent a few minutes healing his wrist.

Changing into fresh clothes, he opened the door and found himself face-to-face with his father. Taking a step back, he tried to find words. But his mouth hung open, and he remained silent.

His father's serious, gray eyes looked him over. "Can we. Talk?"

Grabbing his arm, he nodded. He stepped into the hall and started to close the door when his father peered inside and saw Heather on the bed. His father shifted focus to him, raising an eyebrow.

His face grew warm. "Nothing happened."

"Wouldn't be bad. If it had," Scott commented. "She's a good. Person."

Before closing the door, Caleb looked back at Heather again. His father was right. She was.

He helped his father through the apartment and out onto the patio. Even in the middle of the summer, the cool morning air was refreshing. A brisk breeze blew over the city, and the strings dangled in the air.

The two stood in silence as they looked over Chicago. He wasn't sure what to expect from this meeting, but he didn't have the words necessary to speak first. What could he say?

A quarter of an hour passed before his father finally spoke. "Your mother. Always liked to. Tell stories. Of far off struggles. And beings. Beyond our comprehension." He let out a series of violent coughs. "She said. That your purpose. Was far more. Important. Than any Scribe. Who had ever lived. I have always. And will always. Believe her."

Caleb remained silent. He wasn't sure where this was going, but he was more than acquainted with his mother's fantastical tales.

"Because of that. I believed. Making sure you. Were ready for such. A life. Was of the. Upmost. Importance. It is the. Reason why I never stopped. Your training. I told myself the ends. Justified. The means."

Caleb's shoulders sagged. This wasn't what he wanted to hear. Excuses.

"However," his father continued, "that is not. A good enough. Reason to. Subject you to. That kind of life. To expose you to.

Torture and pain. I was so focused on the man. You could become. That I lost sight. Of the child that you were." Scott looked over at his son, his eyes soft and full of regret.

He met his father's gaze. Grabbing his own arm, he did his best not to look away.

"Like you said. My job as. Your father. Was to keep you safe. And I failed. I should have. Protected you. And asked you. What you wanted. Out of life." His father paused and took a breath. "And I am. Sorry."

A storm of memories flashed through his mind. All the times he had called out for help. Being plagued by fear. Wishing someone would save him. And no one had.

But he also remembered all the times he laughed with his father. Taking care of the man. Listening to his endless stories and just spending time with him. Despite everything, Caleb couldn't imagine the kind of man he'd be if it hadn't been for his father.

"Dad," he said. "I love you. I wouldn't be me if it weren't for you. But, at the same time, this isn't something that can be fixed in a day. We'll have to work at it. But...I need you in my life."

A sullen smile crossed his father's thin face. "I can accept that. I will earn. Your forgiveness. I swear it." His father wrapped a pair of bony arms around Caleb, gripping him as tightly as his weak body would allow.

Caleb didn't hesitate to return the embrace. Warmth and a sense of safety flooded him. This problem indeed would take time, maybe even years, to fix. But he wanted to fix it. And a little more weight had been lifted off his shoulders.

The two separated after a minute, and a strong gust barraged the patio.

"It's a bit. Nippy. Let's go. Inside."

Heather and Aalia sat around the table in the study with Opp at their feet. Aalia looked paler than usual, and dark bags hung under her eyes.

"Aalia," he said, "you okay?"

Her head snapped towards him, her eyes wide. "Oh. Yeah. I'm just not feeling well."

Wilson stepped into the room, carrying several plates filled with eggs, sausage, and toast. Setting them down, the old man went back and retrieved a bowl of oranges and bananas. "Breakfast is served."

Everyone sat at the table. Apart from Aalia, they all dug into the food. As they did, Heather caught Aalia up on the events from the previous night.

"In short," Wilson said, "another one of our plans has fallen through."

"Do we have. Any other. Ideas?"

Caleb shrugged. "I can start going on patrols again. I'm not sure how effective it'll be, but at least we wouldn't be sitting around and doing nothing."

Heather shifted in her seat. "There is another thing we can do." Everyone looked at her, and she continued, "I have to confront my father when he's back in the city. Aalia, did they mention when he'd return at the meeting last night?"

Her shoulders shot up. "They said the timetable was a week or two."

"In that case," Wilson said, "Mister Fleischer will patrol the city. Then when Mister O'Brien returns, we'll all help Miss O'Brien confront him."

They all nodded in agreement. Scott pulled his journal from the medical stand and began to scribble.

"Almost done?" he asked his father.

"Almost."

For several hours, his father worked, and everyone watched, transfixed. At one point, Heather left and returned dressed in a fresh outfit.

He watched in fascination as his father thought, pondered, and wrote. How much time had he spent as a child watching this very thing? When it came to incantations and being a Scribe, his father was nothing short of a genius. To see him work was akin to watching an artist paint. He wished he could have seen his father before the sickness.

Another half an hour passed, and his father threw down his pen with sudden enthusiasm. The man flipped through the last few pages, rereading the notes. After a few minutes, he looked up with a grin. "I think. I've got it."

His father explained the incantation to him, walking Caleb through how it could work. They discussed how to mold the soul, the correct way to hold it in their mind, and how to vary its strength. It took them an hour to cover everything.

"It has to be that dense?" Caleb asked, looking at the math.

Scott nodded. "This one. Will drain you. Don't use it. Recklessly."

After wrapping his head around the incantation, Caleb delved into himself. He flared his soul, stoking the golden flame in his chest and giving it life. Manipulating it, he spread it throughout his body, molding and shaping it. Thinning his soul out, he proceeded to seep it into his blood, fusing them together.

With the golden flame running through his veins, he held the incantation in his mind, letting the imagined effects saturate his soul.

He repeated this cycle again and again over a few hours. Once his soul was fully attuned to the incantation and it was within his blood, he grabbed his satchel. Opening a side pocket, he produced a small black box.

Inside was a razor blade, a fountain pen, and a tiny glass vial. He removed the rubber stopper from the vial and set it in front of him. Taking the razor blade in his right hand, he made a clean incision on the back of his left. Blood spilled down his hand, which he held over the vial. The small container filled up, and then he cast an incantation to heal the small cut.

Opening the tome to the three-quarter mark, he found the first page with free space. He dipped the fountain pen into the blood and wrote out the incantation. As it dried, he cleaned up the supplies and tossed them back into his satchel.

"So, that's how you make an incantation?" Heather asked.

He nodded. "I can explain it in a little more detail. Give me a second."

"It's exciting. Stuff," Scott teased with a wink.

Blowing over the wet blood, he tried to get it to dry. As he did, Heather suddenly perked up. She leaned over to Wilson and whispered something into his ear.

Once the page was dry, he returned his tome to the satchel. Heather wiggled in her chair, bursting at the seams with curiosity.

"Okay, okay," he said. "Obviously, you know that we write our incantations in blood. But before you can do that, you have to move your soul throughout your body just like I taught you. The time it takes varies with the incantation's complexity, but once you do it, you can write with your blood."

"It's that simple?"

"It can be tricky to get down, but it's that simple in theory. So long as you understand the incantation."

She tilted her head. "What do you mean?"

"Just like when using an incantation, when creating it, you have to understand it and hold it in your mind. They can range from fairly simple to incredibly complex."

"Can you make incantations do anything?" she asked.

"In theory, yes," he said. "In practice, no. I could hypothetically make an incantation to give someone immortality, but the energy cost to do so would kill me a thousand times over, at least. We're limited by the strength of our souls."

"Have you ever had to make an incantation weaker to make it possible?"

"Yes. There's one incantation I can cast that will limit the scope of someone's soul, but tampering with someone's soul is incredibly difficult. To make the incantation practical, I make it weaken my own soul as penance. Both of our souls are weakened, but if I had an ally, they'd now have an advantage." A thought occurred to him, and he stood. "Come here."

She walked over to him.

He picked up his tome and opened it to the desired page. "I'm going to cast an incantation that will prevent you from moving. Ready?"

She nodded.

"Stay still your highness; I will now bind us."

Yellow glyphs appeared beneath their feet. A golden barrier grew from it and surrounded them both, restricting both their movements. At the same time, it felt like a cage had been placed around his soul, nearly severing his connection to it.

He held it for a few seconds before letting it go from his mind, releasing them both from its effects.

"That felt weird," she said.

"It's a strange sensation. But that's a good one to break down. If you think about it, in theory, I could just seal your movements. But most Scribes usually have multiple enhancements in effect, and trying to combat that can be tricky. I could limit both our movements as penance, but there's the possibility that you could still cast incantations. So, to be the most effective, I can seal both our movements and both our souls, taking us both out of the fight."

She thought over his words a moment, then nodded. "I think I get it."

"Yeah, there's a lot of thinking involved in being a Scribe. It's why I told you that, usually, it's the smarter Scribe that ends up winning."

"Okay," she said, paging through his tome. "Why do incantations have to rhyme?"

"Actually, they don't have to. If you really wanted, you could make an incantation an assortment of words that made no sense. But when you're in the middle of a fight and trying to hold multiple incantations at once, you have to recall the ones you need to use. If they're all nonsense, you're going to have a tough time being effective."

Heather's gaze shifted between him, his father, and Aalia. "You all had to learn all of this as kids?"

Aalia shrugged, looking as if she were barely paying attention. His father nodded.

Heather shot her friend a look, then faced him. "Can we do some more exercises?"

Caleb led her through the motions of manipulating her soul. His father watched him teach with a joyful smile. After she was warmed up, he instructed Heather on how to infuse her soul into her blood. He watched her soul as she tried, though it was a tall order. It took the better part of an hour before he sensed a small part of her soul leak into her veins.

"That's it!" he told her.

"I only managed it for a second," she said with a disappointed expression.

Scott tapped his bony fingers on the table. "Don't sell. Yourself short. It took me. Weeks my first. Time."

"It took me half a year," Aalia chimed in.

Heather perked up and smiled.

He let out a sigh and packed his tome into his satchel, setting them both against the wall behind him. They all devolved into casual conversation until Wilson returned to the apartment.

Heather shot Scott and Caleb a wide grin. "I've got a surprise for you both."

He arched an eyebrow as Wilson revealed grocery bags full of noodles, marinara sauce, ground beef, and various other supplies.

"When we first met," she said, "I denied you this meal, but you told me it was your favorite. So, after yesterday, I figured it would be a good way to cheer ourselves up."

A warm feeling bubbled in his stomach as a smile crossed Caleb's face. Some of his favorite memories from his childhood were smushing hamburger meat in a bowl to make homemade meatballs.

They all headed into the kitchen and prepared the meal together. Wilson prepared the garlic bread, and Scott stirred the sauce. Heather and Caleb made the meatballs, and Aalia steamed some vegetables. Oppenheimer watched them from the floor with ravenous eyes.

When the meal was finished, they each brought a plate into the study. As he always had a kid, Caleb cut off a piece of meatball and slipped it under the table for Opp. His dog ate it eagerly, licking his lips afterward.

Wilson brought out a bottle of wine and poured glasses for everyone, though Aalia barely touched it or her food.

Scott regaled them all with more stories. Laughter filled the room, and Wilson shared a few of his more lighthearted war stories.

Once everything began to settle down, Caleb let out a sigh. "I suppose I should get going soon."

"Very well," Wilson said. "Keep the military patrols in mind, Mister Fleischer."

"Actually," Heather said, "you don't have to go out, Caleb. You're still recovering. And you looked for six months and didn't find anything. We have our other plan."

The front door of the apartment opened, and they all exchanged glances. Everyone was in the study.

Wilson was the first to move, shooting up with his sidearm in hand. Caleb stood as well and looked to Opp. No barking. The Guild wasn't ambushing them. Who was coming?

A middle-aged man in a blue suit sauntered into the room, an air of superiority apparent around him. The man's dark brown hair had patches of white, just like the bushy mustache that sat beneath his nose.

Heather's face contorted into a scowl. She stood, her hands balling into fists. "Dad?"

Dad? This was the head of the Guild?

"Hey there, Mouse," he said to her, though his eyes were locked onto Caleb.

The front door opened again, and Opp began to bark three times over and over. Caleb snapped his fingers, bringing an incantation to his mind. But his tome didn't come.

He spun around to find Aalia holding his tome tight to her chest, her own floating in front of her. Tears flooded her eyes, and she gave him a desperate look. Silently, she mouthed a single word. Sorry.

Agents Trenton and Eckerson strolled into the room, their tomes at the ready. Wilson stalked across the room, moving to stand next to Heather.

"Dad," she said, "what's going on? Why haven't you returned any of my calls or texts?"

"I'm here to save you from these dangerous men. You and I have a difficult talk ahead of us, and it was one I wanted to have in person."

Scott rolled his medical stand forward. "Hey there. Michael."

"Betrayer," Michael responded with venom.

"Let's talk. About this like adults. Old friend."

Disgust painted Michael's face. "You lost the right to call me that the moment you made a deal with the devil."

Caleb's eyes drifted to Opp. Should he make a move? But in such a small space, with how outnumbered they were, there was no way a fight would be casualty-free. And his father still looked calm. Perhaps the man knew something he didn't.

"Dad, stop this!" Heather demanded.

Scott shuffled forward. "Please. Give me a chance. To explain. No one has to. Get hurt."

All Michael did was shake his head. Eckerson shot towards Caleb, throwing a right hook into his gut. The blow knocked the air from his lungs. He grabbed his stomach, tears coming to his eyes as he fell to his knees.

"My new hand works just fine, monster," the large man said.

Trenton approached Scott and bound his hands with zip ties, then placed a black bag over his head. Eckerson forced Caleb to the floor and restrained his hands as well. The last thing he saw before the agent forced the bag over his head was Heather throwing her fists at her father.

Unable to see and cut off from his tome, they dragged Caleb

from the apartment. His heart raced, and sweat dripped down his face. Where were they taking him? His chest tightened. He didn't want to know the answer.

Chapter Seventeen

How long had he been chained to this metal chair? Hours? Days? With the black hood still covering him, Caleb's ability to tell time had become nonexistent. When they had first arrived wherever they were, he had tried to move the chair, but bolts held it to the ground.

A rough hand ripped the hood off his head. Blinding light assaulted his eyes, and he quickly shut them. No sooner had he done so when a powerful fist shot into his stomach. He doubled over, the blow expelling the air from his lungs. Vomit surged from his mouth and onto the ground. Breathing rapidly, he tried to catch his breath and spit out bile.

He blinked several times, adjusting to the light level. Agent Eckerson stood over him. Smooth, yellow barriers surrounded the man's fists, and a tome floated around him. Hatred reserved for vermin burned in the man's eyes.

Unsure of how long he'd have a chance to look, Caleb quickly scanned his surroundings. They were in some sort of warehouse.

It was empty save for a few wooden boxes around the periphery.

Ten feet in front of him, his father was chained just as he was. Scott was only vaguely conscious, twitching in his chair occasionally. The medical stand was nowhere in sight. Thankfully, no wounds covered the man. His father couldn't take much of a beating in his state.

To his right, about thirty yards away, his tome sat in the middle of a purple glyph. His soul was completely cut off from it. But its placement seemed odd. Why was it so close to him?

Eckerson slammed another fist into his cheek. Pain seared across Caleb's face, and he recoiled from the blow, spitting blood onto the concrete.

He looked at the man with defiant eyes, waiting for the questions to come. But neither Eckerson nor Trenton, who stood off to the side, asked him anything.

The punches were infrequent but consistent. His torso was the most common target, but there were a few headshots for good measure. He took the blows, letting the pain consume him. This wasn't his first torturing.

All at once, his father sprang to life. The sickly man looked around, his gray eyes settling on Caleb. Scott's father's face grew worried, and he convulsed against his chains. Bony limbs flailed about as the man shook.

"He needs his medicine!" Caleb yelled.

Eckerson backhanded him across the face. "Quiet down, abomination."

His father eventually stopped moving, but a small puddle of blood pooled beneath him. There was a deep cut on the man's foot, and one of the rusty chair legs was stained crimson.

The sight of his father started a fire in Caleb's gut. He fought against his confines. There had to be something he could do, some way to get them out of this mess. His whole life, his grandfather had raised him to fear the Guild above anything else. Now that he was in their clutches, there was nothing he could do to fight against them.

Seconds ticked into minutes, which melted into hours. Eckerson didn't relent from the onslaught, and every inch of Caleb screamed in pain.

Every half an hour or so, his father would convulse again. The man's feet made a mess of the blood on the floor, but he did not look at Caleb again.

A vehicle started outside of the warehouse. A black SUV with tinted windows drove through the large opening and into the structure, parking fifty yards away. Engine still running, the passenger door creaked open. Oppenheimer barked from inside the vehicle, but it was Michael who emerged.

The well-dressed man strutted across the warehouse, his head held high. The leader of the Guild inspected the two prisoners, a smirk on his face.

"Oh, how the mighty have fallen," the man said to his father. "The name Scott Fleischer once invoked fear and respect. Now look at you." Michael then turned his attention to Caleb. "And there's you. For a miscreant, you can take a hit, I'll give you that."

"Eckerson hits half as hard as my grandfather."

"Ah yes," Michael said, waving his arms in an extravagant gesture. "The legendary Karl Fleischer, the man who looked down on everyone. Who enjoyed reminding them of what his family's name meant. If I'm honest, this whole situation was meant to lure him here. I'd very much like to erase him as a nuisance. But it seems you aren't worth saving to him."

"He left the city over a day ago. You'll never find him now."

"So it seems. A cruel and cowardly man."

"You don't need to tell me what kind of man he is."

"Do I not?" Michael asked. "You know, when your family was banished from the Guild after your birth, your grandfather approached us to make a deal. We agreed to stop hunting him."

"I know. He convinced you I was dead."

Michael chuckled. "Do you think we took him for his word? No, he delivered us an infant corpse as proof. I have no idea how he managed to fool the DNA tests we conducted, but we'll look into that."

Caleb was silent. What innocent baby had his grandfather killed? Unfortunately, it sounded exactly like the man.

"Well," the man continued, "if your being here isn't going to deliver Karl to me on a silver platter, then I have no use for you." Michael produced a handheld radio. "All units, all units, this is Alpha. Silver Wolf is not returning to the den. I repeat, Silver Wolf is not returning to the den. Fan out and return to previous duties. Out."

Several sets of footsteps sprinted across the roof of the

warehouse as Michael put the radio away. "You're going to die now. Just know, with your family out of the way, I'm going to bring humanity to new heights."

Images of explosions, collapsing buildings, and screaming people filled his mind. The utter destruction a hydran could cause.

And then he saw Iibere, and the golden glyphs that covered each of the filken the Guild had sent after him. "Have you ever talked to the filken?"

Michael walked away without an answer.

"They have names!" Caleb yelled.

The Head of the Guild paused briefly before continuing to the SUV.

"Please don't. Do this, Michael," his father pleaded. "We can help. Turn the Guild. In a different. Direction."

Michael ignored the man's desperate appeal. He opened the door, releasing the sound of Oppenheimer barking again. Caleb heard Heather's soft voice trying to comfort the dog to no avail.

"Kill them," the Head of the Guild ordered before getting into the vehicle.

The SUV reversed out of the warehouse.

His father convulsed again, the sound of clanking chains filling the space.

"Kill the abomination first," Trenton ordered, her voice apathetic.

"Yes ma'am," Eckerson responded. The barriers around the man's fists vanished. His tome flipped through its pages. "I told you, monster, that you'd regret not killing me. Today, you pay that price."

Caleb closed his eyes, trying to control the whirlpool of emotions inside of him. The fear of death. The guilt for the city in crisis. The regret for dragging his father to this fate. And the heartbreak of not getting to say goodbye.

"Caleb!" Scott yelled.

Jolted from his thoughts, he opened his eyes to find his father staring at him with a broad smile on his face. Scott took in a large breath before saying in one go, "Save Chicago, and remember that I love you."

The two agents turned to face the sickly man as he took in one more massive breath. Too late, they noticed the words written in blood upon the floor.

"Come on here boy; The horse of Troy," Scott called out. A smile still rested on the man's face as his eyes rolled back in his head, and his body went limp.

A portal appeared in the air to Caleb's right. It opened straight into Michael's SUV. Heather looked back at him with a horrified expression. Next to her sat Oppenheimer. Caleb clicked his tongue twice, and Opp ran straight at him and jumped through the portal.

The moment Opp was in the warehouse, the portal collapsed. Despair and rage erupted inside Caleb, but he kept his face straight and his mind focused. The next few seconds were crucial.

As the two agents looked back at him, Caleb snapped his fingers. But his tome didn't move. Instead, Oppenheimer's collar flew off and floated in front of him. On the inside of the collar, written in blood, were a handful of phrases.

The words glowed red. *"No longer bound by the clock slave; It is time for a real shock wave."*

With Caleb and Opp at the epicenter, an explosion of purple energy and air burst out in every direction. The blast launched the two agents off their feet and blew a hole in the roof. Debris rained down, and he shifted his mind to a different phrase on the collar.

"With blood of iron, and heart of coal; Make my body stronger than my soul."

Strength surged through Caleb, and his battered body felt refreshed and new. He tore out of his chains as if they were made of paper and stood.

He sprinted at the purple glyph with Opp right on his heels. Sliding across the concrete, he grabbed his tome and removed it from the seal. Opp's collar fell to the ground as his soul connected to his tome. Holding out his hands, he summoned his scythe.

Eckerson and Trenton lay collapsed on different sides of the warehouse, rubble surrounding them. They both began to stir.

Caleb spoke his speed incantation and sprinted towards Trenton. It was smartest to take out the more rested opponent before they recovered. And all he could see was red.

She came to a knee as he reached her. He spun his scythe and swung it at the woman's head. Trenton dropped to the ground and avoided the attack. Anticipating this, he brought one of his enhanced legs back and delivered a powerful kick straight into her face.

Trenton rolled back, the force of the blow nearly caving her face in. Without a moment's hesitation, he closed the distance between them, rage still burning inside of him. In one swift motion, Caleb brought his blade down into his opponent's chest, killing her.

A voice shouted from behind him. Jumping to the side, he narrowly avoided a ball of flames as it flew past him, singing his clothes. Eckerson stood across the warehouse, his crystalline ax in hand.

Several volleys of fire shot out at him as he darted across the structure. He weaved in and out of the attacks, moving closer and closer to the large man. Coming upon his opponent, he unleashed a storm of slashes, swinging his scythe with focused anger. Despite the ferocious attacks, Eckerson managed to stay on his toes, ducking in and around the scythe.

Time was short. His opponent hadn't just spent who knows how long without sleep, water, and getting attacked. He couldn't win a war of attrition.

Taking a few steps back, Caleb spun his scythe above his head, building momentum. As he did, he brought a new phrase to mind, the third incantation straining him. With practiced efficiency, he brought his weapon down in a powerful arc at Eckerson's torso.

The wide arc was easy to dodge, and the man ducked under it. The agent came back to his feet and stepped forward as Caleb followed through on his attack. Eckerson raised his ax as Caleb's tome opened to the new page.

"Traveling through time and space; fly me to another place," he whispered.

A portal opened in front of his scythe's path while a second appeared behind Eckerson's feet. His blade passed through the portals and severed the agent's legs at the shin. The man yelled and fell to the ground, blood gushing out of the stubs of his legs.

Releasing all three incantations, Caleb stood over the man, glaring down at him. Eckerson met his gaze and started to hyperventilate, panic filling the agent's eyes. Caleb's hands shook as Eckerson desperately tried to crawl away, slipping in his own blood.

He glanced across the warehouse. At his father's body. His lifeless body.

Focusing back on Eckerson, he said, "You were right. The day came where I regretted letting you live. I should have killed you back then."

The man held up a desperate hand. "Please, don't. You didn't back then, and you shouldn't now."

As the man pleaded with him, Caleb thought of his father smiling. Laughing. Telling stories. But those images gave way to thoughts of his grandfather. And the eternal question.

"Please. I was just following orders."

"So am I," Caleb said in an ominous tone. "Do you know what Fleischer means?"

Bringing the scythe over his head, he swung it down into the man's face. Crimson blood sprayed everywhere. More thoughts of his father filled his mind. He slashed at Eckerson again. And again. He hacked the man's corpse to pieces, a terrible scream escaping him.

His arms grew tired and fell, his scythe vanishing. Opp cautiously approached him from behind, but he ignored his companion. His eyes were glued to what had been a person only moments before.

"It means butcher."

Time seemed to stand still. The furious haze that clouded his mind subsided, and he looked down with sobering eyes at what he had just done. He doubled over and vomited, his stomach turning inside of him.

What had he done? He looked down at his hands. The two agents' blood covered them.

This is what his grandfather had always wanted him to be. A murderer. Now he was truly a Fleischer.

Wiping away his mouth, Caleb's head turned on a swivel as he tried to find his father again. The shockwave had knocked the chair off its bolts, and his father's body lay on the ground, still bound by chains.

He sprinted across the warehouse, though he wasn't sure why. There was no sense in running. His father was already dead.

Collapsing at Scott's side, his hands shook. He wanted to reach out and hold his father, but he was too afraid. As if touching him would make it real.

Tears welled up in his eyes. Not his father. Please, no. Anyone but him. His hands crept forward, touching the man's face.

"Please, Dad," Caleb muttered, his voice weak. "Come back." He gripped his father's shirt, shaking the man in a vain attempt to wake him. "Come back. Please come back. I have to forgive you." He began to wail. "You can't die until I forgive you. I can't do this without you. I'm not strong enough."

Tears streamed down his face. His grip on his father's clothes grew tighter. Unable to contain himself any longer, he leaned forward and buried his face in his father's chest.

And he screamed.

Chapter Eighteen

Caleb's scream carried on. Once it died out, only his sobs echoed through the warehouse. His chest heaved. Clenching his fists, he tried to control his breathing. Time was short, and he needed to move. But he couldn't compel his body to do so.

His father was dead.

Slamming doors snapped him back to reality. He lifted his head from his father's chest and realized Oppenheimer was barking next to him. His dog licked Scott's face, trying to nudge the man into moving.

Caleb reached out and pet the top of Opp's head. "He's gone, buddy." He closed his father's eyes and picked up his body. His tome floated in front of him as he shuffled out of the warehouse. Opp trotted beside him, letting out continuous whimpers.

Michael and Wilson stood in front of the SUV outside. The noon sun shined down upon them, heat radiating off the concrete. Michael's tome was already out.

Wilson had his pistol drawn but lowered it upon seeing

Scott's body. The butler's eyes shifted between the warehouse and Michael, but he did not raise the pistol again.

"You're full of surprises, Fleischer. I'll admit that much," Michael called out.

Caleb stared in silence. His eyelids hung half-open. What did it matter? His father was dead, and he was standing on his last legs.

"I'll have to put you down myself," Michael continued. "Shouldn't take too long, given your current...state."

The man was right. There was little fight left in him, and it certainly wasn't enough to duel a master. Let alone the Scribe in charge of the entire Guild. His mind raced as he tried to think of a plan, some tactic he could use to overcome the Scribe that stood before him. But he simply didn't have the strength.

Michael's tome flipped through its pages, and the man opened his mouth to speak.

The rear door of the SUV flew open, and Heather vaulted out. "Caleb!" she yelled. She sprinted towards the warehouse with tears in her eyes. Pushing past Wilson, she tried to sidestep her father, but he caught her.

Her tear-soaked eyes locked onto Caleb, a helpless look on her face. She thrashed against her father's grip. Michael leaned down and whispered something, and she stopped.

Loosening his grip, Michael stood and faced the warehouse again, keeping a hand on his daughter. The floating tome flipped through its pages once more.

Caleb remained motionless, not knowing what to do.

But Heather acted first. Swatting her father's hand way, she leaped forward and grabbed the tome from the air. She wrestled it to the ground as it fought against her.

Anger flooded Michael's face, and he took a step towards her, but Wilson's hand shot out and grabbed Michael by the shoulders. Delivering a powerful kick to the back of the knees, he threw Michael against the pavement. Wilson helped Heather up, and they sprinted towards the SUV.

Heather jumped in the back while Wilson took the driver's seat. The wheels spun to life, and the SUV accelerated down the pier. They swerved around Michael and drove straight at Caleb.

Once they were twenty yards from him, the tires skidded, and the vehicle spun around. The SUV reversed the rest of the distance and screeched to a halt a few feet away from him. Heather opened the rear hatch and yelled at him to jump in.

Caleb helped Opp into the vehicle and placed his father's body in the back. The SUV took off the second he was inside. Closing the back door, he climbed into the rear seats with Heather. His satchel waited for him on the floor.

The vehicle veered out of the harbor and sped towards the highway.

Heather looked him up and down, her eyes still wet. She reached out and cupped his cheek. "Caleb...you...your dad. I'm so sorry."

Her touch was a strange mixture of comforting and painful. And he had no words for her. The last twenty-four hours hadn't been a picnic for her either. Instead of saying anything, he leaned forward and wrapped his arms around her. She returned the embrace, and they enjoyed a short reprieve.

Michael's tome shot from Heather's lap and crashed out the window, no doubt returning to its owner. They were going to get company. Soon.

His father's smile flashed through his mind. Closing his eyes, Caleb pushed the thought away. The present had to come first. Heather, Wilson, and Opp had to come first. What was he going to do to get them away from the Guild?

"What's the plan, Mister Fleischer?"

"I don't know. But get ready for company."

Wilson pushed down on the gas, and the engine revved. They merged onto a completely empty highway. Had the martial law already had this much of an impact? Maybe it was fear of the plague. Or both.

"We need a plan," Heather said, drying her eyes.

Engines sounded from the rear. Three Humvees accelerated towards them, and he had to squint to see the soldiers inside, along with what he assumed were Scribes.

Caleb's breathing was ragged, and he tried to bring it back under control. "Heather, please open your soul to me."

She looked at him and nodded. He joined his soul to hers, and a golden string connected them. Energy and power surged through him, temporarily pushing his fatigue away.

Keeping an eye on Heather, he limited the amount of her soul he was drawing at once. He needed her to stay conscious.

His tome flipped open. "Wilson, keep it steady."

He spoke the words and cast a portal in front of them. A second opened a mile down the highway beneath them. Wilson kept them stable even as they drove onto the new road. Looking back, the three Humvees had stopped. They didn't appear to see them. A small victory.

Until a portal opened in front of them, and two military trucks appeared. Wilson cursed and slammed the brakes, turning them around in one swift motion. They fled from the new hostiles, back towards the first highway.

Rolling down the window, Caleb stuck his head out and looked at the side of the SUV. A purple glyph clung to the vehicle. A tracking incantation. His mind raced to think of a counter when another portal opened. The original three Humvees sped straight towards them.

He hung his head low. There was no escaping the Guild.

"Caleb," Heather called out, shaking his shoulder. "We need you to stay focused."

Meeting her eyes, he nodded. His tome flipped through its pages. *"Missile of gas and steel; The power is unreal."*

Yellow glyphs appeared over their SUV, enhancing it. Similar glyphs appeared around the three Humvees. Gritting his teeth, he held the enhancement twice in his head, doubling its strength. His eyes widened. He barely felt the effect of holding the words twice in his mind. Glancing down at the golden string, he realized another one of its advantages.

"Brace yourself," Caleb told Heather.

She nodded, and he held the incantation a third time. A fourth. And yet his mind wasn't splintering. His connection with Heather allowed him to share the burden. But she was growing pale and shaking.

He had to be careful. But with this power, the Humvees didn't stand a chance.

"Wilson," Caleb said, "do you trust me?"

"Tell me what to do, Mister Fleischer."

"Do *not* stop."

"Yes, sir."

Lightning, fire, and blasts of golden light flew at them as the Guild cast their attacks. The incantations bounced harmlessly off their protection, and Wilson did not waver.

The Humvees raced towards them, the distance between them shortening every second. They were counting on a three on one advantage, but they had never witnessed the power of a golden connection before. Today was the day they were going to learn.

Their SUV crashed head-on with the center vehicle. Its front bent in and the Humvee flipped over them. It crashed into the pavement and rolled a dozen times. Caleb looked down at the golden string. It was a hollow victory, but at least the Guild experienced its power firsthand.

He shifted his focus to the two remaining Humvees. They had reversed course and sped straight towards them again. The two trucks followed intently. This was a losing game. Outlasting their pursuers wasn't going to work.

Bringing a second incantation to mind, he focused on the left Humvee. *"Traveling through time and space; Fly me to another place."*

A portal ripped open in front of the left vehicle, transporting and sending it straight at the right Humvee. The two cars collided and stopped in their tracks, scraps of metal flying everywhere.

"How are you feeling?" he asked Heather.

Sweat dripped down her face, and she was as pale as him. "I'm fine," she said through short breaths.

He released both incantations and pinched the bridge of his nose. But the reprieve only lasted a few miles. Helicopter rotors cut through the air above them, and the two trucks were gaining ground. Speaking the words, he reapplied the SUV's enhancements.

The moment the protective glyphs appeared, a storm of gunfire rained upon them. The bullets deflected off the SUV, but his soul strained from the burden.

"It's an Apache," Wilson said. "They're not playing around."

Missiles rested under the helicopter's stabilizers. If the Guild wanted, they could end the chase right now. No doubt Heather's presence was the only reason they were still alive.

The bullets ceased, but the helicopter continued its relentless pursuit. Two more Humvees merged behind them, joining the trucks. A variety of incantations shot out at them and barraged their enhancement. Caleb strained his mind to keep their defense supplied with enough energy.

"We've got trouble ahead," Wilson called out.

A line of S.W.A.T armored trucks blocked the highway two miles in front of them. Caleb could easily portal around them or try to plow through them with his enhancement, but what was the point? More would come. Even a golden string couldn't fight an army.

"Wilson," he said, "I'm going to portal Heather out—"

"You will not!" Heather yelled.

His head snapped to her, his eyes growing wide.

"Caleb Fleischer," she huffed, "I forgave you when you tricked me out of that apartment. I forgave you when you sent me away from the elderon. But I'll be damned if you do it a third time. You do not get to make my decisions for me, do you understand?"

He stared at the fierce determination that burned behind her eyes. Guilt bubbled in his stomach, but she was right. She usually was. "Okay."

Her fervent expression softened. She cupped his cheek and said, "We're in this together. To any end."

Nodding, he looked to the rearview mirror. "Wilson, we're going to have to stop."

Wilson met his gaze in the reflection, eyes full of understanding.

"No," Heather said, shaking her head. "Portal all of us away."

He shook his head. "By now, they'll have thermal vision tracking us and the entire area. Anywhere my portal could reach, they'd know. We were going to stay to keep them distracted. To get you safe. But now..."

"Then the three of you teleport away," Wilson said.

"Absolutely not!" she yelled. "You're not staying behind!"

Wilson applied the brakes, and they slowed.

"There has to be something," she said frantically. "We still have to save Chicago."

They came to a stop a dozen yards from the blockade, and Wilson sighed. "There is a loser in every battle, Miss O'Brien."

Caleb nodded. And the Guild would never kill Heather. At least she'd survive.

The four vehicles halted behind them, and the helicopter hovered above. After ensuring that no attack was coming, he released the incantation protecting the SUV. His tome dropped to the floor, and he severed his connection to Heather. He took in a deep, surrendering breath as the string vanished, and his fatigue returned.

A voice through a loudspeaker shouted at them, "Come out with your hands up. No guns. No Tomes. No sudden movements."

Wilson shut off the vehicle and took out the keys. The old man looked back at them both and asked, "Are you two ready?"

Caleb nodded. He had made his peace with death in the warehouse. He wasn't going to falter now. His eyes darted to his father's body, and the man's smile flashed through his mind again. He signaled for Opp to stay. Hopefully, at the very least, his oldest companion would manage to survive this encounter.

With hands up, they all exited the SUV. The helicopter's rotors boomed above as it sent gusts of wind upon them. A chorus of screams ordered them to get on their knees. He and Wilson complied. Heather sprinted forward.

Several screams sounded to hold fire as she came upon a soldier. They yelled at her to stop, but she ignored them. Without hesitation, she threw a sharp jab straight at the soldier's nose. The soldier stumbled, and Heather lunged at a Scribe. The Scribe took her weight and restrained her.

"Don't hurt them!" she yelled. "I'm ordering you not to hurt them. My dad is your boss!"

Caleb looked down as they gently brought her to the ground, holding her in place.

"All units prepare to fire," one soldier called out.

They all raised their rifles. Caleb closed his eyes and held his breath. Heather's face flashed through his mind. Her smile. Her green eyes. His chest tightened, and his stomach sunk. It would be so easy to look at her one last time, but he didn't want her to see him die. So he squeezed his eyes shut even tighter.

"Three...two...one...fire!" the soldier yelled.

Gunfire echoed across the highway.

But nothing happened.

He felt no pain. No metal ripped through his body. He opened his eyes a crack. Dozens of bullets floated inches in front of his nose, suspended in place.

The soldiers exchanged nervous glances before firing again. The bullets shot out and stopped, just like the others.

He stared at the small bits of metal in disbelief.

A frigid, snow-white hand touched his shoulder. The figure in the black cloak stood over him, its face hidden by the shadow of its cowl. The figure sauntered forward, approaching both soldiers and Scribes. She passed the hovering bullets, and they fell harmlessly to the ground.

Each Guild member looked at the figure in absolute horror. The incantations they screamed drowned out the Apache. A flurry of fire, lightning, water, glyphs, and golden light shot at the figure. Each attack vanished before touching her.

The figure glanced up at the helicopter floating above them. She raised her hands, and the rotors disintegrated. It plunged to the ground, but a few feet above the pavement, it slowed and floated down safely.

The soldiers took aim at her, but before they could fire, an invisible force ripped the guns from their hands. The guns drifted in the air before the same force tore them all in half. They fell to the ground, useless.

"Heather, dear," the figure's melodic voice said. "Please rejoin Caleb."

Heather stared at the figure before pulling away from the Scribes holding her, facing no resistance. She sprinted to Caleb and knelt next to him, giving him a confused look.

The figure raised its hands and spun them in small, slow circles. A golden mist spread in every direction, engulfing the whole highway.

As the fog surrounded them, Caleb's stomach lurched, as if they had just come to a sudden stop.

The mist cleared. They were in a completely different part of the Chicago underneath a bridge. Heather and Wilson were at his sides, and the SUV was behind them. The tracking glyphs had vanished.

An invisible force opened the rear door. Opp jumped out and darted straight at him. Caleb embraced his dog and held him. A wet tongue licked his face.

The figure stood facing them. She reached up, grabbed the edges of her cowl, and pulled it back. The mystical shadow that perpetually covered her face dissipated, revealing a beautiful woman.

Her skin was as white as snow, and her hair as yellow as the sun, giving off a soft aura of light. Her features were soft and delicate, but her icy blue eyes held remarkable strength in them.

But Caleb's attention shifted to the SUV. His blood boiled, and his stomach fell. His father's body still awaited him in the trunk.

He charged the woman. Grabbing her cloak, he held her close to his face, his eyes stinging with tears. "Bring him back," he seethed. "Bring him back now."

The woman looked at him with soft, sympathetic eyes. "You know that is not how it works."

Tears fell from his eyes. "Please. I'm not ready to live without him."

His arms fell to his sides. She shuffled forward and put cold hands on his shoulders. Pulling him in, she embraced him.

"It is okay," she said, "Let it out."

Caleb pressed his face against her shoulder and began to heave as tears streamed down his face. He gripped her black robes, his nails digging into his palms. She rubbed his back as he sobbed, his mind filled with images of his dad laughing and joking. Of the man scribbling in the small journal. The sound of the rolling medical stand drowning out his thoughts. Things he'd never experience again.

"Scott was a good man," she said. "One of the best I have ever seen walk this Earth. But his strength, conviction, and most importantly, his heart, live on in you, Caleb."

After a long while, his cries finally died out. His eyes had run out of tears. Slowly, he backed away and cleaned off his face.

Wilson and Heather approached him from behind, each placing a supporting hand on his shoulders.

"Caleb...who is this?" Heather asked.

Sniffing, he glanced between the woman and his two companions. "This is Aeria Cestius, the Guardian of Death. My mother."

Heather took a step back, her eyes growing wide. Her gaze shifted between him and his mother several times before a look of understanding spread across her face. It was as if several of her questions had been suddenly answered.

His mother smiled at Wilson and Heather and bowed her head. Her face grew sullen when she glanced at the SUV.

"May I see him?" she asked.

Caleb considered her request. Part of him was still angry with her, as he had been for all these years. She was the reason his father was sick. She was the reason the world had labeled him an abomination. A monster. An outcast. But, at this moment, all those reasons seemed beyond petty.

Nodding, he led her to the back of the SUV. He opened the rear hatch to reveal his father's body.

His mother's eyes grew misty. She approached Scott and gently brushed a hand against his cheek. "You're as cold as me now," she said with a hollow laugh. Letting out a sigh, she leaned down and gently kissed Scott's forehead. "Goodbye, my whimsical warrior."

Aeria stepped away from the vehicle and gave all three of them a careful look, stopping on Caleb. "My son, I have made many decisions leading up to these events and the events that have yet to come. I have broken my vows both by giving birth to you and now in saving your life, directly interfering with the mortal world. I will have to answer for my crimes."

He met her gaze and nodded. "Mom," he said, then hesitated. "Thank you for saving us."

A warm smile took her face. She leaned in, and her cold lips brushed against his forehead. "Remember, I will always love and believe in you."

Before he could say anything more, his mother vanished into thin air. He looked at Heather, and her eyes locked onto him.

"Should we bury him?" she asked.

The words hit him like a truck. His father was dead. It still didn't feel real. Would it ever?

Taking in a deep breath, he shook his head and said, "No. Scribes are cremated."

"We can't keep the SUV," Wilson offered. "It has GPS trackers and is too recognizable."

All three of them walked over to the vehicle. As best as they could manage, they cleaned off his father's body. His lifeless corpse. No more jokes. No more words of encouragement. No more chances to tell the man he forgave him.

Caleb approached his father and cupped his cold cheek. Tears dripped down his face, and his hand shook. Biting his lower lip, he crossed the man's arms over his chest. Leaning down, he whispered his final words. "I love you, Dad. I promise I'll save

Chicago."

Taking a few steps back, he snapped his fingers. His tome flipped through its pages while Wilson gathered anything useful from the vehicle. A soft hand wrapped around his. He glanced over to see Heather giving him a melancholy smile. She gave his hand a tender squeeze. Opp trotted to his side and whimpered.

Caleb wiped the tears from his eyes and spoke the words, "*By mark of brimstone; Be scorched to the bone.*"

A ball of flame surged from his tome and set the SUV ablaze. They stood a safe distance back as the fire consumed both his father and the vehicle. Orange and red flickering flames danced and cackled.

Sighing, he looked up at the canopy of purple soul strings. "We have to go into hiding," he told them. "The Guild and the military will be after us from now on."

Heather stroked his hand. "I'm not gonna leave you now."

Wilson stepped forward and placed a hand on her shoulder. "I go where miss O'Brien goes, simple as that."

Caleb nodded and shifted his gaze to the Chicago skyline. The strings wrapped around it like a web, constricting and suffocating it. Killing its people.

"Okay then," he said. "From this moment on, we're all fugitives on the run from this city. And we're the only people that can save it."

End of Part Three

Part Four

Chapter Nineteen

Immortality, for those that did not know, was more of a curse than a blessing. Watching loved ones age and die in an endless loop. Combined with isolation, such a life was nigh unbearable.

Thoughts like these plagued Aeria Cestius' mind as she walked through a dense forest. Lush grass grew warm under her bare feet, which took her in a random direction.

Sunlight poked through the thick, leafy canopy and illuminated the path before her. All around her, the forest sang with life. Birds called to one another and flew about. Insects collected pollen and burrowed underneath the soil. Large mammals grazed and took care of their young while nocturnal creatures slept.

But where life blossomed, death followed like a shadow. Plants withered and died, their remains fertilizing those that came after. Old age and disease preyed on the weak. Predators feasted on corpses and supported their young.

Life led to death, and death fed life. And there was time, the force that connected the two.

This was the world Aeria saw wherever she went. Endings and beginnings. The great cycle through which the universe hummed. Through which *every* universe hummed. It was an honor to be part of the machinery that kept it all spinning.

Thousands of years ago, the first Scribes had given her and the other guardians their designations of Life, Death, and Time. It was a typical human phenomenon, and the names stuck. But she had no particular power over death, just as her peers had no abilities associated with their names. They shielded humanity from external, planet-ending threats. Nothing more. Or so her vows dictated.

If she had her way, the Guardians would take a more active role and concern themselves with internal threats as well. History had cursed her with endless examples she could point to, but Chicago was an obvious, current debacle.

Her two peers disagreed, however, and thus the vows had prevented her from interfering. For the most part.

She had first broken it by giving birth to her son. Then today, an hour ago, she broke it again by saving his life.

But she had known what was at stake should she have done nothing. She was the only one on Earth who did. The other Guardians, the Guild of Life, nobody knew the truth that lay just beyond their reality. Nobody knew of Winter's War.

She had told Scott and Caleb vagaries, hints, but not the depths the real truth held. It was an actuality they were not ready for.

And now, Scott would never know.

Aeria's chest tightened, and she stopped in her tracks. She placed a hand on the rough bark of a tree for support. For several seconds, she struggled to take a breath. It was strange, to be so affected by the death of someone who shouldn't have been alive at all. Love had that effect on people. Even immortals, it seemed.

The thought brought a tinge of guilt. Ten thousand years of life had a strange effect on one's memory. Though she had once been a normal human, she did not remember her parents, husband, or even her children from that life. All she knew was that a group of filken had taken their lives during the Speculon invasion. That had been before she received her powers from the eldest hydran that chose to save humanity.

From the time she had become Death to a quarter of a century ago, her contact with humanity had been quite purposefully limited. She certainly hadn't grown close with any of them. But Scott had been different. A human who captured her heart. Someone she could create a child with.

Conceiving a child had never occurred to her through her millennia as a Guardian. Even if it had, she wouldn't have pursued it. Such a move would draw incredible ire from her colleagues with no real benefit to be gained.

That changed when she learned the truth of reality from a messenger on high. Even now, she could picture his orange, brown, and red hair.

Learning that she needed to have a child was one thing. Finding a father had been another. Humans often left much to be desired. They had vast tendencies for greed, violence, and apathy. Even into the current era, they had remained tribalistic and short-sighted.

Thus, she considered finding a Scribe who could meet her standards to be a fool's errand. The fact that such an individual who met those standards had carried the last name of Fleischer still surprised her. For centuries she had watched that family rise to prominence on a tsunami of blood and cruelty. They had a penchant for rage, aggression, and selfishness that was high, even for humans.

And then there was Scott Fleischer. Unlike his ancestors, he had not mirrored the cruel and harsh upbringing he suffered as a child. Instead, it molded him into a man that stood against everything his family valued.

He fought not to advance himself, but to protect those weaker than him. He grew close to people not to take advantage of them, but to connect and grow with them. He saw suffering people and did all he could to make them smile.

She recalled the first time she had spoken to Scott. The memories of their world travels, of his smile, and her final proposition to him flooded her mind. She slipped into these memories, eager for a temporary escape.

Aeria followed Scott as he completed an assignment in Japan in 1992. A filken had eluded capture from a few inexperienced Scribes for months. Three people had died, and the Guild contacts within the government hadn't been happy. Karl sent Scott to show he was taking the issue seriously. In less than twenty-four hours, he found the filken, killed it, and saved a young boy it had been feeding from.

The Guild fed the rest of the government some story of serial killings and pinned it on a known criminal. That night, Scott was celebrating with the mayor as his reward for helping the town. It was an evening of drinking, laughter, and games. And at the center of it was Scott.

Aeria stood in the corner of the banquet hall, concealed from everyone's senses. Over the millennia, she had learned two things about figuring out who a person truly was. First, watch them when they had power over others. Second, watch them when they were alone.

She had already seen Scott in a position of power. His abilities as a Scribe and standing in the Guild had granted him considerable leverage over most people he interacted with. And yet, he had never abused such an advantage.

So, she waited and observed, watching the alcohol flow and the laughter roar. But no party lasted forever, and the people trickled out one by one. Scott was one of the last to leave, but, eventually, he gave the mayor a hearty hug and departed.

She followed him out onto the street. His broad shoulders slumped, and he hunched over, swinging a backpack on. He slid his frequently gesturing hands into his pockets, and his eyes were glued to the ground.

Trailing him through the quiet town, she noticed his pace was slow and methodical as if he were a man without a destination. Despite not looking forward, Scott managed to weave around the other pedestrians with ease.

They reached the outskirts of the town as it transitioned to rural countryside. A train station stood across the empty road, and Scott shuffled towards it.

Only a few individuals occupied the platform at the late hour, most of whom were businessmen. Scott paid no attention to the other travelers and made his way over to a row of payphones against the wall. Reaching into his pocket, he pulled out a few coins and stuffed them into the machine.

She walked close to the wall so she could overhear him.

"Hey, Dad, it's me. I wanted—"

She guessed he had been cut off. He was speaking German, but every language was known to her.

"Yes, the filken is dead. It took me a few hours, but I found it."

A brief silence on their end.

"Yes, the local government paid the fee." Scott's face twisted in discomfort. "No, I didn't ask for more money."

She couldn't make out Karl's words, but his voice had grown louder on the other end.

"You know I know what it means. But they're good people. I'm not going to extort them." Scott's eyelids drooped, listening to his father's response. "No, I'm not coming home tonight. I'll be on a plane sometime tomorrow."

Scott hung up before a response could come. For a long while, he stood in front of the payphones, not moving, his hand still on the receiver. After an extensive sigh, his hand fell to his side.

He bought a ticket and sat on an empty bench. A cold breeze blew over the station, and in the distance, the light of a train came upon them from the country.

Everyone waiting in the station stood except for Scott. The man collecting tickets for the train approached him. In an instant, Scott became the person he had been at the party once more. He stood and smiled, broad-shouldered, as he and the ticket man talked. They exchanged a laugh, and the man returned to the train.

Once the locomotive departed, Scott sat back down. His shoulders sagged once more, and his face went blank. The station was now empty, save the employee behind the counter, who drifted in and out of sleep.

An hour of silence went by before another train approached the station, this time coming from the city. Scott boarded it and found an empty compartment. Aeria took the seat across from him, wanting to keep a close eye on him. As the train left, Scott's gaze was glued to the mountains out the window.

After a while, they were deep into the country. Scott's face was expressionless, and his brown eyes were empty as if no life resided in them. It was a look that should not have appeared on a face so young.

Scott reached into his backpack and pulled out a golden tome. His head swiveled about to see if anyone was watching before muttering an incantation.

A portal opened in their compartment, and a second one appeared on the mountain in the distance. He stepped through it and vanished from the train. Without missing a beat, Aeria gathered her massive soul and teleported to his side.

Scott had brought them to the edge of a cliff a few hundred feet up the mountain. The view from their perch took her breath away. Beneath them, lush hills rolled into an expansive, green valley. The only sign of humanity in the grassland was the solitary set of railroad tracks and the locomotive they had just come from.

Across the valley rose another small mountain chain. Combined with the range they stood upon, it created a protective fortress around the plains.

Even as an immortal who traveled the world over, she never tired of sights like this. This planet never stopped surprising her. And in return, she never wanted to stop protecting it.

"I can tell you're there, by the way," Scott called out.

She took a step back, staring at the man in confusion as his feet dangled over the cliff's edge. Looking into herself, she verified her soul was still feeding the correct incantations. They should have completely shielded her from detection by any of his five senses.

Curiosity killing her, she removed the incantations. "How did you know?"

Scott nearly fell off the cliff as he jumped to his feet in shock. He spun to face her. "Who the hell are you?"

Her mouth hung open. She shook her head, giving him a questioning look. "I thought you knew I was here?"

"I always say that when I'm alone," he said, his breath short and eyes wide. "I never thought it was actually true."

Aeria stared at the man before a gentle chuckle rolled out of her. She struggled to remember the last time she had laughed.

"Who are you?" he asked again.

Realizing her cowl still shadowed her face, she pulled it back.

His eyes grew even wider, then narrowed in confusion, then wide once more. "You're not...you can't be. Are you?"

"My name is Aeria, the Guardian of Death."

His eyes darted back and forth. "Right...how much did I drink?"

"Quite a bit. But this is real."

Scott looked down for a moment, digesting the information. "Should I be attacking you?" he asked, glancing at her out of the corner of his eyes. "I think my Guild hates you."

She rolled her eyes. "You are a powerful Scribe, Scott. But you would not last five seconds against me."

"Fair. Are you here to kill me?"

She remained silent. The answer, unfortunately, was yes. Though it was not in the manner he was thinking. But she wasn't going to lead with that.

Strolling to the edge of the cliff, she sat down and beckoned for him to do the same. The young Scribe hesitated for several seconds before plopping down next to her.

Aeria cleared her throat. "I am not here to fight."

"Why then?"

"To create hope for a bleak future."

He stared at her in confusion.

"You told a lot of stories at the party," she said. "Tell me one."

He hesitated a moment. Then he told the story of a filken that had managed to evade him in San Francisco. It had hidden under trolley tracks and absorbed the souls of those who rode it. He'd bluffed his way through engineers to get down to the maintenance tunnels before he'd finally been able to slay the creature.

After the story, she asked for another. And another. And another still. She then asked more pointed questions. About his father and the Guild. She knew the legacy of the Fleischer family, but learning it from someone firsthand was different.

They talked all through the night and into the new day with the rising sun. She looked at him, giving Scott a pointed expression. "You told your father you would be returning today."

He winced. "I did."

"Travel the world with me instead," she offered.

He grinned and nodded.

For the next year, they scoured the globe together, traveling from country to country and continent to continent. They visited every famous city and natural wonder they could think of. They spent their days in the frozen tundra of Antarctica and the sand dunes of the Sahara. She brought him to the outer limits of the atmosphere and the deepest depths of the oceans.

But none of it was as beautiful as Scott's soul. During their time together, she laughed and smiled more than she had in the last ten millennia combined. For the first time, she felt truly alive.

Thus, in a hotel room in Berlin, she told him a partial truth. About the message she had received. What her child would be responsible for.

He sat in silence for several minutes. His hands shook, and a nervous smile spread across his face. "That's a lot to take in."

"More than you know," she said. "I want you to father that child, Scott. This would be... a sacrifice for you. I don't imagine you will survive our binding."

Scott chuckled and gave her a wink. "I'm not a man so easily killed."

"Scott—"

He held up a hand, a more serious expression taking his face. "Having a child is a great endeavor in life. Having a child with someone you care for, even more so. And fathering the child you describe...well, there can be no higher calling."

A weak smile spread across her face. "Are you ready to give your life for that belief?"

He grinned. "What's the point of having a life if you can't give it for those you love?"

Aeria leaned over and kissed him. Butterflies flew in her stomach as their lips touched, and she pulled him down to the bed. They tore off each other's clothes, and their flesh became one.

As they moved together, her soul opened and consumed his. If one could have seen it, it would have been like the sun swallowing a candle. When they finished, she looked down upon him, cupping his cheek. Scott looked up at her with a weak smile before he began to convulse.

She climbed off and knelt beside him, taking his hand in hers. She wanted to make his death as peaceful as possible, but she couldn't grant him a quick end with her own hands.

Scott spat up blood, and his brown hair fell out in clumps. He struggled to take breaths, and he clawed at his flesh, breaking the skin. She held his hand tighter. It was too painful to watch.

Through all the pain, however, he did not die. He looked up and winked at her with a hollow gray eye. She smiled and reached out with her soul. His was no longer powerful. It was beyond brittle. But it was still there. She didn't think it could be possible.

"I told you. I was not. Easy to. Kill," he said, taking a painful breath every few syllables.

She smiled through tears, kissing his hand. She moved to speak when pain tore through her abdomen. Scott's transformation had captured her attention so thoroughly that she had failed to notice her own.

Her stomach had grown bulbous, and she experienced her first contraction. Giving birth as a Guardian, it seemed, was on a different timetable. She wished someone had given her an instruction manual.

She fell to her back and spread her legs. Scott crawled to her side and took her hand. Over the next hour, pain ruptured through her as she gave birth to her child.

An infant's cry filled the room.

Taking the baby in his arms, Scott showed her their miracle. A boy.

Aeria, covered in sweat, reached over and severed the umbilical cord. "What should we name him?"

Scott thought for a moment, then said, "Caleb."

Her mind returned to the present. She was surprised to find herself on her knees, her wet face buried in her hands. The night Caleb was born, she had been ready for Scott to die. But now that he was dead, it was more than she could bear.

For over an hour, she remained there, unmoving. Finally wiping away her tears, she stood and put one foot in front of the other. She continued through the dense forest, letting the music of nature drown out her memories. It was a brief reprieve.

She came upon a meadow that, upon inspection, appeared mundane. But it was far from ordinary. This was the spot where she had received her powers as a Guardian ten thousand years ago.

Stepping into the clearing, Aeria raised her hands and poured her soul into the black soil. A gazebo of golden light rose from the ground. She walked up translucent stairs and entered the structure. It transported her to another dimension.

A white, empty plane opened around her in every direction. The only object to occupy the endless void was an ornate altar. Four marble columns stood upon a raised platform. One column was green, another was red, the third was orange, and the final was white. Suspended between the four pillars floated a purple, metallic sphere that emitted a golden aura.

Two individuals stood waiting for her. The first was a tall woman, her dark skin a sharp contrast to her white robes. The other was a thin man with copper skin and a bushy, silver beard dressed in golden robes. The Guardian of life, Mirembe, and the Guardian of Time, Hakeem.

Mirembe crossed her arms and tsked. "Glad you could finally join us."

Aeria shrugged. "Sometimes, I actually like to walk through the world we protect."

Raising his hands in a gesture of peace, Hakeem said, "It matters not. We are all here now."

"I trust you understand why we are having this meeting?" the Guardian of Life asked.

Aeria leaned against the white pillar and looked up at the floating sphere. "I can make an informed guess."

"Aeria, my friend," Hakeem said. "You directly interfered in mortal affairs when the fate of the world or existence was not in the balance. Such an act is in direct violation of the vows we took when we accepted our roles as Guardians."

"I am aware of our vows. And *I* wasn't the first to break them."

"Do not deflect," Mirembe said. "You have broken them

twice now in such a short time span. We looked past you spending so much time with that human male. We looked past you giving birth to that creature. But now, what do you offer as justification?"

"If you ever listened to me, you would know my actions were protecting both the world and existence itself."

"Ah, yes. Your little stories about seasons and the creation-consuming war. Unless you have direct proof, we shall continue not believing you."

Hakeem let out a labored sigh. "Since you took your time arriving, Mirembe and I had a chance to discuss without you. We have reached a decision. You are no longer permitted to interact with mortals without one of us present. If you violate this, we will be forced to slay the boy as recompense."

Aeria narrowed her eyes at them. "If you ever try to harm him, you will have to go through me."

"If we have to," Mirembe stated.

"What about Chicago?" she asked them.

The Guardian Life waved a dismissive hand. "Mortals die every day. The Guild won't let a single hydran devastate the planet."

Without another word, the two of them vanished, and she was alone once more. The meeting had gone better than she had expected, no doubt thanks to Hakeem's influence. But she knew they were serious. For Caleb's safety, she would have to respect her vows from this point on.

After she left the mystical gazebo, she continued to make her way through the woods. The days passed like seconds, and soon, snow-covered the forest around her. Five months had passed, and she remained amongst the trees, watching from a distance, unable to interact with mortals any longer. All she could do was hope that Caleb could prevail.

Chapter Twenty

Caleb dashed through the blizzard assaulting the Chicago streets. His tome floated in front of him while Heather and Oppenheimer sprinted behind him. They turned down an alley, heads on a swivel.

"Did we lose them?" she asked.

Shadows darted across the buildings above them to serve as their answer. Two Scribes landed on either side of the alley, trapping them. Oppenheimer barked three times and growled. It was going to come down to a fight. Like always.

He dropped the large duffle bag that hung off his shoulders. It landed with a thud and a metallic clank. Summoning his scythe, he stood back-to-back with Heather. He cast his speed and strength incantations.

"Mousetrap?" he asked her, opening his soul.

"Let's do it," she said, responding in kind.

A golden soul string shot from his chest and connected to hers, their souls becoming a singular, powerful entity. His eyes darted between their two opponents. One brandished a simple small sword, and the other awkwardly held a mace.

Caleb faced the small sword, and his tome opened to a new page. *"By mark of brimstone; Be scorched to the bone."*

The Scribe jumped high above the ball of fire, and Caleb immediately spun to face the mace. His tome glowed red. *"I am king of this stage; Chains will be your cage."*

Golden chains shot out of a yellow glyph and pursued the mace wielder. Taking advantage of his connection to Heather, he held the incantation twice in his mind, allowing the normally slow chains to dart down the alley with blinding speed.

As the mace wielder desperately dodged the chains, the small sword Scribe came over the fireball and headed towards the ground. Heather reached into her coat and pulled out a piece of parchment. It glowed red as Heather muttered, *"No matter the power you may wield; Stand firm against my mighty shield."*

The small sword Scribe landed just as a dome of golden light appeared around him, trapping him. At the same time, Caleb's chains wrapped around the mace wielder, slamming the Scribe into the ground and rendering her unconscious.

Releasing the chains, he ran towards the trapped Scribe. Heather released the barrier, and he unleashed a volley of slashes. The small sword Scribe tried to parry, but his footing was poor, and Caleb knocked him to the ground.

"Please," the young Scribe said, scrambling back. "Don't rip me apart like you did Agent Eckerson."

Caleb's eyelids dropped, the agent's screams filling his mind. What he had done spread through the Guild. His grip on his scythe tightened, and he looked down on his opponent. The boy couldn't have been older than eighteen. Far too young for the Guild to be placing him on guard duty.

"What's your name?" he asked the Scribe.

"D-Devin."

"I'm not going to kill you, Devin. Please radio to your backup and tell them your location. Tell them you and your partner need medical support."

Devin hesitated before complying.

"When you come to, talk to the filken. Ask them their names."

A bewildered look spread across the young man's face. Caleb raised his scythe and rammed the end of his staff into the boy's face, knocking him out.

He turned to Heather, severed their connection, and picked up the heavy duffle bag. "I wonder if any of them has actually listened to me. Let's get out of here."

Creating several portals, he brought the three of them a few miles from the scene. They hid in an empty warehouse. Caleb brought a new incantation into mind. *"Begone, machine; Our heat, unseen."*

A red glyph appeared beneath them, completely hiding their heat signatures. Just in time. Helicopter rotors sounded on the horizon. He counted at least two. No doubt there were drones overhead as well.

Heather sat down, catching her breath. "Well, that didn't go as smoothly as last time."

"At least we made it out," he said, his eyes on the duffle bag.

Ten minutes passed, and heavy machinery rumbled outside. He peeked out the window to see a tank rolling down the street. Several smaller armored vehicles flanked it as well as a platoon of armed soldiers.

"I don't think I'll ever get used to that," she said. "You see pictures of military occupations in history books, but you never think you'll see it up close. I've never seen Chicago so depressed."

He shrugged. "I wonder what the rest of the country thinks."

The siege of Chicago had only grown more desperate in the last five months. The Guild had stopped all traffic in and out of the city. Only the military brought in supplies. The cellular towers were deactivated, and regular internet connections were severed. They were completely cut off from the world.

"No doubt everyone is being told the army is keeping everyone safe. Not that they're a puppet of the Guild. Of my father." She dug her toes into the ground.

He put a hand on her shoulder. "We'll stop them."

She smiled weakly. "As soon as you finish that new incantation."

"Yeah." If he were lucky, he'd finish it tonight.

They waited another half an hour. The noises had vanished, so he released his incantation. It took him a moment to recover from holding it for so long, but they quickly made their way back out onto the street.

The canopy of purple strings hung over them as they ran. As winter had come upon them, the number of strings had grown to over a million. More than a quarter of the city had become victims. Who knew how many more were doomed to the same fate?

Last time they had gotten their hands on a newspaper, the death count had risen to a thousand, and the hospitals were overflowing with patients. Thankfully, thus far, Cassandra wasn't on the list of the dead. No doubt thanks to the seals they had placed on her for months.

They stopped in an alley a few blocks from their temporary shelter. Three pieces of paper hung on the brick wall, each saying "Wanted." One was a picture of Caleb's grandfather. The second was of Wilson. And the third was of him. It was blurry since they didn't have any real photos of him. But it was him nonetheless. Enemy of the State.

The rundown brick building wasn't much to look at, but it was their home. Most of the windows were boarded up or broken. The paint had faded, and he could smell its foul odor from the street. It reminded him of his house back in Orion.

An abandoned room on the third floor served as their base of operations. Snow covered the floor, and the broken windows allowed the cold winter wind inside. Three sleeping bags broke up the emptiness of the room. In the center sat a small metal crate where they would burn fires. Thick blankets lay at the sides of the sleeping bags, and a large suitcase sat in the far corner of the room.

He walked to the luggage and set the duffle bag down. Unzipping it, he revealed two dozen cans of food. He took stock of what they had managed to gather. Eight cans of meat. Five cans of fruit. Fourteen cans of vegetables.

"Not a bad haul," she said, standing over his shoulder.

"It's one of our better takes."

They had raided one of the military ration sites. The only place they could find food now. One of the many ways the Guild kept control over the populace.

Static crackled from his satchel. He opened the main flap and produced his father's journal and a military-grade radio. He pressed down on the transceiver button twice without speaking.

Wilson's voice came over the radio. "Homebase, this is

Bloodhound. Cargo acquired. Returning in T minus one hour. Over."

"Bloodhound, this is Sunflower. Acknowledged. Athena and I are at Homebase. Out."

He set the radio down, a smile cracking on his face. It was impossible not to brighten up whenever he used the nickname Heather had assigned to him.

Reaching down, he picked up his father's journal. It was all he had left of Scott. That, and memories. Caleb paged through the notes, reminiscing over the incantations the man had created throughout the years. He reached the final project. The last incantation he had learned from his father.

As he turned the pages further, however, his handwriting replaced his father's. Over the past few months, he had created a handful of his own new incantations. And now he reached the notes for the one he was presently working on. He pulled out a pen and began to scribble his thoughts.

"So much hard work is about to finally pay off," Heather said.

He nodded as she pulled out her parchment. "You going to do some exercises?" he asked.

"Yupperooni. Gotta keep improving. Can't let you have all the fun."

Returning her smile, he found himself staring into her eyes. His face grew warm, and he focused on her mouth. Sweat formed on his hands. He shook his head and cleared his throat, returning his attention to the journal.

For the next hour, he worked. He jotted down ideas and wrapped his mind around how the incantation could work.

The sound of footsteps came from the stairs, and a familiar voice called out, "It's me."

Wilson walked into the room. He took off the rifle strapped to his shoulder and started a fire in the metal crate.

"Your contact delivered?" Heather asked.

The old man nodded. "Steven is an old friend. Thankfully, he hasn't bought into the Guild's propaganda. He got me the mayor's itinerary through the next week and guaranteed the next two days. If we're not ready by then, he says he can try and acquire a new one."

"Two days," she said hesitantly. "That'll be Christmas."

"Given the current situation, all essential government personnel are working through the holiday. Will you be ready by then, Mister Fleischer?"

He nodded. "I think so. If I take first watch tonight, I'll probably finish before you two wake up."

"Very good. And tonight's mission was a success?"

"We got the food," Heather said. "But two Scribes chased after us. Led to a fight. They were beginners, though, it seemed."

"It feels like it's getting harder and harder to travel through the city," Caleb said.

Wilson stroked his unkempt beard. "Yes, Mister Fleischer. The army just stationed another five hundred soldiers yesterday. And tomorrow, another air wing is arriving."

Caleb considered the new information as Wilson grabbed a can of meat and vegetables. Reaching into the suitcase, the man pulled out two rusty pans and a grilling plate. Placing the grill over the fire, Wilson opened both cans and poured them into the pots.

They passed around the meal once it was warm. It was bland and unsatisfying, but it kept their stomachs full. Caleb made sure to set aside some meat for Oppenheimer.

"I wish we could make food with incantations," Heather said. "What's the point of having magic powers if you're still bound by the Laws of Thermodynamics?"

They chuckled and finished the meal. As Wilson cleaned, Heather looked out the window. "How certain are we that the mayor isn't already in the Guild's pocket?" she asked.

"I don't know," he answered. "All we know is your dad had Aalia's mom run against Mayor Ivers. Hopefully, that means Ivers is not associated with them."

"And once we get her on our side," Wilson said, "she'll have contacts outside the city we can reach and turn them against the Guild."

There was no way it was going to work, even with the help of this new incantation. Every attempt they made to get ahead of the Guild had ended in failure. Why would this be any different? But sitting around and waiting for the hydran to hatch wasn't an option. They had to try something. Anything.

"That is," Wilson continued, "if you're still against our other option, Mister Fleischer."

Caleb clenched his hands. No, not anything. "We aren't torturing someone. Even a Guild Officer."

"Very good, sir."

Heather said her goodnights and climbed into a sleeping bag. Wilson took out his rifle and began to clean it.

Scribbling into the journal, Caleb tried to focus on his work. Every few minutes, however, his eyes flickered to Heather, sleeping on the floor. Butterflies fluttered in his stomach. It was such a strange feeling. One he hadn't felt before. But it could only be one thing, right?

He cleared his throat. "Wilson?"

The old man looked up from the rifle. "Yes, Mister Fleischer?"

His face grew warm. This was a stupid question. "Have... have you ever been in love?"

Wilson tilted his head. "I have. Once."

"What was it like?"

Setting the rifle down, Wilson's eyes grew distant. "My friend, Bobby. We were more than best friends. We dated all four years at West Point. He was my everything. My safety. Whenever the army threw shit at me, he was there. Whenever I felt like I couldn't keep going, he was there. We helped each other. Grew with each other. Tried to maximize each other's happiness and minimize our sadness. I think that's what love is like, Mister Fleischer."

He looked at Heather as the man spoke. Is that what he felt? How was he supposed to tell? When his peers started dating back in middle school and high school, it felt like they had all been given instructions that he had not. But with Heather, for some reason, perhaps he was starting to understand.

Wilson smiled at him. "I'm going to get some rest, Mister Fleischer. Miss O'Brien will take the second watch, and I shall take the third."

"Good night, Wilson."

The old man drifted off to sleep, and Caleb continued his work. Nearly two hours later, he closed his father's journal and smiled. He had finished the incantation. Over the next hour, he moved his soul and seeped the words into his blood, holding the incantation in his mind as he did.

Cutting his hand, he dripped blood into the vial. After he healed the cut, he wrote out the incantation in the first open space in his tome. Four incantations below the last one his father had given him.

Closing his tome, he stared out the window at the canopy of strings. He fought against memories of his father that tried to plague his mind. He did the same for intrusive thoughts of his grandfather. But as he stared at the strings, images of a hydran appeared. The destruction it could wreak. The millions of people that could die. And they were running out of time.

Heather's watch alarm sounded, and she stirred awake. Rubbing her eyes, she sat up and looked over at him. "I had a dream about Aalia."

His jaw clenched at the mention of Aalia's name, but he tried to keep his voice steady and impartial as he asked, "Are you worried about her?"

She scrunched her face. "I don't know. Is there a word for being worried about, angry at, and missing someone all at the same time?"

He thought of his discussion with Wilson. "I think that's all part of love."

Heather looked up at him. "Yeah, you're right."

Caleb averted his gaze, his cheeks growing warm. "I finished the incantation."

Her shoulders shot up. "That's great! We should go to City Hall tomorrow."

He nodded. "Convincing the mayor we aren't out of our minds isn't going to be easy."

She smiled. "Don't worry, we'll get her on our side. Get some sleep, Caleb. The watch is mine."

Chapter Twenty-One

"Are you ready?" Caleb asked the old man.

"Yes, Mister Fleischer."

His tome floated in front of him, open to the incantation he had finished the night before. Wilson stood looking out of the windows of their temporary home. Heather sat eagerly to the side, watching them with Oppenheimer at her feet.

Old nerves stirred inside Caleb as he held the new incantation in his mind. How many years had it been since he had tested a new incantation on someone else? He suddenly felt three feet tall and covered in bruises. His grandfather screamed at him incoherently in his thoughts.

Shaking his head, he took in a deep breath. *"As blind as you may be; I allow you to see."*

His tome glowed red and a white glyph appeared on Wilson's back. The old man took a step forward and glanced in every direction out the window.

Wilson drew a sudden breath. "Well, I'll be. You two weren't joking when you said they were strings."

Heather's eyes widened. "You can really see them?"

The old man nodded.

"The effects will last for half an hour," Caleb said.

Wilson nodded and pulled the mayor's itinerary from his pocket. "She's in meetings with the military council until eleven hundred."

"Gives us a few hours to make our way to City Hall," he responded.

"Yes," Wilson said. "Let's pack up and gather what we need. We'll leave in ten."

Caleb returned his tome to his satchel and checked his radio to confirm it had enough battery life remaining. Walking over to Opp, he knelt and held his forehead against his companion's temple. "You're gonna have to be on guard today, buddy. It's gonna be rough."

Heather walked over to him. "You nervous?"

"A little. Everything rides on today being a success."

Wilson cleared his throat. "We do have a backup plan, Mister Fleischer."

He shot the old man a pointed look. That plan was unacceptable.

"Very good, sir." Wilson bowed his head and headed down the stairs.

Ensuring they had everything they needed, he and Heather followed the man out onto the sidewalk. Opp kept tight on their heels as they shuffled down the street.

As rudimentary as their shelter was, it did provide some level of protection against the elements. Outside, the early morning air was especially cruel. Caleb rubbed his hands together and zipped his windbreaker all the way up. Winter was the worst.

Sneaking across the city was slow, but their progress was consistent. Darkness covered their first hour of travel, but once the sun rose above the horizon, they took more caution with each step. The streets were still abandoned, save the roaming military convoys. Wilson always noticed them before either Caleb or Heather did, signaling for them to stop. Once they had, soldiers and tanks rolled down the street thirty seconds later.

Two hours into the journey, they happened upon a platoon of troops shepherding a large herd of civilians down the street.

It must have been their assigned ration day, waiting in line by a supply depot.

They walked the entire journey, not relying on portals at all. Should things go wrong, Caleb would need all the energy he could save. And when hadn't things gone wrong? Even still, they arrived at City Hall with time to spare.

"*Shadows hide me from my enemy's eyes; Make me impossible to recognize,*" he muttered under his breath.

He poured enough of his soul into the incantation to cover all four of them. Giving Opp the signal to remain silent, he let Wilson know they were hidden. Peering around the corner, they stared at City Hall two blocks down the road.

The building was constructed of white stone and took the form of a massive cube occupying its own city block. Windows covered the lower two levels to form the base of the structure. Tall, round columns divided the upper floors.

It was an impressive structure, but the small regiment of soldiers that surrounded it made it even more imposing. Dozens of soldiers stood behind barricades, weapons at the ready. A tank sat at each corner of the building, their turrets on a constant prowl.

"That's a lot," Heather commented.

Wilson observed the troops through his rifle's scope. "I'd say half of them are two hours into their watch. The other half about six."

"The soldiers will be easy to get around," Caleb said. "It's potential Scribes that have me worried."

Lowering the rifle, Wilson checked his watch. "We have fifteen minutes before the mayor's meeting ends. If she sticks to her normal habits, she'll go back to her office to eat lunch by herself."

The four of them bunched up and shuffled across the street. Thankfully, the pavement on all sides of the building had been freshly plowed. Hiding their bodies was one thing, but having to worry about footsteps would have been a headache.

They took their steps in unison as they approached the barricade. A small gap opened between two groups of soldiers. Caleb held his breath as they crept by. None of the troops noticed. They hugged the wall and shuffled towards the entrance.

Large windows flanked either side of the doors that led into the ornate building. A grand marble lobby sat beyond them with reception desks on either side. A rich crimson carpet led visitors to flanking rows of elevators, extending to the far wall.

The windows on the far bulkhead revealed a courtyard that rose through the heart of City Hall. Muttering an incantation, Caleb opened a portal in front of them and into the center yard of the building.

The mayor's office was on the ninth floor. Counting the windows, he cast another incantation and portaled them back into the structure. They stepped onto the marble floors of a hallway. Gray brick walls surrounded them, though several pieces of art covered most of the surface.

A solitary doorway adorned the interior wall of the passageway. The mayor's office. Four soldiers stood guard outside it, looking aggressively bored. Two muttered to each other, and one of them snickered.

Unfortunately, the door was closed. Portaling to where one couldn't see was incredibly taxing and risky. How many stories had his father told him of Scribes appearing in the middle of objects, dead? No, they'd have to wait.

But the wait was not long. A short woman appeared around the corner of the hall. She wore a formal, violet blouse. Her dark hair was held in a tight bun, and wire-framed glasses sat upon her nose. Her brown skin was paler than the photos they had been given, no doubt due to the purple soul string jutting from her chest.

She wasn't a Scribe. But she was dying.

Two advisors accompanied her, handing her various documents while they walked. The small group reached her office door, and Mayor Ivers said her farewells before stepping inside. The door to the office closed, and the advisors walked down the hall and out of sight.

Nodding to Heather and Wilson, Caleb stepped towards the soldiers. Without exchanging a word, they each took position. He stood in front of the two on the left, Wilson and Heather each in front of one on the right.

In a whisper, he cast his strength and speed enhancements. His mind strained from holding all three at once, but it would only be for a moment. Wilson produced a handheld taser while Heather brought out a piece of parchment.

They exchanged a glance, and Heather muttered, *"Stay still your highness; I will now bind us."*

Yellow glyphs appeared beneath her and the soldier she stood in front of as barriers surrounded them. The entrapped woman stood paralyzed and confused, unable to signal for help. The other troops didn't notice.

Caleb released the cloaking incantation. The soldiers jostled, their mouths agape. His hands snapped forward, palming both soldiers' faces, throwing their heads against the wall behind them. The blows were hard enough to knock them out, but he tried to keep it as light as possible. They were only doing their job.

Wilson charged his target, holding their rifle down with one hand and shoving the taser into their neck with the other. With the flip of a switch, the taser clicked to life and stunned the soldier.

As the three soldiers fell to the ground, Caleb released his two remaining incantations, letting his mind relax. Wilson stepped to the final soldier and nodded at Heather. She released her incantation, and the barriers vanished.

"Now," she ordered.

Wilson shot his hand forward and tased their final target.

Caleb took stock. Someone probably heard the commotion somewhere, but there appeared to be no immediate threat.

Moving quick, he threw open the door to the office. Bookshelves adorned the walls to his left and right, and a red carpet covered the floor. Just before him sat a small coffee table surrounded by a couch and two chairs. The only other major piece of furniture in the room was a large, ornate desk on the far side of the room.

The mayor shot up from her chair, staring at them. "It's you! Caleb Fleischer and Wilson Price. Have you come to kill me?"

Wilson pushed the couch in front of the door to block it off. Caleb looked down at Opp, giving his companion the signal that it was okay to bark. But no sound came. The mayor truly wasn't a Scribe.

Locking eyes with Mayor Ivers, he said, "No, ma'am. We've come to save this city."

Before the mayor could respond, Heather stepped forward. "Ms. Ivers, I don't know if you remember me. You've worked with my father, Michael O'Brien, in the past. I am here to ask you to listen to us."

The mayor's brown eyes flickered from him to Heather, and a moment of recognition flared in them. "I remember you, Heather. Though, if I recall correctly, your father very heavily supported my opponent in the last election. And now you've brought two fugitives into my office, past my security, and in your current state of...appearance. Why should I trust you?"

Caleb held his hands out in a gesture of peace. "I can't tell you why. But I can show you if you would be willing to trust me for thirty seconds. Please."

Her eyes shot to the gun in Wilson's hands. "I suppose I don't have much of a choice. Thirty seconds."

He nodded and held out a hand to her. Hesitantly, she took it, and he led her to the large back window of her office. He held his tome in his hand, wanting to limit the number of surprises he was about to spring on this poor woman. Her world was about to change.

Bringing the incantation to his mind, he placed his palm against her back. *"As blind as you may be; I allow you to see."*

A yellow glyph appeared on the mayor's back, and she startled away from the window, her hands covering her mouth. "What are those?"

"They're called soul strings," he said. "They're what's causing the Sleeping Plague."

"But...what are they?" She took a step forward, her eyes glued to the window.

"Without going into too much detail too soon, there are creatures from another world that feed off our souls with those strings. Controlled by some bad people, like Heather's father, the creatures have created those strings all over your city."

She shot him a skeptical glance. "For what purpose?"

"To create chaos. To summon a terrible force of nature they can exploit to seize power."

It was then that the mayor finally noticed the string coming from her own chest. She tried to grab it, but her hand only passed through it. "Then...this means..."

His eyes softened. "Unfortunately, ma'am, it means you're already a victim. I don't know how much time you have, but we've come to ask your help to stop it."

The mayor didn't answer at first, her gaze fixated on the purple strings. He didn't blame her. It was a lot to process, and he did not relish thrusting this responsibility upon her. But it had to be done. They needed her on their side if they were ever going to begin turning things against the Guild. They needed someone with power.

A moment of silence passed as the mayor slowly examined them individually. Her eyes were focused and harsh as if she were trying to peer into their very being. "You expect me to believe this? To believe any of this?" she asked, taking a step back. She looked at the glass of water on her desk. "You slipped something into my drink."

He walked towards her. "Please, we're telling the truth. If you don't help us, everyone in Chicago is going to die." His tome flipped through its pages. "I can prove to you that I'm telling the—"

Opp barked three times.

Caleb spun on his feet to see a portal open in the room. Four individuals emerged, each with a yellow, crystalline weapon and a tome floating in front of them. And he knew one of them. Aalia stood with her staff in hands, avoiding their gaze.

Caleb let his tome float in front of him but made no move to cast an incantation. The Guild had them dead to rights.

But then a different Scribe stepped towards him. The man was short and wiry but had an air of command about him. In both hands, he carried crystalline daggers. "We were wondering if you would try this play, abomination," he spat.

"Aalia," Heather muttered, staring at her friend.

"No response?" the leading Scribe said. "That's fine. We'll kill you and the butler and take Heather home."

Ignoring the man, Caleb looked across the room at Wilson with his rifle raised. They both knew the same truth. They could not win this fight without casualties.

"You won't risk open combat," Caleb said. "Not with the mayor here."

The lead Scribe let out a laugh and flicked his wrist, throwing one of the daggers. The blade pierced the mayor's skull. With a sudden, violent twitch, the mayor fell to the floor.

Caleb glared at the man, his hands clenching into fists. Fire burned in his eyes.

"Oh ho," the leading Scribe huffed, "is this the famous Fleischer anger I've heard so much about? Or is this your mutt half?"

His fists shook. "Do people's lives mean nothing to you?" he yelled.

The man's eyes narrowed. "Anything for the Guild."

What was he supposed to do? The moment his tome flipped a page, the Scribes would attack. He looked at Wilson. Slowly but deliberately, the man mouthed, "Just go." He shook his head. Abandoning the man wasn't an option.

Aalia opened her eyes and looked up. She slammed her staff into the Scribe's head nearest to her.

Every head in the room snapped to her.

Taking advantage, Caleb summoned his scythe and charged the lead Scribe. He swung his scythe and cut off the distracted man's right leg. The lead Scribe screamed and fell to the ground.

Kicking the man's tome away, he focused on the remaining Scribe, but Wilson had already raised his rifle. The old man pulled the trigger and shot the Scribe clean through the heart. It was a true sign of overconfidence, springing this ambush without strength enhancements already active.

Blood pooled beneath them, and Caleb looked away. Why did people always have to die? Why?

"Mister Fleischer, focus. We have to escape before backup arrives."

The lead Scribe clutched his bloodied stump. "You'll never get away, monster. We will find you and kill you."

With a heavy heart, he ignored the man and looked out the window. Speaking the words, he cast a portal incantation.

"Please," Aalia said, stepping forward, "let me come with you."

Caleb glared at her, but Heather pushed him towards the portal. "Just go!" she said.

All five of them, Opp on Caleb's heels, jumped through and appeared in a random alley. They repeated this process three more times, quickly getting a dozen blocks away from City Hall.

The snowy ground swayed under Caleb's feet as he recovered from the successive portal incantations. Once his vision returned to normal, he marched towards Aalia.

"Caleb...please," she said.

"You sold me out to Michael!" he roared. "You got my father killed!"

Heather stepped forward. "Caleb, calm down—"

"No, he's right," Aalia said, standing tall. "That decision is on me. Michael discovered you all were staying at my place, and he threatened my mother and brother if I didn't help capture you all. But that doesn't absolve me of guilt." Tears formed in her eyes. "I was so happy when I learned you had survived, Caleb. And I was devastated when I learned about Scott. He was a good man. I'm so sorry."

She was sorry? His blood boiled. His father's laugh sounded, and the image of the flaming SUV burned in his mind. Sorry wasn't good enough. He stepped forward.

A soft hand reached out and clasped his shoulder. He turned to see Heather's green eyes, somehow both warm and afraid.

All at once, the rage bubbling in his stomach simmered. He took a step away from Aalia.

He knew what Fleischer meant. His grandfather had tortured the concept into his consciousness. But he rejected it. Never again would anger dictate his actions.

His eyes stung and grew wet. "I'm sorry, Aalia. You didn't have a choice. This is the Guild's fault, not yours."

Tears streamed down her cheeks. She held out a hand to him, a weak smile taking her face. "Allies?"

Without hesitation, he shook her hand. "Friends."

"Miss Laghari," Wilson said, "perhaps you could give us some information about—"

An explosion shook the city. Looking in the direction of City Hall, they saw flames and debris climbing high into the sky.

"They're framing the mayor's death as a terrorist attack," Wilson said confidently.

Leaning against the brick wall of the alley, Caleb's mind tried to catch up on everything that had just happened. This was supposed to be the day they took a step forward against the Guild. Now, the mayor and everyone in City Hall was dead, they were no closer to stopping the strings, and the hydran was still coming.

Slowly, he slid down to the cold ground. Bringing his knees to his chest, he wrapped his arms around his legs and buried his face in his thighs.

Chapter Twenty-Two

The silence in their makeshift home the next morning was deafening. Not a word had been spoken on the journey home the day before. Caleb sat against the wall, his face buried into Opp's side. Images of the mayor falling to the floor filled his mind. It had been such a monumental failure. Even changing into his last pair of fresh clothes did little to brighten his mood.

Heather glanced at him every few minutes from across the room. Wilson prepared some breakfast of beans and peas. Studying from her silver tome, Aalia sat in the far corner of the room, away from the rest of them.

The beans were bland, but he ate them nonetheless. His stomach was desperate for any sustenance.

After they finished eating, Aalia cleared her throat. "We're gonna have to talk about our plans eventually."

He looked up at her, saying nothing. What else could they do? The Guild was too powerful. A hydran was unstoppable. They had lost.

"There's always Wilson's plan," Heather suggested.

"What's that?" Aalia asked.

Wilson sighed and rubbed his beard. "We would engineer a scenario to lure a Guild officer. Capture them. Then I would use my training from the army to extract information."

Aalia looked down, thinking. "That could work. It would have to be a pretty high-ranking member. I'd say at least two-thirds of the lower ranks still don't know the full plan. Only the upper echelon knows where the hydran egg is."

"What would it take to lure them out?" Heather asked.

Considering a moment, Aalia's eyes fixated on her friend. "You would. Michael is out of his mind trying to get you back."

Caleb looked up. "We're not doing that."

"Mister Fleischer, I must ask you to reconsider."

He shot up. "No!"

He knew he was being foolish. They had no options left. This was their only path forward, their only chance of saving Chicago. But torture? That's what the Guild did. What his grandfather did.

"I know nobody's asking for my opinion," Aalia said, "but if it were up to me, we'd sneak out of the city. Get Heather to safety. There's no winning this."

Heather crossed her arms. "We are absolutely not abandoning Chicago."

Wilson walked forward. "I would be the one who performed all the...unsavory aspects of the plan, Mister Fleischer. It wouldn't be on you."

"I'd be condoning it," he said.

Heather put a hand on his shoulder. "I didn't like the sound of it all that much either, but it's the only thing we can do to find the egg."

He shook his head and stepped away from them both. Grabbing his satchel, he shoved his way to the exit. Opp stood to follow, but he signaled for the dog to stay. "I'm going for a walk."

"In broad daylight?" Heather called out after him.

"It's Christmas. The military is easing restrictions for people to attend services."

He was out the door before Heather could reply. Grabbing a snow cap from his windbreaker, he stuffed his curly hair up into it, covering it completely.

A cold wind swept over him when he reached the street,

stabbing at his face. He pulled his hood over his head and walked in a random direction.

While in the more worn-down area of the city, he remained cautious. But the convoys were more sparse than usual. No doubt keeping track of the influx of pedestrians.

It took him an hour to reach the heart of the city. All around him, people exited their homes dressed in full winter gear. He kept his head down, but nobody gave him a second glance. Everyone kept to themselves.

Integrating with a group, he flowed with the crowd as if it were a river. His grandfather had always told him it was infinitely easier to hide in an ocean of people than in isolation.

Over half the people in the street had a purple soul string extending from their chests. How much longer until it was all of them? Or would the hydran kill them first? The thought sent shivers down his spine.

But a worse thought came. Would it be worth torturing a single person to save them all?

He pushed the thoughts from his mind.

A group of soldiers stood in the road, handing out newspapers to each person passing by. It was certainly filled with propaganda, but he accepted one nonetheless, keeping his head down.

"General Robert Cromwell Arrives in Chicago" was printed in bold on the front-page headline. Skimming the article, he found it was in response to the City Hall bombing. He wasn't sure how much of it could be believed, but it reported that three hundred people had died along with the mayor.

Flipping past it, he found the section listing those killed by the Plague. His eyes darted across the page. Cassandra's name was nowhere to be found. He let out a breath and lowered the paper. Heather would be happy. But everyone was running out of time.

He tucked the paper into his satchel and continued moving with the herd, his eyes fixated on the feet in front of him, trying to avoid the haunting image of the strings. Due to his lack of attention, he had no idea how he ended up on a lush blue carpet. Oak pews rose on either side of him. Wooden columns climbed up white walls and molded into a beautiful vaulted ceiling. It was a cathedral.

Too late to push back out the door, he took a seat in the

rearmost pew. Most of the patrons gravitated towards the front, leaving him alone. The priest spoke, but he didn't listen to a word she said.

Given his knowledge of the world, he had never believed in any religion. Still, he had to admit that he understood the appeal. Being able to trust in some benevolent, all-powerful entity to watch over him would ease so many apprehensions. And yet, here he was.

He thought of Wilson's proposed plan and what it would mean if they carried it out. Was there nothing this city wasn't going to ask of him?

It was more than just Chicago, though. Any glance at a history book would show the same thing. Time and again, for thousands upon thousands of years, humans conquered, killed, enslaved, and oppressed each other when there hadn't been any need.

It was the easiest thing in the world, not to hate someone. And yet people failed this common task so often. He had failed it.

Caleb's mind wandered to his mother and the words she had spoken to him after the elderon fight. She had always been cryptic, but even for her, the words were strange. Autumn rises when Winter falls. They made no sense to him, and yet she had said them with such conviction. Why hadn't he just let her finish? Maybe it would have made more sense.

He had disappeared so deep into his mind, he didn't notice the service had ended. The parishioners had come and gone, and he hadn't even seen them exit. At the front of the church, the priest stood, reviewing some papers. She looked to be about forty, with tan skin and dark brown hair.

Shaking his head, he stood and made his way for the door, but the priest's voice stopped him. "Caleb Fleischer, is it?"

He froze. His name echoed through the empty building, paralyzing his thoughts. Nobody else was in the cathedral. Just the two of them. Spinning, he faced the priest.

She stepped away from her altar and walked towards him, raising a hand. "Don't worry. You have nothing to fear, my child. I have no interest in feeding you to the military."

He arched an eyebrow and stepped away from her. She reached into her red and black robes and produced a folded piece of parchment. The sight of paper sent his heart racing, and he brought his fingers together, ready to snap.

She unfolded it to reveal his wanted poster. His hands shook. What was she planning? Sweat dripped down the side of his head, and the priest continued to move towards him.

"If this is to be believed," she said, "you are a very dangerous individual. Responsible for both the attack yesterday and the strange happenings five months ago."

Flashes of the elderon fight tore through his mind. His hand shot to his stomach, but there was no wound. He met the woman's eyes, his fingers still pressed together. "I'm not responsible for any of that."

"I know, Caleb. I was there five months ago. I was with my family after my son's recital. Things started exploding, people were dying, and we had no idea why."

The bodies of the dismembered patrons of the pub sprung into his thoughts. How their blood painted the floor. He hadn't saved them.

"And," she continued, "in the middle of it all, was you, Caleb Fleischer. This young man, impossibly leaping around and screaming for people to run. Protecting them. Bleeding for them. We ran to higher ground to hide, but I watched you through the window. I saw what happened to you. I witnessed what you did for us."

Her words slammed into his chest, knocking the wind out of him. Why? Why had they had such an impact on him?

The priest was feet from him now. "I can't say that I understand what happened that night. But, between watching you then and during the last hour, I know you're no criminal. This city is sick, I know that. God has decided to test us in a most challenging manner, and I know there isn't much I can do to appease him." She paused, studying him intently. "But you...you're different. You're trying to save us, aren't you?"

She placed a hand on his shoulder. His eyes shifted from the woman's warm smile to her soft eyes. All he could do was nod as tears welled in his eyes.

"Thank you, Caleb Fleischer. I see great light within you. You are one who is loved by God. Please, help Him forgive the sins of this city."

The words made him uncomfortable, yet... "I will," he finally said.

"*Can* you save it?" she asked him.

Her question hung in the air. Could he? No, he couldn't.

"I don't know," he confessed. "Yesterday...that was our last chance to do something."

The priest's shoulders fell. "Then we are already lost?"

He took several careful breaths. "Can I ask you something?"

"Of course."

Grabbing his own arm, he looked down. "There may be something we can do. But...it involves hurting someone."

"Oh," she muttered. "Is the individual in question responsible for the Sleeping Plague?"

He nodded.

She pursed her lips. "I am a Christian, Caleb. I believe our God is a loving God. That He sent His only son down to Earth to die for our sins," she said. "But I am also well read on the Bible. His words. There are violent passages. War. Murder. Things that make me uncomfortable.

"When I was young, I had trouble explaining it. And, eventually, I came to a conclusion. We humans are imperfect. We've messed up the world God created. In order to fix it, in order to do the right thing, it is required a few people to get their hands dirty. For everyone else to live in peace."

The words sat heavy in his stomach. They were too familiar. What does Fleischer mean?

"The important distinction is," she continued, "that we only harm when we have no other choice. That we stop people who would hurt others. That we become the shield for the weak."

He lifted his eyes, locking with hers.

"Can you be a shield, Caleb?"

He thought of Heather. Oppenheimer. Wilson. Aalia. His father. Chicago. The endless web of purple soul strings.

"Yes," he said, "I will be their shield."

A broad smile spread across her face. "I know you will. Now you must go, my child. The military will be inspecting the cathedral in twenty minutes. Follow me. There's a tunnel in the crypts you can use to get away from here."

He followed her to the back of the building and down into the lower levels. The wet smell of dust surrounded him as she turned on a few inadequate lights. They arrived at an old wooden door, and she removed a key from around her neck. With a quick motion, she unlocked and opened the door. "Good luck, Caleb Fleischer."

"Thank you," he said and ducked into the cramped tunnel. Before she shut the door, he turned back to face her. "I never asked your name."

"Reyna. Now, go!" She slammed the door shut and locked it.

Nodding, he disappeared down the passage. The lights soon vanished, and he pulled out his tome. *"I make this light; Please aid my sight."*

A small orb of golden light appeared above his tome and illuminated his path. The corridor was narrow and uneven. Bits of earth poked out, and he found himself weaving in and out of them.

Twenty minutes passed before he reached the other end of the tunnel. A rickety spiral staircase brought him up to an alley in a random part of the city. A cold wind barraged him the moment he stepped out onto the snow-covered pavement.

There was no sign of the military. Gathering his bearings, he assessed where he was and headed home. He took a long and roundabout path back, giving himself time to think.

The sun had dipped below the horizon by the time he returned. Heather, Wilson, and Aalia gathered around the fire, sharing a meal. Opp rested at Heather's feet, asleep. Her green eyes looked up and saw him, a warm smile spreading across her face. And it was at that moment Caleb found his answer.

Humanity had a vast tendency for cruelty. But there were those that fought against the mold. There were those who fought for honor and duty. There were those who fought for love. And there were those who sacrificed their wellbeing for the greater good.

He was their shield.

Heather held out a pot of beef stew. "We saved some for you."

Accepting the pan, he took a hearty bite before passing it to Wilson.

"Listen, Mister Fleischer," the old man said after his bite, "I'm sorry for pressuring you. I don't want us to leave anything on the table. Not if we think it might help."

Taking a measured breath, he glanced around at his companions. "You were right. There's a difference between doing cruel things for selfish reasons and doing it for just ones. Tomorrow, we'll go with your plan."

They spent the rest of the evening planning. Aalia brought up her objection once more, pleading for them to leave Chicago, but Heather shot the idea down.

When they finished, a thought crossed his mind. Reaching into his satchel, he produced the newspaper. "I got this today," he said to Heather. "I checked. Your mom's not on the list."

She let out a sigh of relief, but Wilson shot up from his seat. "Mister Fleischer, may I see that a moment?"

Arching an eyebrow, he handed the man the paper. The old man's eyes took in the front page, a strange expression crossing his face.

"Everything okay?" Caleb asked.

Wilson hesitated before looking up. "It's nothing, Mister Fleischer. Nothing."

Caleb arched an eyebrow but didn't press the issue. A few minutes passed, and both Wilson and Aalia hunkered down for the night, leaving Caleb and Heather alone.

They sat next to the fire with only the sound of the wind to accompany them. She leaned forward and stoked the flames, brightening them. When she sat back, Caleb realized how close she was to him. Her shoulder brushed against his, and his cheeks grew warm. Too nervous to move, he kept his eyes focused on the flickering orange flame.

She cleared her throat. "I got you a present." She brought a small business card out of her pocket and handed it to him.

It was one of her father's cards. But she had crossed off Michael's name and job. Instead, she had written Caleb's name in by hand, and underneath the title, it said: 'Not a Scribe.'

A strange feeling simmered inside of him as he looked at the small piece of paper. He had never been sure what he exactly wanted to do with his life, but being a Scribe certainly wasn't it.

"I figured after we save Chicago, you can finally quit," she said. "And I'll pursue my career as a therapist."

He locked eyes with her. She always radiated such warmth; it comforted him even in such troubling times. "I think that's a good idea. We've both spent enough time living lives that doesn't make us happy."

She closed her eyes and smiled at him. Resting her head on his shoulder, Heather moved closer to him. His face blazed. Swallowing past a lump in his throat, he placed his hand over hers, their fingers interlocking. It was a moment he wished would last forever.

But there was one thing life had taught him. The good times never did.

Chapter Twenty-Three

Heather sprinted down the street toward the military convoy. She screamed so loud, her throat cracked, desperately trying to get their attention. The soldiers marched around three armored personnel carriers. Lungs on fire, she forced her legs to move faster as she barreled towards them. More than once, she slipped on the snowy pavement, but she managed to keep herself from falling.

They finally saw her. One of them barked an order, and three soldiers formed a line, raising their rifles at her. They ordered her to freeze. She stopped in place, throwing her hands into the air.

"Please!" she yelled. "My name is Heather O'Brien. I'm begging you to help me."

The line of soldiers continued to point their guns at her while two new soldiers approached. They patted down her body, checking for any weapon.

"She's clear," one of them called back.

"Bring her over," the woman in charge ordered.

Each soldier grabbed her by an arm and led Heather to the now stopped convoy. The leading officer pulled out a smartphone and held it up to her face.

"It's her," the leader said. "Radio it in. Please follow me, Ms. O'Brien."

While one soldier spoke into a radio, the leader brought her over to one of the vehicles. "Please, take a seat," the woman said.

Heather climbed in, and the leader offered her a canteen. Forcing her hands to shake, she accepted the container and took a small sip. Handing it back, she wrapped her arms around herself and rocked back and forth.

"Ms. O'Brien, if I may...what happened?"

Her head snapped to the officer, forcing her eyes to be wide and distant. She opened her mouth to speak, but let the silence drag on for several seconds. "I...I can only tell someone who works with my father."

"I understand. They're on their way. Do you need anything?"

She let out a visible shiver. "A blanket. It's so cold."

The leader walked to the rear of the vehicle and returned with a scratchy, gray blanket. Heather wrapped it around herself and continued to rock. She kept her eyes forward despite the constant movement and talking around her.

No more than a quarter of an hour passed before two black SUVs pulled up to the convoy. Six men and women exited and approached the leading soldier. They exchanged a few words, and the leader pointed over to the vehicle Heather sat in.

She waited for the approaching Scribes to get about ten yards from the vehicle before she jumped out.

The woman walking in front wore violet rimmed glasses that were framed by her light brown hair. Her pale skin only had a little more color than the snow on the ground. Heather recognized her as Miranda Cross. The last leading officer of Operation Moonlight Sonata. She wrapped her arms around the tall woman's chest. "You have no idea what they put me through," she wailed. "It was horrible."

Miranda stroked her back. "You're safe now."

Heather pulled away and looked up at her with wet, hopeful eyes.

"Would you mind telling us what happened?"

"Who are you?" she feigned ignorance.

"I'm Agent Cross. I work closely with your father. He asked me to look after you." Miranda took Heather's hand and led her to the SUV. "Now please, answer my question."

"You don't understand what that monster did to me," she said. The words were sour in her mouth, but she had a job to do. A role to play. A persona to sell. "My father warned me, but I thought he was a good person. It was a lie. I finally managed to get away, and I ran to the closest military convoy I could find."

"The abomination can fool many people, and you should have never trusted him, but at least you're okay."

"Can you please take me home?"

"Of course, dear."

They stepped into the SUV, Miranda and Heather sitting alone in the rear. Buckling her seatbelt, Heather looked out the window as they drove off towards the penthouse. They were well over half an hour away, even if there was no traffic.

"Ms. O'Brien," Miranda said, "could you tell us the location of Caleb Fleischer?"

"He's in an abandoned apartment building on Jefferson. Red brick. We were on the third floor, I think."

Miranda pulled out a smartphone and typed a message. Taking careful glances, Heather noticed no one besides her were wearing their seatbelts. Hopefully, it was the same for the SUV behind them.

Needing a pretext, she quickened her breathing and feigned a fit of hyperventilation. She leaned forward and put her head in her knees, taking deep breaths. Miranda rubbed her back, trying to calm her. As she did, Heather's right hand slipped down to her boots, pulling out a folded piece of paper.

Sitting back up, she hid the paper in her fist. "Sorry. I'm okay."

Miranda nodded and turned her attention outside the vehicle, scanning the area. Heather took a deep breath and cleared her mind. Quietly unfolding the paper, she looked out at the SUV following them.

Holding an incantation in her mind, she whispered the words under her breath. *"No matter the power you may wield; Stand firm against my mighty shield."*

A square, yellow barrier appeared in front of the rear vehicle. Its brakes screeched, but it crashed nonetheless, coming to a dead stop.

A few seconds passed before a large fireball flew in from behind and consumed the wrecked SUV.

Miranda and the two other Scribes with her looked back in horror. Their vehicle came to a stop, and Heather held another incantation in her mind, releasing the first as she did. Staring straight at Miranda, she muttered, "*Stay still your highness; I will now bind us.*"

Yellow glyphs formed beneath both their feet while a barrier surrounded them. Heather was unable to move, but she knew it was the same for her target. The two Scribes in the front glanced back at them in disbelief as machine gun fire began to barrage the vehicle.

Wilson monitored the scene through the scope of his rifle. Heather entered the leading SUV with three other individuals. Three additional foes entered the second vehicle. He still grappled with the notion of using her as bait, but it was the only way they could properly execute the plan. What's more, she had more than proven herself capable. He needed to learn to stop overprotecting her. She was no longer the child he had raised, but a strong woman.

He knelt atop the apartment building he occupied with Mister Fleischer and Miss Laghari a few blocks ahead of the military convoy. Winter had been especially cruel this year but being so high in the air chilled him to the bone. He adjusted his cover to better shield his ears before looking back through the scope, waiting for the vehicles to move.

One. Two. He counted the seconds the SUVs weren't in motion. Three. Four. Five.

Mister Fleischer sighed. "It never ends, does it, Wilson?"

"What's that, Mister Fleischer?"

"The fighting. The killing. The Guild kills. We kill. The cycle repeats."

Jungle trees jumped into Wilson's mind while the sound of

gunfire crept from his memories. "This is a war, Caleb. It ends when one side wins." His answer didn't seem to bring the young man any comfort. "Come, Mister Fleischer. We have work to do."

Miss Laghari leaned over the edge of the building. "They're on the move."

Wilson looked back through his scope. "They're heading north."

Mister Fleischer muttered some cryptic words. A moment later, the air pressure around them shifted.

"It's in front of me," the young man said.

Nodding, Wilson stood and slung his rifle over his shoulder. Stepping where Mister Fleischer had motioned, he found himself in an alley several blocks ahead of the SUVs. He had lost track of how many times he had traveled via these portals, but he still hadn't adjusted to the sensation.

His two young companions appeared next to him, their books floating in front of them. While they waited, he verified his weapon's safety was off and a round was in the chamber. Perhaps his bullets would be of zero use against opponents who literally wielded magic, but he was going to fight nonetheless. Being a non-combatant wasn't in his blood. Perhaps Heather had picked that up from him.

"Ready?" Mister Fleischer asked.

Wilson nodded, and the young man placed a hand on his back. More cryptic words escaped Mister Fleischer's mouth, and a strange sensation spread through Wilson's chest as if taking a sip of coffee on a cold day. Looking up, he once more saw the swarm of purple strings swinging above them.

It was still difficult to accept such things as possible. In his younger years, he had gone through so much. War had given him a lifetime's worth of experiences in a single year. Yet, the world still seemed to have a few surprises up its sleeve.

The thought got his heart pumping. Even after all these decades as a butler, he had never stopped being a soldier at heart.

The SUVs had nearly reached them, but it was Heather who would dictate when the attack began. Holding his breath, he counted the seconds as they passed. One. Two. The vehicles drove by them. Three. Four.

A wall of golden light appeared in the path of the second vehicle. It was beyond amazing that Heather could construct such a thing from her mind. Or, more accurately, her soul.

The rear SUV collided with the barrier. Miss Laghari conjured a massive fireball and launched it at the wrecked vehicle. Flames consumed the metal, and screams erupted from inside. The smell of burning flesh tore through the street.

Without his consent, Wilson's mind was thrown into the past. Saigon. The Tet Offensive. Children screaming as napalm burned their flesh. His fault. Forever his fault.

Shaking his head, he snapped back to the present and tried to lower his heart rate. Raising his rifle, he took aim at the first vehicle.

"They're shielded," Mister Fleischer said with his eyes closed.

Wilson pulled the trigger. He didn't fully understand how Mister Fleischer could tell Heather was protected, but he trusted the young man. At the same time, Miss Laghari and Mister Fleischer charged the burning wreckage. Their job was to finish off the survivors. His was suppression.

As he unloaded on the front SUV, the two unhindered personnel exited. Stepping out of the alley, Wilson brought the scope to his eye. He lined the sights over the nearest Scribe's head. The woman took out her book, and he knew his time was short.

He felt the wind against the back of his neck. The frigid temperature of the air. Slowing his breath, he took the shot.

A hole appeared in the Scribe's forehead, and blood painted the black SUV.

Before Wilson could even take his finger off the trigger, the second Scribe jumped over the vehicle and faced him. Without hesitation, Wilson fired three shots at his opponent. Two at the chest, one at the head. All three bullets bounced harmlessly off the man.

Cursing, he switched his rifle from semi to automatic. He unloaded the remainder of his magazine at the man, but the Scribe only stood there. His gun ceased firing, and Wilson threw it the ground. Reaching to his belt, he ripped off a metal canister.

Pulling the pin from the grenade, he lobbed it at his opponent's feet. The canister popped and spewed orange gas. The Scribe coughed and choked, clutching his eyes.

Not wasting a moment, Wilson removed his sidearm from

its holster. His other hand shot to his pant leg and withdrew a specific magazine. Forty-five caliber hollow point rounds. Mister Fleischer always said that their magic depended on concentration. He was going to put this Scribe's strength to the test.

Sprinting, Wilson waded into the cloud of smoke. Years of army training and granted him a temporary tolerance to military-grade tear gas, but he didn't have long. Leaping towards the incapacitated Scribe, he held his firearm point-blank to the Scribe's head and pulled the trigger.

His opponent's head snapped back, and he fell to the pavement. The floating book fell to the ground, and blood spewed from a hole in the Scribe's head. The bullet had only traveled two inches into the man's head, but it had been enough.

"Holy shit, Wilson," Miss Laghari said, appearing from behind him with Mister Fleischer.

Adjusting his shirt, Wilson holstered his sidearm. "I cannot allow you youngsters to take all the risks."

The three of them marched towards the SUV. Miss Laghari located the trapped Scribe's book and took ownership of it. Satisfied, Mister Fleischer gave the signal, and they prepared to move their target to a more secure location.

Wilson wrapped the final chain around the woman, securing her completely to the chair. A fire crackled next to them, giving off enough light to see. They were deep in an abandoned subway tunnel that had been closed off by the military. Nobody would come this way for a good long while. Plenty of privacy.

Shuffling over to his three companions, he said, "You all can leave now. I'll call you back when I'm finished."

Mister Fleischer shook his head. "If we're doing this, I need to witness it. I cannot absolve myself by not being here."

Heather nodded in agreement.

"Let's get it over with," Miss Laghari requested.

Wilson looked at his comrades with remorseful eyes, but he did not argue. This was their decision to make, though he wished it wasn't on the table at all. So young and thrust into a war they never wanted to be a part of. For the briefest of moments, he saw not the three young adults he had come to love, but the soldiers he once led.

Taking in a deep breath, he put on an impartial expression and faced Miranda. Pulling up his own chair, he took a seat across from the woman, moving the metal box that contained the fire, so it sat between them.

She sat bound in her chair, glaring at them. They had extensively searched her, ensuring she had no backup paper on her person. Miss Laghari had also used some magic to seal the woman's book.

Without directly looking at Miranda, Wilson drew his combat knife and poked it at the wood in the fire, stoking the flames.

"Is that supposed to intimidate me?" she spat.

He remained silent.

"There's nothing you or the mutt back there can do to get me to jeopardize our mission."

He remained silent.

"You are terrible at this, you know?"

He let out a soft, sincere chuckle. "I had this friend back at West Point. His name was Bobby. We had this detailer, this giant of a man who always told us the army had molded him into a creature who couldn't love. Every fucking day he'd tell us this while giving us shit. 'Price! Cromwell!' he'd yell. 'Get your no-good asses over here. I have no sympathy for you. I lost the ability to love pathetic meat bags.'

"Well, one day, Bobby got so fed up with the guy that when the man said it, Bobby yelled back, "Come to my bunk tonight, and I'll remind you how to love.'

"The man stood there, stared Bobby down, and cracked a smile. You see, Bobby always had that gift. He got to you, made you laugh and smile. It was in his DNA. I was never good at that sort of thing."

Miranda stared at him in confused silence.

He cleared his throat. "No, me, I was good at something else entirely. When we were over there in the jungles of Vietnam, we quickly learned that this wasn't going to be a normal war. Our enemy, he liked to hide. He dug his little tunnels and scurried about. One second, he'd be here, the next he'd be there. Let me tell you, it made it difficult to find him.

"So, that's where I came in. I'd get my hands on one of them northern soldiers, alive and well. He and I would spend some quality time together, and before the day was over, we'd know exactly where his friends were hiding. That's how I came to get my nickname. The Vietnam Bloodhound."

Before Miranda could speak, he raised his hand and thrust the knife straight into her knee. She let out a blood-curdling scream as crimson blood oozed down her leg. He gave the knife a powerful twist, causing her scream to intensify.

"The funny thing was," he continued calmly, "that even in an environment like that, Bobby found a way to stay positive. Whenever we were alone, he'd break down. But in front of the men, he was a rock. It's what made him such a good leader. He'd make them laugh, give them hope even when there was none. I turned out to be a good soldier, but I was never a good leader, not like he was."

Miranda's scream had only just transitioned into a sob when he pulled the knife free. Not waiting a moment, he grabbed the woman's wrist and drove the knife straight through her hand. Another scream.

"Of course, after the war, I knew I couldn't stay in the army. I had seen too much. Done too much. But Bobby? No, he was a career man. We stayed in touch, but time erodes all things. A bond like that doesn't go away, though. Not ever."

He removed the knife and plunged it straight into her shoulder.

She let out another shriek and stared at him with desperate eyes. Tears streamed down her face, and she shook her head. "Ask me your questions," she pleaded.

He shot her a confused look. "What questions? You don't know anything." Tearing the knife out, he thrust it into her thigh.

She thrashed against her chains. "I know everything! I'm the head of this project! I'm in the inner circle! I work directly with Michael!"

Wilson twisted the blade. "Very well then, madam inner circle. Where's the egg?"

"It's under the water in Burnham Harbor. Right by Soldier field!"

He rotated the knife even harder. "No! Tell me where it really is!"

She broke out into uncontrollable sobs. "I swear, that's where it is."

Removing the knife, he studied her cautiously. There was truth in her eyes. He was a little surprised by how easily she had broken, but that was the problem with the Guild. They were the sole superpower in their world. Nobody existed to even think of challenging them. In such an environment, what need was there to train officers to resist torture?

"You sure she's telling the truth?" Mister Fleischer asked.

Wilson nodded. "I have enough experience to know when someone's honest with me."

Miss Laghari stepped forward. "It checks out. Burnham Harbor is one of the many locations the Guild has taken direct control of."

Sighing, Wilson held the knife towards Miranda. "How do we destroy the egg?"

She glared at him with seething eyes. "Destroy it? You can't! You've gained nothing from this. The hydran can't be stopped. Certainly not by an army dropout, a mutt, a traitor, and a spoiled brat."

He sheathed the blade.

She squirmed frantically in her chair. "Please, let me go. I can get you inside. I can help."

He shook his head. "I only have one more question." Unholstering his sidearm, he aimed it at her. "If I don't like the answer, I will kill you."

"I'll answer, I swear!"

"If your plan succeeds, how many innocent people will die?"

Miranda's mouth hung agape.

"That's what I thought." He pressed his pistol between her eyes, and without hesitation, he pulled the trigger.

Chapter Twenty-Four

Caleb kept his face straight during the interrogation, trying not to let it get to him. But his stomach churned, and his throat ran dry. Once Wilson pulled the trigger, Heather doubled over and clutched her gut, gagging several times. He ran towards her, but she raised a hand to stop him.

"I'm okay," she said, spitting.

The four of them stood in uncomfortable silence. It was then that he realized how ragged they had all become. Their clothes were dirty and torn, dirt and grime covered their faces. They all had lost weight, and dark bags hung heavy under their eyes. Wilson's beard had grown unkempt and wild. It fit the side of the man he had just seen better than the polite butler he had grown used to.

But it was not just Wilson who had carried out the act. It was the old man's hands that moved the knife, but all four of them were culpable. Caleb doubted he'd ever be able to forget what had happened here today.

Heather took a step forward, looking them all up and down. "What we did today is unforgivable. But now we have a responsibility. We have to put an end to this to save the millions of lives in this city so that at least this wasn't done in vain."

He nodded, but the sentiment didn't make him feel better. All he could think about was his grandfather congratulating him. Squeezing his fists, he forced the thought from his mind. This wasn't about being a Fleischer. This was about being a shield. And he had a city to protect.

Every second that passed brought them closer to the completion of the Guild's plan. Despite this, the four of them returned to a new home they had set up. They had zero chance of success if they stormed the Guild HQ without rest and food. They'd need their strength.

Oppenheimer greeted them as soon as they walked in. Caleb gave his dog a weak smile, petting him softly. While his friends got situated, he walked across the room and stared out the window.

The sight of the strings had become so familiar, they were normal. They were part of the Chicago skyline. And they seemed so peaceful. There was no noise. No screaming or gunfire. No sirens or explosions. They were a silent killer strangling the city, and even now, most of the city didn't understand what was happening to them.

Wilson prepared a meal, and they ate in silence, passing around what could very well be their last supper. When they finished their first pot, the old man prepared second helpings. One way or another, they wouldn't be needing backup rations.

Bellies full, the five of them sat in a circle, staring at the fire. What words could they exchange at a time like this? What comforts or well wishes could dilute the truth of what was to come? So, instead, silence fell heavily.

Caleb stared into the flames, reflecting on the last year of his life. So much had changed in such a short amount of time, and yet it had all felt so long. Getting to know Heather and Wilson.

Discovering the strings. Confronting his grandfather. Being tortured by the Guild. His father's death. Those experiences had changed him. If he stood across from the man he was a year ago, would he even recognize himself?

"So much has changed," he said absentmindedly.

Heather bit her lip. "Caleb...do you wish I had never shown up at your doorstep?"

He glanced over, finding guilt in her eyes. "No," he admitted. "This year has been hard. Downright terrible. But...I think it's what was meant to be. And I don't mean in some sort of fate kind of way. Just that...being here next to you, Wilson, and Aalia trying to save this city...it was what needed to happen. No matter how this turns out."

"Yeah," she said, then dug into her pocket and produced a folded letter. "I need to ask you a favor. If...if something happens to me tomorrow, promise me you'll get this to my mom."

He frowned. He wanted to assure her that nothing was going to happen to her. That she'd was gonna make it through, no matter what. But he couldn't. All their lives were on the line. So, instead, he accepted the letter and stuffed it into his jacket. "I promise."

She nodded, her usual smile absent. He couldn't blame her. The situation they were in. The things they had seen. It would steal the cheer from anyone.

He tried to think of what else he could say. Instead, she moved closer and leaned against him. He reached his arm around her shoulder and held her tight. There was a comfort in her presence, in feeling her warmth against him. It didn't make the reality of what tomorrow would bring vanish, but it helped.

As the night wore on, the fire began to wane, and the four of them tried to sleep. Opp cuddled against his sleeping bag, and he kept an arm around his furry companion. Despite his exhaustion, he tossed and turned through a restless night.

The next morning, Caleb prepared breakfast after Wilson stepped outside their hideout. Corn and canned meatloaf was the meal of choice. He stirred the pots, trying to focus only on the food and not the task that lay before them.

An hour later, Wilson returned in a car he parked on the street. They ate in silence, and Caleb made sure to set some out for Opp. None of them bothered to clean the pots when they finished.

He donned his satchel, and triple checked his tome was inside. Aalia carried hers in her hands. Heather ensured her small piece of parchment was inside her boot. Wilson reloaded a few rifle magazines and donned in his gear.

After they finished preparing, he knelt in front of Opp, resting his head against his dog's temple. "It's going to be a rough day, buddy. But I know you'll look out for all of us."

Opp let out a playful yap and licked at his ear.

A smile took his face, and he looked over to his three companions. "This is it, I suppose."

"Let's go save Chicago," Heather said.

Without another word, the five them packed into the small car and took off towards Burnham Harbor.

Careful to dodge patrols, it took them two hours to cross the city. However, as Soldier Field came into view, he could see their destination. He wasn't sure how Burnham Harbor appeared normally, but presently it was a makeshift fort. Steel walls surrounded the whole harbor, topped with barbed wire and manned by armed sentries.

Soldier Field had also been altered. The floodlights atop the stadium now pointed outwards instead of in. Soldiers, tanks, and other military machinery sat in rows in the parking lot.

As they approached the harbor's walls, Caleb played their plan through his mind. As Miranda had said, they couldn't destroy the egg. The four of them were incapable of such a feat. They only had one card to play. Heather. Her father was the mastermind behind all of this. She had to get them close to him. He was the key.

Wilson stopped the car two hundred yards from the gate to the harbor. As they exited the vehicle, Caleb could see several Scribes on the wall pointing in their direction. Good, the Guild had noticed them.

With a snap of his fingers, he brought his tome out of his satchel. His scythe appeared in his hands, and he appreciated its familiar weight. Aalia summoned her staff, and Wilson brandished a knife.

Heather nodded to the old man and turned her back to him. Wilson then lowered his hand and placed the blade against her jugular.

Signaling for Opp to follow, they marched towards the harbor. His stomach twisted into knots and sweat dripped down his head. A cold wind blew in their faces, carrying the frantic voices of the Scribes on duty.

"Open the gate!" he yelled upon reaching it.

A flurry of shouts escaped from behind the barricade. Moments later, the sound of turning gears rumbled through the air, and the gate opened.

Hundreds of Scribes greeted them, their tomes out. Some of their tomes flipped through their pages, no doubt ready for an attack. Others, however, shifted uncomfortably, their faces painted with fear. They were downright terrified. He remembered Aalia's words about the common Guild Scribe not supporting this monstrous plan.

But none of them cast an incantation. Heather was right. Her father had ordered them all to stand down.

Without hesitation, their group of five waded through the sea of enemies, making their way towards a large platform on the peninsula. Each step felt like an eternity. He had never seen so many Scribes in one place. Scanning the whole harbor, he saw at least two thousand. All staring at him. Some probably hating him.

He tightened his grip on his scythe and swallowed past the lump in his throat. This had to be done.

As they moved further into the compound, he saw a truly heartbreaking sight. Stacks on stacks of metal cages. Many housed filken, some trapped elderon. Purple glyphs dotted each and every one.

This is where the Guild had kept the captives they used to create the strings. This is where Iibere had been held prisoner. All those creatures, forced into a life they had never asked for. Exploited by the Guild.

Pushing the image out of his mind, Caleb stepped up to the large platform that overlooked the harbor. They made their way up the stairs, and he could see the whole area clearly. The Guild members gathered around the platform like an audience, staring at the stage where Michael was waiting.

"Congratulations, abomination, you got Miranda to talk," the Head of the Guild said with mild frustration.

Caleb looked down at the mention of her name. Her screams filled his head.

Michael turned to face the harbor, pulling out a radio. At his command, dozens of cranes surrounding the water came to life and lifted in unison.

From the depths of the harbor emerged an enormous sphere of purple light. Sixty feet in diameter, the light it produced was blinding. This was it. The cursed object Caleb had been searching for all this time. The destination of over a million soul strings. A hydran egg.

Paying no attention to the display, Heather tapped on Wilson's hand. The old man lowered the knife from her neck. Without a wasted breath, she stormed towards her father and slapped him across the face.

Michael rubbed the red mark on his cheek.

Tears streamed down Heather's face as she glared up at the man. "I still haven't had the chance to scream at you!" she yelled. "How could you?"

As she spoke, Caleb directed his mind inward, opening his soul to his surroundings. The vast pressure of the soul emitting from the egg nearly floored him, but he kept his composure. Now was not the time to falter.

Michael opened his mouth to speak, but she slapped him again. She motioned to the Guild members and the strings that choked the city. "All of this is your fault! All the people that have died. Scott! And Mom! Because of you, she's in a hospital barely clinging to life!" She shoved him back a few steps. "Say something! I dare you to justify this to me."

"Heather," the man said, "this would have happened with or without me. The Guild can't be stopped. At least with me in charge, it can happen for the greater good."

Closing his eyes, Caleb stoked the golden flame of his soul. Focusing, he sought out Michael's.

She shook her head in disbelief. "So, Mom and everyone else has to die for your greater good?"

"Your mother getting sick was an...undesirable consequence.

But look at history, Mouse. Progress is always achieved by crossing an ocean of blood. It will be tragic. It will be horrible. But after this is all over, the world will be better for it. I promise you."

She stepped back, staring at her father in disgust. "I don't care what you promise. I care about what you do. And if your next action is anything other than putting a stop to this, I will never forgive you."

Pain crossed Michael's face. "It seems that I must sacrifice even your opinion of me for the world's sake." The man raised the radio to his lips.

But Caleb reacted first.

Flaring his soul, he forced it to connect to Michael's. A purple soul strings shot from his chest and into the man's.

Michael's eyes widened, and he fell to his knees. Perhaps this was the first time the man experienced having his soul stolen. Caleb didn't envy him.

He walked across the platform and stood over the Guild Leader. "Your soul is mine, Michael. Do what I say, and I'll release it."

Michael glared up at him, his breath growing ragged. "You swine!"

"Order the Guild to destroy the egg. All of them together, they can do it."

The man shook his head.

"Do it!" Caleb yelled, drawing more energy from the purple string.

Michael doubled over and clutched his chest. Finally, the man brought the radio up to his lips.

A deafening crack sounded through the harbor before Michael could speak. Green light washed over them, and Caleb unsummoned his scythe. The massive egg shook as fissures began to spread across its surface.

He watched in horror as the egg began to hatch.

End of Part Four

Part Five

Chapter Twenty-Five

Caleb was frozen in place. His head shook, denying the hatching egg in front of him. It couldn't be. They weren't too late. Please. They couldn't be too late.

But as the cracks along the sphere's surface spread, his heart thrashed against his ribcage. He had to run away. Had to get Heather out of danger. Now!

But he couldn't move. Even as he gasped for breath. Even as he stifled a scream in his throat. He had vowed to be a shield. How could he flee?

"You fool!" Michael screamed at him. "Release me! I'm the only one that can control it!"

Sweat pouring down his face, he stared at Heather's father. What choice did he have? Disappearing into his soul, Caleb severed the purple soul string that bound him to the Guild Leader.

Michael stood, his tome floating in front of him. The man gestured his hands like a showman and stepped towards the egg. Cheers and applause erupted from the crowd of Scribes below.

He tried to grasp the nature of their reaction. Was it peer-pressure or disillusionment that fueled their ignorance? Did they not know how much danger they were in? That this city was in?

Aalia ran across the stage and grabbed him by the shirt, pulling him close. "Fleischer, focus! We have to get Heather away from the harbor."

No words escaped him. He was unable to take his eyes off the disaster unfolding before him. And he knew what Aalia seemed to not.

There was no escape. Nowhere in Chicago was safe now. She was about to say more when a thunderous blast cut her off.

The egg shattered.

Fragments of light burst in every direction and spilled over the ground, vanishing. A massive creature, thirty yards tall and twenty yards wide, hovered where the egg had been moments before. Its body was dark green and bulbous with tiny hairs protruding sparsely across it. Six insectoid legs wriggled to life, and slimy fluid dribbled off them.

Four insect-like wings buzzed from its back, keeping it in the air. A small, oblong head rested atop its body. Two purple compound eyes vibrated and observed the world, and a pair of hairy, three-part antennae twisted and turned in every direction.

A hydran.

The millions of soul strings that had wrapped around the egg had vanished. The souls of Chicago had successfully incubated this beast, and the skyline was clear. Finally, after a year, the strings were no longer strangling the city. But this was nothing to celebrate.

Michael walked to the edge of the platform, staring up at the hydran. The man's tome flipped through its pages, and a wicked smile crossed his face. *"Hear me, fiend, I am god; I go where few have trod; Your free will I disband; Heed my every command!"*

Purple glyphs appeared all over the beast's body. Michael furrowed his brow in deep concentration, holding out his arms towards the creature. It screamed telepathically.

The high-pitched wail pierced Caleb's eardrums and brought most of the crowd to their knees. He fell to the ground, clutching his head. It was as if a stake were being driven through his skull. Through gritted teeth, he brought his vision back into focus just as the hydran tilted its head towards Michael. The glyphs on its body had vanished, and its screaming ceased.

Caleb sprang to his feet. With a powerful leap, he tackled Michael away just as the hydran shot a ray of red energy from between its antennae. The beam tore through the stage and shot deep into the earth.

Michael stared at him in disbelief. "You...you saved my life?"

Silence hung over the harbor. For a brief moment of peace, nothing moved. And then the hydran lurched forward. A never-ending series of energy beams discharged into the crowd. Panic spread like wildfire as the sea of Scribes broke into a stampede. Desperate screams filled the air as the people cried for help.

Caleb rolled off Michael and stared in horror as the hydran hovered over the harbor. Craters and corpses littered the ground like a warzone. The beast attacked indiscriminately, leaving no part of the crowd untouched.

Heather ran over to him, helping him to his feet. Goosebumps ran up her arms, and her face had gone deathly pale. "Caleb...what do we do?"

"I don't know," he admitted. There was nothing they could do.

Michael stood next to them, watching in horror. "The incantation...it didn't work."

He stared at the man, mouth agape at the sheer display of hubris. "Of course it didn't! You're just one man!"

Michael glared at him. "I am not just a man. I'm Michael Lancaster, Master Scribe, and the Head of the Guild of Life. I usurped the legendary Karl Fleischer. I was the only up and comer that could keep pace with Scott Fleischer. I am not capable of failure."

It was only then that Caleb realized how far the man had slipped into delusions of grandeur.

A barrage of incantations flew across the harbor at the hydran as the Guild desperately tried to kill it. Each attack bounced harmlessly off the beast's exoskeleton. It continued to hover, firing into the crowd.

Wilson ran over to them, his eyes wide and glued on the bulbous creature. "Can the military combat that thing?" he asked the group.

Caleb ducked under flying debris. "There hasn't been a hydran on the planet since the stone age."

It must have been hard for the old soldier, seeing one of the creatures for the first time. No doubt the whole city would be in a panic soon. And unlike Wilson, they'd have no explanation for the sudden appearance of a monster.

Michael looked over at the butler. "If the military has any chance, it has to be while it's still in its larval form. If it molts, there won't be any weapon the military has that can kill it."

"How long before it molts?" Aalia asked.

The Guild Leader's eyes narrowed at the young Scribe. "We have no idea. We let it gestate for two years, so it's had time to develop. It could molt in thirty seconds or thirty months. There's no way to know."

Caleb glanced down at his shaking hands. No matter how hard he tried to control them, they wouldn't stop shaking. A hollow coldness spread through his chest, and it took him a moment to figure out why.

It was quiet.

The hydran was no longer attacking. The beast's head tilted side to side as sporadic incantations pelted it. It rotated through the air until its gaze rested upon the skyscrapers comprising the heart of the city. It flew towards the buildings.

Caleb's gaze lingered on Chicago's skyline before resting on Soldier Field. The tanks, helicopters, and missile launchers. Then his head snapped to the Scribes still occupying the harbor. How many more were stationed throughout the city? Would it be enough?

He marched towards Michael, standing inches from the man. "What was the plan?"

The man's face grew red and hardened. His mouth remained tightly shut.

"Dad, answer him!" Heather yelled.

Her father's face contorted. "The plan was to control the monster. But seeing as how that fell through, we have to put it down. But it's not possible. I have three thousand Scribes stationed in the city."

Only three thousand? The man was a fool. It would take at least three times that many, and there were millions of Scribes in the Guild. Surely they would have had more to spare. And yet, here they were.

"I have an idea," he told everyone. "But the Guild has to do exactly what I say."

Contempt filled Michael's eyes. "Are you daring to order me, you abomin—"

Wilson threw a quick jab at the man's mouth. "You will not speak ill of Mister Fleischer, sir."

Michael stumbled back, his hand wiping blood from his mouth. The mention of his last name seemed to trigger some sort of primal rage in the Guild Leader. The man moved to speak, but Heather cut him off.

"Dad, this is your fault! All of it. The people that are dying right now have their blood on your hands. Put the Guild to use. Listen to Caleb."

The distaste did not fade from the man's eyes.

Caleb stared into them, unwavering. "It's either working with us or death."

Michael clenched his hands. "What's the plan?"

He frantically looked around. "We need a car. One that can carry all of us."

The Guild Leader produced a radio. "I need a vehicle at the platform now."

Trying to control his breathing, Caleb stared at the hydran as they waited. Sirens wailed in the distance, and helicopters took off from the stadium. He cursed under his breath. They needed to hurry before the military threw themselves at the beast in vain.

An SUV pulled up to the base of the platform, and a Scribe exited. Wilson took the driver's seat, and Michael sat next to him. He, Heather, and Aalia helped Opp into the rear and sat in the back.

"Where to Mister Fleischer?"

"Soldier Field," he said, looking at Michael. "You have contacts with the military here, right?"

"I did before the new general was stationed here," the man seethed. "He didn't take too well to me."

Caleb cursed. His plan hinged on the Guild getting them in with the army.

"I can get you inside, Mister Fleischer, if that's what you are needing."

"You sure?"

"Yes, sir."

He nodded and kept his eyes on the hydran. It had left the harbor and now floated over the smaller buildings in the area. Three helicopters rained machine gun fire upon the creature before unleashing a volley of missiles.

The weaponry deflected off the hydran, and it barely seemed to notice. Tanks approached from below, firing massive shells at it. It finally stopped and examined the machines attacking it. Tilting its head again, it studied them.

Red energy shot from between its antennae in a continuous stream, engulfing the helicopters and tanks alike.

Wilson pushed harder on the accelerator, and they sped towards the stadium. Even from within the SUV, Caleb could hear bullets and shells harmonizing with the screaming populace. Several stacks of black smoke rose in tall columns as the hydran continued its advance.

They pulled into the stadium parking lot. Soldiers surrounded the SUV screaming with their rifles raised. With their hands up, they exited the SUV and dropped to their knees.

"Civilians need to evacuate while the army deals with that... thing," a soldier yelled. "Why did you come here?"

Wilson looked the soldier in the eye. "Captain, in my left breast pocket, there is a wallet with an ID card. Please remove it."

The captain approached him. Reaching into Wilson's jacket, she produced the wallet and ID card. Her eyes grew wide. Another soldier glanced at the ID, his reaction mirroring the captain's.

"You recognize my name, correct?" Wilson asked them.

The captain nodded. In the background, Wilson's name carried from soldier to soldier, some even whispering, "Vietnam Bloodhound."

"Please," Wilson said, "take us to see your Commanding Officer. I have intel that is of vital importance."

The captain barked a few orders and shuffled them into the stadium. Men and women in uniform ran chaotically as a roar of voices consumed them. Soldiers pointed, yelled, and passed papers frantically.

They followed the captain deep into the stadium and out

onto the open space where the field was normally set up. A giant, temporary structure had stood to serve as the military's headquarters.

Rows of monitors and other equipment lined in the interior of the makeshift building. Most of the displays showed the hydran from various angles. Half the soldiers sat at desks and shouted into phones.

The captain helped them navigate the maze of desks and brought them to a muscular, elderly man. This man stood at the front of the room, inspecting the largest monitor with his hands folded behind his back. The captain saluted the man and spoke to him in a hushed voice.

It was hard to describe the air of authority that clung to the man. Any slight movement he made, the room seemed to move with him. Three silver stars adorned the collar of his camouflaged shirt. His silver hair and clean-shaven face were as sharp as his uniform.

The captain waved for them to approach. Wilson was the first to move, the rest of them keeping pace.

As they approached, the uniformed man's gaze shifted between Wilson and Michael, but his face was unreadable. "Willy?" the man asked.

"It's been a few years, Bobby."

The two men locked eyes a moment before embracing each other.

"Too long," the man said.

Wilson nodded and turned to the group. "Everyone, this is Lieutenant General Robert Cromwell. He's one of my oldest friends."

Bobby gave them all a curt nod. "Not to sour the mood, but the situation is going to hell in a handbasket. Why are you here? And it best not have anything to do with that snake." He motioned towards Michael.

"No, I'm here because of this young man," Wilson said. "This is Caleb Fleischer, and he's here to help."

Caleb grabbed his own arm as he stepped forward, not meeting the intimidating man's eyes. Words escaped him. His gaze shifted to the monitor that displayed the hydran.

Robert studied him for all of five seconds before shooting Wilson a questioning look.

"I know, I know," Wilson said, holding up his hands. "But listen to him."

The general nodded and looked at him. "Well, son?"

Still unable to speak, Caleb nearly took a step backward when he felt a soft hand interlocked with his. Heather stood behind him, giving him a reassuring glance. Her thumb softly rubbed over his fingers.

Clearing his throat, he stepped forward. "Sir, I have a plan for stopping that creature."

"Do you know what it is?"

"Yes sir, though I don't think we have time for the long explanation. If you're willing to accept that it's an immensely powerful beast from another world, we could skip to the part where we fight it."

"I can, but you'll owe me an explanation after this is all over. What's the plan?"

"I've seen missile launchers throughout the city. Do you have planes and other stuff that can deal a lot of damage?"

"We have a wide arsenal at our disposal that can deliver heavy payloads, yes."

"Are you able to time an attack all at once?"

The general nodded. "We have that capability, yes."

He considered his next words with care. "Throughout this city, there are people with...special abilities. If we can coordinate a strike between them and the military, it may just be strong enough."

Robert rubbed his chin and studied the large monitor on the wall. The man then faced Wilson. "You trust this young man?"

"With my life," Wilson answered without a moment of hesitation.

An unfamiliar lightness passed through Caleb's chest as Wilson's words echoed through his mind. It was only three words, but they tugged at his heart and brought tears to his eyes. But he fought them back. He'd have to process everything when this was over.

The general nodded. "We currently don't have a better plan other than deploying WMDs. I'm on board to try anything else."

"How long will it take you to get ready?" Caleb asked.

"At least forty-five minutes. Equipment will have to be moved and calibrated. I'll need to station soldiers to paint the target as well."

Forty-five minutes? He swallowed past a lump in his throat. That was so much longer than he had hoped. But he'd have to find a way to make it work. Nodding to the general, he faced Michael, giving him an expectant look.

"The Guild will do as I instruct, don't worry. We can coordinate a strike."

He took in a deep breath. "Okay then, we have a plan. General, do you have a radio I can borrow to communicate with you?"

Robert snapped his fingers. A moment later, a soldier brought a radio and handed it to him.

He clipped it to his windbreaker and faced Aalia. "Give me your Guild radio."

She complied.

"Alright," he said, "Heather, Michael, and Wilson. We'll go out and stall the hydran anyway we can until everyone is ready."

"One caveat," Robert chimed in, "Michael stays here. I know he's involved with this somehow, and I will not allow him to be on the loose.

Caleb's expression soured. He needed Michael to smooth the coordination with all the Scribes.

The Guild leader seemed to sense this as well. Producing his own radio, he said, "Attention Guild of Life, this is Alpha. Treat all orders coming from my daughter, codename..."

"Athena," she said.

"Codename Athena as if they are coming from me. This is absolute and binding."

Caleb nodded, satisfied, and gave Heather's hand a reassuring squeeze.

"What about me?" Aalia asked.

Wilson cleared his throat. "Miss Laghari, no doubt there will be sedition amongst the members of your organization. Some may be unhappy working with Mister Fleischer and Miss O'Brien. Go find senior members you trust. Organize them, disperse them amongst your people. Rally everyone to our plan."

Aalia nodded and walked up to Heather, embracing her and whispering something in her ear before vanishing into a portal.

As everyone else prepared, Caleb knelt and called Oppenheimer over. His dog rushed to him, and Caleb embraced him tightly. The two of them had been on so many adventures together. He always felt so invincible whenever he had his oldest companion around. But where they were going, Opp could not follow. What could a dog do against a hydran?

"Wait here for me, buddy," he said with a smile and a wink.

Opp let out a reassuring yelp and licked at Caleb's face.

It took all his willpower to stand, but he managed it. Looking over to Wilson and Heather, the three of them held each other's gaze for a long moment. His hands were still shaking.

"You guys ready?" he asked.

"Let's finish this, once and for all," she said.

"Lead the way, Mister Fleischer."

Chapter Twenty-Six

Black smoke engulfed the sky above Chicago. The hydran floated amongst the skyscrapers, paying no mind to the barrage of incantations colliding with its exoskeleton. Caleb sat in the rear of the SUV as they sped towards it. His eyes narrowed as he watched it. Something was out of place, but he couldn't put his finger on what.

Wilson swerved down an off-ramp, and Caleb jerked against the vehicle door. Military vehicles drove ahead and behind them, escorting them towards the beast. It was still ignoring all the attacks being volleyed at it. What was going on?

Taking a gamble, he looked over at Heather. "Tell the Guild to stop attacking."

She met his eye line for a moment before speaking into the radio. "This is Athena. Cease all attacks against the hydran."

Less than a minute later, the incantations had ceased. And he figured out what was off.

The hydran wasn't attacking anymore. The gargantuan creature hovered a few feet from an apartment building, slowly rising higher into the air. It almost looked as if it were studying the structure, tilting its head from side to side.

"What's it doing?" Wilson asked.

"I'm not sure," he responded. The creature had certainly displayed its ability for destruction, but every book he had read described them to be beasts of only rage and chaos. Yet it almost seemed calm. His mind drifted to Iibere.

Wilson reached back and put a firm hand on his knee. "Don't lose conviction, Mister Fleischer. We've seen what it's capable of. It is imperative we put it down."

He locked eyes with the old man through the rearview mirror. He knew Wilson was right, but it didn't make him feel any better.

"I am their shield," he whispered to himself.

In a little more than thirty minutes, they had driven to the streets beneath the hydran. It floated from building to building, inspecting each of them. They got out of the vehicle and looked up at it. The more he stared at it, the more his gut told him not to attack. Caleb couldn't put the reason into words. But he didn't have a choice. He had to save the city.

Pushing the feeling away, he looked at Heather. "Pass the plan on to the Guild."

"Attention, this is Athena," she said into the radio. "We're coordinating an attack on the hydran with the military. In fifteen minutes, on my signal, all Guild members will attack the hydran. Find a high up position where you can see it."

Within seconds, portals opened on the tops of the buildings around them. With a snap of his fingers, Caleb summoned his tome. He focused on the top of the building the hydran was presently inspecting. Muttering the words under his breath, he created a portal in front of him and his companions.

Heather helped Wilson as they stepped forward and onto the roof of the skyscraper. Five other Scribes occupied the space with them, each staring at him in confusion and fear. It was better than contempt, at least.

The buzzing of the hydran's wings drowned out the loud wind that swept over them. The area surrounding Burnham was ablaze. The flames danced violently, and more smoke spewed into the air. Fires also dotted the beast's path from the harbor to downtown. This was it. The proof of what the hydran was capable of. He couldn't let any more destruction come to this city.

A pair of antennae poked over the top of the building. Within seconds, the whole of the beast was above them. Panicked gasps sounded behind him.

Looking back, he saw the other Scribes' tomes flipping through their pages. He held his hand up, stopping them. They looked at him as if he were crazy, but he held his hand firm and shook his head. Their expressions scrunched, but they nodded.

Caleb's heart raced as he faced the hydran. With deliberate slowness, he extended his arms in a non-threatening gesture. He directed his tome to float behind him, out of the creature's view. He took small steps forward, keeping his gaze steady.

"Work with me here," he whispered.

The hydran stared at him as he closed the gap. Its buzzing wings kept it in place, and its compound eyes shifted in and out of focus.

"You don't want to hurt anyone, do you?" He swallowed past a dry throat as his toes reached the edge of the roof.

The hydran was only a few feet away from him. His mind raced, and he fought every survival instinct that urged him to run. He leaned towards it. Unlike a filken, it didn't smell rancid. It smelled familiar. Almost like freshly cut grass.

Tilting his head back, he met its gaze. It had no humanoid facial features, but there was something familiar in how it looked at him. That look is what stayed his hand from attack.

Without taking his eyes off the hydran, he asked, "Wilson, how much time until the attack?"

"Eight minutes, Mister Fleischer."

So little time. Was it enough to call off the attack? He'd have to change everyone's mind. Convince them of what he believed.

With sweat dripping off his face, Caleb reached up a hand. "Please," he whispered.

The hydran shifted its focus to his hand, studying it curiously. The pitch of its wings grew softer as it leaned forward slightly.

"It's okay," he said, trying to hide his anxiety. His heart thudded in his ears.

Unwilling to back down, he placed his hand on its face. Its exoskeleton was surprisingly cold, nearly freezing, but he didn't back away. With caution, he petted the creature.

Slow, almost gentle clicks filled his mind. He smiled and continued to rub its face, a sense of relief flooding him.

A yell echoed from another building. Before he could react, a bolt of lightning struck the hydran in the middle of its body.

The creature reeled back and let out a terrifying shriek. There was no sign of damage, but it buzzed around frantically nonetheless.

Clutching the sides of his head, Caleb fell to a knee as its wail tore his mind apart. Dozens of incantations shot at the creature from various directions, crashing into it.

Desperate, he turned to Heather and yelled, "Tell everyone to stop attacking, now!"

She spoke the order into the radio, and the incantations stopped, but it was too late. The hydran faced one of the buildings that had attacked it. Caleb forced an incantation into his head, and his tome flipped to a new page.

"Traveling through time and space; Fly me to another place."

A bolt of red energy shot straight at the cowering Scribes that had attacked the beast. His portal tore open directly in front of them, capturing the energy and sending it up through the sky.

He hoped beyond hope that the hydran would calm down. That its attack had only been a reflexive response. But it shrieked again and opened fire. Glass shattered and concrete crumbled as screams consumed the city.

"I'm sorry," he muttered under his breath. "Heather, I need your soul."

Without looking back, he opened his own to the world. As he did, he cast a new portal incantation. The first appeared directly beneath the hydran, large enough for it to pass through while the second formed amongst the clouds.

Heather's spirit reached out to him, and he accepted it, creating a golden connection with her. The strength and power of her soul fused with his, and he rose to his feet, a new incantation in mind.

His tome opened to the final page with writing. Pouring his soul into the phrase, he locked eyes with his father's final gift. The incantation the man had given him before his death.

He focused on the portal among the clouds, and drawing a powerful breath, he yelled, *"Bear witness to my one-track soul; I trap this fiend in a black hole."*

Above the portal, a small sphere of golden light appeared. It hung stationary a moment before pulsating and spinning. Purple light appeared from thin air and shot towards the sphere. It grew larger and larger, fading from gold to violet. It sucked air towards it like a vacuum and grew forty yards in diameter.

Even in the city below it, he could feel the suction pulling on him, his hair waving wildly. Thanks to his portal, however, the hydran felt the incantation's influence up close.

It was pulled immediately through the gateway and straight into the large sphere. He closed the portals, trying to limit the effect on the city. Even still, the buildings shook as glass and rubble were sucked into the air.

The hydran's screech tore through their minds as it struggled against the suction. He gritted his teeth, drawing massive amounts of energy from his connection to Heather. The creature fought against their very souls, and it took everything to keep the beast from moving.

"Three minutes, Mister Fleischer."

Caleb nodded. His legs shook and felt like jelly. A stabbing pain tore through his mind. Never had a single incarnation put such a strain on him. He forced his eyes to open wide and refused to blink, afraid that if he broke eye contact for a moment, he'd lose control of the hydran.

"Heather, tell the Guild to get ready," he yelled.

She spoke into the radio, but he couldn't make out her words.

His skull felt as if it were splitting in half. His heart raced, and his eyes stung from exposure, but he held firm. In a few minutes, it would all be over. This last year, everything he'd been through...it could all end. Here and now. And then he could go home.

"One minute, Mister Fleischer."

His knees slammed into the roof. His chest burned, and he could hardly take a breath. But his concentration remained intact. So close. So close.

"The military is firing," Wilson yelled.

A succession of explosions sounded from every direction. Distant objects blurred straight at the hydran.

"Twenty seconds until impact!" Wilson shouted.

His body felt as if it were on fire. Taking a labored breath, he yelled, "Heather, now!"

She spoke into the radio.

"Ten seconds until impact!"

His mind screamed for relief, but he did not relent.

Thousands of voices called out in unison. The red lights of tomes dotted Chicago like ornaments. A storm of attacks rose out of the city like a magical flood as every offensive incantation possible rushed towards the hydran.

'Five seconds until impact!"

He let out a desperate scream. Through sheer force of will, he directed his mind, body, and soul to maintain the incantation. His fingers dug into his legs, drawing blood.

The missiles, incantations, shells, and every other attack hit the hydran in a crescendo of destruction. A shockwave shattered every window in the city as an explosion surged from the epicenter.

The blast threw Caleb to his back, but he clamped down harder on the incantation in his mind. The giant violet sphere sucked in the fires of the detonation, preventing them from consuming the city.

And then everything went quiet, and ash fell from the sky. Finally, he released the incantation. Every fiber of his being celebrated the absence of the burden, and he glanced up at the massive cloud of smoke hanging over Chicago. Closing his eyes, he tried to catch his breath.

Cheers and applause erupted from the city, but Caleb's stomach turned over itself. He wished he hadn't had to kill the creature. What other choice had there been, though?

Heather and Wilson knelt on either side of him, wrapping their arms around him. She rubbed his back while the old man helped him back to his feet.

He released his golden connection to Heather, giving her soul back to her. The roof swayed beneath his feet, and it took him a moment to adjust. That incantation had taken more out of him than he had thought.

It had been nearly a year since Heather had shown up at his door and enlisted him to save her mother. Although the task had led down an unpredictable path, the enormous weight of it was finally off his shoulders.

Once and for all, he could stop being a Scribe. His life would return to its quiet, normal—

A piercing screech filled their minds. Beams of crimson energy shot out of the smoke cloud. The hydran emerged from the haze, its exoskeleton cracked all over and two of its wings missing.

The fractures on the beast's skin spread and widened before shattering in every direction. Where its massive, bulbous body had once floated, a small figure now hovered.

It stood only ten feet tall with a somewhat humanoid figure. Its oval-shaped body was strangely muscular. Dark green, it had a slight purple sheen to it. Four powerful, single-joint arms had replaced its six legs. Each limb was capped off with a three-part pincer.

Just as he had always seen in his grandfather's book, a round head rested upon a short neck. Two small, compound eyes rested in the center of its head, and their red color contrasted with the purple antennae jutting from its head. Six insectoid wings flapped at an imperceptible speed, holding the creature in the air.

He stared at it with a blank face and sullen heart. They hadn't killed the hydran. It had molted into an adult.

Chapter Twenty-Seven

Terror. No other word could describe the blanket of fear that covered Chicago. Absolute terror.

Caleb stood motionless as the hydran stretched its new body. It floated side to side as it looked at its own pincers, clamping them open and shut repeatedly.

Once more, an uncomfortable feeling confronted him that he could not place. Something in its behavior didn't sit right in its gut. What were his instincts trying to tell him?

But the feeling didn't matter. They had failed. He had sold the city on a plan, giving them hope that they could survive, and now he had robbed them of that hope. His grandfather's voice rampaged through his mind, asking him what he had expected to happen. He clenched his fists, and his eyes began to sting.

The hydran raised one of its pincers. A dense crimson ball of energy formed above it. Caleb stared helplessly as it threw the sphere towards the outskirts of the city.

The energy rocketed towards the shorter buildings that

dotted the area. The instant it made contact, it exploded into a scorching red dome that consumed the area.

His eyes widened, and he could feel the heat of the blast from where he sat. A crater nine blocks wide was all that remained when the explosion had cleared.

How...how many people had just died in the blink of an eye? Debris and ash rained upon the city. All the stories hadn't been wrong. It could destroy them all.

If he didn't stop it.

Screams tore from the city below. Caleb's gaze shot down to see the air itself split open. Stretching for hundreds of yards, a jagged portal opened to a foreign, crimson sky. The Speculon. The strength of the hydran's soul had torn a hole in the barrier.

A chorus of telepathic howls escaped from the portal as beasts of the Speculon crawled through, twisting from their inverted realm and onto the Chicago streets. Hundreds of filken and dozens of elderon swarmed the city, attacking anything that moved.

Iibere's voice rang through his thoughts. *Forgive the crimes you have seen my kin commit. It is easy to sin when you are starving to death.*

Columns of smoke rose from every part of the city. Spheres of crimson energy flew out in every direction, tearing through buildings. Wails harmonized with the explosions as the assault on Chicago truly began.

Desperate cries screamed as bodies fell from buildings. One smaller building collapsed in on itself, spewing a tidal wave of dust and ash onto the streets.

Caleb felt sick to his stomach. Everything he had feared had come to pass and more. People were dying. Clenching his fists, he stood. He had to do something. Anything.

"Heather," he said, "tell the Guild to assist the military with the rift. The soldiers won't be able to see those creatures. Wilson, work with her to coordinate the defense."

They both frantically spoke into their respective radios. He turned his attention back to the hydran and nearly fell over, the roof spinning beneath his feet. If he took a single step, he was sure he'd collapse. Taking a breath, he looked up at the floating beast.

The hydran wasn't attacking at the moment, but how long

would that last? After seeing what one of its attacks was capable of, he knew he couldn't give it a chance to strike again.

Heather looked at him with soft green eyes. She took his hand in her own, giving it a worried squeeze. He leaned into her, appreciating her warmth and stability. His mind, body, and soul were exhausted, and he wanted nothing more than to sleep. But the massive weight was on both his eyelids and shoulders.

"What about the hydran?" she asked him.

Taking in a deep breath, Caleb's tome flipped through its pages. He pulled their personnel radio from his satchel, clipping it to his jacket. He then asked one of the Scribes on the roof for their Guild radio before sending them down to fight at the rift.

With both radios hanging from his windbreaker, he looked back to the hydran. "Heather," he said, "please open your soul to me again."

She squeezed his hand harder. "You can't, Caleb. It'll kill you. You can't fight it."

He turned to her. Defeat consuming him, he pierced her with desperate eyes. "If I don't, who will?"

She didn't respond, tears streaking down her face.

"Heather, please. I have to try." He had to be Chicago's shield.

Letting go of his hand, she nodded and backed away. Her soul opened to him. Even from a few feet away, its abnormal strength and warmth washed over him. Reaching out with the rest of his own, a golden connection formed between them.

Her energy flooded him, and he felt renewed. Closing his eyes, he took a single moment for himself. A brief, peaceful reprieve. But it passed. The city needed him.

Filling his lungs with air, he yelled, *"From sky to page; Feel the storm's rage."*

A river of lightning shot from his tome, consuming the hydran in a flash. Squinting, he saw no damage on the creature. Even the exponential power of their two souls wasn't enough to harm it. But its attention was now focused on him.

Under his breath, he muttered his strength and speed enhancements. Crouching, he jumped from building to building, air and smoke rushing past him. He had to lead the creature away from Heather and Wilson.

He landed on a new roof, the concrete cracking beneath

his feet. The hydran's compound eyes were still fixated on him. Holding out his hands, he summoned his scythe and brought a third incantation into his mind, the golden string allowing his mind to handle the burden with ease.

Another stream of lightning sprang from his tome, and the hydran flew around it, zooming forward. Undeterred, Caleb cast a portal directly in the creature's path. Another opened to his right. The hydran traveled through the openings and appeared directly in front of him. Pouring their souls into his muscles, Caleb swung his scythe with all his strength at its head.

With nearly imperceptible speed, the hydran spun around the strike. His blade dug into the roof as the creature soared away from him.

Removing his blade from the pavement, he released the portal incantation. His tome flipped through its pages, and he muttered, *"I am king of this stage; Chains will be your cage."*

A yellow glyph formed beneath his feet. The circle of light spun, and a dozen crystalline chains slithered out like serpents. They shot out towards the hydran, trying to ensnare it.

The buzz of its wings rose in pitch as it darted through the air around the chains. Furrowing his brow, Caleb maintained his focus as the chains formed a web around the beast.

They circled and spun around it, but no matter what they turned or shape they took, the hydran evaded their clutches. Refusing to concede, he brought a fourth incantation into his mind, his thoughts straining only slightly.

A minuscule portal opened behind him after he spoke the words. A new chain formed from the glyph and shot through it, appearing from the second portal behind the hydran. It flanked the creature, wrapping around its lower arm.

Stopping in place, the hydran stared curiously at the light wrapped around its limb. Within a second, the twelve other chains ensnared the beast, constricting it. The creature didn't struggle against them, simply staring at them instead.

Caleb didn't waste a moment. Releasing the portals, he pulled a new phrase into mind. *"From fossil in soil; I have now struck oil."*

A jet-black glyph formed in front of him, aimed at the hydran. A geyser of oil spewed at the creature, engulfing it in seconds. Once it was covered, he released the incantation and immediately brought in another one. *"By mark of brimstone; Be scorched to the bone."*

A large ball of fire ten feet in diameter shot out of his tome, flying towards the oil-soaked creature. But he wasn't finished yet, bringing a final incantation into his thoughts. Through gritted teeth and a sweaty brow, he screamed, *"From breeze to gale; Feel the sky's wail."*

The air around his tome spun, spiraling into a gust of wind. It consumed the fireball as it fled towards the hydran. The rotating oxygen in the gale turned the ball of fire into a swirling vortex of flames.

The firestorm consumed the hydran, igniting both it and the oil that covered it. Its surprised wail filled Caleb's mind.

Scythe firmly in his hands, he jumped towards the inferno. He poured his and Heather's soul into the strength enhancement. With the creature distracted by the flames, he swung his weapon down on its skull.

His blade bounced off its exoskeleton with a resonating clank, not so much as denting it. Seemingly amused no longer, the hydran burst from its chains and backhanded him with a pincer.

The simple swat knocked the air completely from his lungs, even with his golden string fueled enhancement. He flew back towards the building he had leaped from. Smashing through a window, his body tore through several stories of concrete, carpet, and desks.

One of the floors eventually didn't give way, only cracking from catching him. He writhed back and forth on the ground, clutching his ribs, trying to draw a breath. His enhancement had kept him alive, but pain burned through his body.

Coming to his knees, he coughed up a small pool of blood, gasping as he tried to inhale. The attack had been the equivalent of a light slap, and it had nearly killed him. The hydran had been humoring him as if this were playing a game.

"Caleb? Caleb, are you okay?" Heather's voice came in over their personal radio.

Reaching up to the device, he managed to mutter, "I'm alive."

Cursing under his breath, he crawled across the carpeted office he found himself in. Even in this skyscraper, the sound of gunshots and screaming reached his ears. He had to trust that the Guild and military were keeping the creatures spewing from the rift contained. One problem at a time.

Reaching the window, he came to his feet using the glass as support. Resting his head against the cold surface, he looked upwards to see the hydran swatting out the last of the fire that had engulfed it.

Despite everything he had thrown at the beast, it barely appeared as if he had inconvenienced it. Shaking his head, he took a few breaths, trying to form some semblance of a plan. Even with the golden connection, he was reaching his limit. Anything he tried would have to be quick and powerful. His tome floated in front of him but did not flip through any pages. No ideas came to him.

The hydran raised one of its arms and opened the three parts of its pincer. A dense crimson ball formed with the creature's gaze locked onto the area of the city he, Heather, and Wilson currently occupied.

His heart raced, and panic flooded him. He couldn't portal it away if he didn't know where or when it was going to throw the attack. And from what he saw before, the attack moved too fast for him to intercept.

He released his strength and speed incantations, nearly collapsing without them. His tome flipped through its pages, only one idea coming to him. *"Stay still your highness; I will now bind us."*

A yellow glyph appeared beneath them both as barriers wrapped around them. Despite the seal, the hydran continued to move, the barrier around it warping with its movements. Caleb's eyes widened, and he held the incantation's phrase twice in his mind, doubling its effect.

The hydran still moved. It raised its arm, readying to throw the attack. Tears formed in his eyes as he held the sealing incantation a third time in his thoughts. The beast visibly slowed, but it still raised its arm higher into the air, its head snapping his direction.

Desperate, he held the incantation four times. Five times. Six. Ten. He pushed his connection with Heather to its limit, but now it felt as if his consciousness was fracturing. And no doubt Heather was feeling the burden even more. If he pushed any further, she might have not consciousness.

But the hydran was stationary.

"Please," he begged, tears streaming down his face.

The crimson ball of energy dissipated as the hydran let out a high-pitched shriek. Its body vibrated against the barrier confining it before it shattered like glass. The creature flexed and stretched its arm and stared at him.

It flashed forward and rammed a pincer through the glass. He wanted to jump out of the way, but his body wouldn't move. He had no strength left. The hydran pulled him through the window and out of the building.

Outside once more, the orchestra of bullets, shouting, and screaming throughout the city washed over him. The rift sat in the street beneath them. The number of beasts emerging had gone down significantly, though a few still leaked through.

His body went limp in the hydran's pincer as its grip steadily tightened. His muscles strained as it clamped down on him. But the pain barely registered as Caleb met the creature's eyes. It glanced at him curiously, its hairy antennae rubbing over his face.

Survival instincts kicking in, he reached up and tried to pry the pincers away from his body. He had to get free. He had to keep fighting. He had to save everyone.

But the creature's grip did not budge. Clenching his jaw, he pulled harder and harder as the hydran studied him.

His arms felt like they were made of jelly. Taking in a breath, he summoned the resolve for one last burst of effort. Nothing. Heather's voice came over the radio, but he couldn't make out the words. It was time to give up.

Caleb closed his eyes and let his arms fall to his side.

Chapter Twenty-Eight

The cold December air surrounded Caleb like an unwelcome hug. He hung hundreds of feet above the ground, just over the tops of the Chicago's skyscrapers. An explosion ruptured a few blocks away. He clenched his eyes shut as the hydran clamped down harder on his torso.

He counted his heartbeats as he waited for the end. He struggled to make out Heather's voice as she screamed repeatedly through their personal radio. He wanted to reach up and respond, but his body refused his orders. Even with her soul sustaining him, he was running on empty.

After sixty heartbeats, he opened his eyes. The hydran was still staring at him, tilting its head to the side. Its grip tightened. Was it trying to see how much pressure he could endure? How hard it could squeeze until he popped?

The pain increased, but he kept his face blank, not wanting to indulge the creature's curiosity. Once more, he tried to pry himself free, but it was no use. Even if he did manage to release its grip, it would only result in him falling into the rift.

He met the beast's eyes. "Please, just get it over with."

The hydran cocked its head to the other side when he spoke. Several random clicks sounded in his mind as if it were trying to speak back. Hydrans could speak, but it seemed this one was still too young. He stared at it, confused, as its grip tightened even further.

He gasped with pain and scrunched his face. It was all he could do to keep himself from screaming. Opening his mouth, he prepared to plead again with the beast.

But Heather's voice over the Guild radio cut him off. "Guild of Life, this is codename Athena. Right now, many of you are helping the military push back against the Speculon. You are putting your lives on the line, and that makes what I'm going to ask that much harder.

"At this very moment, Caleb Fleischer, son of Scott Fleischer and the Guardian of Death, grandson of Karl Fleischer, is in the hydran's clutches. He is there because of me, because a year ago I dragged him to this city to save my mother. Once he discovered the soul strings, he stayed in Chicago because he saw it as his duty. When the Guild sent an elderon to kill him, he didn't run and hide; he stayed and fought for the people of this city. When he learned he'd be opposing the entire might of the Guild, he didn't give up.

"I know you've been taught to hate Caleb. That he's an abomination. That he should be feared. I may not be able to change your mind here and now, but I can tell you what I have seen. I have seen him bleed, suffer, and struggle for the sake of others. You've seen what the Guild has caused today, so atone for your transgressions. Open your souls to Caleb and lend him your collective strength. Either we all climb out of this hell together, or we doom ourselves and millions of others to death."

He listened, her words tugging at his chest. There was no response over the Guild radio. Against his gut instinct, he opened his soul. No other souls opened for him to connect with.

Her words had been kind and heartfelt. They had been desperate and sincere. But he knew it would take more than words to convince people that he wasn't a monster. It would take more to show his birthright wasn't to be feared.

How could he expect others to open their souls to him when

it had taken over two decades for him to accept himself?

The Guild radio cackled. "I believe in Caleb Fleischer." It was Aalia's voice.

Hundreds of yards away, a soul opened to him. Reaching out with his spirit, he connected to it, and a golden string stretched out into the distance. Sudden warmth and strength flooded his body, giving him renewed energy.

Gritting through the pain of the hydran's grip, he reached and tried to pry the pincer open. It wouldn't budge.

"I believe in Caleb Fleischer," Michael O'Brien's voice came over the radio, a slight tinge of repugnance hanging on the words.

Another soul in the direction of the stadium availed itself to him. Caleb connected to that one as well, more power accompanying it.

More and more voices trickled over the radio like the first drops of rain before a storm. Two...three...seven souls opened to him. He connected to them all, pulling harder and harder against the hydran's grip.

Then, all at once, an imperceptible amount of chatter echoed over the radio as hundreds of individuals spoke at once, calling out their belief in him. Tears welled up in Caleb's eyes as he struggled to understand his own emotions. Thousands of souls opened around him. All in all, a majority of the three thousand Scribes in Chicago availed their souls to him.

Golden soul strings wrapped around his body like a robe of light, its fibers extending out in every direction. Out into the city itself. Power surged through Caleb like he had never felt, never even known possible. It was as if an ocean of adrenaline and strength was pumping into him. His eyes widened, and his limbs twitched to life.

His tome floated next to him. Caleb yelled out his strength incantation and strained against the hydran's grip. He grunted, and the hydran shrieked as he pulled its pincer enough to create a gap. He delivered a powerful kick to the creature's body and freed himself.

He fell towards the rift, the hydran just staring at him. His tome flew down after him, flipping to a new page.

"With birds, I'd like to share; Being lighter than air," he muttered.

A yellow glyph formed around his waist, and he hovered in

place. With the aid of every Scribe's soul, he was able to control the incantation with exact precision.

Rotating through the sky, he positioned himself to face the hydran with renewed determination. All around the city, the sounds of the military fighting off filken and elderon echoed. While the Guild members were sharing their souls with him, their attention was no doubt still on with helping the soldiers.

The hydran was his responsibility.

He flew straight at the beast, slamming his shoulder against its exoskeleton. His arms wrapped around its body, and he pushed it out towards Lake Michigan. The further it was from the city, the safer everyone would be.

For several hundred yards, he managed to push it back before for it grabbed onto him. With a tug, it ripped him away and threw him through the air. Cursing, he used his flight incantation to stop his momentum and shot back at the hydran. He tried to grab it once more, but it dodged. Each time he tried to trap it, it danced around him, playful clicks filling his mind as it did.

Caleb reached out towards it, shouting his speed incantation as he moved. With a sudden burst of speed, he grabbed the creature's arm, feeling its cold exoskeleton. Before he could move it, the beast slammed an arm straight into his back.

Pain surged through his torso, and the blow propelled him downwards. Air rushed past him as he fell, everything around him turning into a blur. He pumped everyone's soul into his strength enhancement just as he crashed straight through the top of a skyscraper.

He plowed through the hundreds of floors and crashed into the ground in seconds. His enhancement had prevented any serious injury, but a piercing ringing buzzed in his ears. His vision faded in and out for a moment before he regained his focus. Only now was he beginning to understand how much the hydran had been toying with him before.

Caleb shook his head, trying to get his bearings when a long, ominous creak tore through the building. The structure had already taken a lot of damage before he had crashed through it. Its supports began to shake, and it seemed to moan, barely able to keep standing.

Eyes wide, he flew out of the door and onto the street. The building was about to collapse in on itself, teetering back and forth. Citizens ran through the street, running towards an army convoy as filken chased them.

He yelled at them to get away from the skyscraper. Then more screams reached his ears. Dozens of people stood on the top floors of the building, waving for help. One person fell.

Gritting his teeth, he flew up as his tome flipped to a new page. The falling man's screams filled the air as he reached him. Matching his speed to the man's descent, Caleb caught him and leveled out. The young man clung to him desperately, crying.

The building let out another wail. Focusing his soul onto it, he yelled, *"I am king of this stage; Chain will be your cage."*

A massive golden glyph formed around the base of the entire structure. Thousands of golden chains shot out of it, wrapping around the interior and exterior of the building, stabilizing it.

His tome flipped to a new page. *"Summoned from frozen Hell; The winter citadel."*

All around the skyscraper, white glyphs formed. Gargantuan columns of ice grew out of them, growing out to the building, holding it in place.

He landed next to an army unit and set the man down. "Keep him safe," he told them. "And get some backup to evacuate this building. I don't know how long it'll stay—"

A powerful force launched into him and lifted him off the ground. The hydran wrapped its four arms around Caleb's body as they flew higher into the air. Its hold on him was tight as if it were afraid of him trying to escape.

Even as it carried him away, Caleb maintained his incantations holding the collapsing building. The army needed time to evacuate everyone. As he did, he struggled against the beast's arms. Unable to escape, he brought his head back and crashed it into the hydran's face.

A surprised shriek escaped it, and its grip loosened. Throwing his arms out, Caleb broke free and flew back, putting distance between them.

Holding out his hands, he summoned his scythe. The hydran studied him and tilted its head to the side before letting out an angry, telepathic scream. In a flash, it was in front of him, throwing a powerful punch at his chest.

He dodged to the left, but the attack clipped his shoulder,

sending him into a spin. Before he could even out, another blow slammed him from above, sending him back down towards the city. He had fallen a few dozen yards when the hydran appeared beneath him, landing another punch into his gut.

Blood and vomit shot out of his mouth as the attack launched him back up into the air. Pain spread through his stomach, and he tightened his grip on his scythe. The hydran came at him from every angle, throwing powerful attacks at every part of his body. Each time he tried to counterattack, the creature had vanished and was coming at him from a new direction.

The blows piled up, and his body turned black and purple. Muttering under his breath, he created a portal underneath him. Escaping through it, he floated a few hundred yards away from the beast, trying to take a momentary reprieve.

But there could be no escape. The hydran's head snapped in his direction, and it barreled towards him.

It hadn't moved more than thirty yards before a chorus of a thousand voices echoed from the city below. The Guild, united with their connection through him, launched a wave of simultaneous incantations from every part of Chicago. The hydran shrieked as it weaved in and out of the thousands of attacks. There were too many, however, and they consumed it.

Heather's voice came in over their personal radio. "Caleb, the Guild and the military have pushed the majority of the filken and elderon back. There are no more coming through the portal. We're not sure why; maybe something on the other side is stopping them. The Guild has been working on another idea. Hold on a little longer, okay?"

He nodded, only to remember she wasn't standing next to him. Taking in a deep breath, he watched as the hydran emerged from the swarm of incantations. It raised one of its pincers and formed a red ball of energy.

Pouring energy into the flight incantation, Caleb soared towards the creature, brandishing his scythe. It readied to throw its attack, and he swung his weapon. He caught the creature midswing, his blade snagging the hydran's wrist.

Even with his enhanced strength, the scythe only partially cut its exoskeleton. But he interrupted its momentum, and it accidentally threw the ball of energy straight up instead of down. The red sphere flashed through the air and exploded, consuming much of the sky for several seconds.

Drops of purple blood trickled down the hydran's wrist. It let out a series of angry clicks and flashed around Caleb, the movement so fast it blurred. Another volley of jabs tore into him, and pain quaked through his body.

As he tried to dodge the attacks, something pricked in the back of his mind. Thousands of new souls were opening across the city. The souls were weak, far weaker than a Scribes, but in thirty seconds, there were over ten thousand of them, with more appearing every moment.

"Caleb," Heather's voice said over the radio, "the Guild has gathered the evacuees and helped them open their souls. Chicago is with you."

Closing his eyes, Caleb reached out to the souls. They were appearing so fast he couldn't keep track of them. It was hard to believe so many people were able to give such blind trust. But the last year had made the people of this city desperate.

Hundreds of thousands of golden soul strings joined the ones he had already created. He looked around at the new skyline. Golden soul strings fell over the city like a blanket. They wrapped around every building and shot from every citizen's chest. After a year of being plagued, confined, and oppressed, Chicago was fighting back.

Caleb flew after the hydran, catching up to it in an instant. Wrapping his arms around the massive creature, he tried to direct it towards the lake. Its pincers clamped down on his torso, and it threw him off.

Cursing under his breath, he weaved in and out of the hydran's oncoming attacks. His speed now outmatched its, but he was physically weaker. But the advantage was his if he kept his wits about him.

The hydran must have come to the same realization. It let out a desperate screech and thrashed out with all four of its pincers. He ducked and weaved around the attacks, circling the beast.

He swung his scythe at its back. It partially dodged but still suffered a shallow wound. As it cried out once more, he brought a new incantation into his mind. Through the golden strings, he could feel the other Scribes do the same.

A gigantic fireball launched from his tome after he spoke the words. A thousand voices sang from the city below. Incantations flew up and joined his, surrounding and consuming the hydran.

From within the storm of spells, he could hear it shriek, no doubt trying to avoid as many attacks as it could. While he floated and watched, the same uncomfortable feeling crept into his gut as earlier. An unease about the attack. What was wrong?

Before he could place the source of the feeling, it escaped from the mass of attacks and flew straight up. He chased after it with blinding speed, the city just a blur of color beneath him.

Once upon the creature, he swung his scythe down, severing off one of its arms. The Hydran writhed in pain as he circled underneath of it, slamming the butt of his staff into its face. Its exoskeleton cracked.

And then a sound he had never heard before resonate in his mind. It was soft. It was melodic. And it was heartbreaking.

The hydran was crying.

It slowly floated away from him, its three remaining hands clutching its face as it convulsed in pain. Purple blood rained down on the city from its multiple wounds. Looking down, he saw they had circled right back above the rift to the Speculon.

Readying his weapon, he moved to strike the final blow, wanting to give it a quick and painless death. But when he tried to fly, his body refused his commands. Something about the hydran stopped him, the same sickening feeling that had plagued him since it had hatched.

It looked at him, its compound eyes vibrating softly. It made distinct clicking sounds in his mind as if it were trying to speak to him.

And then, finally, after all this time, he figured it out. Why it made him uncomfortable. And he knew what he had to do. Reaching up to the Guild radio pinned to his jacket, he pushed the button to talk.

“Evacuate any remaining people in a ten-block radius around the rift. Do it as quickly as you can.”

Chapter Twenty-Nine

Scribes barked orders over the radio, and military vehicles sped through the city. While the military evacuated the remaining citizens, Caleb stared at the wailing hydran. Purple blood covered parts of its exoskeleton and poured from the stub where one of its arms had been. It writhed and wriggled in pain, letting out chirps that resembled sobs.

It reaffirmed his conclusion. All this time, something about the way it behaved had bothered him. Something in the way it moved. In the way it sounded and acted. It reminded him of something else. Something different than the monsters the hydran had been portrayed as by his grandfather.

This hydran had only been born an hour ago. It was a child. Even if it had molted into its adult body, it still had no sense of the world. It couldn't speak yet and had no bearing of its surroundings. The first thing it ever experienced was being attacked and controlled. Any other living creature would have acted the same. He would have acted the same.

How could Caleb kill it knowing this? But it couldn't stay in the city. Its potential for destruction was too great. Too many lives depended on him, and he couldn't simply walk away. He had to be their shield. But there was a third choice.

He floated towards the creature, holding out a gentle hand. It uncovered its face and glared at him. It shrieked and charged him, lashing out with its three remaining pincers. He weaved in and out of the attacks, making no attempt to fight back. If its attention was on him, no one else was in danger. All he had to do was buy time.

The more it wailed, however, the more his heart felt as cold as the winter air. This conflict had produced too many victims. So much death, suffering, and destruction that benefited no one.

"I'm sorry," he whispered to the hydran.

It didn't understand him, of course, and continued to chase him. Its shrieks haunted his mind as he dodged its strikes. He tried to wrap his arms around the creature, trying to subdue it, but it just brushed him off. Its physical strength was overwhelming.

The Guild radio clipped to his chest crackled to life. "Fleischer, the area is clear. Whatever you're going to do, do it now!"

He took in a deep, long breath. The moment of truth had finally come. As he ducked under another attack, his tome flipped through its pages. Holding the incantation in his mind, he focused his attention through the rift and deep into the Speculon.

"Bear witness to my one-track soul; I trap this fiend in a black hole," he yelled.

A few hundred yards through the rift, his father's incantation took form. It grew into a large sphere of light, sucking everything towards it. Even from above the city, he could feel its pull, using his flotation incantation to resist it.

Despite the energy he poured into his father's incantation, the hydran was able to fly against it. He could form it closer to the rift, but that would only increase the risk of collateral damage. Even as it was now, he had to be expedient before whole parts of the city were sucked in.

He had to force it down close enough so it couldn't escape the suction. Flying towards the creature, he swung the staff of his weapon at it, trying to swat it downwards.

With a shriek, the hydran caught the weapon between two of its pincers. With a powerful tug, it flung him down towards the rift. Cursing, he poured the city's souls into his flight incantation.

He stopped fifty yards above the rift. Gritting his teeth, he fought as the incantation pulled on him. Air rushed past, and it sounded as if freight trains were storming past them. Debris and furniture flew out of the buildings around him, sucked down into the Speculon.

The hydran flew down to him, looking as if it were going to attack. Once it descended low enough, it let out a panicked shriek as the incantation took hold of it.

They both flew against the suction, neither of them making any upwards progress. If he lessened the incantation's effects, it would also free the hydran. His mind raced for ideas, but the buildings around the rift began to shake and vibrate. With every passing second, he put the city more and more at risk. Caleb knew what he had to do.

Closing his eyes, his tome flipped through its pages. With a shaking hand, he reached up to the personal radio. "Heather, I'm sorry. Goodbye."

There was a momentary pause. "What are you doing?" her voice belted over the channel.

He wanted to respond, but the hydran started to pull away. He was out of time. Forming the incantation in his mind, he whispered, *"Stay still your highness; I will now bind us."*

Yellow glyphs appeared beneath them, and barriers surrounded them. The hydran's wings ceased buzzing, and his flight incantation vanished.

His father's incantation sucked them both down. He looked up at the city he was about to leave. To the planet he was about to see for the last time.

"Caleb, please don't! There has to be another way!" Her voice cracked in desperation.

More than anything he wanted to respond. But it was a futile hope. Just like the hydran, he was completely trapped.

Her sobs echoed through the radio. "You've done so much for me. For my family. For this city. It can't end like this! Not before I tell you that I—"

He and the hydran passed through the rift, coming out the other side. His radio produced static as the incantation pulled them up from the rift that tore through the dry, purple grass and to the crimson sky. Thousands of filken dotted the plain, all staring up at them. In the distance, nine adult hydran zoomed towards him, each significantly larger than the child he had just fought.

Ignoring them, he looked down to see the rift closing now that the hydran wasn't in the city. Relief flooded him as the golden soul strings vanished. The connection between the two worlds had severed. After all this time, he had finally succeeded. He had kept his promise to his father. He had kept his promise to Iibere.

Caleb closed his eyes. The sound of multiple hydran wings buzzed in his ears, but he didn't care. Even as exhaustion and fear flooded him, a small smile appeared on his face. He had defeated the strings. Cassandra would live. Chicago was safe.

Opp's bark filled his mind. Caleb's oldest companion would get a good life. Wilson would get the chance to reconnect with Bobby. And although he'd never get to see her again, Heather would finally get to pursue her dreams.

This wasn't a bad way to go out. Not bad at all.

"—you," Heather frantically yelled into the radio she clutched with desperate hands.

The rift began to close. She screamed his name and lunged forward. Wilson's powerful arms wrapped around her, holding her back.

She thrashed against him, falling to her knees. "He needs our help, Wilson!"

"Heather, he's gone."

Tears rained from her eyes as the golden soul string hanging from her chest vanished. The street below had returned to normal with no sign of the rift. Every golden string was gone.

"It's not fair," she said, her voice cracking.

"War never is," he whispered, rubbing her back.

She leaned into him and looked up at his face. His eyes were red and misty. She had known the man her whole life and not once had she seen him cry. She clenched his jacket and buried her face into his chest.

Thunderous cheering erupted all over the city, nearly shaking it. Fighter jets soared overhead, and the cheering evolved into chanting "Fleischer" over and over again.

Heather broke down into sobs.

Between the applause and her own cries, she barely heard the footsteps behind her. A new hand grasped her shoulder, and she looked up to see Aalia standing over her. Her friend gave her a sympathetic look, and Heather reached up and took hold of her hand.

"The three of you saved everyone," Aalia told them.

The thought didn't comfort her as she tried to dry her tears. But they kept falling, and her face was drenched.

She used Wilson's support to stand, looking at the battered city as it cheered. Smoke rose from flame-engulfed buildings, and dust continued to settle on the debris-filled streets, but for the first time in nearly a year, she could see the skyline without strings. She would have smiled if she hadn't had to bite her lip to stop herself from sobbing.

"I'm sorry," Aalia continued, "but General Cromwell asked me to bring the three... two of you back to the stadium."

Heather nodded. She had to leave this place. Reaching down, she picked up Caleb's empty satchel and held it loosely in her hands.

"Let's go," she said to Aalia and Wilson.

Heather sat with a blanket wrapped around her. A cup of untouched coffee rested in her hand. The drink had long since gone cold as she stared aimlessly into the distance.

Most of their time back at the stadium had been full of waiting. Soldiers ran around screaming at each other and making phone calls. Every quarter hour or so, some random soldier would tell them they'd only have to stand by a little longer. She believed it less and less each time.

Wilson sat next to her in his own chair. Neither of them

spoke. What was there to say? They had achieved the goal they had pursued so long. Only it was at a price she had not been ready to pay. She hadn't been ready at all.

She studied the brown leather satchel in her lap. Holding up to her face, she realized it smelled like him. The scent brought random memories back to the surface. Meeting him in Orion. Seeing him cast an incantation for the first time. The roof of the hospital. When they had first connected their souls

They had been through so much, and she had never stopped to truly appreciate the time they had spent together. There had always been so much going on, so much they had been working towards. She had failed to see the forest for the trees.

"We need to let his town know," Wilson said quietly.

She nodded. "Those that knew him deserved to know the truth."

"I'll take care of that after we leave," he said.

Reaching out, she placed a hand on his arm. "No, please. Let me do it. I need to."

"Of course, Miss O'Brien."

Aalia had gone to handle Guild matters, as she put it. The Guild leadership was in disarray. Not only had their operation failed and backfired, but some officers that weren't in Chicago were displeased her father had openly supported Caleb. The most extreme officers were livid. Her father had a daunting task in front of him if he were to keep the Guild from revolt.

While she was lost in these thoughts, amongst a sea of camouflage, another soldier approached them. "Mister Price, Ms. O'Brien, if you would please follow me."

The soldier led them through a maze of corridors, papers, and personnel until they reached a metal door. It led them into a cold, small room with a single steel table in the center. General Cromwell sat in one of the four chairs around the tables, manila folders in front of him.

Sudden barking grabbed her attention. Oppenheimer sprinted at her, nearly leaping into her arms. She smiled weakly and embraced the dog. Kneeling, she tried to keep her tears at bay. He licked at her face before she pulled away, staring at him. He looked to the door, waiting.

Her lips quivered. "Opp... he's not coming."

Oppenheimer tilted his head before walking into the hallway, glancing around. He returned and stared at her, his face less jovial. Holding out Caleb's satchel was all she could do to keep herself from crying.

Opp sniffed it a moment before studying her face. Small whimpers escaped him as he took the satchel in his mouth. He paced to the corner of the room, laying in a small ball with the satchel at his center.

The general and Wilson stared at each other as if speaking in silent code. Walking over to the table, Heather took a seat and stared at her messy reflection on its surface.

The general cleared his throat. "Wilson, Ms. O'Brien, I've been reading some of the cursory reports my soldiers managed to gather. I know the events are still fresh and...personal for you. But I would greatly appreciate hearing your accounts of what exactly happened here. If you could, please start from the beginning."

She paused, not sure what to say. How could one even tell this story? Her mind drifted to the past. How had any of this started? Finally, she talked about the rumor she had about Scott Fleischer from the doctor well over a year ago.

Once she began, it all poured out of her. She told him everything, from showing up to Caleb's house to this very day. The laughs, the struggles, the loss, and the sacrifices they'd all endured to save this city.

After she finished, the room seemed to exist in its own vacuum of time, none of them moving or saying anything. The occupants of this room were the ones who hadn't clapped when the rift closed. Who hadn't cheered. Who had reflected on the cost of victory.

"This is a lot to take in," Bobby finally said. "This has been a strange assignment from the beginning. The way every level of government and command handled things had an unusual feel to it. Learning more about this...Guild, as you call it, explains much."

The general paused, and she looked down.

"Would you like to speak to your father?" he asked.

Her eyes widened, and her hands balled into fists, but she nodded.

"If it were up to me, I'd send him to the darkest cell I could find and keep him there until the end of time. But I've already gotten calls from the Pentagon ordering his release. I'm going to keep him in custody for as long I can manage, but I don't know how long that will be. I want to learn more about this organization and its level of influence. I have a haunting feeling I can't shake, and I need more intel. But you are free to come and talk with him whenever you'd like."

Bobby stood and spoke into a radio. He and Wilson exchanged some hushed words, and the general departed. A minute later, her father walked in with two armed soldiers. Handcuffs bound his wrists, and he wore some sort of electronic collar around his neck.

Her father took a seat across from her. He reached out to take her hand, but she pulled it back, glaring at him.

He cleared his throat. "I heard what happened to the boy—"

"His name was Caleb!"

He stared in silence as if trying to find the right words.

Wilson walked over to her and placed a hand on her shoulder. "Miss O'Brien, I shall take Oppenheimer and go check on your mother. I'll meet you at the hospital after you finish here."

She nodded, and he exited the room with Opp. Her thoughts shifting to her mom, Heather wanted to finish here as quickly as possible.

"We can go see her together," her father said.

She shook her head, firmly holding the man's gaze. "You aren't allowed near her or me after this conversation. Not until you make right what you have wronged. Mom was nearly killed because of you. I don't know if I can ever forgive you, but if you want to earn it, then turn this monstrous organization into a force for good. Fix Chicago, and make the rest of the world a better place."

"It's not that easy, Mouse. The Guild is a complex—"

She slammed a fist down on the table, sending tingles up her arm. "I don't want your excuses! When faced with the decision between the difficult, right choice, and the easy, wrong choice, a good person takes the hard path. Cause if they don't, who else will?"

"That's a nice ideal, but—"

"It was that idealism that saved this city, Dad! You were the cause of its near demise."

Her father seemed to try and find a response. With Wilson

and Opp absent, the room felt even colder. She wrapped her arms around herself and lost her sense of location for a moment, the sounds of the battle returning to her mind. The hydran's shrieks. Barking orders into the radio. Caleb's goodbye.

"Mouse?" her father asked, presumably not for the first time judging from his tone.

She blinked and looked at him, collecting herself. "Please leave," she whispered. "Don't contact me or Mom until you've atoned for what you've done."

He opened his mouth to speak but didn't. Standing, he walked to the door and opened it.

"One last thing," she said. "I'm not going to become a surgeon. I'm going to be a therapist."

The words gave him pause, and he closed his eyes. "I love you, Heather."

He left the room with the soldiers, the door closing behind her.

She sat there alone, resting her head on the table. She wanted to leave, to go to the hospital and see her mother. But her body felt as if it weighed a ton. What she really wanted was to sleep and forget. To push away the memories she didn't want to have.

It was unclear how much time passed, but eventually, she managed to leave the cold room. She asked a random soldier if she could get a ride to her mother's hospital. A dispatch quickly provided her with an escort.

The hospital was hectic. Bloodied people sat against the walls, and the hospital staff rushed around frantically. She reached ICU room three hundred and three. Opening the door, she stepped inside to find Wilson and Opp.

"There you are," a voice she had not heard in a long time said.

On the hospital bed, her mother sat with her eyes open. Cassandra was eerily thin and frail but awake nonetheless.

Heather leaped forward and threw her arms around her mother, holding her tightly. "I'm so glad you're okay," she said with a raspy voice, not wanting to cry again.

Her mother returned the hug, rubbing her back. "I suddenly woke up, and it sounded like I was in the middle of a warzone."

She leaned back, staring at her mother's soft face. The entire series of events that had consumed her life for the last year had started to save this woman she loved so much. "It's been a long year."

Cassandra played with Heather's hair. "Wilson also tells me that I have you to thank for being alive."

"Yeah, Wilson and I did everything we could to help. Us, Aalia, and a young man named Caleb Fleischer." She looked down and gripped her mother's bedsheets as his name left her lips.

Cassandra smiled, then her expression drooped. "Tell me about him."

Heather smiled weakly, staring at her mother. Part of her couldn't believe that her mom was awake. That it was finally, truly over.

She pulled a chair to her mother's bedside, holding the woman's hand. And she told the story of Caleb and the strings.

Chapter Thirty

Heather adjusted her seat in the car. She looked out at the snow-covered farm fields. They were beautiful. An advanced psychology textbook sat in her lap, open to its final pages. Rolling down the window, she let the cold January air rush past her face. The road they sped down was vaguely familiar, and memories of her journey from over a year ago returned.

"Almost there," Wilson said, his eyes focused ahead.

She nodded and looked to the backseat at Opp and Aalia. Opp's face was glued to the window, his tail wagging feverishly. He hadn't budged since he started recognizing the landscape. She didn't have the heart to tell him that no one was waiting for him at home.

Aalia was passed out, her tome laying on the seat next to her. It had been difficult for her to get away from the Guild for the trip, but she had insisted.

Heather looked forward, deep in thought. It had been a week since her mother had woken up, and she had barely left her side during that time. But her mom was a long way from being able to check out of the hospital, and another engagement required her attention.

"Turn here," she told Wilson as they came to a four-way stop.

It had taken some research, but she had managed to call a few people from Orion. After asking around, she had gotten the number for a man named Jordan Jackson. After they had talked, he gave her the number of his daughter, Sally.

The two of them spent a long time on the phone over that week. The world had heard all about Chicago. Millions of videos flooded the internet, showing the hydran and the destruction the city suffered. That, and the young man that fought it. Sally had many questions.

It hadn't been easy for her to tell Sally what had happened to Caleb, but Heather hadn't held anything back. Sally deserved to know the full truth.

All in all, Sally had been strong in dealing with the information. News of Caleb's death had sent her through the wringer, but she couldn't be faulted for that. Since then, Sally had made the necessary calls and organized the town.

"It's that one, right there," Heather said, pointing at the familiar house.

Wilson pulled the SUV into the driveway. Oppenheimer pawed eagerly at the window and let out an excited yelp. She got out of the vehicle and opened the door. He sprinted out and ran straight at the rundown house.

She shook Aalia's shoulder. "Hey, we're here."

Aalia opened her eyes and looked around. Getting out, Aalia and Wilson walked up the driveway. Heather pulled out her textbook and Caleb's satchel. Stuffing the book into it, she made sure not to crumple the piece of parchment inside.

She went up to the house and saw the yellow bike in the front yard, covered in snow. Caleb told her it had been a birthday present from Scott. She frowned; it had barely been used. Picking it up from the snow, she wheeled it around to the backyard. Carefully, she laid it to rest where Caleb had always said the sunflower field would grow.

Sighing, she returned to the front of the house and opened the door. A musty smell greeted her as Opp jolted into the living room. He then ran into the kitchen, whimpering.

She knelt and held him in her arms. "I'm sorry, Opp. They're not here."

He let out a few whines and laid down next to the empty chairs at the table. She spent a few moments petting him before standing.

Wilson took a last look around. "I'll go grab our changes of clothes, Miss O'Brien."

She nodded. Aalia plopped down on the couch while Heather walked down the hall. Entering the last door on the left, she stepped into Caleb's room. Dirty clothes littered the floor, and a few books poked out from underneath the bed.

Paging through a few of them, she found they were about the Speculon or Scribes. Stacking the books, she made a mental note to bring them home when they were finished.

Standing, her eyes fell onto his unmade bed. She shuffled to it and straightened the sheets. Climbing into the bed, she buried her face into the pillow, shutting her eyes tight.

It smelled like him.

Wilson's footsteps sounded outside the door, but she didn't look up.

"I'll hang your dress on the door, Miss O'Brien."

She nodded and waited for him to leave. After a brief pause, she stood, closed the door, and undressed.

She took her time changing into her black dress and cardigan. Once she had changed, she set her old clothes on his bed, folding them neatly.

Walking out of the room, she found Wilson in a suit with two high heeled shoes in hand. She slipped them on and walked out to the living room. Aalia had changed into a blazer and slacks. The three of them gathered Opp and returned to the SUV.

Using the address Sally had provided, they drove across the small town of Orion until they arrive at a gated plot of land. Hundreds of cars sat parked in and out of the cemetery. Sally had said most of the town was going to be in attendance.

After they parked, Wilson pulled a roll of newspapers out of the trunk. They walked amongst the graves and the people of Orion. Many of them gave her sideways glances, no doubt trying to place her.

They walked up to where most of the town was crowded. Two caskets rested over freshly dug graves. Heather knew Scribes were cremated, not buried, but this was for Orion.

A young woman stood at the front of the crowd. The woman approached her, giving her a warm embrace. "Heather?"

She smiled weakly. "Yes. It's good to finally meet you in person, Sally."

A stocky, bald man walked up and placed a powerful hand on Sally's shoulder. "Good afternoon. We talked on the phone, I'm JJ." The man's eyes were red and misty, and he looked as if he were barely keeping it together.

Sally looked down. "It would have been his birthday today."

Wishing to move from the thought, Heather motioned to her companions. "This is my best friend, Aalia Laghari. And this is Wilson Price."

They all exchanged greetings. Not knowing what else to say, Heather took her place in the crowd, standing close to Aalia and Wilson with Opp in front of them.

Sally began the service. The whole town listened in silence as she spoke, recounting both the official news and Heather's story of what happened in Chicago. It was strange, hearing the story told by someone else. Heather stood like a statue as she listened to everything she, Caleb, Aalia, and Wilson had done.

Sally concluded her speech. "We all knew the Fleischers as a strange part of our little community. How many times did we endure a long-winded story from Scott we had already heard a thousand times, only to end up laughing again anyway? How many times did Caleb walk amongst us in silence, none of us knowing that he kept us safe all these years? They both gave their lives to save millions, and we owe them to at least be remembered. So please, everyone, bow your heads and join me in a moment of silence to thank them."

Heather lowered her head along with everyone else. The cold air nipped at her face as she closed her eyes, but she didn't flinch. After the silence ended, the town slowly passed by the graves, everyone each paying their respects. It took a few hours for all of Orion to shuffle through, but soon the crowd had dissipated.

Sally, Wilson, Aalia, Opp, and Heather stood over the graves as the caskets were lowered. Snow fell softly over them as workers poured dirt into the holes and laid patches of grass over them.

They all stood in silence, each mourning in their own way. She thought of Caleb. How he would grab his arm whenever he was uncomfortable. Or how it had felt when they first connected their souls. She thought of his smile, his laugh, and his concentrated face whenever he studied his tome.

Pain tugged at her chest as more memories forced their way into her mind. She was never going to see him again. She had forced him into her life, and the world had torn him out of it. She clenched her fists. It wasn't fair.

Wilson held out the roll of newspapers and opened them to reveal a bouquet of sunflowers. They each took a few in hand and set them upon Caleb's gravestone, watching the snow blanket the yellow petals.

"He was a sunflower forced to bloom in winter," she whispered.

After she stood there for some time, Heather readied herself to walk back to the car. But, before she left, something about Caleb's gravestone caught her eye. It had his name, birth date, and date of death written upon it. But what caught her eyes was the quote in the center of the stone. She read it again and again, trying to understand it. For a reason she couldn't explain, the words resonated deep within her soul.

"Sally," she asked, "did you choose the words on his gravestone?"

"Yeah, why?" Sally asked. Walking over, she stared at the engraving, and her eyes grew wide. "This isn't what I picked! I need to go figure this out." Pulling out her phone, Sally walked away from the graves.

Heather spent a moment considering Sally's words, and her eyes flickered up. Across the cemetery stood a strange, almost glowing boy with red, orange, and brown hair. She blinked and tried to get a better look, but the boy had vanished. Frowning, she looked down and read the phrase one last time.

Autumn rises when Winter falls
Stand and fight when destiny calls

End

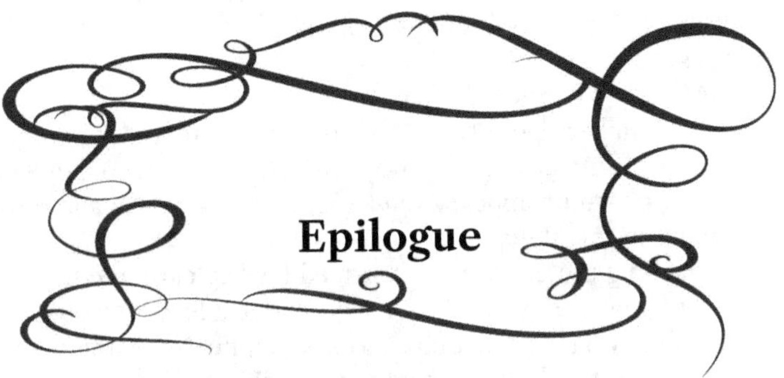

Epilogue

The ride had been unbearably loud. Michael spilled his drink more than once, thanks to the turbulence. He pinched the bridge of his nose as the helicopter finally landed at the Guild of Life compound in eastern Germany. It had taken two full months for that bullheaded general to finally comply with his agents in the Pentagon.

Maintaining control of the Guild while detained had been tenuous, but he had managed. Escaping would have been easy, of course, but Heather wouldn't have appreciated that. He would earn her forgiveness. He would atone.

The Guild was going to become a force for good. No more living in the Fleischer shadow. No more appeasing officers who only cared for themselves. This was no longer about his ego but about the good of humanity.

It wasn't going to be easy. Reforming any organization was a tall order, especially one as ingrained and zealous as theirs. But once he brought the officers into line, the rest would fall in order.

Grabbing the briefcase next to him, Michael exited the helicopter. A cyclone of wind rushed around him as the rotors came to a stop. He stepped into the limousine that waited for him and poured himself another glass of whiskey. Taking a sip, he enjoyed the smoky taste that burned the back of his throat.

As they drove through the compound, he considered what calls he needed to make first. There was Davis in D.C. and a few other ranking officers who needed his attention. It was going to be a busy few months, but it would be worth it.

Once they arrived at the main building, he stepped out of the vehicle. A group of Scribes keeping guard saluted him, their tomes at the ready.

"At ease," he ordered them.

The familiar sight of the black tile floors greeted him once he was inside. As he made his way through the quiet, cold building, a Scribe would appear from a room every so often and render him a sharp salute.

Reaching the elevators, he swiped his key card and took it to the top floor. Only his office resided on that level. It would be nice to finally have a quiet place to work alone. No distractions.

The elevator doors opened to his office. A rich purple carpet covered the floor, and black walls surrounded him. Large bookcases adorned the left and right walls, and a large, ornate desk stood in the center of the room.

He walked over to the desk and grabbed the decanter off it, pouring himself another glass of whiskey. After drinking it in one go, he poured himself another. On his desk sat a manila folder labeled "Operation Chimera."

But it was already open, the papers inside strewn everywhere. He narrowed his eyes. It was only then he noticed the shadowy figure in the corner of the room.

"Karl," he said with venom in his voice.

Karl Fleischer stepped out of the shadows and crossed his arms. "Hello, Michael. Fancy running into you here."

Calmly, Michael took a seat at his desk. He set his briefcase on its surface and quietly unlatched it. Reaching under his desk, he pressed a small button hidden in the corner. "You know you aren't welcome here, Karl. Now more than ever."

The old man looked around the office as if admiring it.

"Well, you know, old friend, things change. I fancy a long, productive stay here."

"You're out of your mind. The Guild tossed you aside after your bastard of a grandson was born."

Karl let out a false chuckle and rubbed his chin. "No, you took advantage of my momentary political vulnerability. You took my Guild away from me. But since then, you have brought the organization to ruin. You failed in Chicago and exposed us to sections of the military that were not under our control. You got my grandson *and* son killed. Those are things I cannot forgive."

Before Michael could answer, three portals appeared in the room. His top three ranking officers entered, answering his distress signal.

Fei, a woman with no emotion on her face, aimed her crystalline bow at Karl. Alexander, in his flawless black suit, held a warhammer. Vlad had his typical look of disinterest painted across his face but held his sword and shield nonetheless.

"That's good and all," Michael said, "but your time has run out. It seems I must put an end to the entire Fleischer family." He signaled for his officers to attack.

They didn't move.

"Oh," Karl said smugly, "I should have mentioned. They can't forgive you either. While you were playing house with Cromwell, we had a good long talk. They've grown tired of your ineffective leadership. It's time for someone with real conviction and vision to take the helm once more."

Anger boiled inside Michael as he stared at his subordinates, their blank faces telling him everything. After everything he had done for them, now they turned on him? Right when things were about to turn around.

He stood and snapped his fingers, but Karl's tome was already out. A yellow, crystalline spear flew at him.

Jumping to the side, he dodged the attack. His tome floated in front of him, and he held an incantation in his mind. But before his tome even flipped through its pages, something stabbed through his back.

Karl's spear had impaled him. Looking back, he saw two portals behind him, redirecting the weapon back at him.

Unable to draw a breath, Michael collapsed to the carpet. A pool of his own blood formed underneath him. He struggled to look up as Karl stood over him with cruel eyes.

Karl tore the weapon from his chest. His vision blurred, but he could see the tip of the spear just above his head. Knowing his time was short, he imagined both Heather and Cassandra's faces. He tried to mutter an apology to them, but only blood spurted out.

"The Guild is mine now." Karl chuckled and drove the spear into Michael's face.

Acknowledgments

The Winter Saga is my life's work and STRINGS is my debut novel. It's a dream come true to reach this stage after pouring a lot of sweat and tears into this story.

But none of this would have been possible if not for the amazing friends and family supporting me the whole way. There is an endless list of people I could thank, but I wanted to take a moment to highlight some especially extraordinary people.

Tyler, my lifelong friend and confidant
Eva, my crabcakes, my gold medal winner
Tina, my Mama Bear
Ello the Grey, my kin
Matthew and Jay, my brothers
Susan Hickey
Amelia
Jose Alejandro Amaya
Emma Rowan
Emily Elaine
Valeriya Kott
Jaime Dill
Jenn Jarrett
Tiffany Sprague
Hannah Ball
Charlie Knight, editor at cknightwrites.com
Jonas Steger, cover designer at Fantasy and Coffee Design

About the Author

Born and raised in the Midwest, Ryan Hickey was accepted into the United States Naval Academy in Annapolis, Maryland. After graduating with a Bachelor of Science in Chemistry and a minor in Japanese, he served in the United States nuclear submarine force. Once he departed from service, he moved to Seattle to pursue his dream of becoming a published author. STRINGS is his debut novel.

Find him on Twitter: @RMH_Winter

and online at www.lordofwinter.com

CPSIA information can be obtained
at www.ICGtesting.com
Printed in the USA
LVHW082035120121
676325LV00040B/1051